CW01261882

About the Author

William Anderson retired from his Chief Executive Career with a London PLC to pursue his interests elsewhere. These include, amongst others, writing, history and climbing mountains. He spends his time between his home in northern Scotland, Europe and the Middle East.

The Mubarizun has been some time in the making. If you enjoy the story, please leave a review.

The author can be contacted at andermubar@gmail.com.

First Published in 2020

The moral right of William Anderson to be identified as the author of this work has been asserted in accordance with the Copyright, Designs and Patents Act 1988, United Kingdom

All rights reserved. No part of this publication may be reproduced or transmitted in any form or by any means, electronic or mechanical, including photocopying, recording, or any information storage and retrieval system, without permission in writing from the publisher.

This book is a work of fiction. Names, characters, businesses, organisations, places and events are either the product of the author's imagination or used fictitiously. Any resemblance to actual persons, living or dead, events or locales is entirely coincidental.

The Mubarizun

William Anderson

In times of war and not before,

God and soldier we adore,

But in times of peace and all things righted,

God is forgotten and the soldier slighted.

   - Rudyard Kipling

Chapter 1

It was the usual Grampian spring weather when he left the house, cool with some wind and threatening cloud, but importantly the sun was shining. He walked down the rough drive which was access to his croft and along the metalled road toward the Linn of Dee, access to the high mountains in the Cairngorm massif. The river roared from the input of flood melt over the last few weeks as if celebrating its youthful origins before going on to more placid descents further down river.

Finlay had dressed, packed his rucksack for a long couple of days in the mountains, planning to ascend the Lairig Ghru, down to Rothiemurcus and return via Ben Avon to his home on the upper banks of the Dee River.

It had been five years since his retirement from the British Army and far from spending a long and happy period with his wife he had coped with her illness and eventual death. Prolonged and emotional hospital visits felt like endless purgatory, almost as if he was in hell itself for those long months. Extreme exercise of whichever shape or form was the easiest way to seek some solace, particularly after a lifetime spent as an infantryman. He enjoyed the outdoors, even the wind, rain and snow, and above all, the sleep inevitably brought about by pushing his ageing body to the limits. It seemed to reduce the time he had to dwell on his loss. Finlay's army pension was sufficient to buy a simple four room croft in the mountains, a Landcruiser to cope with the hard Scottish winter and give him a liveable income for the rest of his days.

As he turned off the metalled road onto the Land rover track up the Linn of Dee the cloud moved north toward the path he was about to ascend but meantime the sun shone and warmed him as his body started to shake off the stiffness of the initial walk. He paused to check his smartphone before he lost its signal to see if he had a message from his children. They communicated with him most days but due to the time zone differences sometimes the messages were rather irregular and sporadic. Nothing so far.

Finlay turned off the vehicle track on to the single track which wound its way up toward the dark granite cleavage between Ben Macdhui and Cairn Toul in the distance. The gathering cloud made it look foreboding when compared to the bright sunshine behind him. It was a familiar route these last three years, he tackled it with conditioned ease despite the mountain clothing and heavy Bergen rucksack. As one footfall followed the other, he was lost in his thoughts in the wilderness. He hardly registered the mountain hut that was Corrour bothy as he walked past it to the steepening ascent to the pass covered with winter snow. Flurries of more snow had started to fall now as he walked up the rough stone path. The sky became ever more grim and dark, wind stiffening, he pulled his fleece headgear down lower over his ears and raised and tied the hood of his Arcteryx jacket.

*

Saeed Abdul Raheem lay in the ancient building in old Sanaa, enjoying the relatively cool breeze that flowed through the bottom floor, pulled upwards by the wind tower. It had crossed his mind many times that the great cultures of Islam had invented air conditioning centuries before the West had done so, using God's gifts to naturally combine and bestow comfort on his subjects. His mind switched to more pressing matters, he had to meet the Iranian to discuss payment and delivery of the product to the port of Bandar Abbas where it would be transhipped after preparation to its destination. He would need to get out of the Yemen, not easy with the Arab coalition and US Special Forces on the ground and drones watching from above. He rose from his mattress and donned the traditional sarong and loose cotton shirt of the Yemeni Red Sea fisherman. He wrapped his head dress around head and mouth, threw his old Browning Hi Power in his duffel and walked out into the warm Arabian mountain evening to await his transport to the coast.

*

Daniel Dubois had left the hotel three days ago; his portly frame had not fared well climbing the path from Colymbridge Hotel on to the frozen mountain path. He was terrified and ill prepared for the challenge ahead, unsure of his destination or ultimate fate. He had been advised by his so called friend to get out of French suburbia to somewhere rural where any tail would stick out like a sore thumb. It was a common strategy used by security services, or so he was led to believe. He suspected anyone that was in his vicinity for more than a few minutes of being in the employ of the people that were hunting him. He knew he had been followed to the UK but felt he had evaded his pursuers. Daniel was not an athlete, he smoked and drank to excess, never exercised, his frame was flabby and pale from working over a desk indoors. He had not regretted anything so much in his life apart perhaps from working in his last job. He had finally gone from an acclaimed physics academic to a fugitive and he had never been so ill equipped. He had tried to compensate by spending a lot of money on outdoor clothing, boots and a tent but soon discovered the reality of the great outdoors. His body was a mess, huge blisters had appeared on his heels. His legs were so painful he could hardly stand, knees cut and bruised from slips and falls on the path and the cold permeated through his tent and sleeping bag.

Daniel had moved the tent at the top of the pass several times depending on wind direction, finally settling below a huge glacial boulder next to the water pools that had accumulated at the top of the pass before plunging into the Dee valley. He lit the stove and decided to eat the last of his supplies before moving on to Braemar village where he could recover in a hotel with good food and a hot bath. It looked clearer over in that direction and he thought he could make it by nightfall.

Despite his predicament on the snow swept hill pass, he felt that no one was following him. Daniel had spent enough time in this purgatory to be assured that no one was up here much less anyone that would be appointed by his former associates.

The only sound he could hear was the increasing wind blowing on his tent through the Lairig Ghru and the hiss of his gas stove heating his meal.

Chapter 2

The crates had come from North Korea having been transported through the series of islands that form the Yalu river delta, following the conduit of century's old trade. The reality was there was little security among the myriad of little islands that made the delta, it was almost impossible to police. The wooden crates had arrived in a freight handling yard in Dandong and were packed in a container with agricultural components, themselves all packed in similar secure wooden boxes. They appeared the same, had the same documents and description as the FOTMA Chinese tractor engines and harrow machines. They had the same stamps on the boxes.

The duck green forty feet long container DES113 was then placed on to a truck which travelled to the container port of Dandong and was cleared through Chinese customs along with the other three hundred and forty three containers that had arrived in the port that day. The random checks had looked at four of the containers, within these, not one packing case had been opened to examine what was inside. There was no need to pay bribes, in itself a risk, for anyone to look the other way. The syndicate responsible for shipping the crate simply relied on the volume of traffic.

Chapter 3

Saeed didn't look like he was from Palestine. He had the short stature, slight build and darker features of a Yemeni tribesman from the mountains or one that made a living from the sea. He looked younger than his fifty five years. He was well into adulthood in his first Intifada in the late eighties, had learned how to conduct covert insurrection against the Israelis from his time in the PLO. He graduated into management of the organisation and migrated eventually to the Mubarizun.

The Palestinian had discovered the key to his business of freedom fighting was to control the money. While he had been involved in violence, he believed this was for the foot soldiers, the thugs, who would have dealt drugs or run prostitution rings on the streets of Gaza or the West Bank if they weren't gainfully employed resisting the Israelis. Saeed was educated, multilingual and highly intelligent. He was at equally at home in a business suit in a large Western bank as he was smuggling in the tunnels that passed through the Egyptian border into Palestine. He looked just at home as the other ten dark skinned Yemeni fishermen as he stepped down from the quayside in Hudaydah on to their seventy foot motorised fishing dhow. He greeted the crew warmly in Arabic and found a space on the deck to make himself comfortable before she sailed.

*

Daniel turned off the stove so he could hear well. There was a noise other than the wind like a rock rolling down the slope above him or a footfall scraping on the path. He held his breath and listened, perhaps he had imagined it as the tent blew in the wind. He exhaled slowly and edged on his stomach toward the zipped entrance to the small mountain tent.

Daniel's lack of experience of the outdoors and lifetime spent in noisy cities had not conditioned his senses well, the mind need to be unconsciously trained to differentiate natural noise. The streets of Paris, Nantes and Toulouse had no calls for such skills. His primary sense in such places was vision and the internals of a tent were not an aid to that sense.

He slowly drew the zip down and looked through the slit at the shoreline of the lochan in front of him, his view was limited with his head inside the tent. He slowly pushed his head through the entrance so he could see laterally around his campsite. The last noise Daniel Dubois heard in his life was the swoosh of an ice axe and a crack as the pick entered his skull below the occipital bone where the lower part of his head met his neck. He lived long enough to feel a boot on the back of his head and a sharp tug pull the weapon out of his skull. By the time the blood started flowing down his cheeks and onto the granite slab where he had pitched part of his tent, Daniel was dead.

Two men stood over his body, one short and stocky, the other taller man dropped the ice axe and pulled Daniel's body down to the shores of the Pools O'Dee. The shorter man wrapped up the tent and belongings and proceeded to push them into the dead man's rucksack along with some stones, both men lifted the body into a sitting position and strapped the rucksack to his back, securing the front webbing. They then took one of their own climbing ropes and pulled it through one of the main back straps of the large rucksack, looped it back on itself and pulled both of the tails of rope across the other side of the lochan. Pulling on both parts of the looped rope they pulled the body, complete with backpack, into the centre of the pool and pulled on one tail of the rope removing it from the body. Daniel Dubois was now resting on the bottom of the pool weighed down by the granite stones that had been in the pass for millennia. The short man coiled the rope and placed it diagonally over his shoulder, threw the ice axe into the pool and slapped the taller man on the back before they both headed south in the direction of Corrour bothy and Braemar. Neither man faltered nor seemed hesitant in the whole process. They had executed the man and disposed of the body like they had done it several times a day in an abattoir.

Finlay could see little more than thirty feet ahead as the snow fell at an angle from the north into his face, but he felt that almost imperceptible sense of something ahead. He'd lain in many ditches and culverts in his life, entered buildings and ventured into various forms of wilderness from sub-zero arctic terrain in Canada to hot desert sands in Libya. Had developed a very familiar sense of threat just before hearing or seeing something which confirmed that danger lay ahead. He's felt this before being ambushed by militia in Bosnia, prior to in IED hitting his convoy in Iraq and before Waziri tribesman had started to ascend toward his OP in Helmand. Was it trained into him or was it a sixth sense or even occasionally his imagination in hindsight, he couldn't tell, but he knew he was right. There was a threat.

For a fraction of a second he couldn't fathom why, the pass was too wide and it was too cold and not enough snow for avalanche, there was no large river or flash flood risk. It was highly unlikely there was any threat from animal or a human on the pass. As he slowed and looked ahead he heard footsteps, the noise being carried toward him on the wind. He reached behind him into the back of his Bergen where his decade's old Fairbairn Sykes knife was clipped in for ease of access, unsheathed it and held it in his pocket. He felt a little ridiculous, it was just hill walkers or climbers descending the pass, as he's come across every time he's gone out on one of his long walks in the Cairngorms. Must be getting jumpy having been a recluse for so long.

The two shapes walking toward him were obviously used to walking long distances in the mountains, they appeared to carry their stride efficiently down the slope, they had no sign of being tired or demoralised with the weather. As he was ascending, he stopped and pulled into one side of the stone steps to allow them to pass. He held the knife concealed up against his right sleeve. As he did so the climbers allowed some distance to open up between themselves, the taller man brought up the rear and was carrying an ice axe in his left hand, Finlay was standing to their right as they descended. The shorter man nodded to Finlay as he walked past but said nothing, the taller man, a few steps behind watched Finlay but made no comment or acknowledgement as he passed. The first man turned and watched his compatriot pass him as if making sure of something. Finlay walked up a few of the steps and looked back at the men descending the glen.

The perception of threat had got worse as they had passed on the narrow stone steps to the point the hairs on the back of his neck had stood. Why had the tall man carried the ice axe in his gloveless left hand when he didn't need it, and the shorter guy checked his friend in passing Finlay? And why was there something like looked like fresh blood on the tall man's left boot? One ice axe between two climbers?

He walked on, the feeling of uneasiness remained with him as Finlay walked further up toward the col. The wind picked up, snow flurries thickened. This was not forecast, Cairngorm weather was a law unto itself. He decided to shelter before he reached the stirrup of mountain that formed the saddle between Cairn Toul and the massive bulk of Ben Macdhui, if this persisted after an hour he would head back down the pass. He also wanted to make sure the two men who had concerned him hadn't turned and followed him back up the hill. Finlay took his mountain tent out of his rucksack and quickly pitched it with practiced skill behind a boulder to keep the worst of the chill off. He sat looking south down the path, though there was little visibility, and brewed some soup from his store of dried food, blending it with water from the pools.

Slowly the snow subsided and the sky brightened, the wind still blew, cold and unwelcoming from the north, the direction he was headed. At least the descent with the force of gravity would counteract the wind if he decided to go on.

As he made the decision to continue Finlay noticed something strange. Where that rocky path started to curve round the Pools O'Dee there was a large granite slab that descended into the water. A red line seemed to be weeping through the light snow that had fallen on the slab, the old soldier had seen something familiar. Subconsciously he had remembered the same picture almost forty years ago in Armagh. A snow covered sloping field, and a man, possibly not even out of his teens, baggy jeans and a tank top barely covered by a cheap and dirty Parker jacket, lying facing upward. A large hole in his chest was the gaping exit wound of a .303 round from a Self-Loading Rifle. A thin line of blood had soaked upward through the snow as the flakes had attempted to cover the evidence. The first time he had seen what a large combat round can do to its victim.

He walked over to the slab and bent down, his nose almost touching the ground. It smelled of metallic rust, iron in blood - something had bled a great deal here very recently but there was no sign of anything as the sun broke through the clouds. The blood was there in some quantity, started behind him and stopped at the water's edge. An injured animal would not go toward relatively deep water if it were in distress and the slab was clearly only a few feet from the water's edge. He walked east up the slope of the mountain until he could look down on the lochan. As the sun shone directly down on the surface of the pool he could see an orange colour around ten feet down. Now he was concerned, something was wrong. He squatted on his haunches and considered his options. Calling the mountain rescue based on his suspicions could mean he be the laughingstock of the team he knew well from his mountaineering days and occasionally socialised with since his retirement. The police would only convey his information to the same people. Finlay could walk away but he knew he'd be back up here within a week considering the situation again.

The only answer for an inquisitive mind was action. He quickly stripped off all his clothing, laying his clothes inside the pitched tent, moved quickly down to the water's edge and waded quickly into the pool. It took his breath away, he could manage three to four minutes in the freezing water, no more. The first few dives served to find his bearings, he could feel only rocks. He grabbed something metallic just as he was going numb, and pulled it to the surface, swimming quickly. An old paraffin stove dark red with rust, he threw it out of the pool. He dived again, felt his way along the bottom, visibility almost non-existent as he raised the peaty sediment between the rocks. Nothing.

One last shot, he climbed out the water to his previous vantage point, shivering to the point it was hurting him and looked down. He saw the dark sediment slightly to the north of where he had seen the orange colour, it was no longer visible. Finlay descended to a stone that he had noted previously as being in line across the lochan with the coloured object, south of the patch of sediment and waded back in. He dived down, was about to give up before he froze to death and felt some material between his fingers. It felt like a jacket, as he felt around he could feel a soft shape, backpack, shoulders, then a head, then, finally round the front of the head, a face. There was a dead person in the pool, a man by the feeling of the stubble on his face.

He moved quickly out of the pool to his tent, dried himself and got inside to avoid the wind-chill while he dressed. The cell phone had a good signal, he'd brew some hot tea before he made the call to the police.

He sat and brought the heat back into his body and considered the situation. The police would want to know why he suspected the men he had passed. How he knew the body was in there, why would any normal climber dive into the pool, so cold and inhospitable on a cold spring day? Better to call "Henry the Fifth."

*

Saeed had enjoyed the relaxed boat trip from Hudaydah to Djibouti, the sea breezes had cooled the nights and the sound of the sea against the old wooden hull of the dhow was oddly comforting for his spirit. Maybe because it was something that had occurred for centuries and was embodied within him, perhaps touched by God. He had cleared immigration as Omar Fakhoury, an Omani national on fisheries business in Djibouti. The Palestinian had reserved a room at the Djibouti Kempinski and decided to spend some time relaxing in the luxurious surroundings, a contrast to the relatively austere surroundings he had experienced in the Yemen these last few months. Here he was under the noses of the Western military that occupied the city and airport. He would exchange his casual clothes that he'd donned from his duffel at the end of his dhow journey for that of a business suit which he'd obtain from the Mubarizun safe house. He would shave his beard and wear glasses before boarding the flight to Istanbul. Saeed's greatest concern was the host of Western intelligence agencies that had trebled their budgets in recent years to fight extremism worldwide. The Mossad would also have a file on him from his years in the homeland. He knew they still shared little and almost jealously guarded the information the various agencies had on known "terrorists" - as everyone that fought for their freedom was now known in the West. He also knew that the fractious resistance movements in the Middle East had traitors who would give information for cash. Infiltrators from intelligence agencies who looked and acted as he did and operatives who would simply betray another organisation to elevate their own standing in the rankings of high profile actions against the West. Sometimes the line that existed between resistance fighters and bandits was a very difficult one to draw.

Saeed had few contacts, only a handful of senior fighters knew his name and appearance. He moved on his own, rarely socialised with his own kind and never bragged of his exploits as many did within ISIS and Al Qaeda. That is why operations were compromised, operatives killed – the intelligence agencies relied on it. His bond was with his people in Palestine and his God. Heaven was assured by his actions, his humbleness and principled lifestyle, not by the award of accolades from his fellows or peers in this life. The few people that made up the Mubarizun were intellectuals like him, their job was to manipulate the foot soldiers of the various organisations in the Arab Peninsula, North Africa and Asia. To supply the finances and oil the machinery of the resistance. The men that made up the organisation could be counted on one man's fingers, no publicity was ever sought, the name Mubarizun was never mentioned outside of the tight circle. They were happy to let the publicised organisations take the credit for small actions, claim the glory on the internet and make the headlines in the newspapers. They would also be the organisations that would suffer retribution from the Western security apparatus. The Mubarizun would, by that time, be on its next mission, always one step ahead. This mission may be different.

*

Henry V's real name was Henry Darcy, he was from a very wealthy English family that could trace its ancestry back to the Norman Conquest and indeed one of his ancestors was listed prominently in the Domesday Book of 1086. His two elder brothers and he had both been Guardsman. While Henry didn't quite have the same aptitude for day to day soldiering as his siblings, he was a sharp young officer and was earmarked as a candidate for Military Intelligence at an early stage in his career. He had joined the Secret Intelligence Service in 1986 and flourished, been involved in the Middle East, China and Eastern Europe at various stages of his career but he had blotted his copybook in Korea. A couple of operatives were hung out to dry and Henry had got the blame. Henry's superiors had decided it was time for a change even though he was a talent and he was transferred to internal security, MI5, very much against his will. He had complained so vociferously prior to his transfer, some of his colleagues at Vauxhall Cross had nicknamed him, rather unkindly, "Henry the Fifth", and it had stuck.

He had walked just under a mile to Thames House across the Lambeth Bridge carrying his briefcase with the meagre belongings from his desk which he had occupied for twenty years. You were not encouraged to take much from the building. He remembered it well, the handshakes and well wishes after the night on the town, the cold and wet Wednesday morning walk and feeling of foreboding he had walking to his new job. His hangover had not helped his outlook on life as he had walked or the rather cool reception he had from his new boss when he arrived. SIS employees were viewed as mavericks by MI5 department heads, rarely accountable for their actions abroad, they knew Henry's record and it confirmed their theory that these SIS guys were cowboys, one step up the ladder from the CIA.

He had been inserted into the section headed by the Deputy Director General, placed to one side in the International Terrorism Department that had the responsibility of looking across the other sections in MI5. His job was liaise with the Strategy and Capability sections to ensure that both fitted with the outlook of his own department which was continually on the front line. While this was regarded as a side-line to the operational role that almost everyone sought within Britain's internal security service, he found, at least initially, as he grew older that the broad scope suited his skills. He spent time on looking at how technical surveillance could be improved within the shores of the country and how future strategy could blend with current thinking on the internal threats from Islamic and Irish extremism. He had even looked at Animal Rights extremists, while a minimal threat, they were technically knowledgeable on cyber security and he evaluated resultant threats they could pose.

After some time Henry V's enthusiasm for the work subsided, there were times he got little results, his own department met the initiatives he had proposed with passive resistance, made the right noises but nothing happened. Henry V was now marking time until he retired.

He had managed to get a desk and an office that looked out over Millbank and the Thames where he could watch what was going on outside when not performing some mundane cross departmental task. He stood looking down on the street with his hands in his pockets when the cell phone on the desk rang.

'Henry the bloody fifth, how are you my son?'

'Jesus, there is a voice from the past, hello Fin, I thought you were a recluse, up in some monastery in Jockland. Clad in a tartan habit, vows of silence and all that shit?'

'Hardly Henry, just enjoying the peace and quiet, until a couple of hours ago.'

'Tell me,' retorted Henry, years of friendship and camaraderie allowing the brevity.

'I just found a stiff in a loch when I was out for a walk, looks as if he has had a job done on him by someone that knows the business, a hit and hide done in short order. Met two blokes on the way down the hill before I found it. They sent a shiver down my spine well before I found the Johnny in the water.'

'Have you told local plods?'

'No, but need to very soon, before someone else walks past.'

'Ok, put keep the stiff hidden if you can and I'll get our Glasgow boys to get there quick, need to get permission from DG for internal operation first. I'll let you know when to call plod.'

'Finlay, tell me one thing ... what is your involvement?'

'Absolutely none Henry, I am out of all that crap, this is about a sense of civic duty, nothing else.'

'Not going freelance and getting an old pal to clean up.'

'This would hardly be the way to do it if it was, number five, have some faith in me.'

'Had to ask, alles ist klar.'

In the murky world of espionage, nothing is clear, thought Henry.

Chapter 4

Colonel Sohail Al Qubaisi walked around the run down old apartment in Bur Dubai while the forensic team were packing up. He bent down and picked up a schematic diagram of what appeared to be some kind of machinery, he couldn't tell, may be useful, he picked it up after donning latex gloves and placed the drawing in an evidence bag.

The United Arab Emirates had largely been free of terrorist related acts for many years, there were a couple of exceptions involving Israelis and a Hamas' Mahmoud al Mabhouh and a deluded woman who decided to make a strike for ISIS in Abu Dhabi. Sohail knew that this was because of an excellent network of intelligence and informers throughout the Emirates who kept close tabs on the numerous different nationalities that lived in the country. He had been directly involved in the Mabhouh investigation run by Lieutenant General Antar. They knew that the Mossad had descended on a Dubai hotel room, armed with British and Australian passports.

The Colonel knew that the Mossad had killed many people around the world when it was assumed that the deaths were by natural causes - as the initial assessment of Mabhouh's death had appeared to be. He had led an unhealthy lifestyle and was considerably overweight, so a heart attack had been diagnosed as a preliminary cause of death. On further investigation it appeared that he had initially been electrocuted with a Taser, then a paralytic muscle relaxant had been injected into his leg, paralyzing him almost immediately. After this a simple act of placing a freezer bag over his head and wrapping it round his neck with masking tape was all that was needed to suffocate the Hamas man. All traces of the ambush had been erased, had it not been for a diligent forensic scientist that picked up traces of the muscle relaxant in the body. Colonel Sohail had wondered how many heart attacks had been passed off this way.

There were also rumours of the Palestinian Authority being complicit in the murder after Jordan handed over two suspects who had appeared to help in the logistics of the assassination. Sohail felt there was a lot more behind the killing than that. Mabhouh was not a big player in Hamas, he had been complicit in the kidnap and killing of two Israeli soldiers, however. The Mossad would not have exposed themselves to this type of publicity unless there was something bigger behind the assassination. Mabhouh had also been involved in procuring arms from Iran and other countries, this was the path they should seek to look down. That had been eight years ago but now they had found evidence of his associates from Hamas living and working in Dubai. Paperwork that showed very large amounts of US currency had moved between banks in the Emirate and beyond.

The apartment he was searching had also been occupied by individuals with British passports. Since the Israeli assassination immigration had earmarked certain nationals with North African, Israeli or Pakistani names. The individuals who had occupied the searched property were British subjects of Pakistani origin. Their names, in this case, had not needed to be tracked by immigration or by Dubai's internal security. The British Secret Intelligence Service had handed the names over as possibly being involved with ISIS. They were 'clean skins' without a previous terrorist link, however they were two brothers, and one had a previous criminal history.

Mumtaz Ansari had a history of burglary, violent street crimes, mostly against women, and drug abuse. He had been disowned by his traditional first generation Punjabi parents and family, served some time in prison where he had decided to turn his back on crime and embrace Islam. It wasn't the traditional, caring and liberal form of Islam practiced in the UAE, it was more extreme akin to Wahhabism. Though he hadn't preached hatred publicly the UK internal security had followed him and his friends to a mosque suspected of such preaching and identified him as a risk. It followed a typical path for extreme terrorism, criminal history, disowned by relatives and suddenly a reformed and religious zealot had been born. A route that a prospective terrorist would find hard to cover. He was the elder brother of Abdul who had kept links with his brother throughout his departure into criminality but had always been devout in his beliefs. Again, the support of the younger brother and the combined descent into extremism was a well-trodden road. The Boston nail bombers were an example.

They had both entered Dubai on a thirty-day tourist visa, met with a wealthy resident of the UAE on several occasions, attended the local mosque in Bur Dubai before departing for Singapore. The Colonel had ensured that his men had maintained twenty four hour covert surveillance on the brothers. They had met with a wealthy Syrian businessman named Hassan Makhlouf. He was a multi-millionaire in Middle Eastern real estate, investing primarily in the UAE, Saudi Arabia and Jordan. He had no criminal record with the exception of being investigated by UK authorities after an allegation of insider trading in his FTSE listed Company, Blue Crescent Homes. The allegations were never proven. Makhlouf had residences in several countries ranging from UAE, Jordan through to London, Geneva and New York. It did not make sense to Sohail, why would two working class brothers with little wealth have a succession of meetings with such a wealthy high ranking businessman in Dubai. Colonel Al Qubaisi had watched a number of hours of video surveillance of meetings between the three men. Makhlouf and the elder Ansari brother had done most of the talking, Abdul had played the role of bystander observer, watching the surrounding tables and occasionally going outside of the meeting venue to smoke a cigarette or make a phone call. They had dined together in expensive restaurants on four occasions, the Colonel could see the two British men were not used to such surroundings. Abdul often playing with his food and seemed unsure of table etiquette. During the last couple of restaurant meetings Makhlouf had appeared bored, going through the motions, as if their stay had reached a conclusion and was at an end. They would need to look closer at Makhlouf's background and dealings in the United Arab Emirates. He would talk to the state security financial investigation team.

Colonel Al Qubaisi told his men to conclude the search and submit the forensics before walking out into the warm Arabian Gulf sunshine.

*

The Ciragan Palace Kempinski sits on the edge of the Bosporous in a stunning location, it surely must be one of the finest settings in the World. It sits on the European shore overlooking the passage to the Black Sea with the Anatolian part of Turkey in clear view. It literally sits on the edge of the sea. Constructed by a Sultan in the 1800s and restored more recently, its original baroque internals were restored to all their glory from a ruin. It is perched on the edge of the huge geographical cleft between Europe and Asia which long represented the division between civilisations, Istanbul changing hands many times between the Christian and Islamic religions since both were in being.

Saeed Abdul Raheem had a loyalty card for the hotel chain which he presented at reception. Once again, as his false identity was registered in the hotel's database, he looked around the famous building and marveled at the abilities of Islamic culture to produce such art and form to align with the functionality of a hotel.

'Omar, I see you arrived safe and well,' a voice from behind him mentioned his alias in fluent Arabic.

Saeed turned without hesitation to see Ebrahim Khorasani. 'Ebrahim, my friend you tread gently, I did not see you come in.'

'I think you saw me some time ago. Come let us sit over here and we can catch up and perhaps conclude our business of these last few months.'

Saeed eyed the Iranian with a bemused smile. He knew Khorasani's position in Iranian Intelligence or VAJA, a murky organisation of which little is known and with close links to the Revolutionary Guard. Even the Mubarizun with its long intelligence tentacles struggled for accurate information on the Iranian Intelligence

Ministry. Khorasani, in contrast to Saeed, was a tall man, thin to the point of being emaciated who smoked at least sixty of his favourite American Marlborough cigarettes every day. Saeed also knew he drank Scotch Whiskey, he could smell the stale remnants of it now while he sat down on one of the plush couches that decorated the huge reception hall.

'I assume you have received the latest payment through Dubai and Singapore for the goods?' said Khorasani as he sat on the chair opposite Saeed.

'Yes we have, and the agricultural shipment is on its way, being transhipped through Singapore to Bandar Abbas. We only need one more payment before the next vessel leaves Singapore. It should be with you in three weeks at the port.'

'We are supposed to see the technicians for removing the goods from the container shortly afterwards at the end of the rail journey, is this confirmed?' retorted Khorasani

'Yes, as agreed'

'They have to go through the correct visa procedure, we have not seen applications as yet, the leader of the group is French?'

'That's correct, he will travel from Europe to Tehran and meet the rest of his team there', Saeed gazed up unblinkingly at the Iranian Intelligence Officer as he spoke, trying to detect any overt suspicion in the Iranian's eyes. He was difficult to read. He waited for a counter but none came.

VAJA had been tracking the Frenchman, they had been infiltrated on a number of occasions by Mossad and were very suspicious of foreigners so no deal, particularly this one, was taken on trust. Everything was treated with suspicion. Khorasani knew they had lost track of the scientist but could not let this Palestinian weasel know his concerns. He could flush it out though.

'I would be grateful if you could contact your man and tell him to apply through our consulate in Paris, that would be quickest, or failing that the embassy in London. We need to apply through normal channels to avoid raising suspicion internally. Oil industry business is the best way to get a visa, we can organise a letter of invitation.'

'Consider it done', said Saeed, 'now would you care to join me for lunch?'

*

Finlay sat cross legged in his croft by the fire he had just lit in the hearth, a strong black coffee in hand and reflected on the events of the last few days. He had hidden himself until a Wildcat helicopter had arrived with an MI5 clean up team. One was a diver and without donning his breathing gear, he dived into the pool. He attached an airbag and compressor to the dead man's rucksack before inflating the bag and bringing the body to the surface.

The helicopter crew had been told it was a joint special forces exercise that had gone wrong and the body had to be repatriated. The body had been taken to a morgue in London which had a military annex and listed as an unknown combatant until it could be identified. Henry V was heading the project and liaising with his old friends from SIS, but not before asking Finlay if he could return to the fold to help out.

They had worked together with Henry since his days with the Parachute Regiment. As a Captain Finlay had entered selection for the Special Air Services in the late 1980's and passed the onerous recruitment procedure but to his surprise was not offered a position in the elite regiment. He was approached by a branch of Military Intelligence known as the Special Reconnaissance Unit or SRU which was founded in the 70's to deal with the IRA though it had carried out more activities than just reconnaissance. The SRU, as far as the general public was concerned, was a murky Northern Irish entity. What they didn't know was that it had morphed into being firmly intertwined with MI5 in Ulster before also being adopted for similar types of activity abroad with SIS. Finlay's brief was to bring military know how and skills to a four man cell who's primary job was surveillance of organisations intent on causing harm to the United Kingdom. Finlay's primary job had been to protect the other three members of the cell, being a combat soldier. He had always believed pre-emption is the best method of defence.

Major Lamont had excelled at his work for many years but after some time he had felt the murky shadows had encapsulated his life. He had spent cumulative years away from his wife and family and the stress had started to wear him down as he had grown older. He had retired and spent the happiest few months of his life on a military pension working in various relatively mundane jobs from flying a desk for the Forestry Commission to VIP security to supplement his income.

It was two years since Ella had died of cancer, he had effectively been a recluse, given up any supplementary income to look after her during her treatment and final palliative care. He thought her death would come as a relief but it felt like it had torn out his very soul.

Finlay had spent two years only communicating with strangers when purchasing sustenance, travelling or in passing them in the mountains. His only social contact had been kept with the local mountain rescue team. He had journeyed to Europe, ascended the toughest challenges, spent long durations in mountain chalets and tents in the Alps, Himalayas and Scotland - seeking out the hardest of climbs. He talked with no one unless he had to. It was as if he had been betrayed by someone or had lost trust in humanity itself.

The rock faces and peaks climbed had been hard. He'd pushed it to the very limits as if seeking an end but had always managed to come though as he instinctively knew how far to push without causing his death. Finlay had fallen once in the shadow of Mont Blanc while climbing the Colton MacIntyre Ice wall. As always the old soldier went solo, ropes had supported him but he had to descend and ski back into the valley in the coldest of winter conditions with a broken wrist, his only failure. He had been on course to climb it in three hours, close to a record, an astounding feat for a man of his age. Yet no one knew of his exploits. He kept a log, though not sure why or who would ever read it. It gave some structure to his quests in the hills to what was an otherwise seemingly pointless series of tasks, other than to simply occupy his body and mind. So he wouldn't think of Ella and the time he had lost with her.

The fire was burning well now so he closed the vent in, his coffee had gone cold. He walked over to the small drinks cabinet he kept in the corner of the living room of the cottage and poured himself a Harris gin, returning to his customary armchair by the fire. He savoured the drink.

Perhaps it was fate that had thrown this body in his path, this would give him something to work on. Henry V was right, he had to do something with the remainder of his life to bring some meaning to it. Having a half-hearted, and failed, attempt to fall or freeze to his death was not the answer. He would wait to find out the identity of the body and cut a deal with his old comrade and see how it all developed. Finlay had no doubt on his physical fitness in handling the task, his mind however, needed some on the job training.

Chapter 5

While Captain Campeti of the three thousand TEU m.v. African Tide container vessel discussed the voyage plans from Singapore through the Indian Ocean and Gulf of Oman with his Chief Engineer in his office, the Chief Officer of the vessel worked through the loading plan in the Wheelhouse. The containers had to be rapidly but carefully loaded in a sequence that could be accessed easily while the ship transited from Singapore to Bandar Abbas. Then it was Jeddah and on to Djibouti. The first discharge to Bandar Abbas was loaded last in Singapore above the deck superstructure. Included in the list of cargo was DES113, listed as FOTMA tractor parts. He had to hand the plan over to the Second Mate before who was about to go on his six hour cargo loading watch. He then had to welcome four Iranian passengers on board who were bound for Bandar Abbas. Despite being a cargo vessel her certificate allowed her to carry up to twelve passengers on board, though it was a rare event, apparently they were travelling with some valuable cargo that would need to be accessed during the voyage. It was listed as live fish in JBK3703 air conditioned unit.

Chief Officer Kravits was relatively new to his position, one of a new generation of Ukrainian seafarers that had not come up through the Soviet system. He was looking forward to his first elevated monthly pay going into his account and was pleased he was appointed to one of the newer container vessels in the Singaporean fleet that plied relatively warm, benign waters. He felt he has done his time in the North Atlantic and Pacific during his training and junior officer years. Kravits was looking forward to a quiet week after exiting the dreaded Malacca Straits en route to the Middle East. He seemed to get on quite well with Captain Campeti, though he was a little excitable, perhaps because he had a green second in command. He was also pleased that the Chief Engineer came from Ukraine so while the common language for the international crew was English, he could socialise occasionally in his native tongue.

He handed over loading and ballast responsibilities to the next officer of the watch and went down to the gangway in the ship's hull door to welcome the passengers on board. Three men and one woman greeted him at the head of the walkway in English and asked if their luggage could be brought on board. An older man was in charge of the party, the younger woman was listed as his wife on the passenger manifest, both Directors of the fish importing business. The two younger men wore the casual uniform shirts of the business and were technicians.

'These must be very important fish,' commented Kravits.

The older man replied, 'they are Caspian Sea Sturgeon, genetically modified in Japan to produce more Caviar'. Very important for our business in Iran.'

Kravits nodded while noting the two younger men didn't appear to understand the conversation or were not interested in breaking the ice.

The older passenger continued, 'my name is Cyrus Sia, I am pleased to meet you.'

'Chief Officer Vasily Kravits, welcome to the African Tide.'

'Thank you Chief'. Kravits ignored the fact he was being addressed with the wrong title. 'We need daily access to our cargo, to check and feed our animals, starting from now.'

'Yes Mr Sia, we will have to wait until all our cargo is loaded and rig a walkway access to the container.'

'Very good, please inform my men when this has been done and the unit is on ships power.'

Chief Officer Kravits escorted Sia and his wife to the owner's suite on the officer's deck and then showed both technicians to much smaller cabins on the crew's deck where the Filipino crew resided.

Kravits returned to the Wheelhouse and briefed Captain Campeti on the loading sequence and timing as well as the arrival of the passengers before returning to his cabin to get some sleep.

Chapter 6

Finlay arrived at City airport in London where there was a large black Jaguar waiting to take him to Thames House. He was in a reflective mood as he drove through the streets and dark overcast sky above. He'd spent a lot of time in London, both in his youthful days in the military and in later years in his role with the SRU. It had been a long time since he's been in the city, the hustle and bustle of the capital was something he had hated, however he found it strangely comforting as he drove past Canary Warf, along past the Tower of London toward Southwark Bridge.

It was the longevity of London and its history that re-assured him that his support of his country had been worthwhile. It had been fought over and assaulted for over a thousand years, been the birthplace of true democracy - bombed by everyone from religious fanatics to anarchists through to foreign states and modern terrorists. It was still here, thriving, its historical landmarks and memorials reinforcing that foundation of resilience. Thumbing its nose at these threats which appeared to have left no lasting marks on its façade.

The Jaguar drove along past the City and toward the north side of the river toward his destination, he saw the Tower of London, St Paul's and eventually Westminster Palace and Big Ben. Further reminders of civilisation and what he had attempted to help preserve.

The car glided to a halt outside the arched entrance to MI5. Finlay thanked the driver and strolled through the arch into the vestibule entrance. Very few people outside of the security services and maintenance staff had seen inside the building. Apart from the usual array of security apparatus inside, it was an austere place, there was very little warmth in the surroundings, furniture, fixtures or fittings. There were a lot of electronic surveillance devices, parts of the building were subject to checks every week, such was the sophistication of electronic bugging devices. He was met by a chaperone from Henry's Strategy Section and taken up to his office.

As Finlay walked into the small office, he saw Henry lying prone across a desk through the raised sash window with his elbows on the external sill smoking a cigarette.

'Henry, I'd recognise that shiny backside anywhere!' exclaimed Finlay

Henry Darcy stubbed his cigarette on the well pocked windowsill and flicked it into the air before wriggling back into the office and sitting on the table swinging his legs.

'They have a smoking room but it's full of arseholes, so I've made my own arrangements,' Henry jumped on to his feet and shook Finlay's hand. 'Great to see you Fin it's been a while.'

'Looks like you're busy Henry,' Finlay grinned.

'Actually I am, especially since I took your call, Director wants to keep it in house and not let my old employers over at the Cross get a hold of it.'

'How do they have jurisdiction? It's internal to UK borders, go to be right up your street though not your section.'

'That's the problem my good man, shut the door.'

Finlay shut the office door and sat down across the desk from Henry, despite his best efforts Henry stank of cigarette smoke. He noticed his old friend had aged, well grooved crows' feet around the eyes when he smiled, hair receding and thinning, his face pale and teeth yellow from his office habitation and chronic smoking. There were also signs of a well grown paunch under his grey threadbare sweater.

'This fellow you found up in the wilds of Bonnie Scotland was a French Nuclear Scientist who had taken the King's shilling from our North Korean friends, disappeared off the face of the earth eight years ago when he was part of the French nuclear weapons programme.'

Finlay frowned. 'I thought the North Koreans were a nuclear power by then?'

'We believe he was instrumental in the development of those original weapons. The stuff they originally made was the size of a plumber's transit van. His particular skill was in making warheads small enough to fit on a ballistic missile. As you know the West has got so skilled at this, they can fit ten or more warheads on one ICBM.'

'So, he has been doing this for North Korea.'

'Yes.'

'And they decide to take him out in case he spilled the beans.'

'That's what doesn't necessarily make sense, the North Koreans want us to know their capabilities, in fact more often than not, have exaggerated them.'

'Perhaps he failed', contemplated Finlay.

Henry grimaced 'Yes that's possible, but why not kill him in North Korea, much easier. They had hired help, I assume, your two suspects didn't look like Koreans?'

'They looked Southern European or possibly North African.'

'Dubois had been out of North Korea for some time, it appears, under an alias, he was living in France, had an expensive place in Provence by all accounts. He suddenly upped sticks and disappeared again.'

'He wasn't an outdoors man, fat bloke, soft, so what is he doing in the middle of nowhere. There must be better places to hide?'

'No idea. Anyway the Nuclear Proliferation boys at SIS want to takeover, we've managed to fend them off saying its internal but I don't know how long for. Our leader's upstairs are pushing the boat out, willing to spend a bit. I've told them you are ideal. All you'll have to do with your previous record of employment is sign some forms to get on board and of course get paid. Boss wants to see you as well.'

'Who am I working with, prefer someone I know?'

'Glad to report it's me Finlay!'

'You are fucking joking, Henry, you're not a field man!' Finlay didn't know whether to laugh or cry.

'It's never too late my dear chap, I've been so excited I haven't slept properly, sick of being stuck in here.'

Finlay stared at his old friend. His teeth yellow, he was overweight, took no exercise and his idea of fresh air and the great outdoors was hanging out the window to smoke fags. Having said that he had an extremely sharp mind and knew the spook business better than anyone he had worked with. He was also a known entity he could trust relative to a stranger. Just don't expect him to climb any ice walls in a hurry.

'Alright what's next?'

'We need to trace Dubois' steps next Finlay, the DGSI have been round his Chateau in France, suggest we take a look over the place, just secured permission from them. They are going to pass on details of his funding once they get access, they've already been over to look at the body and we are passing on what we can in terms of autopsy report. They don't know about your involvement though, let's keep it that way for now. Once you go upstairs and get the paperwork done we'll be on our way.'

*

The fishing town of Bir Ali located on the Gulf of Aden had been a trading port for thousands of years, the population while now, was largely Islamic Yemeni from the mountains, was also descended from traders throughout the Indian Ocean and Arabian Sea. Archaeological excavations in more peaceful times had uncovered wine jars that had originated from Egypt and Greece, inscriptions that had shown craft and people's from around the Indus valley. They had even unearthed a third century synagogue.

Since the more recent resurgence of war in the Yemen the village people had not prospered well. Though the foreign fighters from Al Qaeda and fisherman turned traders had profited from the illicit trade in arms and food, it what was a country subsisting on famine relief from Yemen's rich neighbours and the West. A number of dhows had traded with the Yemen, Oman and the UAE, bringing in food and clothing which fetched a high price from those Yemeni locals that could afford it. There was little policing of the trade once at sea, most naval efforts were directed against piracy or protection of the LNG terminal further down the coast.

A mixture of dhows and fishing boats sat alongside in the small port, some anchored offshore from the beach and were accessed by small wooden fishing boats which lightered them while they were waiting for a berth. One such dhow had just entered port after making passage through the Red Sea.

Externally it appeared to be well weathered due to its time spent on the ocean. Internally it was very well founded with two large powerful Cummins diesels and sizeable fuel tanks, enabling a high cruising speed and extended range. The tanks and engines appeared to have been retro-fitted more recently. A visitor to the craft would have wondered why an old wooden fishing boat was being used to access the large cargo dhow when there was a sizeable rigid inflatable lying inboard of the deck crane under a canopy with two 300hp Mercury outboards on it.

The dhow had a small crew of five men who had worked to get as much of the cargo off loaded to a lighter barge they had hired. They had winched it back and fore using the anchor windlass and a pulley secured to the beach by a large cement weight. She wouldn't have to wait for a berth on the quayside any longer, they would be finished discharge within 48 hours. Like most of the inbound craft there was not outbound export cargo due to the war in Yemen, though the Captain knew he had to wait for a human cargo. He had been paid handsomely for this trip and had been promised considerably more by the Palestinian in Hudaydah that dressed as a Yemeni. He had distributed the share money in time honoured fashion to his crew who were delighted with the return they made. They couldn't quite understand how the customer could make so much from selling in such a poor country, particularly when it was in US dollars. They had just heard they were taking people out of the country. The crew had expressed their concern to the Captain who had told them their payment would cover the risk, he re-assured them by telling them the Coastguard had been taken care of. The Palestinian had rewarded him for previous excursions by replacing the old Stork engines installed in his vessel and fitting large fuel tanks giving him greater fuel economy and range. Captain al Shafer had taken part ownership with Fakhoury as part of the deal which had saved his ailing business.

The gentle winter breeze and swell from the sea caused the dhow to range a little and tug at her anchor while the sun set over the mountains overlooking the village. From a distance the scene would not have looked so very different from when those Hellenistic traders had landed their worldly goods on the very same beach two thousand years ago.

Chapter 7

Chief Officer Kravits squinted out of the Wheelhouse of the African Tide as she departed the Malacca Straits with Northern Sumatra on his port side and Malaysia on the starboard. He could still smell the jungle on the seaward breeze, a mixture of rotting vegetation and smoke from fires. The region had been a hotbed of piracy fifteen years ago but was relatively safe now, the only real hazards being navigational with so much vessel traffic both north and southbound in such a narrow and shallow waterway. Added to this was haze in the summer months from extensive Indonesian bush fires. As the ship navigated into more expansive water before turning west at the tip of Sumatra, the risks lessened considerably.

He looked at the weather forecast printed off the desktop computer next to the chart table, it looked as if the weather was going to blow up as they crossed the Bay of Bengal. He had accompanied Sia and his wife and the two technicians to inspect the live fish cargo in JBK3703 the previous afternoon just after the ship had sailed from Singapore. He was amazed by the size of the sturgeon and the amount of equipment that had to be fitted inside the air conditioned container. The tanks had to be cooled at the right temperature and seemed huge even for the size of the giant fish. One technician told him in very broken English this was to ensure the fish exercised and remained healthy so they could provide useful breeding material at their destination on the shores of the Caspian. Food had to be administered twice a day from a storage area at the back of the container.

He noticed that Sia or his wife rarely spoke to the two technicians in Persian but conferred in English, certainly while he was there, perhaps out of courtesy or so that he would know the process for the fish. He would need to tell them about the weather as it may affect the large water tanks the fish were kept in.

Captain Campeti, the Chief Engineer and Kravits had entertained Sia and his spouse the centre table in the dining saloon for dinner, they had taken lunch and breakfast in the large owner's suite which had its own living room and dining table. Sia had been engaging, he was a well-travelled and wealthy man who had frequented a lot of the countries the professional seafarers had been to. His wife said very little, she seemed less worldly and a lot younger, perhaps a second marriage or Mr Sia perhaps had more than one wife. Kravits wasn't sure if Iranians were allowed more than one spouse, he noted that both shunned any offer of alcohol so he's assumed they were practicing Muslims. The Chief Engineer of the African Tide like a few glasses of wine with his dinner, he had got the impression that Sia had not approved, particularly when he got overly friendly with Mrs Sia on the first evening they dined together.

He glanced over at the electronic chart screen and noted the speed of the vessel as she changed course slightly to the north-west. The ship had to get to Bandar Abbas and comply with a strict timetable, software on a computer calculated the weather, tides and estimated time of arrival in the next port. This was linked to the huge marine diesel engine's fuel consumption efficiency and the resultant calculated speed was set thousands of miles before arrival. He checked the computer's calculation against his own figures once a day.

The African Tide also had two radars as required by international law, as the officer on watch he scanned these regularly to pick up any vessels he may not be able to see. Small wooden fishing boats without radar reflectors were always a problem particularly at night when the boats had their lights switched off to save battery power. Many fishermen had disappeared near the Malacca Straits without any of the crews of these giant ships being aware of their fate despite colliding with them. The sheer size of the ships gave no indication at night that they had run over these tiny boats, the only metal on board being the little outboard engines, almost undetectable on radar.

At 4 pm he was relieved of his navigational watch by the second mate and decided to take a walk round the deck to inspect the container lashings and the loading guide system for pneumatic leaks. He requested the engineering officer of the watch to start the system up and he could go forward to listen for leaks when the deck was quiet. Away from the superstructure there was little noise but the sea breeze created by the ship's motion and the distant hum of the accommodation and hold ventilation.

Chief Officer Kravits marked the deck with a sure mark pen where he could here leaks net to the distribution box and worked his way forward. He would inform the engineers which repairs were required highlighted by his markings. He rounded number one hatch where JBK3703 was located and heard raised voices, intrigued, he rounded the container quietly, listening carefully. There was obviously an argument going on between one of the technicians and Sia's wife, quite a heated exchange. He decided not to interfere and turned to attend the other side of the vessel. One thing that struck him was the language they were speaking sounded like Arabic or Hebrew, more guttural, vowels being produced from the back of the throat. It didn't sound like the Persian he had heard before when he had attended nautical college in Odessa with Iranian cadets and discharged his ship in Iranian ports.

There were a number of languages spoken in Iran, so perhaps it was one of them he hadn't heard, Kurdish or Armenian perhaps. Maybe a fish had died.

Chapter 8

Ebrahim Khorasani sat in his office in Tehran staring at one of his European operatives within VAJA through a stream of cigarette smoke. The man had arrived the day after Ebrahim had returned from Istanbul via Charles De Gaulle with a short stay at the Paris embassy.

'Explain to me why you can't locate Dubois?' he growled.

'Colonel, he was last seen at his home in Southern France, prior to us requiring him to come here for the project.'

'Well when did he leave?'

'We lost track of him three weeks ago. He must have left his home at night and gone over a wall or fence at the back of his garden, it's a big place we couldn't keep eyes on the whole perimeter.'

Khorasani felt the blood rising in his neck with anger, he raised his voice an octave, 'I told you this was one of the most important surveillances this organisation has carried out, and you have lost the target, you think the Mossad would have lost this man? He was a fat unfit scientist, not a James Bond!'

His operative looked averted his eyes from Khorasani, his fear of the consequences of his failure to track Dubois very evident. He stared at the edge of Khorasani's desk.

'We are still trying to find him sir.'

'Get over to Gaza and talk to our people in Hamas, go to Beirut and speak to Hezbollah, they may know more, don't come back here until we locate the scientist.'

The shipment was due to arrive in one week, they could not advance the weaponry without the Frenchman. It was the one individual they needed to head the team and they had lost him. He would need to answer to the revolutionary council on the progress of the mission by the end of the week. VAJA used Hezbollah for some of its clandestine work, based in Beirut most of the senior operatives spoke French and the first contact with Dubois had been made in Southern France through one of their Lebanese agents.

Ebrahim Khorasani had been the architect of assassinations, interrogations under physical and mental torture for over twenty years. He had a mixture of success and failures, was trusted with his network to get the job done. His dedication to the Iranian regime had never been questioned. This failure would set the project back months or even years. Hundreds of millions of scarce Iranian foreign currency, mostly dollars, had been spent on procuring and shipping the equipment from North Korea since the United States had re-imposed sanctions. He felt that the project was starting to go wrong and the pressure was causing many sleepless nights.

He stood up and walked over to the mirror in his room. The reflection showed a suit that looked two sizes too big for his thin frame, scuffed shoes and a fraying shirt collar done up with no tie - as was the Iranian custom since the revolution. He took a comb for his pocket and brushed his hair back, an attempt to make himself presentable before he visited his mistress. He needed to have some whisky and distract himself with the attentions of his lover to take his mind off this damned project. He donned his coat and walked down the stairs, stopping only to light a cigarette in the doorway to the building before walking out into the cold air of the Tehran winter. It was slowly turning into spring.

*

Zarrin Rahmani occupied an apartment in Elahieh, in one of the recently built high rise apartments in the affluent area of Northern Tehran. She had moved to the district from a much poorer area in Southern Tehran and found the quality of life in the high risers nestling below the beautiful Alborz mountains to be much better. The air was cleaner despite the traffic in the equally narrow streets and it was much greener. The parks and gardens were well maintained and reminded her of the City of London's west end. She had been educated there as a student and had loved the City. Zarrin was a tall naturally elegant woman in her late thirties, her dark hair and emerald green eyes turned many heads in the streets of Tehran despite her dark hijab which she only wore when she had to. It was a useful garment helping conceal her identity when she was in Ebrahim's company in public. She had met him ten years ago and become his mistress very quickly. He had paid for her apartment and got her a job in the government administering civil planning for the sprawling city. She had found him to be a kind and attentive lover in the beginning. A combination of his higher salary as a Revolutionary Guard Colonel in VAJA and the money he made from his trips abroad had kept her in relative comfort.

Zarrin walked over to the hidden drinks cabinet which was essentially an electrical distribution box. It had all the switchgear bolted into a latched door which opened into a large alcove in the wall containing a combination of illicit spirits and wine bottles, mostly scotch whisky for Khorasani.

Despite the luxury she lived in Zarrin was aware she was getting older, her life for the past decade had been a monotonous one of being a kept woman. Despite Khorasani's kindness she knew she was being watched, probably because he was naturally suspicious that she may carry out an illicit affair during his prolonged visits home to his wife and children. She knew the consequences of betraying him in any way and she had a secret which was starting to make her nervous. Her tedious existence was sometimes highlighted by infrequent short interludes of sheer terror. Zarrin was looking for a way out.

Chapter 9

Finlay stared at his friend when he got off the flight to Nice and stood at the car hire counter. At least he was nondescript. He wasn't sure if it was by accident or design but Henry and his colleagues in either five or six seemed to have a knack in blending in. His slightly pot-bellied frame with old jeans, training shoes and a well-used jumper could have come out of a spy training manual. Henry's sallow complexion and pock marked face served to add to the visual mediocrity. He'd already suggested Finlay stood in the car hire queue while he went off to smoke a couple of cigarettes after two whole hours of abstinence. He trotted off outside with a cigarette dangling from his lips, reminding him for the third time since they left Thames House "don't forget to get a receipt". He'd returned to find the transaction had not been completed and was obviously contemplating going for another round of smoking. Henry knew Finlay wouldn't let him smoke in the car.

'How long does it take to get there, Fin?'

'Couple of hours perhaps, depending on traffic.'

'Ah, you should probably drive, I may get confused, what with these French people driving on the wrong side.'

'Fine.'

'If I crack the window open ever so slightly you can get a venturi vacuum effect as the car moves along, which acts like an extractor fan, you won't smell a thing.'

Finlay didn't comment, he'd been brought up with squaddies smoking and it actually didn't bother him too much but he knew Henry would take advantage if he was sympathetic. They completed the hire of the car, found the vehicle, an older Ford Mondeo, and set the navigation system supplied by the hire company to the address they were looking for just outside San Tropez.

They made good time in the off season traffic and were surprised to be guided to a relatively rural area overlooking the Bay of

Pampelonne. A wrought Iron gate stood open with an unmarked police car parked just inside the walled enclosure on the driveway to the Chateau. Two casually dressed men introduced themselves as the local Police Nationale and confirmed they had been asked to give the two British agents access to the site by their own DGSI as it was linked to an internal matter in the UK. Finlay was surprised by the non-attendance of their security service personnel but Henry retorted that the men in attendance may well be DGSI but wearing police uniforms. Perhaps their view was making a fuss would only serve to alarm the UK security services further. Better to give the impression is wasn't a big deal.

Finlay was surprised at the size of the building and grounds which were surrounded by a two metre wall topped with wire fencing. Security cameras were positioned both on the boundary as well as inside the grounds and on the façade of the building as they approached. Internally it did not look as if Dubois had spent a lot of time on decoration or furnishings, in fact it looked as if he had barely moved in. Henry and Finlay had discussed how they would approach the search while they had driven from the airport. They systematically searched each room, lifting carpets, checking under tables, behind paintings as well as the more obvious places like the cupboards and beds. Henry knew a few tricks such as pulling out the kitchen appliances, screwing off the back covers, he did the same with televisions and speakers and they found nothing of interest. They accessed the loft space and the basement, still nothing. It didn't appear as if the building had been ransacked or searched by anyone else, all appeared quite innocuous.

Finlay agreed to look around the grounds while Henry searched the large garage area. He looked at each security camera as he wandered around the ground to see if anyone had disabled them whilst making a clandestine entry, nothing.

Finlay returned to the Chateau and found Henry sitting in the large living room, one of the few decorated and furnished rooms in the house which had been modernised by knocking through into the next room. A mezzanine area was accessed from the lower living room which contained a large dining table which, in turn, led to the kitchen. The house had been built on a slope, the lower part of it served as the large living area with large glass doors that led to a balcony overlooking San Tropez.

'There is something not right with this room Finlay', mused Henry, who appeared to have poured himself a healthy glass of wine from Dubois' stock in the kitchen, 'if you look from outside the house from the living to dining room and then to the kitchen slopes up the hill, eventually to the bedrooms at the back of the chateau. The house wasn't originally built like this, the kitchen would have been in the basement with servant's quarters, the original hall and entertaining area was built on a levelled part of the site which would have included the dining area.'

'And the dining room is on a mezzanine level,' retorted Finlay

'Yes which is slightly higher than a man, either that has been raised on a brick or cement plinth or it's a space.'

Both men walked up to the mezzanine level, moved the dining furniture to one side and rolled the rug up along the wooden floor, no misalignment of the wood flooring that would indicate an access was evident. They walked down to the living room again and checked the side of the mezzanine. Henry went round to the side where a narrow walkway between the external wall and the raised floor gave access to a cupboard located on the side. He tried pushing it sideways, it didn't move at all. Finlay went to the end of the access and put his fingers between the mezzanine and the wall and pulled the large full height wooden cupboard. The cupboard, despite storing a large weight of crockery swung out easily until it fitted the narrow access perfectly, anyone standing in the living room and looking at it would have assumed that it was located on the wall at the end of the access when in reality, as Finlay saw from behind the cupboard there were steps down into a sizeable room located below the dining room floor. He let Henry get past the cupboard and both men descended into the hidden space after Finlay switched on the light. The room was very neat and organised. Computers printers and a large TV screen covered the back wall of the room. A long drawing desk occupied the centre of the floor, along with a sizeable CAD drawing printer. Large drawings were rolled up and occupied long horizontal filing cabinets against the side walls.

'How the hell do we go through all this stuff and know what we're looking at?' said Finlay as he unrolled a drawing.

'We need to let the French in on this or we take as many pictures as we can and close it all up,' replied Henry. He looked at the drawing Finlay had unrolled on the desk. 'They know one of their nuclear scientists has disappeared but I'm not sure how much else they know. I'm sure they don't know about this room and what we suspect in contains or it would all have gone. They will be very embarrassed about one of their boffins going feral for cash. We haven't got much time before those cops come up here sniffing about to see why we are taking so long. Let's get the computer hard drives in the car and take a few drawings with us that look as if they could mean something, we can pretty much get that in a suitcase, the rest we leave and shut the door.'

Finlay went up to the master bedroom and found a suitcase while Henry unbolted hard drives from two of the computers. He then looked at some drawings, made a good guess at what he thought looked interesting, folded them and put them at the bottom of the case. He then took as many pictures of the hard copy drawings as he could with his cell phone while he waited for Henry to finish his task. When the case was packed Henry returned to their car and took some of his clothing from his own suitcase and covered the drawings and hard drives inside the case. It would pass a cursory examination on the way out.

Finlay looked at his companion as he zipped the suitcase up inside the boot of the car, 'we could lose the lot if they search the car,' he grimaced. Finlay grabbed the case and ran down to the wall and fence he had inspected earlier behind the chateaux and threw the case over the top. Henry understood the plan immediately and started the engine while Finlay approached the car. They drove down to the gate and were stopped by the two policemen who spoke to Henry in French and asked him to inspect the car and its contents. As they did so the sky started to darken and rain started to fall slowly on the scene by the gate overlooking San Tropez. Both visitors from the UK looked thorough miserable as they stood outside the Mondeo and waited for the policemen to complete the search.

'Well done Finlay,' Henry muttered under his breath as the two policemen took everything apart, searched the cases and even the engine compartment, albeit apologetically making excuses about instructions from their superiors and the spooks at the DGSI. They departed and once out of sight of the chateaux gate, Finlay ran up to the back fence and retrieved the case.

They elected to drive back to the UK and take the ferry to lessen the likelihood any further scrutiny of their luggage. Finlay drove and Henry smoked.

*

The man called Omar Fakhoury had flown from Istanbul to Dubai, as an Omani and a GCC national he didn't need a visa to enter the country. He booked himself into the luxurious Royal Mirage Hotel on the verge of the turquoise sea of the Arabian Gulf with the original Dubai Palm a few hundred metres from the secluded beach. Saeed had stayed in the hotel many times and regarded it as just reward that gave him a little respite from his calling to conquer the crusaders. His clandestine life and faith required a frugal existence to be kept but sometimes in a place like this you can hide in plain sight. The spring weather was very pleasant when he had arrived the night before so he had arranged his meeting at the open air seafood restaurant overlooking the beach.

He had arrived early as was his habit and sat looking out to the Palm and open sea to his left, he noted the grey skies and dark clouds moving in from the sea. There was a humidity in the air that had the feeling of a thunderstorm, an almost electric energy awaiting to release itself as the clouds moved slowly toward land.

Hassan Makhlouf arrived on time and greeted him warmly, both men had known each other since childhood on the West Bank when the Syrian had help bank roll the Intifada. Unlike most Syrian resistance fighters, Makhlouf had originally had a foot in both camps of Hamas and Hezbollah until they had irreconcilable differences in the last two decades.

Makhlouf was a bulkier man used to the good life and food of Dubai, unlike the relatively diminutive Palestinian who also dressed very simply compared to the more ostentatious Syrian. They looked an odd couple but not necessarily out of place in such a cosmopolitan city with a melting pot of cultures.

Saeed looked across at his old colleague, noting the fatter jowls and buttons straining on his expensive silk shirt, 'Hassan, you have put on weight.'

'And you have not, my friend, you need to enjoy things in middle age, you are no longer being starved by the Israelis on the West bank. Live a little.'

'Allah feeds me every day Hassan.'

'And me, I have a role at the point of our spear also, but if I show myself as a conservative Muslim in this country, with my wealth and nationality, I will attract attention. My role cannot be a pious one, perhaps you are more fortunate than I.'

Saeed smiled, while he felt that Makhlouf was dedicated to the Mubarizun, he suspected this was an excuse for the man to live how he wanted but he was invaluable as the treasurer. The man that could bank roll their project.

'Have you found your Frenchman Saeed?'

'Omar, please.'

'You see microphones in every flower pot… Omar. You are paranoid living this life,' laughed Makhlouf.

'No he has disappeared, the Iranians are seeking him also.'

'We can't undertake the project without him.'

'I believe we can, the device has a simple trigger, three or four steps, we can activate with human hands, no complicated timing devices. We only need an electrical supply.'

Makhlouf leaned of the table and whispered, 'This has the power for such a bomb?'

'It has the power for conventional explosives which in turn detonate the material inside a ball.'

'We have to get the machine first Hassan, that is my next step, once we have it in our hands, we can see. We have drawings with instructions from Dubois. Our plan was to go through the process with him prior to target delivery. We will eliminate him immediately after project completion, to ensure it works. Our contacts are looking for him, if we can't find him, we move ahead ourselves.'

'How far are we from having it in our hands?' retorted Makhlouf

'Only days.'

'Where will you intercept?'

'That is known only to the interceptors.' There was a policy within the Mubarizun not to disseminate information to those that were not required to have it. Makhlouf knew this, thought Saeed, he should not ask me. The dangers of being rendered by the enemy were very real – "need to know" was key in the organisation. Saeed Abdul Raheem alone had the full picture.

Makhlouf nodded understandingly, 'OK let me know about further funds, should they be required, I have to be careful here. While it is a lot easier to move money than Europe or the U.S. there is pressure from the American FCPA people to investigate laundering. I don't want to fall into that trap, I need as much notice as I can get.'

'I understand, we need fifteen million Euros deposited in my bank in Switzerland to fund the ongoing delivery of the project, the interception money is here and we don't require further funds for that. It has been paid for.'

Both men continued to talk over a light meal washed down with a fruit cocktail. As they ordered Lebanese coffee the dark clouds rumbled and cracks of lightning seemed to fly from the clouds on to the Palm. This was followed by a large burst of sheet lightning that lit up the sky in spite of the daylight. As the large and heavy drops of rain started to fall Saeed turned on his seat and peered up at the sky. He turned to Makhlouf who was rising from his seat to move into the shelter of the restaurant, 'This is surely an omen of things to come for our enemy, my friend, power is returning to those that strike in the name of our cause.'

As both men walked into the beach restaurant a man dressed in a traditional Emirati head dress and white kandora took his telephone from his pocket. He moved underneath a sun umbrella to make a phone call as the preliminary pattering rainfall turned into a tropical downpour.

Chapter 10

The African Tide was now four days into her voyage and four days from Bandar Abbas. The Bay of Bengal had proven to be windy with a short swell disrupting the passage toward the Arabian Sea around the southern side of Sri Lanka. The port of Galle was on the starboard side. It appeared that the wind had abated and shortly after getting into the lee of the island from the easterly wind it became calm as the container ship turned north.

Chief Officer Kravits decided to take a walk around the deck once more while his Bosun and seamen took to washing down the decks with fresh water before commencing a deck maintenance and painting programme. It appeared the weather was good now all the way to Iran.

As he took the leisurely stroll he reflected on the past four days. While the crew were comfortable in the weather conditions, after all it was hardly storm force, his passengers had suffered from seasickness. The initial excitement of the voyage had had worn off, it appeared, and given way to monotony. The technicians had been in the fish container only on two occasions, showing little interest in monitoring the fish when the weather was bad, though the container on such a high sided vessel was accessible in poor weather. He had overheard Cyrus Sia instructing his technicians, he assumed, to get out and monitor the livestock. It appeared they were reluctant to do so, both looking rather pale and tired, sure sign of seasickness. He also watched them from the Bridge as they swayed up the deck on the rolling ship, one stopping to vomit over the side handrail. He smiled; often fresh air helped with seasickness. Unfortunately the eyes picking up the movement of the horizon finally gave the stomach the last lurch it needed to regurgitate its contents.

A couple of things didn't add up, firstly they were not speaking Iranian, he had asked Sia what dialect he spoke at dinner. He had told him it was Persian and seemed to be quite agitated when Kravits had pushed the issue further on dialect. Also, his Indian Bosun had told him that he spoke some Arabic, after some time working in

Oman, and he had overheard the technicians talking, clearly in Arabic. They had spoken about how all the fish would be dead on in the next couple of days, neither seemed to care, he would have thought their jobs with Sia had depended on their survival. The respect they showed for their boss didn't reflect the nonchalance of the conversation relayed to him by his Bosun on the subject of the prized fish. Perhaps the container was a cover for smuggling narcotics in which case they were taking a big risk, committing such a crime in Iran.

And then there was the woman, he didn't believe the body language between Sia and his wife was one of husband and wife. She was considerably younger of course but the relationship was more like a father and daughter. He decided as he was walking down the deck he would have a look in the container if he could get in it. Kravits looked down the deck he had just walked on from the bow of the ship and saw no one apart from his deck crew at work. He then moved across to the other side of the ship and looked down the walkway, no one. He walked up the steps that had been rigged for the container JBK3703 and saw that is had been locked with a fairly large steel padlock. He would see if he could try and get the key. Kravits would tell the Captain of his concerns in the meantime.

Chapter 11

Finlay had been tired on the long non-stop journey from San Tropez, they had elected to cross the channel between Calais and Dover, customs had been informed by intelligence to let the car through without a search. They were taken to the front of the traffic que with a police escort and by the time they reached the M2 it was the middle of the night. Henry called ahead to the office and ensured that the doors were opened in the early hours by security so they could leave the computers and drawings they had removed from Dubois' property in a safe place. Finlay had elected to drive all the way, not trusting Henry's erratic driving style, while Henry had dozed, smoked or been organising their arrival on his cell phone.

As they neared the city centre of the Capital and drove toward Henry's Millbank headquarters Finlay noticed that a set of headlamps had been following him from the motorway. He had noticed the shape of the headlamps and the lack of proximity of the vehicle, seeming almost reluctant to catch up but very keen to overtake any slow moving vehicles behind him. He knew about tails from his days in the SRU and his tours of Northern Ireland. This was a tail.

'I think we've got company Henry,' he spoke as he peered in the mirror.

Henry sat up from his slouched position in the passenger seat, 'Let me call the security boys at Millbank.'

As they pulled up to the rear entrance of the building a police car with armed police received them. Some of the security staff emptied the vehicle, carrying the hard disks and drawings up to Henry's office. Finlay stretched on exiting the vehicle and strolled round to the front entrance of the building. The car that had been following him was nowhere to be seen. There were a series of parked cars in permitted spaces but they didn't seem to be occupied. There were no people around apart from London council cleaning crews who always worked through the night to clean up the city. Finlay pulled his jacket collar up around his neck to protect himself from the chill of the night after the warmth of the car journey. He went back into the MI5 building to say farewell to Henry before going back to his hotel.

As he exited the Millbank building he walked up toward his Premier Inn hotel in Westminster, he glanced behind him and saw two figures emerging from a side street around fifty yards behind. A low mist had covered the Thames and the streets were clear of people and damp. There was little wind so the sound of their footsteps reverberated on the street, it sounded like they were wearing boots. From their silhouettes he could see they had caps on. It was probably nothing, construction workers perhaps or council cleaners. As he walked up toward Westminster Abbey they appeared to be gaining on him. He neared a short set of steps to a town house doorway, turned sharp right and stood at the top of the steps. The two men walked past, one of them glanced in his direction but neither men broke their stride. He waited a couple of minutes and walked back down on the pavement to resume his journey. There was no sign of the two men. As he turned left on to Victoria Street a black Mercedes saloon pulled up, two burly men exited and walked toward him, both men wearing thick jackets and baseball caps, one red cap, one black. Most men would have taken time to react to being approached so quickly but Finlay's sixth sense had been activated once again as he heard the vehicle pull up beside him. Black cap, the first man, had a large rubber club in his hand and raised it over his head, Finlay could see the intent in his eyes below the baseball cap. In a fraction of a second the Sykes Fairbairn was in Finlay's hand, it flashed in the light as Finlay jabbed the point right through the inside of the elbow of the first assailant's raised arm, removing it as quickly as it went in. The second strike went in underneath his left jaw and came out through his tongue, he observed in a fraction of a second through black cap's mouth. Finlay had difficulty in getting his knife straight back out so he stepped left holding the man up with the hilt of his knife. The second man was pulling something from his coat pocket but it was stuck momentarily. Finlay let go of the Sykes handle thus dropping black cap who fell heavily on the ground. He stepped right grabbing the man's floundering arm, his right hand came up under red cap's throat and pushed his head with some force against the wall of the granite building next to him. Red cap swung a punch which caught Finlay on the side of the head. While holding his arm Finlay stuck his thumb in red cap's eye, the thump to the side of his head caused him to momentarily loosen his grip. Red cap finally managed to pull a snub nosed revolver from his pocket and attempted to raise it toward Finlay's head. The old soldier held the hand firmly and bit red cap's nose as hard as he could. As he felt the salty blood in his mouth red cap loosened his hold on the pistol allowing Finlay to grasp the barrel and pull it out of his grip. He spun it round and fired a round into the second assailant's leg. The force of the bullet shattered red cap's thigh and he collapsed on the pavement. Finlay looked down at the .38 special he held in his hand, his instinct was to administer the coup de grace to red cap. Black cap looked as if he was already dead. He started to shake as the shock of the fight started to course through his body. Wiping the blood from his hand on black cap's jacket, he pulled his cell phone from the pocket of his jeans to phone Henry. As he fumbled with the phone screen, wet with congealing blood, to get his number, he heard siren's in the distance. He looked down at the two men lying on the pavement, one groaning and semi-conscious the other one completely still. They were both wearing heavy duty boots.

*

When Henry arrived at the Police station in Westminster Finlay was handcuffed and sitting calmly in an interview room, his hands bagged to contain any firearms residue. A burly policeman stood at the door with his arms crossed, two armed officers were stationed outside with Heckler and Koch sub machine guns. Henry was escorted by a uniformed Chief Superintendent who had been contacted by his head of section.

Henry grinned at his partner as he walked into the room, 'Well didn't take you long to get into the thick of things Finlay!'

'Get these fucking things off me Henry.'

Henry gestured to the constable in attendance 'Please take the cuffs off him.' The Chief Superintendent nodded when the Constable glanced at him.

Henry looked down at Finlay as the handcuffs were being unlocked, 'Bags will have to stay until the forensics chaps get here.' Henry waited until the policeman left the meeting room, he had already asked that any external microphones be switched off and the room be isolated from any cameras.

'Your special forces are far as this incident is concerned my friend, your little tiff is on three security cameras and there were two witnesses looking from windows. It is probably clear you were defending yourself but there will be an investigation and a public explanation will have to be forthcoming. Don't worry we'll take care of it.'

Finlay took a deep breath, 'I thought I was finished with all this shit in my life, is one of them dead?'

'No, one is in critical condition, lost a lot of blood and if he survives will need some dental treatment and a bone graft to his jaw. The other won't walk properly again. I've seen the video, all took eight seconds, lightning quick my friend, not bad for an old bloke. Hopefully the critical guy will survive and then it's less likely to crave media attention.'

'Any idea where they're from?'

'We haven't had time to speak to them yet but the delirious chap with the hole in his neck was trying to speak what sounded like Russian according to the ambulance crew. Though with the state of his mouth it could have been anything.'

'Jesus the plot thickens, how did I piss them off?'

'No idea, we'll find out in due course. You shouldn't have pulled the knife out of him, he's lost a lot of blood, maybe you nicked an artery.'

'I'm not losing my knife to some arsehole who tried to cave my head in, I'm emotionally attached to that blade.'

'I bet you are but you'll have to leave it with the cops for now, its evidence apparently.'

Finlay was moved to a laboratory where his hands were swabbed. A picture was taken of his face where the blow was landed and where his hands were cut from the fight. His clothing was bagged and he was given green overalls to wear. Henry went to Finlay's Hotel and picked up some clothing with the police. Finlay showered, donned his fresh clothing and left the police station with Henry. He was not charged but cautioned as per police procedure and sent on his way pending investigation.

*

The dhow Captain sat on the forecastle of his boat at anchor and sipped his sweet char and ate breakfast. He had cooked some lamb and wrapped it in pita with olive oil, tomatoes and over cooked egg plant. The crew had been dining well since the Palestinian had partnered with them. He gazed out over the beach as the early morning sun rose over the hills to the east and started to warm the air. His passengers had been delayed by a day, if they didn't come he would not make his rendezvous which he had calculated and marked on his charts.

His crew had got bored and gone ashore the previous evening drinking elicit black market alcohol despite his warnings about its side effects. During a previous voyage one of his Somalian crew was temporarily blinded. They had returned, waking him as they noisily stumbled on board the dhow from the tender boat.

As he looked toward the road that passed the beach front in front of the town of Bir Ali he saw a Landcruiser pickup truck and white Hiace van draw up. He hadn't checked all his men had returned, this was probably a stray lagging behind from the night before. He could see the driver opening the back doors of the van and counted eight men with heavy rucksacks being emptied out on to the sand, they turned and walked toward the beach where the dhow was anchored. Two pairs of men were carrying heavy boxes between them as well as the rucksacks.

The Captain went below to rouse his men from their drunken slumber. It wouldn't look good to his employer, particularly as he saw one small slim figure exiting from the pickup truck which resembled the Palestinian who called himself Omar. The Palestinian was a devout man, the smell of self-brewed alcohol on the breath of his crew would not go down well.

Two of his men started the small outboard motor on the tender boat tied to the side of the dhow and travelled across to the beach. The Palestinian got into the boat with a number of the rucksacks and one of his men, the Captain hailed them with greetings as they approached the side ladder of the dhow and the remaining crew rigged the stores crane to lift the equipment on board.

'Captain al Shafar, as-salaam alaykum.'

'Alaykum salaam.'

'Kayfa halik.'

'Humdullilah.'

The traditional Arabic greetings over, the men shook hands and went aft to the Captains quarters. Saeed looked around the Captain's austere cabin, there was little in the room, a small desk and writing bureau which also served as a chart table, a narrow bunk and a table with a chest underneath where he must keep his clothing.

'You must use my cabin Omar, if you are to sail with us on this trip.'

'Not at all Captain, I will sleep under the awning on deck with my men. We should only be spending two nights there before we reach our destination.'

'What do we do once we get there?'

'We land on a beach Captain, to pick up some equipment which you must carry for us to another destination, then you must go about your normal business. It will not take more than three to four days' work. You will receive fifty thousand dollars for you and your crew.'

'You must remember, sir, I am not a pirate, but a merchant Captain.'

Saeed laughed good naturedly and slapped Captain Al Shafer on the back, 'you have nothing to fear my good friend, your fine dhow will not be involved in anything like that.'

'We must sail tonight Mr Omar, if we are to get to the area you have requested in time.'

'We sail as soon as everything is on board Captain, I suggest you prepare for departure immediately.'

The eight passengers and five crew loaded the dhow from the small boat in three journeys, at one point the Captain thought the top heavy weight of the boxes and rucksacks would tip the small wooden boat into the water. He hadn't realised that so many men would come with so much equipment. The area marked on the chart as their destination to land the men was just beyond where the Straits of Hormuz narrowed near Iran. There were many naval craft in the area, including fast Iranian patrol boats, he was worried now. He had thought this was a case of dropping and picking up illicit goods as required, he was not averse to smuggling but these men looked like trouble. They were quiet but very sure of themselves, looked fit and focused on the job ahead. He wasn't sure what was in the boxes but he hoped sincerely it wasn't weapons.

The men distributed their equipment and bedding strapped to the top of their rucksacks into orderly areas on the deck. Some lay on the light camping mattresses and sleeping bags, others sat on the side of the dhow and smoked while his crew prepared for departure. When the Captain heard the roar of the engineer starting the dhow diesels down below he signalled to two of his men to let go from the mooring buoy they were tied to. The Captain stood at the Wheelhouse console mounted aft on the raised poop deck. He pushed both control levers to astern and backed away from the mooring and beach into deeper water. The wheel was spun, turning the large wooden dhow in the crescent shaped anchorage south-east toward the sea.

When the power increased on the diesels the Captain could feel the wooden deck throb and the speed of the craft pick up. He could also hear the swish of the seawater against the hull of the broad beamed craft as she eagerly reached out toward the Arabian Sea. As the turquoise hue of shallow coastal water gave way to the deeper blue of the ocean he could smell his cook preparing lunch in the cramped galley as was his custom after departing a port. The smell mixed with the cigarette smoke of his passengers who now had squatted behind the solid bulwark on the side of the boat. This was so that prying eyes from the port wouldn't be suspicious of the numbers of men they could see through any binoculars. The waters shone in the light of the sun as the awning flapped gently in the wind generated from the dhows motion. Normally all these sensations filled the Captain's heart with pleasure. Today it seemed to darken his mood and fill it with foreboding.

*

Finlay had returned to his croft near the Linn of Dee after flying back up north from London. His ageing frame ached from the exertions of the fight, despite the short time it had taken. He had been asking himself why he had got involved again, while he had felt alive and enjoyed the intrigue, the violence had sickened him. When he was a young soldier winning a scrap, be it live combat or in training had enthused him and given him a sense of accomplishment. Now it was almost as if he was conditioned to it, that it would never leave him, as if he was being tested until he slipped up, became too weak or simply failed. A sense of melancholy pervaded.

Henry had told him to go and rest up for a couple of days while his people analysed the drawings and interrogated the men that had attacked him. Finlay spent the time walking to ease the aches, did a couple of short easy climbs on Ben a Bhuird and Ben Macdhui to keep himself in condition. The silence of the mountains and the woods was a tonic after long car journeys and the hustle and bustle of London.

As he walked down off the hill from his latest climbing adventure, he could see his croft in the distance. It was springtime in the Cairngorms. The weak Scottish sun had lit up the purple blooming heather contrasting its bright colour against the dark highland granite in the shadows of the cliff faces. The worst of the winter snow had thawed from the higher ground, keeping the burns that flowed from the mountain full despite a few days with little rain. He could see a colour through the trees in front of his home that wasn't natural. He stopped and peered through the far off trees with his binoculars, it was a car he didn't recognise. He rarely had visitors apart from the odd drop in from his mountain rescue colleagues. He carefully made his way down the track through the trees, checking his flanks and looking for movement in front of his croft. He saw a figure walk back from his front door toward the car, as he took the movement in, he could see it became familiar. It was Elspeth, his heart lifted seeing her familiar shape pull open the door of her car while looking down at her cell phone.

He called the anglicized version of her name 'Elizabeth, I'm here!'

She moved her head, trying to point herself toward the sound she had heard through the breeze in the trees. She turned toward the path, her long hair interfering with her eyes so she had to hold it with one hand.

'Dad, where are you?' she smiled recognising it as his voice. 'Hiding in the bloody bushes as usual.'

'Here.' He strode toward her, a big grin crossing his face for the first time in months.

She rushed toward him through the trees and jumped, hugging him, legs raised off the ground. Finlay marvelled at how much she looked like her mother. High cheek bones and the almost turquoise eyes set in a pale skin.

'Where the hell did you come from Eli, I thought you were in San Francisco?'

'I was dad but I've been texting you and you haven't answered for almost a week, I was coming over anyway to see Brucie but wanted to come to Scotland as I haven't seen you for ages.'

It occurred to Fin that Henry had put an encrypted sim card in his phone and Eli didn't have the number. He'd not got round to purchasing another phone for his own sim card.

'Yes, I damaged my phone when I was up on the hill and have to get a new one.'

'What happened to the side of your head?' She saw the dark bruising through his short hair.

'Slipped when I was climbing again, I'm afraid, not as young as I used to be.'

Eli frowned 'You have to tell people where you are, going off on your own is dangerous, no matter how experienced you are. Mum always nagged you about that and you never listened.'

'I'll be fine Eli. There are a lot more dangerous things in life than me having a dander in the Cairngorms.'

'And you are mountain rescue as well, you should be setting an example.'

'I'll bear that in mind my dear.'

'Let's go for a bite to eat and a drink in the Fife Arms, I'm starving dad.'

'Aye, well let me get a wash and I'll be right with you, tell me your news.'

Eli babbled while he showered, filling Finlay in on the last six months she had spent working in California. The friends she had made, her apartment, job, weather, day trips to the mountains and beaches, the full richness of her American experience. Both of his children had the gift of the gab, unlike the relative quiet thoughtfulness of their father, once again a trait that their mother had. She had been quiet and reserved amongst strangers but talkative and gregarious with people she knew, particularly her family. Ella had loved life like no one else he knew and it showed, she'd brought brightness in to a room whenever she entered, their children were the same, particularly Eli.

She continued to talk with the odd reciprocal grunt or agreement from Fin while he drove the Landcruiser seven miles to the village of Braemar.

They sat over a meal of fresh shellfish starters followed by venison, accompanied by a good bottle of red wine. Eli looked over at Fin's craggy features tanned by the outdoors apart from the slight bruising to the side of his head. His cropped hair now losing its colour to grey, 'you look older since I last saw you - but healthy.'

'Yes, there is nothing like your family to tell you like it is!' he smiled.

'It's been a year since I saw you and your beloved son hasn't seen you for almost a year. Why don't you come with me to Cyprus?'

'I can't Eli, I'm working for the government on a project, paper pushing in London,'

His daughter looked at him, her blue eyes tinged with disbelief. Her mother had opened up to her a few weeks before her death, informed her of what her father had done in the army. That it was important and covert, had been dangerous. Her mother hadn't mentioned that her father had any administrative skills. Even without that conversation, the thought of her father "paper pushing" didn't quite match his character. She also doubted whether such a skilled mountaineer would slip and bang his head in the Cairngorms.

'I see, well I will tell you like it is, if this is something dangerous you are doing just remember Bruce and I are still young. We would still like at least one of our parents to be around into middle age!'

'Rest assured Eli, the worst I'll get is a paper cut.'

They spent the next three days together, walking in the mountains in some rare sunny weather, Eli was a keen cyclist, so they cycled around the Cairngorm massif Land rover trails, hiding their bikes in the brown and purple heather and walking to the mountain summits. They camped one night in Glen Avon before climbing Ben Avon, bathed in a small lochan and cooked over a campfire.

Finlay found a happiness of sorts for the first time in five years, maybe Eli was right, life can be worth living.

Chapter 12

Oudlajan in Tehran was known as the Jewish Quarter where the Jewish population was allowed to live in peace without any direct persecution, unlike parts of Europe. It used to be one of the wealthiest areas in Tehran but had become run down, many of the grand houses had been turned into stores or simply left derelict. More recently the area had had some capital injected into it, despite sanctions, to restore the old beautiful houses to their former glory. It was a project that would take decades to complete with the little funds that were available.

One of the properties was being refurbished by a Jewish contractor, Moshe Cohen. His family had lived in Iran for ever since anyone can remember, probably hundreds of years, even prior to Islam existing in the Middle East. Despite the offer of relocation to Israel in more recent times they had decided to remain in Iran. Outwardly it appeared that there was no persecution of Jews, however there were almost no Jewish people in senior positions since the Islamic revolution. They were allowed to exist and prosper but not to have a say in the running of the country, they were, after all, a very small minority.

Moshe and his team of builders had erected scaffolding inside and around the ancient Jewish merchant's house and were commencing on roof and upper floor wall repairs when Zarrin Rahmani walked on to the site. Moshe looked up from his drawing table of the ground floor just inside the grand entrance to the building, he was surprised to see her.

'Why did you come here?' he said disapprovingly, 'everyone can see you on this site.'

'I can't keep a telephone in case Khorasani finds or traces it and I can't get a hold of you unless you come to me, it's not a good situation,' whispered Zarrin.

They walked round to a covered area that had been set up for coffee breaks within the building site and sat at a small camping table and chairs, Moshe offered her some coffee.

'What is the problem?'

'Khorasani is on something big, he's been on his phone all the time to operatives in Gaza, West Bank and Lebanon. They are looking for a Frenchman linked to Korea who they want to find urgently, that's all I could hear. He is under a lot of pressure. He has talked to Esmail Ghaani a few times whom I am sure you have heard of, he is top of the tree in the Guard. Ebrahim is a thug but he's scared of this man. You need to inform Tel Aviv.'

'Ok. I hope you weren't followed here. If VAJA is following you to the Jewish Quarter to meet me, we are finished.'

She reached out and held his hand, they had been lovers since the operation had begun almost a decade ago. He was all that kept her going through the dark times and the act she put on with Ebrahim Khorasani, 'I want out of this, I can't take any more, I have done my part, more than anyone else I know.'

'Hang on in there Zarrin, we'll get you out once we find out what he is working on. That should be soon, remember I cannot go anywhere, my family is here.'

'You can come and live in Israel, that is accepted here. They won't know you have been involved with intelligence,' she smiled weakly her eyes filling with tears.

'My family is here Zarrin, I could never return,' he repeated.

She was caught in an emotional trap, if she wanted to stay with the love of her life she would have to stay with Khorasani. If she wanted out of the sordid relationship with the spymaster she had to leave Iran and Moshe. She wished Khorasani was dead, she would stay in Tehran then.

Moshe looked at her, 'let's get through this project first and then we can perhaps find a solution.'

He stood up taking her hand to pull her off the camp chair as he did so.

'Don't come her again Zarrin, I will contact you soon, once I get feedback from Tel Aviv. Go out through the back door, there is a gate in the walled garden in case you have been followed.'

She placed her sunglasses over her eyes to hide the redness from her tears and walked out into the alleyway behind the massive Merchant's house. Seeing Moshe to unload some of the pressure hadn't helped, merely aggravated her state of mind.

Chapter 13

Captain Campeti stood over the digital chart watching the track of the African Tide as she turned north-west from Mumbai toward the Straits of Hormuz. She would pass Karachi on the starboard beam in a few hours before entering the heavily policed straits. It was here that the ship's owners would increase the insurance to war risk after recent attacks on the world's tankers that entered the narrow seaway. They would be in touch with whichever vessel the West's navies had appointed to make themselves and their destination known. They would already be on some warship's long range radar or satellite monitoring system.

Chief Officer Kravits had expressed concerns about his four passengers, he felt that their story did not ring true and that they should search the container when they were retired in their cabins. The Captain felt that, unless the security or safety of the vessel was at risk, the contents of what was in the container was not his concern. He had told Kavits this. He had also told him he had no right to breach the clients' cargo container without permission and that he and the Bosun should continue to monitor the situation.

He watched as the sun set off the port bow over the Arabian Sea. Captain Campeti had taken the usual route through the Italian Merchant Marine, had spent time on passenger vessels for many years and joined the container liner business for a quieter life and promotion in his middle age. He spent many hours dreaming of his retirement villa in Tuscany where he planned to grow olive trees and produce the best oil in Italy. His wife had grown used to his long absences and had her own life at home when he was away for months on end. She had her own routine with the family and her friends when he was away. They would need time to adapt, he would need something to occupy his time and ease into retired life.

As the sun dropped further, Kravits put on a dark set of deck overalls from the paint locker and took a hacksaw blade he had ground down in the workshop which would serve as a lock pick. Picking up a bunch of keys, he started down the deck toward the bow where the live fish container was. The sun had almost gone over the horizon and he wouldn't be seen striding down the walkway on the port side of the African Tide which had container cargo stored above its overhead hatch beams. The hum of the engines and engine room fans located at the stern of the vessel slowly dissipated and gave way to the sound of the ocean lapping along the bow wave as the ship pushed through the water. He loved the relative silence and the sound of the sea, away from the sound of machinery and the more formal setting of the Navigating Bridge.

He was of course about to breach regulations as well as the clients' cargo, he could be immediately terminated from his employment and receive no references for another job from his time spent with this Company. He felt the security of the ship was at stake and Captain Campeti was neglecting his duties as Captain under International Law. He couldn't prove anything until he looked in that container.

As the Chief Officer neared container JBK3703 he heard voices, the passengers must have gone up the starboard side of the vessel and not informed the officer of the watch they were doing so. The poor weather had abated so they had obviously felt better. He crept round the side of the unit next to live cargo container and listened to the conversation as best he could. It was most definitely Arabic, not Farsi, Cyrus Sia was giving curt, clipped instructions to possibly all three of his team. Kravits could hear the mechanical sound of some kind of machinery being operated. The familiarity of it started to nag at him. Where had he heard it before? His thought briefly went to his Ukrainian Navy apprenticeship. It was precisely the noise he remembered. Then it dawned on him it was the sound of small arms being readied, magazines being inserted and bolts being cocked to push the first round into the chamber. He would never forget that sound as it brought on the curious feeling of nervousness combined with power and anticipation.

As he furtively peered between two containers he saw Sia step out on to the platform, briefly look around and aim what looked like an

AK47 at a far off imaginary target, before returning inside his container.

He backed off, no point in taking on armed terrorists, that's what they were, clearly. He walked hurriedly back toward the accommodation. Campeti must listen to him now, there was no time for speculation.

Chapter 14

Captain Al Shaffer was scared now. They had rendezvoused with a small truck on a beach east of Salalah before heading further east into the Arabian Sea. More equipment had been loaded. Omar Fakhoury has changed from being a welcoming and affable man to being curt and discourteous. He saw the men under his command becoming increasingly irritated and nervous. He had been snapping at his crew about everything from the use of space on deck for their equipment to bringing up the fact they had been drunk on illicit liquor in Bir Ali.

What concerned him more was how devout these men were. They rigorously prayed five times a day, continuously asked for the bearing toward Mecca. Even when the weather had picked up on their way to the beach equipment meeting, they had missed their meals, a couple had even been physically sick, but they had all gone through ritual ablution and prayer. These men were fanatics in his view, he regretted ever setting eyes on Omar Fakhoury. This was not to be the trading of illicit goods or alcohol. Their mission was nothing to do with making money.

Omar Fakhoury walked over to the radar which he had ultimately paid for during the dhow's extensive equipment refurbishment and peered into the viewfinder while adjusting the range. It was obvious he wasn't experienced in using the equipment.

'Captain Al Shaffer, I trust you know how to track vessels on this radar and identify them using the Automatic Identification System?'

'Yes I do Mister Omar, assuming they have the transponder turned on and they are not naval vessels which don't have them.'

'Ok I want you to find African Tide and track it for me, we are to meet with them to transfer some equipment.'

'Sir are we to do this at night as we may get tracked by naval ships.'

'I will tell you when we are to meet with it. Don't worry yourself we are too far south of the straits to be a concern for these people, simply follow your instructions.'

The Captain looked into the view finder, the rubber sunshield hiding the distress on his face. He spent some time adjusting the range and definition of the system. Radar could only see to the horizon or slightly beyond depending on the atmospheric conditions. He couldn't see any vessel called the "African Tide" only some fishing vessels and a couple of merchantmen which he could check on his internet connection, they didn't have the name required.

'Do you know where the vessel is coming from and where it's bound?' he said without lifting his head from the radar.

'It will be heading west by north-west approximately from the direction of India toward the straits. If it's not in range it should be soon. Keep looking, I will give you co-ordinates for the rendezvous.'

Captain Al Shaffer looked up toward Omar Fakhoury who was searching for something on his cell phone, probably the co-ordinates.

Fakhoury looked up from his phone and grinned at the Captain for the first time since their acquaintance, 'don't worry Captain, everything is very well planned, we will have fulfilled our mission within the next twenty four hours.'

In the setting sun on the deck of the dhow, Fakhoury's thin weather beaten face and spaced teeth looked like a death's head mask to Captain Al Shaffer. Fear gripped him further.

Chapter 15

Captain Campeti stared in disbelief at Kravits. 'How can you be sure it was the sound of weapons you heard?'

Kravits face was red with excitement and the effort of explanation, 'I am telling you as First Officer and Security Officer under the rules of IMO that we are about to be hi-jacked by these people, they are terrorists of some kind! I *saw* Sia with a weapon.'

Campeti had the impression since his First Officer joined the vessel that he was dramatic and full of conspiracy theories, 'I cannot arrest a client and send out a distress on the grounds of something you thought you heard or saw very briefly!'

Campeti attempted to put a re-assuring hand on the arm of his First Officer, Kravits pulled his arm away in disgust. 'I am going to alert the crew and commence rigging fire hoses and fire axes in both deck accesses before they return.'

'You will do no such thing.' Campeti was getting angry now, he turned to see Kravits opening the access to the stairwell and running down the stairs. He couldn't follow, he was on the Bridge to relieve the Second Officer of his watch so he could go to the dining saloon for his dinner. He lifted the telephone to call down to the dining area.

Kravits went to the crew deck and alerted the Bosun and deck crew who started to rig the equipment required in piracy procedures and make preparations in the ship's citadel where the crew could retire to in case of an armed attack. He would return to the Bridge and would seek support from the Chief Engineer so he could assume command from the Captain if he had to.

As Kravits walked past the chart table on to the Navigating Bridge he saw the young Second Officer staring out of the bridge windows at the crew rigging hoses below. This procedure was used to stop pirates boarding ship and combined with the ships speed and ability to turn in or away from the attacking vessel. This could be effective when the assailants were not already on board but Kravits had grave concerns about using it against armed men already on the ship. It may give them time if the high pressure water hoses could stop them from returning up the narrow alleyway. Meantime his men were putting communication equipment and food and water in the citadel.

'Where is the Captain?' he asked his Second Officer

'Looking for you Mr Kravits.'

Just as he turned away to resume his search for the Captain, Kravits heard fire hoses being turned on. As he walked back to look over the bridge bulwark outside on the bridge wing he heard three loud shots followed by a burst of several. He couldn't see what had happened as containers covered both port and starboard walkways forward of the accommodation where the hose nozzles had been deployed. The Chief Officer ran down the stairs jumping three steps at a time down four decks and cautiously moved toward the port access door. As he did so a Filipino crewman supporting Captain Campeti stumbled across the coaming of the door from the deck. Blood had soaked the Captain's uniform from his right shoulder right down his shorts to his legs.

He addresses his First Officer, 'Let's get to the citadel now.' Campeti's face was white, he was losing a lot of blood.

Kravits replied, 'I need to get the rest of the deck crew, who is left out there?'

The crewman responded, almost calmly, 'I think the Bosun is dead sir and the other two AB's I am not sure of, its Santosa and Flores, they are both lying on the deck. I can't see the gunmen because of the fire nozzle spray, not sure if they can see us. I think it may be our passengers who are shooting at us.'

Kravits grabbed a thick padded lifejacket from a nearby locker and put it on as the two men made their way down the nearby stairwell to the citadel in the forward section of the engine room. At least this could afford some protection from buoyancy material if he was shot above the waist. He slowly peered round the watertight access door which opened facing forward - affording further protection.

He edged round the door, the Bosun had obviously rigged the nozzle by inserting it directly on the fire main hydrant, the supply pipe of which ran along the walkway. He had pointed it directly down the passageway and a powerful jet of water around thirty metres long had prevented anyone getting up the narrow alley way without being pushed back by the jet. Kravits could see a similar jet now on the starboard side. His Bosun was lying behind the nozzle with a large exposed wound in his head, and by the way his body lay akimbo on the deck like a broken rag doll it was obvious he was dead. Santosa was lying behind him both legs bleeding from wounds and Flores was trying to drag him back toward the accommodation.

Kravits needed to give them time to get back, he could see a dark shape crawling along the deck below the jet of sea water, obviously soaking wet but not being affected directly by the pressure above him or her. The First Officer grabbed a fire axe next to some equipment left by his men and started to climb around the frame which supported the containers stacked above the hatch, if he could get behind the attacker without being seen by the others he could hit the assailant with the fire axe. It meant going outboard of the vessel, standing on the handrail and walking along the rail while holding on the container hatch extension. He circuited the first frame successfully walked along the next section of rail, the hatch frame spacing, Kravits remembered, was around seven metres. He transited two more, before looking down to see a shape crawling below the jet of water, it was one of Sia's henchmen. First Officer Kravits had never hit another human being with an axe, if he had perhaps he had he wouldn't have hesitated. But hesitate he did before another metallic noise, similar to the one he heard in JBK3703 reached his ears. He looked up, the woman, Sia's wife, stood on the next frame pointing an assault rifle at him. Before he could do anything he felt a huge force hit him in the chest. First Officer Kravits was thrown back from the railing, clear of the side of the high sided m.v. African

Tide. Before he hit the sea fifteen metres below, he had time to remember he hadn't sent out a distress message. Kravits felt he had let his men down.

Chapter 16

The spring weather in the Cairngorms had started to give way to the summer, it was still cool enough that the dreaded midgies were not out in force but warm enough that the trees, heather and shrubs had started to blossom. This time of year as well as late autumn was often the most beautiful in the Highlands of Scotland and was to be cherished. Finlay was dozing outside in his garden having had a decent lunch after his morning walk. Eli was long gone, off to see her brother after spending most of her trip persuading him to come along. Finlay would visit him when he was finished with Henry and his shenanigans. He would complete this project and then have some time with his kids. Eli had told him she had been approached by a business in Miami which could use her IT skills as an encryption specialist in the ever evolving world of cyber security. He could visit her there or in San Francisco in due course, make a trip of it. He would also pop over to see his son in Cyprus for a long weekend.

Finlay's cell phone rang, "Monmouth" flashed up on the screen as the caller. Fin answered it, 'Henry.'

'Where the bloody hell is your house Finlay. I'm supposed to be a spy and I've been driving around these wilds asking half the local yokel population where you live?'

'What are you doing here Henry, why not call?'

'Fancied a trip away from the Smoke old boy, thought I'd surprise you but should have known better. Not many people seem to know who the hell you are.'

'Well I suspect they do now, there is such a thing as Google Maps.'

'I don't trust all that shit, the yanks will track us with it.'

Finlay gave his colleague directions, turned out he was in the wrong glen about twenty miles east of his property. Henry finally arrived with a file under his arm in a hire car which he had already managed to dent. He would also probably be fined when he handed it back judging by the amount of smoke emanating from the window of the vehicle when he arrived.

Henry wore scruffy yellow cords that almost matched his teeth and a thick blue jumper which looked as if it had been darned more than once. He walked in the Finlay's croft with obvious purpose that indicated he had some important news and spread the contents of his file over his compatriot's dining table.

He placed a pair of reading glasses round his neck and pointed at the documents.

'The plot thickens my old pal, it appears our chaps at Aldermaston who've been looking at these drawings are of the opinion that the information is about miniaturising nuke warheads. That is what Dubois has been employed by the Koreans to conduct or should I say had. In essence the North Koreans had the ability to create a nuclear explosion but couldn't deliver it on a practical missile of any kind. The scientists tell me he would have needed something the size of a Saturn moon rocket to deliver his earlier warheads. Dubois had made his name in France making warheads so small they could be delivered by relatively light combat aircraft and cruise missiles. He was so good at it the French shared or swapped this information with their allies in return for other technologies such as stealth aircraft and satellite access.'

'Why did he work for the Koreans?' enquired Finlay

'It was certainly not because of idealism or left wing politics. I got some information out of our nukeprof guys in six, albeit grudgingly. They have had their eye on him for some time but he disappeared of the radar when he went to North Korea. If the French knew he was back on the loose they certainly didn't tell us. He was passed over several times for promotion and was never trusted with the whole story regarding France's nuclear strategy. It appears the main reason for him working for a despotic regime was pure and simple, money. We believe that large sums to the tune of millions of Euros was placed in offshore bank accounts belonging to Dubois. We don't know who killed him yet, could have been some freelancers hired by the Koreans, the French or the Americans. He could have been working for a new client, six are checking connections in the Middle East on both sides of the Islamic divide and also the Israelis.'

'What about my two friends in London, managed to squeeze anything out of them?'

'Thus my comment on the Middle East, it appears they are Chechyns, we don't know who they were working for but they are Muslims. Whether part of a terrorist organisation or state sponsored is still unclear. They've hardly been singing like canaries. I have been in touch with some of our friends in the region and we are making enquiries with their state security. An obvious suspect would be Iran but they have tended to use their own agents rather than foreign nationals.'

Fin looked at Henry as the latter lit another cigarette, he never asked if he could smoke in anyone's property, 'so it appears that making a nuke smaller is a big problem as it can be delivered on a missile or a smaller military vehicle of some kind, there are plenty of those around.'

'Yes Fin, but the issue goes beyond whether a rogue state is the problem, why did Dubois have to be killed?'

'Either by North Koreans who didn't want him telling anyone or by someone else he is working for.'

'Then he would simply disappear at the end of the project in the country he was being paid by. No one would care or be concerned, with the exception of any family he may have had.'

'So what are you saying Henry, these are terrorists that killed Dubois?'

'Or the enemy of the state he has worked for after departing North Korea. We need to consider ambitions in the Middle East, find out if he has connections there. He wouldn't be working for the Israelis as they have had nuclear weapons for some time. More likely an Iranian connection.'

'I thought they were some way from developing a bomb?'

'Who knows?' retorted Henry, 'it wouldn't be the first time we in the West got it wrong.'

Finlay and Henry walked out to the back garden and sat on the small patio, Fin made a pot of coffee and Henry laid out two of the drawings.

'Spot the difference between the drawings Fin.'

Finlay stared at the drawings. He had been trained in his army career in sabotage and demolition with explosives by the Corps of Royal Engineers so had an ability to read technical drawings. It looked like a spherical component of a much larger machine. Part of the drawing was two dimensional, part three with an exploded view of whatever it was. It basically looked like the skin of a football but much thicker, the internals were not shown those must have been part of another drawing. Both drawings were identical with the exception of a square component mounted on the side. One drawing has what looked like a large solenoid striker trigger while the other had what appeared to be a simple car battery and a switch mounted to the side of it.

Fin explained, 'Both are trigger mechanisms for the external implosion devices using conventional plastic explosive. The reason for internal implosion is it is used to trigger plutonium or uranium, the extreme pressure caused by the implosion causes the highly purified core to start a chain reaction which splits the atoms in a nuclear explosion. The implosion has to be very precise but also enables the bomb to be made a lot smaller than a much bigger barrel type bomb. The one on the left has a remote electronic trigger which is activated from afar either by external means or by sensors within a missile for example. The one on the right is a simple manual trigger no different from starting your car.'

A light went on in Fin's head, 'This is what really is stoking your concern, you won't have a manual trigger in a state sponsored missile.'

'Precisely my good man, you are looking at a trigger mechanism for the world's largest suicide bomb, not one that you can wear but maybe one you could drive around Paris in your car.'

'Jesus.'

Chapter 17

Ebrahim Khorasani was becoming increasingly concerned, Dubois had apparently gone to the UK and disappeared off the face of the earth. Had the British Military Intelligence got a hold of him? He had enquired through the intelligence operatives at the Iranian Embassy in Princess Gate London, he was familiar with the operations there after the embassy had re-opened in 2015. They had no information on Dubois and limited ability to find out what was going on inside UK intelligence. They only had one relatively low level operative in Millbank.

The Iranians needed Dubois to help reverse engineer the weapon before re-assembling and making operational. It was at the very highest level of priority and eyes at the most senior level of VAJA and the government, and in indeed the Supreme Ruler, were on him. Without Dubois they would be held up for months if not years. Successful understanding of the weapon would then just result in Iran having to acquire fissionable material, the rest of the technology to deliver the weapon was in hand.

Iran had long considered the most risky period for the country and any serious threat to its ability to become a nuclear power wasn't the prelude to a test, but the space of time from when they had demonstrated detonation to the world to producing a weapon that could be delivered. North Korea, by contrast, did not have an arch enemy in the region that had the mind-set of the Israelis. They had the memory of the holocaust firmly etched in their minds. Iran had threatened to annihilate Israel more than once, indeed it had declared it to be one of the main ambitions and strategy of the Islamic Republic of Iran. The Supreme Leader and government knew that an attack of their facilities would be highly likely which could lead to all-out war. In this case Iran needed a deliverable weapon available in parallel with the test. No other country had achieved this, even the U.S had a short delay before delivering their device to Japan. It only needed a short delay of a few weeks to see comprehensive infrastructure damage inflicted on Iran by Israel.

Khorasani had been tasked to get the first weapons into Iran. He then had to ensure the first device was handed over to the Revolutionary Guard who would make if deliverable on one of their long range missiles, the Shahab 3. The second device that was purchased would be disassembled to be examined by Iran's nuclear engineers before undertaking a demonstrable blast. He was also responsible for the delivery of that device to the Atomic Energy Organisation of Iran at a secret site in Shiraz. The Israelis had already bombed their reactor in the 1980's as well as attacking a Syrian attempt to build an atomic reactor in 2007, so the proposed location of the weapon was known only to a handful of people. The weapons would be shipped as if they were factory parts, even internally in Iran, such was the secrecy.

The ship would arrive in Bandar Abbas in the next couple of days. He would travel down then and accompany the vehicle and VAJA operatives who would provide clandestine security for the transport of the weapons' container north to Shiraz. Arrival of the weapon would be cause for celebration amongst his superiors, he was responsible for the day Iran became a nuclear power, the first country in the Persian Gulf.

Khorasani knew the following failure to provide the technical expertise he guaranteed to come with the bomb would be highlighted shortly thereafter. That would be followed very quickly about security concerns when it became known that Dubois had disappeared. The Mossad had also prioritised Iran's nuclear capability as its main strategic priority. As well as bombing its facilities they had undertaken a kidnap and assassination programme directed at Iranian nuclear scientists. He would be summoned to see the senior echelons of the Revolutionary Guard, anything could happen to him then, his fate would not be under his control. He needed to ensure the safe arrival of the container for now, his men were still out looking for Dubois and were now in the UK. Hopefully he would hear some good news while he was in Bandar Abbas or on the way to Shiraz. After that he was booked on a London flight as a diplomat and he could oversee the search for Dubois himself. It would also keep him away from prying questions on the scientists' whereabouts until he got back.

The other more minor issue he had was his mistress, Zarrin. She had become sullen and depressed in his company more recently whereas she had always been pleased to see him previously. She shunned his sexual advances and, on a few occasions, had caught a look of disgust on her face when she thought he wasn't looking. He would have to deal with that also, perhaps she had a lover or was sick of playing second place to his wife and family. That, he supposed, was always the inevitable outcome with a mistress as she grew older. He would never allow her to take the place of his wife and family, she needed an attitude re-alignment. He would have her followed to see if there was another man in her life.

Chapter 18

Captain Al Shafer stood at the dhow steering position checking the radar. He had removed the viewing cover used in daylight to shield the viewer from the sun as it was now dark. Saeed Abdul Raheem could also see the radar picture now standing next to the Captain. They were on a course of 45 degrees from north. There was a tanker which had entered their radar trace and was about to pass by their stern by 3 nautical miles at approximately 120 degrees. It obviously had left the Straits of Hormuz and was bound for India or the Far East. As they viewed the screen another trace heading at around 285 entered the maximum range of the device. It was moving very slowly indeed. Then both the dhow Captain and Saeed saw the name flash up next to the trace of the ship, 'African Tide.'

'How long before we get to that vessel at full speed captain?'

'Around 30 minutes if we increase speed sir.'

'OK give it everything.'

'As we draw near the ship will change course to avoid us.'

'No it won't Captain, they are going to rendezvous with us.'

Captain Al Shafer visibly relaxed - if the ship Captain was aware of the rendezvous with the dhow then he wasn't being asked to commit an act of piracy on a commercial vessel. This sounded more like smuggling now, despite his fears.

Saeed went down to the deck where his men were.

'Ok get ready we have sighted the ship on the radar, we have been through this many times, focus on removal of the cargo from green container DES113. There are a number of crates we have to remove and place on the dhow from the ship stores crane on the port side of the African Tide. Our brothers on board should have subdued the crew but be careful when we make initial contact in case they have not been overcome. I will call the ship on the VHF shortly.'

The crew of the dhow stood by as the eight passengers readied themselves and the dhow Captain looked on. The man called Omar Fakhoury supervised while boxes were opened and an array of assault rifles, grenades, explosives, grapnel hooks and even an RPG were removed. Two of the men swung the large RIB over the side of the dhow and held it in with rope bowsing tackle so that equipment could be loaded. The rest transferred the personal rucksacks and weapons to the fast RIB while two got in and started the large outboards. Captain Al Shafer watched as two men took their equipment to the opposite side of where the RIB was positioned. They were obviously intending to stay on board in case he and his crew had second thoughts.

He observed Fakhoury and the five men then board the RIB when the African Tide was about one nautical mile away, its navigation lights and deck spotlights clearly visible. Captain Al Shafer was instructed to slow down to 3 knots. They could see the shapes of two men on the port side of the ship's accommodation. The two men that remained on board instructed Fakhoury to slow down further and told his men to lower the RIB on its davit while tying off a painter line from the nose of the RIB to a stanchion off the bow of the dhow. This would keep the RIB pointing in the right direction while dhow would momentarily tow the craft until the outboards could produce thrust in the seawater. It did so very swiftly as the Coxswain of the RIB gunned the big outboards with a growl. The crew hurriedly untied the painter line and threw it to the RIB crew. The outboards turned sharply and the RIB accelerated away toward the African Tide lit up nearby now. Fakhoury was talking animatedly on the RIB VHF radio as they pulled away. He had already greeted someone on the dhow VHF though appeared to be conducting a pre-arranged and coded conversation with the ship. He obviously didn't want to let other ships in the vicinity, that may be listening in, know what was going on.

The dhow Captain was terrified now, this wasn't an affable meeting with the ship, they didn't need to be armed to the teeth for that. Why would the ship let them on board when they obviously meant harm of some kind? He regretted, to his very core, ever setting eyes on Omar Fakhoury.

*

The Second Mate of the African Tide was twenty two years old and he was now the Senior Navigating Officer on board. Captain Campeti had died of blood loss and he had personally seen Chief Officer Kravits get shot and fall into the sea when he was standing on the ship's bridge wing. He stood now in the same position and put the ship to full astern to stop her dead in the water. Cyrus Sia stood next to him with a Kalashnikov strapped to his chest talking on the VHF. He told the Second Officer to calm down and concentrate on stopping the ship to meet up with the dhow ahead. He wouldn't be harmed if he did what he was told. The young man conducted himself as if he were in semi-comatose state. He acted slowly and deliberately, continuing to stare at the auxiliary manoeuvring console on the port wing as if he had never seen it before.

Most of the crew were dead, their attempt to close up the citadel were thwarted by a large explosive charge being placed on the locked dogged down door. CS gas had been thrown into the citadel and members of the ship's crew that had survived the enormous blast through the watertight door were shot as they exited the space unable to breath from the effects of the smoke. Only two engineers including the Chief Engineer and a member of the deck crew were still alive, probably because they were needed.

The woman was the most brutal, she had pushed her comrades out of the way and insisted on carrying out as many executions as possible as the crew exited the citadel. One Indian sailor pleaded to her in broken Arabic, telling her he was a practicing Muslim. She told one of Sia's two men to guard him while she and the other carried out the remaining executions, she then seemed to change her mind and shot the kneeling sailor in the back of the head. Even her colleagues were shocked by her callousness. Cyrus Sia had trained his daughter Miriam well, she appeared to be even more fanatical than he.

Sia had distributed a strong stimulant to his team in the container while they were checking their weapons, called Captagon. It had been around for many years. It would keep his jihadists awake for a long period, bring them a feeling of contentment in their arduous work and indeed even make them feel euphoric in doing so. His daughter had taken a double dose. He was seriously considering forcing some on the young Second Officer who was making a real mess of keeping the huge ship on station. The young man had applied too much thrust on the transverse bow propeller and had to counter with the main propulsion and rudder. The dhow was getting close to the side of the African Tide, Sia didn't want to smash it and Saeed to pieces during the loading process. The RIB was now right alongside and the remaining two engineering crew were lowering the gangway of the vessel from the ships side shell door on his instructions while being supervised by Miriam. His boss was screaming at him on the VHF when they were supposed to minimise their chat on the airwaves. Sia had not meant to kill the Captain, he simply had got caught up in the process of hi-jacking of the vessel and some over enthusiastic shots fired by his daughter. This junior officer was all he had to drive this monster. Luckily the weather was good and forecast predicted to be so for the next few hours.

He looked down from fifteen metres above the RIB and could see its occupants standing up on the small pitching boat to get on to the gangway. Five men jumped across successfully on to the lower gangway platform and the Coxswain hurriedly drove the RIB away from the side of the ship to stand by near the dhow.

Saeed stopped to embrace Miriam as he ran up the steps from the gangway to the main deck for access to the Bridge to meet with Sia. She appeared wild eyed, her fine features flecked with blood and hair wet with sweat. He greeted the woman in Arabic and congratulated her in her success. Normally he wouldn't embrace a young woman but she was a soldier and this was Holy War.

He was out of breath by the time he reached the Bridge several stories above, Sia also embraced Saeed warmly and treated him with friendly deference as his leader.

'This was a perfect plan Saeed you have surpassed yourself this time.'

'It is not over yet Cyrus there is much to do. We must start unloading the cargo, this will be the lance that will strike at the heart of the enemy once and for all.' He slapped his friend on the back.

'I will go down and unload the container if you take command here,' retorted Sia.

'What about him?' Saeed gestured at the Second Officer outside at the wing propulsion control with his Browning pistol.

'He has lost his mind but is the only one that can keep this ship on station, the Captain and Mate are dead and the engineers cannot steer this ship.'

'We have two hours as per our schedule, other ships will ask why we are stationary and if we need assistance. We don't want the dhow near here when the sun comes up in six or seven hours. You should not have killed the Captain, those were not your instructions.'

'I understand, my men are guarding the remaining members of the crew. I will tell Miriam to take over and they can assist your men to unload the container into the dhow.'

'No, get the crew to help, they know the ship and can help if we need equipment. We need to do this quickly, if they don't co-operate kill them, apart from the Chief Engineer. We still need him. No more mistakes like the Captain!'

*

Chief Officer Kravits was still alive. He was getting cold despite the relative warmth of the Ocean. He raised himself out the water by crossing his arms over his life vest and pointing it downward into the water so the vertical buoyance would help him see over the waves instead of lying on his back. He thanked god for Solas and the International Maritime Organisation regulations that stipulated that lifejackets should be self-righting when worn in case of unconsciousness. He'd lost consciousness when the round had pierced the buoyant material in his life jacket and had then deflected grazing his skull. Kravits had woken floating on his back with the ominous sight of the African Tide's stern at least a mile away steaming away from him.

He could see nothing on 360 degrees of horizon but had to remain optimistic, he was in a relatively busy shipping route, had a light on his jacket powered by the saline sea water and it was high visibility orange for searching in daylight. Though he would also be in danger of being run over and sucked through a ships screws if not spotted by the crew from the navigating position. He had spent an hour or so drifting between sleep and consciousness, probably as a result of his head wound. Time spent dreaming of his family, reflecting on his life and what had led him to this point in time. He had remembered events and emotions that he had not felt for some time. He thought of his mother and how she would always search for him if he had disappeared. Like many seafarers he was a bit of a loner, self-sufficient, not prone to establishing and maintaining relationships other than that of close family. As consciousness returned more permanently, his resolution returned. He was going to survive this, go back to his home and take up the fight against these terrorists or pirates or criminals - whatever they were. They had attacked his ship and crew, he had failed, to his knowledge, to save the ship. He wondered at the fate of his men.

Kravits removed his socks and belt and used them as a combined padded tourniquet to strap to his head to stem the blood weeping from the wound. His first and main challenge for survival, he knew from his survival training, was thirst. He could last perhaps 36 to 48 hours before he died of dehydration on a sunny day. While he was cold, the sea was too warm for hypothermia, he could last for two full periods of daylight, perhaps. The light on his jacket at night may be visible to a ship but they would mistake it for a small wooden fishing or sailing vessel with no radar reflection and steer clear of him. Unless the African Tide had issued a distress and they were looking for survivors. He hoped his Second Officer would have had the presence of mind to do so if the Captain hadn't survived or was in isolated captivity.

He raised himself up on his lifejacket every five minutes and rotated 360 degrees with his legs in the water searching the horizon for a ship. There wasn't much he could do if he saw one other than keep his lifejacket light pointing in the right direction so a sharp eyed look out could see it.

He tried to put the thoughts of anything sinister lurking in the water to the back of his mind, another good reason to try and stop the flow of blood. He lay back and floated and tried to conserve energy until the sun rose, he hoped, not for the last time in his life.

*

The USS John S McCain was on her way to the Arabian Gulf for duty which mainly encapsulated having a presence to deter any Iranian aggression. She had just been in Mumbai and as well as attending exercises with the Indian Navy had held receptions for Indian dignitaries and American embassy staff and citizens. Captain Edward Spencer sat in his cabin catching up on his overdue paperwork. He'd volunteered for the Navy to work his way up to his current position and see some action. He disliked the pomp and ceremony of foreign state visits which was necessary for the greatest sea power in the world. He'd prefer it if someone else did it. Spencer was young for the command of a guided missile destroyer at thirty two and was regarded as a rising star. He may get a chance to prove himself in combat in the Arabian Gulf if tensions escalated.

The office phone rang, he looked at the lights on the phone indicating where the call was coming from. The Bridge. He frowned. A warship such as the John S McCain usually always had a Senior

Officer on the Navigating Bridge, there was rarely a requirement for the Captain to attend when the ship was on passage. He answered;

'Captain Spencer, go ahead.'

It was the Watch Officer.

'Captain we have a radar trace of a vessel ahead on a similar heading to us but she has stopped in the water.'

'Have you tried to raise comms with her?'

'Yes Sir, I think she may have broken down and was going to check her status, to see if we could get some help for her but she's not answering.'

'We're too far east for piracy and there have been very few attacks recently - even further west near Hells Gates.'

'Yes sir, perhaps we should take a run past and check visually.'

'Ok let's launch a Seahawk to have a look before we go anywhere near the ship, and sound action stations. It'll be a good live drill to sharpen us up for Gulf.'

The "Big Bad John" as she was fondly known sounded out the call to arms.

*

Saeed was relatively happy on how the unloading had gone so far. The valid tractor parts were pulled out of container DES113 by using the deck mooring winch on the bow. They ran the cable through some fairlead rollers which were lashed on the hatch to produce the right angle to get access to the cargo in the container. These were unceremoniously pulled off the hatch, crashing to the deck. The components that Saeed and his men needed were stored in six crates to ensure the equipment could be manhandled and placed on pallet trolleys. Then they could be pushed down the deck. The crates were still very heavy, however, and needed pulled from the back of container. The men treated these very carefully indeed. Saeed had to shout at his men and the assisting crew members more than once as they became frustrated with handling the heavy boxes. Eventually they got the six boxes off the hatch and down on the deck where two pallet trolleys could wheel them back to the stores crane situated forward of the accommodation.

Saeed was now positioned on the port side rail next to where they were rigging the last box for lifting on to the dhow. The dhow Captain had placed fenders on the starboard side of his craft and used his rudders and the RIB pushing on the dhow bow to keep alongside the high sided container ship. The Chief Engineer of the African Tide was instructed to use the crane to slowly lower the crates on to the dhow. The last one went smoothly, the last few feet were most crucial as the dhow ranged alongside the much larger ship in the swell and the crate banged on the deck. A major slip could be the end of everything in the vicinity of the African Tide. After Saeed gave the signal to let out the hook as quickly as possible and it was disconnected from the crate. He instructed Sia to end their time on board the container vessel. They would now execute the final part of the hijack.

Cyrus and Miriam Sia took the Chief Engineer and other two crew members down to the engine room, after they had descended into the space Saeed walked up to the Navigating Bridge. The Second Mate was sitting shivering in the bridge chair staring into space. Saeed gestured to his guard to head down to embark on the RIB.

He walked round to face the terrified officer, 'you are part of history young man, we will move the world to a different place with what we have taken from you. We will be respected, you're corrupt and ruined society will eventually be annihilated to be replaced by one that is chosen by God. In your own way you will also be a martyr, though of course not a very willing one,' Saeed almost grinned at his own irony.

He walked round behind the chair, raised his Browning and chambered a round before discharging the weapon into the back of the Second Officer's head.

The Sia's returned from the engine room without their charges and met the rest of the hijackers at the gangway shell door including the man most of them only knew as Omar Fakhoury. All of them filed down the gangway and jumped one by one into the RIB. After the last crate had been loaded the dhow had pulled away from the side of the ship and stood off in the darkness away from the African Tide's floodlights. The RIB, heavily laden with ten individuals and equipment pushed toward the dhow. They all made short work of jumping on to their escape vessel and pulling the RIB back into the davits. The dhow Captain, without waiting for instructions from his charge, now back on board, hastily turned his boat west in the direction of Oman.

As the men settled down on the vessel to get some rest they could hear the far off resounding whack of helicopter blades but they could see nothing but the lights of the massive container ship fading into the distance.

Chapter 19

After studying the drawings and going through almost every possible reason for Dubois designing these devices, Finlay and Henry had left the peaceful solitude if the springtime Cairngorms for the hustle and bustle of Millbank in London. Henry had made contact with his old colleagues in SIS who had agreed to put him in touch with their Nuclear Proliferation section. The concerns about Iran and general nuclear biochemical counter proliferation work carried out by MI6 was relatively public and well known. There was a key section that dealt purely with the threat from international terrorists or rogue states acquiring weapons from existing ones, which was not so well recognised. Henry did not know anyone from that section. Partly because he had been away for so long and also because it was a relatively new phenomenon to the old state sponsored form of proliferation.

Both men sat in a meeting room in the famous Vauxhall Cross building and waited for the SIS attendees to come in.

'Place has changed a bit since I was last here,' surmised Henry 'it's gone all corporate bullshit, like a magic circle legal firm or hedge fund office.'

'Times move on Henry, they don't employ washed up Guards officers from privileged posh families who smoke sixty a day and drink themselves to oblivion anymore,' responded Finlay with a smirk.

'Bloody cheek, we kept this country safe for generations.'

'Philby, Burgess and Maclean?'

'That was Cambridge, nest of fucking communists Finlay, and not one a Guardsman. If they had done some decent time in the military they wouldn't have turned into pinkos in the first place. When you put your life on the line for your country you understand what patriotism is. They were all fucking journalists, from memory, no wonder they were traitors, heads in the clouds. How could anyone in their right mind think the Joe Stalin show was the way to go, he was worse than Hitler!'

'Well I hope we're not about to meet some ex hacks, Henry.'

'Wouldn't surprise me in the least.'

Just as there was a lull in their conversation, two men walked into the meeting room and introduced themselves. Both were in their late twenties, fresh faced, short haircuts and sharply dressed in suits, though not wearing ties. One was called Will Bainbridge, he immediate opened up a laptop and started to make up a note, the other, Charlie Jones, seemed to be the most senior and spoke first;

'Nice to meet you both, Mr Darcy, I have heard a lot about you from some of your old comrades in six. All said you were the best, never understood how you were moved on after the Korean affair.'

'Well that's perhaps because they knew bugger all about it,' said Henry, the barb obviously being directed at the youthful MI6 operative rather than his former colleagues, 'we also refrained in my time from using the word comrades, unless of course we were joking.'

Finlay looked at the faces of both men as Henry played out his grumpy old lag act, not useful if he's trying to get information out of them. Neither man showed any reaction other than a slight amusement. Bainbridge tapped a little nervously on his computer and Jones carried on as politely as he had started;

'How can we help you gentlemen?'

Henry V laid out what they had found on the desk and explained the circumstances behind Dubois and his death. He didn't mention how Finlay had got involved, merely hinted at the fact his military covert surveillance experience was invaluable. It took around fifteen minutes to explain the scenario. Both of their new acquaintances grew ever more interested as Henry went on, Bainbridge's note tapping increasing in pace.

Finlay mulled over the situation while Henry talked and poured over drawings in the well-lit room in between sipping from his coffee cup. He knew the last thing his friend wanted to do was divulge this information to this section of the Secret Intelligence Services. It was right up their street and, to be fair, very much in their section remit, more recently laid out in the defence and intelligence review of 2015. It was not in the remit of MI5 and most definitely not in Henry's strategic section of the internal intelligence service. It would involve MI5 if the threat of proliferation was a direct threat to the internal security of the United Kingdom. This was the handle that Henry was firmly grasping while driving the explanation to the SIS men. Rivalry between the two organisations was legendary and while this had led to enemies of the UK benefitting in the past an endless amount of reviews and recommendations had done little to resolve that situation. Henry had sat on both sides of the fence and, while his manipulation of the circumstances was masterly, it was still going to be difficult for these two men to give way to a more tenuous connection that Henry had. Despite the fact that Henry was giving the impression that he had support at the highest level of both organisations, Finlay knew he had not. Even if he had it was always possible politicians could interfere. The biggest immediate problem was he was trying to get information out of MI6, but to get it he was taking the risk of giving most of what he knew. By the end of his explanation Henry had given the impression he could pass on a lot more if he could get a small part of the jigsaw from Jones. The old spy even hinted he could hand the whole shooting match over to Jones's section if further information convinced him enough that there was no risk to the UK. He was banking on the ambition of the young man.

'Mr Darcy, these circumstances, other than the fact Dubois was murdered inside the UK, must fall firmly within our remit,' retorted Jones finally.

'All I am asking for is information that may link the development of this weapon for use inside the UK and if you have it. Of particular concern is the manual trigger device we have shown you.'

'It's a manual trigger, could be triggered *manually* anywhere.'

'And the man that designed it to fit to a small nuclear device was killed inside the UK.'

'But Mr Darcy that may be simply where his killers found him, it doesn't mean he was going to use it here.'

'We believe he was here to train someone how to assemble the device and use it within the borders of the UK. I cannot tell you more than that.'

Finlay was impressed with how quickly Henry had made the last comment up, they had no reason to believe that Dubois was in the UK to train anyone - but that part was an internal security matter and as such Henry didn't have to tell Bainbridge or Jones.

'We may have some information that could be of use to you I shall check the files and let you know,' said Jones.

It was a typical, bring the meeting to an end, non-committal answer. One that could stop the whole thing dead by a follow up call or email. Henry knew that.

'Well I will tell you one thing, Charlie fucking Jones. If an atomic device goes off in this country and kills millions of people, and it discovered you have withheld information, this country will bring back hanging especially for you…. I would suggest your mate taps that into his notes as an aid memoire.'

Both Finlay and Henry got up and left without shaking hands. They strolled purposefully out of the Vauxhall Cross building stopping only to hand over their security passes.

Harry had gambled his ace and now had to wait.

Chapter 20

The Sikorsky Seahawk was the naval version of the famous and ubiquitous US military Blackhawk. It cost well over forty million United States dollars and was the world's most advanced maritime helicopter. It has a multi role ability as most naval helicopters had including anti-submarine and surface capability, search and rescue as well as communicative command and control systems. As it flew toward the African Tide all that was required initially were the eyes of the two pilots and winchman on board. As they approached from the east the helicopter circled the ship from a distance and observed her position in the water. Once they were convinced there was no threat they circled closer to the ship. The pilot flew the aircraft and the co-pilot reported back to the John McCain. They saw she was sinking, the stern was low in the water which would indicate that the engine room had flooded. They saw some very odd things that you wouldn't normally see on a foundering ship. There appeared to be no fire or collision damage above the surface, the emergency deck lights were still on and no crew were on the deck after hearing the noisy thwack thwack of the helicopter rotor blades. Two containers lay open near the bow of the ship which would indicate a cargo breach. Some crates were lying at the side of the forward hatch next to one of the open containers. The helicopter approached both sides of the ship and flew crabbing its way down the decks with its powerful spotlight shining over the accommodation and walkways. Fire equipment had been rigged forward of the accommodation and there appeared to be a streak of blood on the deck on the port side where someone or something had been dragged into the accommodation block.

The co-pilot reported back to Captain Spencer of the USS John S McCain that there were some curious things about a sinking vessel that didn't make sense - but it was safe for the warship to close in on and standby should the crew make an appearance and require rescue. Captain Spencer told the helicopter to standby and remain on station until fuel replenishment required its return. He also instructed the co-pilot to use the surveillance equipment on board to 360 degree video the ship and take close up stills of anything untoward. He instructed them to use their heat sensing equipment to locate survivors in the water in the vicinity of the African Tide. The Captain then issued a mayday message to any ships standing by in the relative proximity of the African Tide on behalf of the stricken ship. Captain Spencer would consider launching the second helicopter with some marines to land on the African Tide but this would require permission from the Pentagon as there was no threat to his ship. He would mobilise the second chopper and make that call. The warship would be in the vicinity in two hours. It would be daylight by the time he got to the sinking ship.

His discussion with the Pentagon culminated in the second helicopter being sent out to take a look at craft in the vicinity of the African Tide but not to board any ship unless piracy or terrorism was suspected. For now it would be information gathering, search and rescue and nothing else. The rest of the West's naval fleet was occupied escorting tankers and subverting any threats from the Iranian navy in the Straits of Hormuz. The Big Bad John was off mission as it was and couldn't spend too long with the African Tide.

The second helicopter was launched prior to the return of the first.

*

Chief Officer Kravits had a very poor night. He was much colder than he thought he could ever be. The worse feeling was the salt in his mouth and the never ending thirst that came with it. In between shivers he had catnapped through the night, dreamt of his youth and had nightmares about shark attacks. He also had dreamt he had been rescued after hearing a helicopter in the distance. When he awoke he was distressed to find it was all a dream. His head was throbbing and being permanently immersed in the water he was unsure how much blood he had lost as it had been washed away from his tourniquet. His head felt worse as he lifted himself vertically again in the water to take a look around. Nothing, though he couldn't see too far, his eyes were nipping with salty sea water. As he lay back again as gently as he could he prayed for rain, then he could assuage his thirst. There were a few white cumulous which indicated the weather would remain fair meaning better likelihood of rescue. Unfortunately not an indication of him drinking fresh water any time soon.

As he lay staring at the sky he saw an airliner streaking across it, moving almost imperceptibly. He gazed at it longingly. He would give his whole life savings from the sweat and solitude of many years at sea to pay for a ticket to be on that flight, wherever it was bound. He understood, really for the first time, how much money and possessions were really worth when your life was hanging on a slim silk thread of chance. His previous resolve to survive had started to diminish and give way to reflection. Was this the way of death? Is it time now for him to gather his thoughts to prepare for something beyond life. He wasn't a religious man by any means, had always been too busy making his way in the world to be concerned about any God or afterlife. After all no one seemed to agree what that entailed. In his view all of it simply led to more atrocities committed in the name of the almighty, it had gone on for as long as man had a history. Probably a reason these animals had attacked his ship, his mood swung back to determination to survive despite his predicament.

He felt a little breeze picking up and sweeping over his face, perhaps it would bring water or rescue. Wind throughout millennia was often a sailor's best friend or his most cynical enemy.

The small Indian fishing boat was called the Varuna, named after the god of all the seas, she was made of wood and ran by a family from Gujarat. Two brothers with their respective elder sons had a half share each on the small ten metre boat powered by an old refurbished diesel engine. There was enough fuel and water on board to keep them at sea for around five days before they had to return with their catch. They had sailed from a fishing port in Gujarat, were at the end of the range of the brightly painted boat and about to start fishing.

The youngest son of one of the two brothers was on the roof of the small wooden Wheelhouse unravelling the net, which was rolled and stretched across the aft deck ready to be deployed when he saw something in the water. They had been listening to warnings of a sinking ship and the possibility of survivors being in the water all night while they were on passage to the fishing grounds. While not understanding much of the chatter, their English was poor to non-existent, they knew the basics of what was afoot by speaking Hindi to other crews from India on the VHF in the vicinity who had better command of English. They were not rich men and didn't have money to waste on diesel to look for survivors but the eldest brother had told the two boys to keep their eyes peeled for anyone in the water. They could all be in that position one day.

The boy saw a flash of orange in the distance and stood upright from his bent position over the net. Drifting buoys and fenders coloured orange were often seen in the water, so he didn't expect anything more than that. His father and uncle were keen to get fishing before it got too windy and start making some money. He looked harder and it looked square as it bobbed up and down on the long swell of the ocean. He called out to his father to bring the binoculars up on to the Wheelhouse roof as he could see something.

Kravits was dozing again. He felt something vibrate in the water, looked to his immediate left and right, the nagging primitive instinct in his mind telling him to be wary of predators. He then lifted his head clear of the water and pulled the tourniquet from his swollen head so he could hear better. Yes, he could hear something sounded like the gurgle of a small water cooled marine diesel. For what felt like the thousandth time he raised himself up vertically using the lifejackets buoyancy, he turned slowly. Then he heard an even clearer noise of an engine, loud enough so he could gauge direction. He turned quickly toward it and saw as he bobbed in the swell the prow of what seemed to be a tiny boat coming toward him. He waved his hands and a few seconds later the sound of a horn blew from the boat in recognition of siting, what now was, the survivor. His heart soared with relief and for the first time in many hours his eyes filled with water that wasn't from the ocean.

The fisherman slowed and looked down on the man from the starboard beam of the little fishing boat. Shouting instructions to the eldest brother on the helm in Hindi. Kravits could see the dark brown bodies above him contrasting with the bright colours of their traditional koli dress hitched up around their thighs. Their white teeth gleaming below their equally white headdresses. It was the finest sight he had ever seen.

The fishermen looked down at the dark haired white man lying in the water dyed bright pink by the sun, his lips chapped and cracked despite the salty moisture of the sea. A large cut on his head that had removed some of his hair. The two boys laughed as the younger brother threw Kravits a rope making the comment that if this man had been a fish, he wouldn't be worth taking to the market in Gujarat.

*

It had been twelve hours since Captain Al Shaffer had turned his dhow away from the great container ship. His new engines had thrust the dhow forward at sixteen or seventeen knots, every plank straining against the thrust of the over specified engines. His vessel had rarely done these speeds for long and the hull certainly wasn't designed for it. The fuel tanks were also going down rapidly as the engines pushed the fat rounded wooden hull through the swell. On the positive side his electronic chart had told him he had travelled nearly two hundred nautical miles, well away from the African Tide and whatever deeds his evil charge had conducted aboard that ship. Fakhoury's men and the woman had slept on deck at night where it was cooler. They had gone below after his crew served them a meal after dawn. The man called Omar Fakhoury knew that drones and satellites could be watching them from above and that they would be oblivious to it. It was warm below decks in the sun but the speed of the dhow helped cool the men as they slept. The dhow Captain could raise his sail to further conceal the deck but at these speeds in the prevailing wind this would actually act against the diesels, slow the dhow down and use more precious fuel.

Saeed Abdul Raheem had barely slept at night and had been awake since dawn. He sat behind the steering position on the raised poop behind the Captain Al Shafer and reflected on the mission so far. It had been very successful but each hurdle was replaced by another. He had stowed his lethal cargo below in the dhow hold and got away from any threat posed by Western navies in the immediate vicinity of the African Tide. That threat would always exist, he was now steaming toward the entrance to the Red Sea and Port Sudan. They didn't know if it was possible to get there on the fuel capacity of this dhow. They had simply retro fitted the biggest engines available with the largest amount of diesel the dhow could carry. They even had supplementary drums they could pump to the tanks in the hold. The twelve hours or more of the twin engines at maximum load had consumed at least a third of their fuel, they would have to slow down or risk falling well short of their destination.

His mujahedeen had slept soundly after the effects of the Captogen high had worn off, most were still asleep, though the beautiful Miriam was awake and cleaning her weapon. Her father was ever watchful of her and how her relationship was with any of the other men. Ironic in that he was happy to let his daughter kill with impunity but not to flirt with his other soldiers. Even Holy War had its limits in a family atmosphere, Saeed contemplated.

Sia and his daughter were Sunni Muslims, originally from the more isolated Larestan region of Iran. There had been tensions in the region when the revolutionary Shia majority had tried to convert these mountain people to their own faith within Islam. Cyrus had travelled to Palestine with his family and had got involved, initially with the PLO, before meeting and being recruited by the Saeed and the Mubarizun. Saeed could always see the value of different cultural backgrounds coming into the secretive organisation. While there was an element of risk to this strategy, it helped in understanding and penetrating other organisations and assisted with cover. Cyrus often advised him how to deal with Khorasani and VAJA and was instrumental in planning the hijack of the African Tide. Using female operatives was also useful. Having said that

Saeed had kept Cyrus Sia on the periphery of the organisation, he was an Iranian after all.

The Mubarizun were originally part of Islamist armies who were the elite, this had dated back centuries. Their origin had been in pre-Islamic times when duels began by engaging the champions of the opposing armies. They carried on this tradition in the Middle East in Islamic times where the duellists equipped with the latest weaponry and armour would engage the infidel elite on the eve of battle. This would then be followed by the main conflict between the massed forces of each army. The Mubarizun victory would morally boost the Islamic forces before the massed ranks attacked. These men were the point of the lance, the army was the shaft. Without the point that could penetrate the skin, the shaft of the lance was useless and without the weight of the body of the lance the light spear point was nothing.

Saeed had come up with the concept after the attack on the twin towers and the massive Western effort against Al Qaeda. The leaders of that organisation were seen, by many to operate in the background, to use the mujahedeen foot soldiers as expendable pawns. He had watched from the side-lines in Palestine and did not wish to be such a foot soldier. His concept was different, he was the leader like the famous leaders and elite of Islamist armies from a thousand years ago. He led from the front, from the point of the spear, by example. He would not endlessly hide in a cave or in a walled house in Abbottabad while co-operating with Pakistani security services. He was, with his handful of comrades around the world, the Mubarizun, the elite, the warrior who was going in before the great uprising to follow against the non-believers.

He stood up and stepped forward to address Al Shafer, 'slow down to cruising speed Captain, we must conserve fuel. Get your men to start pumping from the drums into the service tanks.'

*

The heli-deck on the stern of the "Big Bad John" had been a busy place. Both helicopters had been operating constantly, refuelling and resting pilots since the observation of the African Tide by the first Seahawk deployment. The warship now stood off the African Tide. The hull of the container ship was now below the water as Captain Spencer watched the ship in her death throes. He thought she would last until the evening but the deck containers stacked four high had their own buoyancy and some were floating clear accelerating the sinking. No survivors had been seen and he hadn't boarded the ship since they had no permission. She had become unstable, capsizing or turning on her side was always possible. One Indian fishing boat had reported finding a survivor in the water in very broken English. They would wait until the Seahawk's were stowed, the great containership had gone and pick him up with one of their RIB's and Marines. Less risk involved than using the helicopter and they could question the crew during pickup.

The USS John McCain had to get back on passage to the Arabian Gulf to relieve their sister ship who was due a refit in Hawaii. It had been an eventful three days, he would rest his men on the way up to the United Arab Emirates. There they would replenish some stores, change some of his crew and head back to the Straits of Hormuz for deployment for six months. The footage of his radar, still pictures and videos had all been sent to the Pentagon. He doubted if any more would be heard of the analysis of the data he had sent. It was rarely passed back to the point of generation unless something had to be actioned. Indian and Pakistani coastguard vessels were now moving to the site of the African Tide. Once he had extracted the survivor the warship would handover to these authorities who would attempt to chart the wreck and minimise the spread of any oil spill.

Chapter 21

Finlay Lamont had returned on the City airport flight to Aberdeen as there wasn't much he could do while Henry continued to look for more information on the Dubois files he had. The largest sticking point for them was getting information out of Vauxhall Cross, that would take a few days. The old soldier couldn't sit still for long and packed to go to an old climb he always enjoyed at Lochnagar on the Queen's estate called Eagle Ridge. A hard climb for most but a morning out for an elite climber like Finlay. He had packed his rucksack quickly while watching the news, it was the usual blend of politics and hard luck stories. One item that had caught his attention was that a large containership had sunk under mysterious circumstances in the Arabian Sea just short of the Straits of Hormuz. There was the usual "security expert" dragged on to the news show questioning whether it could be piracy, Iranian involvement or someone trying to break the sanctions. None of which really rang true. There were rumours of one survivor being in US custody.

It had gone from his mind during the walk into the mountain from where he had parked his car in the picturesque Glen Muick. His head had cleared completely as he had climbed the vertical granite fissures using a rope and pitons. He had taken his rucksack with him so he could camp on the White Mounth Plateau above and then walk and climb some other peaks in the region. On the second night westward from the rock climb toward Glenshee he had noticed an old text message on his phone while he made camp. It was from Henry asking him to call. Finlay had done so the next morning when he had managed to get a signal. It appeared that MI6 had been instructed to co-operate with Henry V and that they would continue to lead the investigation. Apparently Henry's elder brother, also an ex Guardsman, was a senior advisor to the Home Secretary and had pulled some strings and leaned on the heads of both intelligence services. Henry felt, while the wind was in their favour, they had limited time to find out more.

The veteran spy, ever suspicious of technology, didn't want to say too much by text or on the telephone but what he did say was in Henry's home-made code mentioning "washing machines and control cards". What Finlay could glean was a drawing of a similar trigger device was found by the UAE security services in Dubai. They had shared the information with both CIA and MI6 ("cousins and uncles") as they felt that it may have been for a conventional suicide bomb and told MI6 that there were British nationals involved. Henry was furious that none of this had been passed on to MI5 already which had certainly helped make the case with his brother. Henry had secured a meeting in Abu Dhabi, the capital of the United Arab Emirates with someone he knew from his Sandhurst days to find out more.

Finlay put the cell phone back in his rucksack webbing and picked up the pace for the long walk back to where he had left his Landcruiser in Glen Muick.

As he walked at a "fast march", or in British military parlance, a "yomp" pace across the boggy plateau carrying the heavier than usual rucksack, it reminded him of the march he undertook with 3 Para as a novice young soldier. They marched 90 miles to eventually engage the enemy at Mount Longdon in the Falklands war. Finlay's memories were most vivid of the combat situations he had been involved in and his very first on the cold and windswept Falkland Islands so long ago were the sharpest in his mind. Like a lot of paratroopers, he wasn't a tall man, of average height and build. In 1982, still just in his teens he was a gangly youth several kilos lighter than he was now. He still couldn't fathom how he had managed to carry a 40 kilogram Bergen and rifle with ammunition that far. He remembered when he heard the news that the helicopters that were supposed to carry him had been sunk on the "Atlantic Conveyor". How his platoon's grumbling gave way to a quiet fortitude, tinged with nerves, as they started to hear the sounds of combat at their anchorage in San Carlos water.

He had been scared on the assault on Mount Longdon where the Parachute Regiment had been outnumbered four to one but had obviously impressed in tight situations, taking a leadership role despite his status as a junior soldier. Within five years he had risen to the rank of sergeant and been recommended for a commission, that degree of rapid promotion was rare even now. He could never forget seeing his first dead body. His most abiding memory was the clank of bayonets being applied to the Self Loading Rifles and the ensuing hand to hand fighting below the granite peak of the cold and dark mountain.

The British Army, had prevailed however, bringing pride and joy to the country and respect from both Britain's friends and enemies. Finlay, who was "trying out" a military career then became a lifelong soldier. It wasn't dogmatic loyalty to his country that had forged his career but the narcotic of excitement and surge of adrenaline high which he had almost unknowingly sought. The camaraderie loved by some serving soldiers and missed dearly by former ones was less of an attraction for him, he was more of a loner. During the long periods between combat postings he had satisfied his lust for the thrill he sought by mountain climbing, becoming one of the most accomplished in the world. His feats were known to the elite climbing fraternity, rarely published in any magazines and journals, if his name were ever mentioned it was usually preceded by "former soldier" or "ex para".

He had realised, since his wife's death, that he was not a young man anymore. While many of his peers had left and taken on civilian advisory or security roles, and those remaining in service were propping up desks, Finlay had continued to be involved in active front line role. Laterally he had been in the clandestine Special Reconnaissance Unit which had been disbanded, the government had always denied its existence, so there were no reunions, no medals, apparently no history. It wasn't an issue for Major Lamont.

He had genuinely wished to retire prior to finding Dubois's body. He felt that it was only appropriate that he helped achieve a conclusion to something fate had drawn him into. This was the last one, he was pushing sixty soon, didn't need the money or the bruises that had come with it.

Chapter 22

Colonel Sohail Al Qubaisi had his surveillance pictures up on slides on the TV screen and was going through the names and what they knew with his team. The intelligence network in his country was world leading. This resulted in a very safe environment for its citizens and many nationalities from around the world that had come to the United Arab Emirates to work. They had learned much from the West but also used the old family and tribal networks in the region to build a picture for state security. The Colonel ran a network of informers within the foreign national communities with ex patriots who had been in the country for a couple of generations, particularly Pakistani and Indian nationals who had made their family wealth in the Emirates.

It had come to the point where the much more well-known western agencies had come to his organisation for help with terrorist and criminal networks who may be trying to money launder in the region. They had better links than any of the other Middle Eastern countries. Saudi was still too isolated and while the internal networking was good their links to other intelligence agencies was not. No one trusted Pakistani, Iraqi or of course Iranian intelligence networks, they were regarded as corrupt and any information that emanated from them was treated with a great deal of suspicion. The only country in the region who came close to his was Oman and that relationship was hot and cold.

The two men on the screen were pictured at lunch at the Royal Mirage, they knew of Hassan Makhlouf who had been long suspected of criminal activity and money laundering around the Middle East. He'd been under surveillance on a few occasions, some meetings apparently appeared more innocent, more recently the one with the Ansari brothers was the first hint of a possible terrorist link. This most up to date surveillance had thrown up a new character. They had matched his identity on their facial recognition software at the airport to being an Omani national called Omar Fakhoury whom they had no information on. The first suspicion of course, was that he was travelling under a false passport and name, however on exit his passport appeared genuine. The Colonel had two choices. He could go to Western agencies to try and find out if he had any other identities or false names or he could conduct an expensive investigation of his own with Omani intelligence which would bear no fruit, they were not always on the best of terms. It could be possible that these people they were watching were planning something in the UAE or, bearing in mind the UK national connection with the Ansari brothers, more likely it was a foreign operation. Information was currency, he needed to get something in return if he was going to divulge anything to another friendly countries' agency.

Omar Fakhoury had not shown up on any databases, but they managed put his image taken from the surveillance and run through facial recognition software. It had identified three possible targets. One was an Afghan terrorist who had been confirmed to have been killed by a US drone strike using a DNA test. The second was a Turkish drugs smuggler, currently in jail in Greece and the third was a little known but long served member of the PLO who had almost disappeared from view in the last Intifada uprising around 2001. He was known as a tough and resilient member of the organisation with links to the purse strings of the Palestinian Liberation Organisation. Indeed, much of the decline of the organisation had possibly been down to him essentially disappearing from view at that time.

There was a note on file that the same individual named Saeed Raheem had somehow been implicated in Arafat's death. Many unfounded rumours had existed at the time, varying from Israeli and American assassination plots to Hezbollah or internal Palestinian plots to dispose of the elderly leader.

The Colonel had investigated further and found very few images of Saeed Raheem, a couple of very grainy black and white pictures with one decent colour image of him in the late nineties beside Arafat. This was the one that gave the facial pattern recognition match to his much clearer lunch meeting pictures of the unidentified man dining with Makhlouf.

There was no video surveillance. This was much more useful than most people realised, mannerisms, physical deportment and any facial expressions can verify identity, often much better than still pictures. Beards, glasses and even plastic surgery cannot hide these traits. No video had been taken of this Saeed Raheem and while they had airport video surveillance of Fakhoury, they had no means to compare the two. New artificial intelligence software was now in the hands of his intelligence service that could analyse an individual's movements and facial expressions and give a positive match that was almost infallible. They needed to get some genuine footage of Saeed Raheem to get more positive confirmation or talk to other agencies that could be aware of Fakhoury's or Raheem's activities.

Colonel Al Qubaisi had recently been contacted by the UK SIS about electrical drawing he had sent them in connection with the two UK nationals having a meeting with Makhlouf. It had taken some time for them to respond, the UK security services were not known for their rapid reaction. It had, however, brought some news of an old friend who he would like to catch up with, they went back a long way.

As a junior officer in the UAE army, the Colonel had trained at Sandhurst. In his class, at that time, was a young budding Guardsman called Henry Darcy. They had become firm friends over the extensive officer training programme and had become well known for pranks played on other trainees and even their training sergeants. They had lost touch since Henry had left SIS and taken up a post with MI5. Colonel Al Qubaisi had been to Henry's home a generation ago, met and dined with the Darcy brothers and had learned of the history of the ancient family. In turn, during a Middle East posting Henry had visited the Al Qubaisi household and learned a great deal of the ancient history of the combined Emirates and Oman.

Henry and Sohail had spent time together driving and camping in the Empty Quarter in their youth. Sohail had shown Henry the date plantations of Al Ain, told him of the rich history of the sawtooth Al Hajr mountains and explained how falaj's were constructed thousands of years ago to supply the tribes of Arabia with water. He had explained how water to them was life itself, how pearl divers had even discovered underwater springs below the surface of the sea which leached out under pressure from the water channels in the high mountains. They had debated whether it was better to have huge reserves of oil or water, which country as the most fortunate.

Henry had gone to the United Arab Emirates before the huge growth had developed in the country, soon after the nation had been forged by Sheik Zayed's philanthropic approach to the binding of the seven Emirates. An example had been set by the ruler which Sohail and his countrymen followed. It was one of respect for other nations, races and religions, the ability to understand the mindset of your opponents during negotiation while maintaining a fierce patriotism and ability to protect your own people. Their friendship wasn't founded in the modern tourist traps of London and Dubai but in the traditional time honoured fabric of Sandhurst and the harsh and endless geography of the Arab Peninsula. They had established a trust between them. They understood honour, for them it occupied a level of priority as high as any other, not a common trait among modern spies. He looked forward to seeing his old friend again.

He carried on going through the slides, instructing his men to try and find as much PLO footage from the 80's and 90's as they could. He knew of one agency that he couldn't talk to that would have a huge archive, perhaps Henry could help him with that.

Like his ancestors understood from the centuries old pearl diving industry. That was currency to trade.

*

Henry had asked Finlay to join him in a meeting room in Millbank prior to flying over to the Emirates, the old soldier had decided to move hotels after being accosted by the two bandits in London. He had enquired of Henry as to whether further information had been gleaned from the subsequent interrogation while they were in custody, his old friend said that it had not. Henry had met him in his office and handed back his Sykes Fairbairn knife, saying he was sick of his complaints about not having the weapon. He'd managed to "pull some strings" with the ex-military anti-terrorist police in the Met.

They moved on to a meeting room with presentation equipment, one of the MI5 data analysts who was working for Henry joined them, a petit and attractive brunette called Anna Siebert. Henry had introduced her rather insultingly as his "computer monkey". She was obviously used to it.

Anna started by introducing, more precisely than Henry, her role. 'We put search words into worldwide media coverage, even social media, where powerful computation with algorithms takes place and, as a result, related subjects can be thrown up. We have done so with the murder of your nuclear scientist, Dubois. One item which is worth showing you is the recent media footage of the sunken container ship African Tide, in the Arabian Sea. As reported in the media, it may have been a pirate attack. This was taken from a Seahawk helicopter launched from a passing US warship.'

Anna flicked some buttons on her laptop and an image of aerial video of the sea flashed up on the large flat screen TV.

The Seahawk footage showed two tankers, both steaming toward the Straits of Hormuz in ballast and in line astern formation three miles apart. A third was fully laden and on passage south-east toward Colombo, presumably to turn east toward Singapore. There was footage of a few small, old Indian fishing boats and three dhows which were of course well known for their trade between India and the Arabian Gulf. One stood out during the examination of the helicopter video, it was a sizeable dhow with no sail on the mast steaming at abnormal speed for such a vessel in a westerly direction. While the infra-red surveillance had been taken from a significant altitude it did show some detail on the deck. A large RIB with two powerful outboards was hanging roped into a large davit. The outboard engines were still showing a significant heat signature on the helicopter's sensors. It was clearly no small craft used for simply taking the crew ashore from an anchorage or any kind of lifeboat. It was not common on relatively small vessels such as dhows or fishing vessels. No one was on deck apart from a helmsman and one individual standing on the stern behind him. There also appeared to be no cargo - on the open deck at least.

Finlay turned to Henry, 'I'm not an expert marine craft but the readout on that screen says this thing is doing 17 knots, you can water ski at that speed. That can't be normal.'

'It isn't, I took the liberty of calling up the Admiralty and they tell me these things do around 8-10 knots in reality. They are made wide beamed, shallow drafted for capacity, stability and the capability of entering shallow water ports, not speed. The RIB is a large fast rescue or interdiction boat, quite heavy and unwieldy. No way it needs to be on a dhow meant to trudge Middle Eastern goods around the region. Would only be used in this context for smuggling or some form of piracy.'

'I see, let's have a look at the chopper footage of the African Tide.'

Anna hit some more buttons on her laptop. Henry ran the commentary, 'I've watched this a few times. Three things. There is a container DES113, doors wide open crates labelled FOTMA lying over the surrounding hatch.' Anna fast forwarded the vessel footage showing her lying at a sharp angle the port side of the deck now immersed in the sea, the swell pushing the water over the deck. The screen then showed a duck green container lying open with its contents strewn over the deck, some of it being engulfed by the waves.

Henry continued, 'that was broken open before the ship started heeling over, it's in earlier shots, someone broke in there to get something. We have checked the manifest with the owner of the ship and the shipper of the container. Its FOTMA Chinese tractor components bound for Bandar Abbas in Iran.'

'Must have been very valuable tractors for pirates to take that level of risk and effort,' said Finlay.

'Precisely, in earlier shots there is no cargo damage on the deck containers, only this one and a container that was being tended for live fish cargo. It appears only this one was a sealed container that was breached. Secondly, there was no sign of the crew apart from the Chief Officer who is now on board the USS John McCain. Yanks aren't letting him speak to anyone at the moment. I can't get anything out the cousins.' Harry sat back raised his hands, exasperated. 'That would save a lot of conjecture, blind alleys and time.'

'And your third point,' enquired Finlay.

'Our surveillance team increased the level of focus on the footage. You can see fire hoses run out and rigged facing well forward of the accommodation, it's part of a civil unarmed ship's anti-piracy procedure. They were trying to defend themselves from something.' Henry clicked on another file which showed red fire hoses running forward from the living quarter superstructure and ending at the fire nozzles lashed to the walkway handrails. As the shot moved aft they could see what looked like a dark red substance on the deck being washed away by the encroaching sea water. 'Looks like blood on the deck Fin, I think the crew were executed, their bodies kept below, somehow one of their officers escaped. He's the key to this. One more interesting thing, according to the manifest the ship was carrying four passengers who were accompanying a live fish cargo, also lying open on deck. They have also disappeared, either victims or could possibly be the hijackers themselves.'

'So you think it's an inside job?'

'Again, during my discussions with the Admiralty I was told that pirates find it almost impossible to get on these high sided container ships because of the freeboard height combined with the fact they are at speed in the ocean. It's more common to board low sided tonnage like fully loaded tankers and product carriers. My naval friends told me it would be a lot easier if someone could slow the ship down.'

'We need to speak to the crew member, until the Americans release him, we can't know definitively what went on,' retorted Finlay.

'I'm working on it, they have to release him soon.'

Finlay frowned, 'how did your intelligent software make this connection with Dubois?'

Henry looked at Finlay, 'that's the reason I have brought you here today. It picked up the number on that breached container. It rather cleverly knew from the manifest information in its database that the container was shipped from Dandong, right across the leaky smugglers border on the Yula Delta from North Korea. When Anna entered the inputs in her search it made the link with Dubois and possible *Nuclear Proliferation*.'

'A bit tenuous Henry,' said Finlay, still frowning, he went on 'why not just ship it to Bandar Abbas, if it's a smuggled nuke?'

Finlay retorted, 'you are forgetting Finlay, we agreed that this Dubois case is most likely terrorism sponsored rather than state, it could be they have stolen someone else's contraband. If you look at the dhow, the breached container, the strong possibility of an inside job to make it all happen. This is an expensive and very well organised operation. As you pointed out why go to that trouble for Chinese tractor parts, there was something else in there these people wanted.'

Anna added, 'we have used this intelligent software before in MI5 Major Lamont, its picked up links with suspected terrorists here in the UK, through mosques and universities attended for example. It makes various nodal links, personal and family circumstances, local and worldwide geographies, origins, even hobbies and habits. Whether people may hang out at the local gym together. It takes both written and video or photographic footage. From transport passenger lists, club memberships to video at Sainsbury's. You would be amazed as to the links it has made. It has saved lives.'

'And this has never wasted your time Anna?' asked Finlay.

He could see she was starting to get irritated by his negative approach to her analysis. Anna shifted in her seat and visibly sharpened her focus on Finlay, 'yes it has more often than not but it has also taken a vast amount of information simply not decipherable to us, and then supplied us an outcome worth looking at.' She paused and turned to look at Henry, then looked back at Finlay, 'it's particularly useful when you don't have anything else to work on.'

The irony of her statement wasn't lost on either of the men, they agreed they might as well take a deeper dive into this lead. Questioning Kravits and Finlay's two assailants was also on the list of priorities, but top of it was the trigger lead in Dubai.

Chapter 23

Ebrahim Khorasani was sitting in the small cargo office of the Iranian shipper of DES113 when he heard the news of the African Tide sinking. He found it very hard to conceal the mixture of fear and rage that was welling up inside of him in front of the junior shipping clerks who knew who he was and were terrified of him. The most senior one passed on the news and luckily was too scared to hold Khorasani's gaze or even look at him. If he had he would have noticed the VAJA Officer turn white and start to shake visibly as he lit a cigarette.

Khorasani had gone to the local VAJA office in Bandar Abbas, one that was used to running illicit contraband for the revolutionary guard as well as using the busy port as an intelligence gathering hub. He had instructed the local intelligence chief to get access to Western news channels where he had seen footage of the ship sinking. Only he knew which specific ship the cargo was on within the organisation. His superiors may put the equation together, or at least be concerned that this was the same vessel even if the sinking was accidental. He had no doubt that it wasn't. The Palestinian was obviously behind this. The delay of Dubois, his failure to find the French scientist and the subsequent loss of the ship and all its crew as reported by CBS was too much of a coincidence.

The question was what would he do now? If he was going to leave the country he had to be quick. He could leave under the premise he was going to find Dubois and what had happened to his cargo, not mentioning the sinking of the ship. He could then either disappear or go to a foreign intelligence agency and divulge the information for protection. Alternatively he could admit what had happened to his superiors and risk execution or imprisonment. There was a possibility in the circumstances they would give him time to fix the problem. All of it was a risk. His mind raced as he thought through the permutations, disappearing in the circumstances would probably mean they would hunt him until generations had passed. He had his money in foreign bank accounts but no other resources.

Going to a foreign agency would ensure some protection but similarly his own people would try and hunt him down with even greater zeal. The only way to protect his family was to admit that something had happened to the cargo. Pretending that it was an accident was not an option, the Western media had already portrayed it as a suspicious sinking.

Khorasani wasn't overly concerned about his family or his mistress Zarrin, they had benefitted from his relative riches over the years, his life was at risk. He needed to clear his mind of the peripheral issues and threats and concentrate on the one directly affecting him. He had Zarrin followed by his men, nothing had come of it in the short term, but he was still suspicious she was having an affair.

He turned his attention back to the fifteen minute news on the television. A dhow sailing in the darkness with a large inflatable secured to it showed up on the footage with a commentary about piracy from the American news channel. That slimy little Palestinian pretending to be an Omani, Fakhoury. If only he knew how to get too him he could decide which route to take. It could salvage things in Iran for him or ingratiate himself with the Americans as long as they didn't know he organised the appropriation of the bomb. He knew they would eventually find out, possibly even from Fakhoury himself. What was the Palestinian going to do with the weapon? It had to be Israel or the US. Fallout would affect the Palestinian population if they attacked Israel, more likely an attack on the West. Getting the weapon into the US would be difficult, perhaps Europe? The duplicity of the Palestinian both enraged him and, in weaker moments, made him respect the man.

While he considered the options. His eyes kept looking at his cellphone, it would be a matter of hours, if even that, before the phone would ring and a very senior figure in Iran would be on the telephone. Perhaps even the President of the Islamic Republic. The fear welled up inside of him, he had chain smoked since the clerk in the office had informed him of the news he had heard from ship's radio. He could still have time to catch a flight to Switzerland, he already had false identities and a visa from previous visits. He couldn't seek sanctuary anywhere in the Middle East and be safe.

Ebrahim Khorasani couldn't be sure yet of where he was going but he was going to run now.

Chapter 24

Finlay met Henry in the hustle and bustle of Terminal 5 at London Heathrow to take the British Airways morning flight to Abu Dhabi. He was surprised to see his assistant Anna Siebert with Henry. She looked casual and relaxed in a light T-shirt and jeans which accentuated her shapely figure, in contrast to the equally casual but very unkempt Henry V. He made apologies, in front of Anna, for having to "bring her along", but had to due to "his failure in remembering the whole plot". It all seemed to go right over the analyst's head, she appeared to take no offence whatsoever.

Finlay's previous comments of doubts on the quality of the output of the information from Anna's intelligence software the day before appeared largely forgotten. She briefed Finlay on the latest developments in the Dubois case in one of the secluded customs interview rooms that Anna had managed to book through Millbank.

One of Finlay's assailants, 'black cap' had finally succumbed to interrogation. Subsequent to being able to converse with interrogators by writing answers down, due to the serious injury to his palette, he had told them of his mission. The two men who were Chechyn mercenaries had been approached by a 'man of Middle Eastern origin' and asked to track Henry. They had followed them in London after conducting surveillance on the MI5 building in Millbank. They had been asked to eliminate both Henry and any security he may have had. They decided to take out the security detail first before dealing with Henry Darcy. There was no more detail to be had, the two men were not aware of who or why the two intelligence men were targeted. They were merely given Henry's name, his whereabouts and a couple of pictures to identify him from. They said they had no information on Finlay, he was simply in the way. Both men had been charged with attempting to murder an Intelligence Officer and were being held in Belmarsh High Security Prison due to being regarded as a major security risk. If the intelligence service were to give an opinion they would have said that the detail the men passed on was probably correct and little further information may be forthcoming. It was felt, however, that their criminal actions and intent were not based on ideology but were purely financial. On this basis they would be open to co-operating to get a lighter sentence. Finlay, as one of the intended victims said he was happy to work with the Crown Prosecution Service and the Metropolitan Police to this end.

It was further confirmed that the CPS had felt Finlay had acted in self defence and no charges would be brought in the circumstances. Finlay was aware of how there was a fine line in a democracy of being asked to defend one's country and charges being brought for excessive force or even murder on men who had felt protected by the uniform or their position. He knew those valid and necessary layers of protection were being stripped away. One of the reasons he had decided to retire. He felt terrorist murderers he was employed to fight were roaming free while some men that had served under him could be charged with alleged "crimes" during a dirty war in Northern Ireland. He could even still be implicated due to his activities within the SRU. The capricious nature of the criminal justice system in the United Kingdom, he knew, was undermining the willingness of patriotic young men to defend the country he so dearly loved. Once again it had reared its vindictive head.

As Anna recapped on the footage and details on the African Tide, the rescue of Kravits and any further information that could be gleaned from the USS John McCain, Finlay caught himself staring at her for a bit longer than he had intended. His eyes flicked to Henry, who normally at this stage in a meeting would be hoping for a cigarette break and looking slightly agitated, was instead smirking at Finlay's visible discomfort. He knew that a slightly sarcastic but jocular remark would be forthcoming from Henry in private. Finlay didn't feel amused, just had an overwhelming feeling of guilt that overtook him while the analyst continued to summarise the details of their case to date.

They boarded the aircraft shortly after the briefing, Finlay sat across the aisle from Henry and next to Anna, at Henry's behest as they could get to know each other better. Finlay learned that she had worked for military intelligence after finishing a PhD in Artificial Intelligence at Imperial College London. The programme that she had used on the Dubois case has largely been written by her. Thus her defensiveness on Finlay casting doubt on its veracity. After a few glasses of wine on the aircraft and dinner Anna opened up about her personal life. She had some boyfriends, even a fiancé at one point but mostly due to her dedication to work she had never actually taken the plunge into marriage. She had doubted that having a relationship with a "spook like Henry" was ever going to be a good idea. She had no real ambition other than to be at the top end of her profession, perhaps go into the commercial world with her successful practical application of AI. She was also, for the first time, going into the field and was very excited about it. Finlay inwardly felt less than enthusiastic, he already had to carry Henry should things start to get physical, but at least he was an ex Guards Officer. Anna had been a civilian and a self-confirmed desk jockey that did a "bit of jogging" was not the support the old soldier needed.

All three dosed after their airborne dinner and were woken by the announcement that the aircraft was one hour from landing. The sun was in the last throes of setting over the Arab Peninsula, they could see the lights of the offshore platforms in the sea and the gas flares as the aircraft descended. It had been a long time since both men had been in the heat of a desert summer, they looked less enthusiastic than Anna who was about to experience it for the first time.

Chapter 25

Moshe Cohen kept a satellite telephone hidden in his makeshift office on the building site in Oudlajan. He had a sizeable filing cabinet which he moved from site to site containing everything from his drawings to his bank details required for his profession as a builder. It allowed him to stay on site when undertaking administrative tasks without having to move constantly across town in busy traffic to his office. He even had it mounted on wheels, it had pull out drawers containing his laptop as well as several for the building drawings, legal documents and letters from the government pertaining to his business. It also contained some petty cash, and as such was securely locked and protected by on site security. While the reasons for having the large steel cabinet on site were completely valid it allowed him to keep his slim satellite telephone hidden in a false backing in one of the drawers. Such a device was highly illegal in his country and anyone found with it in their possession in the Islamic Republic of Iran would be immediately imprisoned. The fact that Moshe was a Jew would be all the proof that would be required for his execution after interrogation, regardless of its outcome.

The mobile nature of his business allowed him to access the phone after hours, as he was generally the last to leave the site and find an area where he could make the call to his handler in Tel Aviv. The call was encrypted and always made from a different location. The telephone looked no different from a cellphone, the state of the art satellite communication technology shrunken down to the smallest components that could be used reliably.

Cohen had grown up in the Jewish Quarter where his extended family had come from. Iranian Jews had an understanding with the Islamic Republic hierarchy as they had with the Shah's regime. His father, mother and three siblings had towed the line, only ever commenting on the brutalities of the regime in the privacy of the family home. His two brothers and sister had married and had families while Moshe, the youngest, had stayed with his parents and had grown the business his father had started. The Iranian Muslims trusted the Jews in business dealings, somewhat bizarrely, more than they did their own kind. It was almost like the Jews had to be honest in case hellfire rained down from the government because of their minority faith. Moshe didn't care as long as the business was coming in from whichever religious community that existed in the country. He had dealt with Jews, Armenian Christians and all of the Muslim communities in Iran. The wealth he had created from his business and his contacts in the building industry had allowed him to purchase many luxury items that were subject to sanctions. Ten years previously he had got the latest flat screen television so he could watch English football. He was an avid follower of Tottenham Hotspur after having visited London with his parents in his youth. Moshe was regularly allowed to leave the country.

The unexpected side-effect of this was he also had access to western media channels which he watched, almost as a by-product of his interest in sport. He saw first-hand the conflict with Israel, how the Islamic Republic was regarded as a pariah in the world and particularly by the home of the Jewish faith. He had watched TV documentaries on the holocaust and seen how the modern media in Iran and some other fanatical countries had denied that it had even happened.

Moshe had clandestinely, via Germany and Cyprus, attempted to visit Israel. Immigration in Israel had originally been suspicious of his Iranian passport, but after extensive correspondence had allowed him into the country. During his entry he had been interviewed by border security, common when entering Tel Aviv, but later realized that this was a pre-cursor to him being recruited. He was approached by a man called Binyamin Amit. He later found out he was the nephew of the ex Director of the Mossad, in a tourist bar in Tel Aviv prior to a visit to Temple Mount. To his own surprise he agreed to sign up immediately. It had started off as eyes and ears in Tehran, his fluency in Farsi meant he could feedback accurate analysis of what was in the media. He then ventured further afield as his cover as a builder was a good excuse to bid for government building works and then he could pry into contracts that were to be awarded for Iranian weapons programmes. As a Jewish contractor he did not have clearance to bid for lucrative contracts tendered by the Revolutionary Guard. They were so corrupt that these usually went to businesses set up by the Guard themselves or their relatives. He could however bid for peripheral work, like remote army barracks or offices that supported the secretive process of trying to enrich Uranium or Plutonium. This was invaluable to the Israeli security apparatus. He would win the occasional contract and wander around the sites chatting to other contractors and listening to the rumours about what the construction activities were really for.

As with any spy embedded in a country with a harsh regime for a long period, poor moral combined with fear of capture and death was often his biggest battle. This was given a much needed boost when in 2015 targets he had identified were about to be struck by the Israeli air force. The politicians had called it off due to pressure from the United States but the value of his contribution to Israel had been confirmed. He was an important cog now in the IDF machine. His life was worth risking.

He had met Zarrin Rahmani just before the Israeli attack on Iran was supposed to take place in 2015. Moshe was struck by her elegant, if slightly too long face, dominated by large clear eyes which twinkled when she told a joke or was being sarcastic. He had been converting a building for a government official in Elahieh and she had been the official who had organised the administrative paperwork for the building renovation. The builder had taken her to an illicit back street bar which served contraband alcohol. She had seen familiar names on the beer cans from her visits to London such as Heineken, Amstel and Magners and laughed about it with Moshe. They had spent the night drinking and discussing everything from their lives and families to the situation in their country. She had known he was Jewish simply by his name and had no issue with it but as their time that night drew to a close she told him of her dark secret. Of her affair with Khorasani, his power and her fear of him. It was intended as a warning to Moshe Cohen, but unrealised by Zarrin it had simply added to her attractiveness. They had made love that night in the semi renovated attic of a senior government official which Cohen had been working on.

So it had gone on, Zarrin had fallen in love with Moshe Cohen, while Cohen was fond of the vulnerable woman and was protective of her, his relationship was one of convenience. It fulfilled his emotional needs for a female relationship, but above all, allowed him to undertake his duty to his people after centuries of persecution. Moshe had gone on with his intelligence activities and as he correctly explained to Zarrin, he hadn't figured out the end game with his family being unable or unwilling to leave Iran. He hoped for an end to the fanatical regime and better times, perhaps that had to be his answer and the reason for him to fight for Israel.

It was late in the evening and his construction crew had all departed for their homes before another early morning start the next day. Cohen took the phone from its hiding place, checked that battery and went out into the street, he knew a park nearby which he could walk through and make the call as scheduled. His handler was known as David, he doubted if that was his real name. Cohen had not met him in person but he had grown a relationship with his handler over the telephone for almost ten years. David had the rasping voice of a smoker, though eventually Moshe had found out the handler had damaged his larynx after an RPG attack on his Merkava tank during one of many IDF incursions into Lebanon as a young man. This was all he knew, small talk was not encouraged. The odd moral raising joke was acceptable, however, which is how he'd found out after making a comment about David's perceived cigarette consumption.

Moshe Cohen was known as Robert, a play on "Bob the Builder", a children's cartoon favoured by the handler's grandchildren. Some humour from within the Israeli intelligence service that was lost, not only on any VAJA operatives that may be listening in, but also on Moshe Cohen.

Moshe pressed the memory button, David answered in Farsi so that Moshe could converse without raising suspicion. Hebrew or English would attract the attention of passers-by in Tehran.

'Robert, how are you?'

'I am well, thank god.' The greeting was always the same, if any different David would hang up.

'Any news on how our business is developing?' his handler enquired.

'No developments, apart from our client is distracted and nervous.'

'I have an update, it appears that a transporter with goods on it has been cancelled. Our client was waiting for it. Not sure what was in it. You can read about it in the paper.' The cryptic conversation was thinly disguised but combined with a state of the art digital encryption was merely a precaution. "The papers" was a reference to Cohen's access to Western television and media.

'I will check,' responded Moshe.

'This is a priority for our business Robert, like never before. It will send us in to a different league. You must talk to your client's friend and get information, even if she loses her job.'

Cohen felt his heart beat faster, his handler was telling him to risk Zarrin being caught or killed, the former would surely ensure his own capture and death.

'That is a big risk to her and to our business David.'

'I know that, my friend, we have never asked this of you and would not do so if we could find a better way.'
'I understand.'

Moshe Cohen hung up without any further conversation. Firstly, he needed to talk to his lover to ascertain if there had been further developments with Khorasani, then he would figure out what to do. It must be critical, he could hear the nerves in David's already hoarse rattling throat when he spoke. Knew he was under pressure to get a result from his spy and he was expected to deliver, the handler's soft leather gloves had been removed.

Cohen called Zarrin on her cellphone and asked to meet her the next morning at a cafe two blocks away from the property where he was keeping is makeshift office. As he walked through the dimly lit streets in the old quarter, he grimly went over his options. None were particularly attractive for him or his lover.

The next morning he arrived at the coffee shop to find Zarrin already there. Cafe's such as these had sprung up all over Iran in the last ten years. In the absence of bars they had become the mobile office and meeting place, as they had in the West. More than that they were the hub of the young and middle class, where they could meet to discuss the problems in the city and country in general. This one, with its large glass doors opened up to its patio for the warmer weather, situated in the grand old street in Oudlajan with cobbled roads and pavement vendors, could have been in Montmartre in Paris or in St Paul's in London. Moshe knew differently. It was also where state security sat and listened for the first whispers of sedition or the hatching of student plans to demonstrate against the regime. As they did in the warm summer of 1999. More recently the general strikes, partly contributed to by sanctions, had caused great concern. The government had clearly threatened violent suppression.

Zarrin was sitting at a table that was surrounded by others that, though engaged in their own conversations, could easily listen in to theirs. He saw a small, more secluded table that was being cleared at the back of the cafe, and taking Zarrin's hand guided her toward it. She squeezed his hand seeking comfort and reassurance as he did so. As they sat down she looked at his face, trying to read whether this meeting was going to be good or bad - to pre-empt his news from his features. Moshe didn't bother with any small talk.

'Zarrin, my love, we need to get you out of Tehran. But first I need to know where Khorasani is and what he is doing.'

She continued to look at his drawn features, the dark brown intelligent eyes set below the creased brow, 'what is going on Moshe?'

Cohen had told Zarrin that he was feeding information back to the US and ultimately the UN to enable a sanctions breaking deal to be done with the West that would be good for the whole country. This would see the end of Khorasani and the regime, which in turn could allow them both to move on. She knew nothing of the real reason for his hunger for information. He had dressed the whole affair up as the two of them being liberal Iranians steering their country toward better times.

'It appears Khorasani has been importing some nuclear material into Iran through Bandar Abbas,' Cohen guessed, 'I saw the US news last night, it was on board a ship called the African Tide. Do you know where he is?'

'He doesn't tell me where he's going specifically but I think it was in Iran as he always tells me when he's going abroad. He brings me back presents from foreign countries and asks me what I would like to have. He didn't do it this time.'
'He may be in Bandar Abbas, where this ship was going to arrive.'

'I can call him, but it is only for emergencies, he'll be suspicious.'

'You need to find out what he has been doing,' said Cohen bluntly.

Zarrin looked shocked, 'how can I do that, he will never tell me, I will go to jail.'

'This is serious Zarrin, we need to find a way.'

'You would risk my life, or have me imprisoned for this spying you do?'

Cohen could see she was retreating away from assisting him. 'Well get him to Tehran, tell him you are sick, I will deal with it.'

'How?'

'Do you want to be with me and rid of this man?'

'You know I want nothing else.'

'Then leave it to me.'

Chapter 26

Gianni de Bastiani cut an imposing figure amongst the elite of Brindisi, and more so occupying his luxurious office in the heart of the city. He was the head of the Sacra Corona Unita, the organized crime syndicate which operated in the Apulia region of Italy and ran trades from the old traditional olive oil business to more modern drugs and human trafficking. He had been approached about a "special consignment" coming into the port by an established client. He didn't mind bringing items into the country which did not affect his trade if the client paid well and was not an enemy of his Albanian partners or his associates, the Ndrangheta on the west coast of Italy. He also had to make sure that none of the contraband would end up conflicting with the trade of his partners. He had been offered five million Euros for a one off consignment. He also knew there was Middle Eastern involvement. He suspected arms and as was his custom, told his client that the cargo would be checked by two of his close lieutenants which was his procedure in cases like these. He had been informed that this couldn't happen, the payment was then agreed at double, ten million Euros. He didn't like it, but it was an offer he was not about to refuse. Who would know which port this had come through if it were to lead to a major problem? His conditions were that the contraband would be received and escorted by his representatives until it left Italian soil. He was, after all, a patriot.

What had concerned him were the two individuals representing his clients that were now in his office. He had expected to be dealing with experienced and veteran career criminals, instead he had been sent two individuals who he wouldn't send out to get his lunch. One was a thin unkept individual who may as well as have been a mute for the amount of sound that had come out his mouth. The other was an overweight thick set individual with long greasy hair in a black tracksuit. His two most senior capos who had led them into his office had found it hard to hide their contempt. They had seen cleaner people arriving in makeshift rafts from Libya and had told him so. The gang leader had wished he had asked for all the money up front instead of just half. He had an office desk set at the back of an enormous marble floor on the top floor of his office building. There was a tastefully decorated wooden paneled anteroom with a camera in it he could watch from the massive flat screen PC monitor on his desk. He had made the two men wait while he was de-briefed by his capos and watched the monitor on the screen while he listened. They were eventually ushered into his office and showed no deference to him as they walked up to his massive mahogany desk. Normally he would ask visitors to sit at the large meeting desk which was raised on a plinth next to the window and had a panoramic view of Brindisi. He decided, in the circumstances, not even to rise to shake their hands. He spoke in English to the two visitors.

'You are Mr Fakhoury's men, I take it?'

'Yes, we are. We have shown your men our identification and Mr Fakhoury's introduction letter,' responded the thick set one in perfect but accented English.

'Can you confirm why you are here?'

'To escort our cargo truck to its destination.'

'Yes, along with two of my men,' de Bastiani searched their faces for reaction, the stocky one frowned and shook his head.

'That was not the deal.'

'Firstly, my deal is with Fakhoury, not his monkeys, anything that comes through my territory, gets escorted for my protection and yours.'

'We don't need your men or your protection.'

'Then I keep the truck here until I speak to your boss and it doesn't move until I am paid in full.'

'Our instructions are twenty five per cent more on arrival Brindisi and remaining when across the Italian border.'

'That was with our escort, those are my conditions, I need competent people who don't attract attention, you two don't fit that description. You are scruffy, dark skinned and smell, you look like illegal immigrants. The Carabinieri will think you stole that removals container that is coming in on the ro-ro ferry!'

'We have been sleeping in our van that we came in so not to leave a trail for the police. We will get cleaned up here and be ready for the ship's arrival,' responded the thick set man, obviously irritated.

'You can do so, but if my men don't escort that truck to the border, you won't get near your cargo, that is final!'

De Bastiani dismissed them with his hand while looking at his two men, they immediately escorted the two track suited individuals from the main office. He called one of his own men Claudio back in Italian, 'I want Stefano and Luigi on this with these two idiots, they don't move anywhere without them. They can go in the truck if there is room or if not in a tail car. In fact supply a car anyway and follow them from a distance and our guys can keep me up to date on progress. Any hitches and the price goes up. I'd also like to find out what is in that truck that is worth so much money. I think this may be some crazy Arab scheme and if we can take their money and shut it down that's okay, but I don't want a war with some idealistic assholes, so be careful.'

He would have to clear this up with Fakhoury. No doubt the two jokers the Arab had employed would feed back his new conditions straight after the meeting and he would hear from him soon.

De Bastiani was a large man, he carried little fat on his frame despite his sixty three years, spending many hours a week in the gym. He still had a good head of dark hair, suspiciously lacking any grey and a long aquiline nose preceding dark brown eyes set in a broad forehead. A scar ran from the corner of his mouth to underneath his right eye, evidence of his battles as a youth on the streets of Taranto. He always wore expensive suits by Armani or Corneliani, handmade shirts and crafted Italian leather shoes that cost the monthly salary of one of his dockside stevedores. He kept clear of publicity whenever possible but wore his wealth and power on his sleeve to show his confidence in his position as well as contempt for the authorities.

He believed appearance meant everything as leader of his organisation. His men needed to respect him, the day that started to dissipate he was gone. He knew his two sons, despite their expensive education, and his Capos, were questioning the passing of this cargo through their territory. They did not want heat from the police if the goods were used in terrorist related activities such as what had happened in Paris and London in the past. Their influence within the Police and Carabinieri would not extend that far. Their income from drugs, extortion, prostitution and human trafficking was allowed to flow as long as it was kept under control. Murder of innocent civilians would ensure they were all imprisoned if the authorities suspected the involvement of the Sacra Corona Unita.

De Bastiani was a risk taker, his underlings did not understand that he had taken many chances on the way to the top. Ten million Euros with little cost to him was not to be sniffed at. If he hadn't done business with this Arab he would have gone through Naples or Genoa, enriching the competition and taking any future business elsewhere. His show of contempt for Fakhoury's foot soldiers was genuine but it also served to show his senior men who the boss was in this deal. He had been involved in the Mafia trials of the nineties, the original war with the Albanians before that and come out the other end unscathed, he would do so once again.

Despite the fact he was a criminal, De Bastiani was disciplined, he woke early every morning and went to his office where he ran both legitimate and illegal enterprises. His prompt timekeeping was legendary, there were cases of employees being dismissed for being ten minutes late, others for continual breach of business processes, from IT security to not being obtainable by telephone. On the illegitimate side of the business, De Bastiani had never sampled narcotics or any of the illegitimate contraband he trafficked, the consumption of which was banned in his business. One driver had taken to sampling the product he was delivering to customers had crashed his van into a tree. The whole shipment had been confiscated by the police. The driver was shot and buried in a landfill site within forty eight hours of leaving the court where his prosecution had begun despite the fact he had kept his mouth shut. The Sacra Corona Unita had a fabric of defined process and efficiency, the whole business ethos being created from the very top. The Arab's cargo would be subject to these rules and the monies paid into the accounts required once the whole transaction had been concluded. The Boss would see to that.

Chapter 27

Ebrahim Khorasani drove his Iran Khodro Peugeot copy toward Imam Khomeini airport located south of the main city of Tehran. He had decided to leave the car at the airport and get on the first flight to Istanbul, from there he could travel anywhere in Europe. He had no time to compose his escape plan beyond that. He would have direct and uninterrupted access to his Swiss bank accounts which he had built up over time. This was from a combination of bribes he had received and contraband he had confiscated from investigating other Iranians as a senior figure in VAJA. He had also obtained Revolutionary Guard funds to pass on as bribes for intelligence. In reality he had paid individuals concerned very little and kept the resultant balance for himself. He had a personal wealth of over six million dollars as a result, enough to start a life somewhere outside Iran and to cover his tracks.

He had seen a couple of missed calls, several from his wife, two from Zarrin and one was from Brigadier General Abuhamzeh, deputy head of the Guard. This was the one he had feared would come through. He would only call once and expect Khorasani to call him straight back as he had always done. Every minute that ticked past would result in him becoming suspicious of Khorasani's whereabouts, he must be calling about the African Tide. The result of any conversation that would take place with his superiors would ensure he could no longer travel. He could not phone him back before he got on the flight. He would return the call from Zurich saying he was in London pursuing a lead on the loss of the North Korean weapon that had gone missing. This could buy him another couple of days. The question was could he get on that flight which left in two hours.

Khorasani pulled into the new airport, it had been built in 2007 and had boomed until the second imposition of sanctions. The combination of a collapse in the Iranian economy and the direct effect of sanctions on airlines had resulted in a vastly reduced trade at the airport. It was very quiet, Khorasani could hear his footsteps echo on the marble floors as he walked toward the check in counter. There were no direct flights to Switzerland and he wanted to get out on the first available flight so he had booked on a Turkish Airlines flight to Istanbul. He would then get a train to Geneva so his superiors couldn't track his destination.

As he walked toward the check-in counter his pulse picked up and he started to perspire, two men stood in front of the business class counter. They were in suits without baggage facing toward him, they obviously weren't checking in. He missed a step but one was looking straight at him. To turn around and walk away would be suspicious. He kept his stride toward the girl behind the counter and presented his passport at the desk. The two men stepped to the side, to his relief one picked up a clipboard and pen, turned and walked to the next set of check-in desks. The other followed. As he started to go through the normal formalities he could feel the sweat running down his back into the waste of his trousers. His forehead had also started to perspire and his hands felt clammy. He felt nauseous. Khorasani looked behind him, a short thick set man was right behind him, the spy looked at the man's feet, he had cabin baggage. The economy queue was starting to fill up, all appeared to be interested only in getting to the desk to get on the aircraft. He could vaguely hear the Turkish Airlines check in attendant tell him the flight was on time, he needed to calm down. He'd almost had a very uncharacteristic panic attack. Khorasani drew in a deep breath as he picked up his passport and boarding card and walked toward the security gate. His phone rang. It was Zarrin again. He answered it.

'Zarrin my dear I am busy can I call you back?' He felt talking to her may calm him down, he could also weave a cover story should VAJA know of her existence and was curious to see what was so urgent.'

'Ebrahim my love, where are you I need to see you?'

'I am in Bandar Abbas,' he lied, 'I have some very important things to be getting on with, what is the problem?'

'I have some information regarding the work you are carrying out.'

He almost couldn't believe what he was hearing. She knew nothing of his activities, immediately his mind was in overdrive, had she been working him? He couldn't believe it, was she with the security services, perhaps even a VAJA operative? They always watched their people closely. It was a huge coincidence she was calling repeatedly when he was trying to exit the country. His superiors didn't know where he was so were they using her to get a hold of him because he wasn't answering Abuhamzeh's call? He looked at the security guard who was asking him to open his hand luggage before putting it through the scanner. He had his telephone earpiece in and continued to talk to Zarrin while doing as he was bid. 'What are you talking about Zarrin, do you understand what you are saying to me?'

'Yes if you can meet me in Tehran I will tell you everything,' she told him, he could hear her voice breaking, while he listened, continually pressing the mute button when it was her turn to speak. He didn't want her to hear the din of security, or worse, a flight announcement.

'I am too busy to meet with you Zarrin. You have been spying on me?'

She could hear the indignation and anger in his voice. Zarrin was simply trying to get her old lover to a destination where Moshe could deal with the questions about the sunken ship and the background behind the disaster. She knew little more but went further, 'it's about the ship that sunk, the African Tide.'

Khorasani immediately pressed the end call button on his handset and pulled the earpieces out. He knew his calls would at some point be monitored, Abuhamzeh may have given the instruction already. He threw the telephone into the security tray and passed through the scanner before retrieving his hand luggage and walking toward the business class lounge. No one appeared to show any interest in him after the security check. He switched the phone off so they couldn't trace his location.

Moshe Cohen was at the apartment in Elahieh with Zarrin and observed her taking her cell phone from her ear and looking at it, 'he has hung up?'

'Yes, he is suspicious and the background noise kept cutting in and out, he was muting the call quickly when I spoke. I heard someone ask him to open a case and put something in a tray, I think he is at the airport.'

'Which one?'

Zarrin shrugged, 'I have no idea, it could be Bandar Abbas or Tehran, he has had time to get back here. Wherever it is, he is leaving the country.'

'Why would he be leaving so quickly after the ship sunk? He is trying to save his skin or he has a destination which involved pursuing intelligence, either way we need to find him.'

Zarrin appeared almost relieved, perhaps this was the answer to her prayers, Khorasani had left the country freeing her from the relationship. This was her chance to persuade Moshe to leave also, unhindered, with her. She touched Cohen's arm and using her other hand, held his cheek, 'Moshe let us go while Ebrahim has left the country. If he is running there are no comebacks for us. If he isn't I am finished, I have virtually admitted I have been spying on him, there is no way back for me.'

Cohen could see how her logic was working, but for him, it was convenient. Zarrin could still be useful bait for attracting Khorasani either in Iran or in a foreign country. He needed to get back to his satellite phone and contact David. He pulled her close to him and pressed himself against her. He didn't have to do that straight away and the thought of sex in Khorasani's apartment with his lover appealed to him.

Chapter 28

A large black GMC Yukon picked them up at the airport and drove them down a large and busy highway on the mainland where the airport was located over the Mussaffah Bridge. One of three which crossed on to the island of Abu Dhabi. The city had changed immeasurably since either Finlay Lamont or Henry Darcy had been there. As they crossed the bridge Henry marvelled at the huge mosque and hotels built on the island side of the narrow channel that separated it from the mainland. He told his companions how it had all been desert to that point only as recently as twenty five years ago. The whole channel shone in the night, the result of reflected lights from the most opulent of hotels on both sides of the water. They continued on for another fifteen kilometers of grandeur until they arrived at a huge set if high rise blocks sitting opposite the massive Emirates Palace hotel. Their uniformed driver informed them they would be staying in the Jumeirah Hotel in one of the towers.

The two men were sharing a room next to Anna and after throwing their luggage in the room all three met in a quiet corner of the bar to discuss their strategy for the next day's meeting. Henry was to do most of the talking with his old friend while Anna would elaborate on the possibility of supplying intelligent deductive software for their cooperation in the Dubois case. Henry would take the call on whether they would divulge the potential link with the Frenchman's murder. It may be better for Henry to talk privately with his friend on specifics.

After the meeting had concluded Henry had excused himself as he wanted to get an early night, the meeting had been scheduled for first thing the next morning. Finlay and Anna had decided to have a nightcap, their conversation soon changed from the business in hand to personal lives once again. Partly lubricated by alcohol, they opened up about their past, the analyst much more so than the old soldier. He was still typically guarded about his military life and his time with Ella. He made it clear to Anna that was off limits after she had ventured into both subjects while on the flight from London. He was happy to talk about his children, how much he craved their company but understood they had to live their own lives. She queried him more on their upbringing and family life together. This once again got too close to the subject of his dead wife, at that point Fin hurriedly made his excuses, declined her offer of a further drink and went to bed.

The next morning the delegation from UK Military Intelligence was escorted into the fifty-sixth floor of the massive tower situated on the Abu Dhabi beach corniche. The journey on to the office from the hotel had taken fifteen minutes. The wide palm lined highways and efficient road traffic system allowed quick transit to a tower which appeared to have no link to a military or security apparatus.

Colonel Al Qubaisi was with three other men in military uniform while he wore the customary Emirati kandora and head dress. He welcomed his old friend and warmly embraced him. They both made the customary jokes about each other to show their intimacy to others, introduced the rest of the attendees and sat down.

Henry started by outlining his concerns that there had been some "noise" that there was a possibility of a major attack on a European city, he did not wish to elaborate on nuclear proliferation at this stage. The MI5 man went further on to say the trigger device and UK connection with the Ansari brothers was a concern. The Colonel then took up the narrative on the part of the contingency from the UAE stating they had footage of the Royal Mirage meeting as well as separate footage of Makhlouf with the two British Ansari brothers. He elaborated on what he knew of Makhlouf, his suspected activities in the Middle East. They formally went through a discussion on what both their intelligence services had deducted from the schematic drawing they had found in Bur Dubai. Both sides of the table agreed it was a trigger device for a sizeable bomb.

Finally Colonel Al Qubaisi came to the subject of a fourth man, one whom they thought was a key player in the whole story that was unfolding. He stated that he was concerned with both sides not knowing each other's levels of security clearance and asked if he could talk with Henry in person, preferably while sipping Arabic coffee on the beach front of the Corniche before it got too hot. Both delegations left the building while Henry and Colonel Sohail sat in the shade by the beach.

The Colonel was straight to the point, 'I need help on identifying the fourth man,' he met Henry's eyes through both of their sunglasses. 'I will give you who I think he is, in turn, I would like you to co-operate on verifying his identification, whoever it turns out to be. I don't want to give you this and it disappears into a big hole and I get nothing.'

The immediate question came to Henry, 'why can't you do it yourself?'

'Because of the agency that has probably got the answer. Politically I cannot deal with them after what they have done here.'

'You don't think we have the answer?'

'I doubt it very much.'

'So I need to speak to either the Iranians or the Israelis and I strongly suspect it's not the former?' enquired Henry.

The Colonel did not answer directly, 'Do I have your word?'

'Absolutely.'

He slid a clear picture of Omar Fakhoury at the Royal Mirage over to Henry, 'this is a close and probably senior associate of Makhlouf. He then slid a very grainy old picture of a man standing near Yasser Arafat. 'And I think this is the same man, his name is Saeed Raheem.'

Henry looked down at both pictures and immediately understood his old friend's dilemma.

'If it can be done, Sohail, my dear fellow, I will get it done. Now let's have some shisha together inside in the air conditioning before I get cooked to death out here.'

The team from MI5 met later in the day around the rooftop pool at the hotel. Colonel Al Qubaisi had talked with Henry at some length while smoking traditional Arabic shisha, they had discussed family and caught up after years of not seeing each other. Little business was discussed further until both men were about to part company. As they shook hands and promised to catch up again soon, Al Qubaisi's cell phone rung and he asked if he could have privacy to take the call. The caller was from the US Ambassador's office based in Abu Dhabi giving both men permission to board the USS John McCain in Sharjah and question the crew member rescued from the African Tide.

Henry relayed this information to Finlay and Anna and they arranged with the Colonel's office to get transport to get to Sharjah port and the warship. The journey took about two hours, all three attended the meeting. They were shown to the officer's wardroom aboard the large guided missile destroyer and were introduced to Captain Spencer and a CIA operative called Billy Franklin. They summoned the marine sergeant at arms, who brought in a dark haired broad shouldered man who had obviously been badly sunburned. His face was still red but the skin was peeling quite badly. He was introduced as Chief Officer Vasily Kravits, originally from the Ukraine. Kravits had passed information on to the Central Intelligence Agency and produced a statement. A copy was passed to Henry V, who then asked Kravits to repeat what they had told the Americans. The Ukrainian went through the story, which was obviously now well-rehearsed. The salient points were his doubt as to whether his passengers were Iranian, the relationship between Sia and his "wife" and the final takeover of the ship leading to him being shot and falling overboard.

Henry led with some questions, 'Did you see another vessel near the African Tide?'

'No I didn't,' replied Kravits in a strong Eastern European accent, 'I was too busy trying to save the crew in the citadel and resist the attack of Sia and his bandits. We were unarmed. It is possible that something was close in the dark but I hadn't been near the radar for some time and received no warnings from the officer of the watch.'

His English was good but he stumbled over some words. He was obviously used to keeping it simple with varying degrees of English aptitude aboard a ship with an international crew.

Henry went on, 'you have seen footage of the ship sinking, what do you think happened after you went overboard?'

'I think our so called passengers took control of my ship and escaped on another vessel or possibly by helicopter - who knows?'

Captain Spencer interrupted, 'we would have detected any airborne traffic from our ship's systems, we were too far away for seaborne radar to pick anything up initially.'

'Why do you think they would do what they did?' enquired Anna of Kravits.

'They must have been after something on the ship that was very valuable, they went to a lot of trouble. I have no idea what that could have been. They killed a lot of men. They were animals, these people, even the girl.'

Anna carried on, 'Do you think that the fish container was just a cover for their weapons as they couldn't bring them with their luggage?'

Kravits looked at the small woman, wandering what she was doing in military intelligence, 'Yes it must have been, so they had an excuse to access the container, we would not have let them access any of the sealed ones normally. Even the crew are not permitted to access, unless we suspect leaks or fire inside.'

Henry interrupted, 'you'll also have seen from the footage that the ship had another container that was breached at some point before the ship sank, did you have any knowledge of that?'

'None at all, the first time I see this, is when I see the film. They must have broken into the green container after I raise the alarm with Captain Campeti.'

Henry continued, 'would you recognise the passengers again in person or from a photograph?'

'Yes, I spent two weeks with them, I would recognise a recent picture of them.'

Henry thought it a long shot, but took the surveillance picture of Fakhoury from his briefcase and showed it to Kravits, 'is this any of the men?'
Kravits shook his head, 'no I don't think I have ever seen him before, certainly not on the African Tide.'

Henry replaced the picture in his case, 'what are your plans now?' he looked at Kravits then glanced across at Captain Spencer and Franklin.

'He's free to go wherever he likes,' Franklin responded, 'I guess you'll want to go home Vasily?'

Kravits nodded, 'yes I need to have leave and relax and get in touch with my family and the Company.'

The MI5 team and the Americans exchanged contact details with each other and Kravits and said their farewells. As they were departing Kravits, seemed to almost sense that Finlay was the man who could deal with the hijackers if they were ever caught. Holding Finlay's wrist he shook his hand, 'if you need help to catch these animals, please call me any time I can help. I want them caught and thrown in a black hole, they are scum, Major. They killed thirty innocent people who were just working for their families on a ship, nothing else.'

Finlay acknowledged Kravits' plea by squeezing his hand. 'We will do our best mister Kravits, I will tell you if it is done, that is my promise.'

*

The three men who sat in the old wood panelled room in Whitehall, with sash windows sealed shut with many decades of what appeared to be cream coloured paint. All came from different backgrounds. Sir Basil Cudlip, the Director General of MI5 was from a very privileged background. His ancestors had owned a significant part of Cornwall and Devon, less so now but much of the income generated from the land over centuries had been plied into city real estate. Sir Basil was the youngest of four siblings and had followed the traditional military route into intelligence as a young man.

Rory Campbell was the Director General of MI6, correctly known as the SIS, he was the younger of the two DG's and curiously had been a submariner in the Navy. He had served on Britain's 'boomer' or nuclear missile submarines so was brought up with stealth as his watchword. He had gone into naval intelligence before transferring into the UK's foreign spy service. His parents lived in a council house in Dumfries, his father had contemplated joining the communist party as a young man. They contrasted in size and appearance as much as they did with their ancestry. Sir Basil was a tall and commanding figure, dressed in a suit he most probably had worn to the office since leaving the army thirty years before. Campbell was a slight dapper man who wore expensive and fashionable three piece suits. He could have been a broker in the City.

The third man in the room was the Tarique Hashmi, the Foreign Secretary to the government. His grandparents had come from Pakistan in the early fifties after the partition from India to seek work and provide a good education for their children. They had succeeded beyond their ambition, the third generation Hashmi's had produced an Oxford educated senior policeman and the government's Foreign Secretary. Like Campbell, Hashmi was a small immaculately dressed man with a liking for more somber suits but very bright and colourful ties.

One key player missing from the meeting was the Home Secretary, Edward Soames who was in the north of England attending the aftermath of a train crash which had produced several fatalities. He was particularly relevant to the meeting as the topic was based around the recent events involving the death of a rogue French nuclear scientist. The Home Secretary felt that his intelligence agency should keep control of the investigation while the Foreign Secretary had been, rather vociferously, putting forward the point that nuclear proliferation was the clear responsibility of MI6. The Home Secretary and he were bitter rivals despite being from the same political party and appearing to have the same principles and ambitions. Hashmi had known that Soames would be commiserating with the loved ones of the dead victims in Yorkshire and as a result had called an emergency meeting with the two DG's. He had asked Campbell to make the case and he was happy to do so after Sir Basil had outlined the developments to date. Sir Basil, even without the support of his boss in the room, was a veteran of Whitehall politics, it was in his blood but Campbell was determined not to be cowed into submission, 'Sir Basil, if we have learned anything in this business it's that we have to send the right breed of dog after the hare or we'll lose it.'

Sir Basil peered over his reading glasses, with an almost sympathetic look in his eye, 'Rory, the lines of demarcation are very clear here. The threat as my team see it, is to the welfare of our country within its borders. Your man, I forget his name, is as green as the snot that probably drips from his youthful nose. Not someone we should let loose if this country has the risk of a massive bomb being detonated within its shores.'

'His name is Charles Jones, and he is one of our agency's top men. Just because he is a relatively young fellow doesn't mean he doesn't have the requisite experience or intellect,' responded Campbell.

'Then why doesn't he get together with Darcy and bloody well work with him? Henry has worked for both organisations and I'm sure he wouldn't mind the assistance.'

'Obviously you haven't been informed, they have met and Henry basically told him to keep his nose out.'

In fact Sir Basil had been well informed and had told Henry to tell MI6 to "fuck off". He feigned ignorance, 'well I'm sure Darcy was just being a little obtuse and didn't mean it like that.' He continued to play the cooperation game in front of the politician.

Campbell went on, 'he has got some psychotic soldier, ex SRU, in tow who almost killed a couple of blokes in central London instead of asking for backup. Their reputation precedes them after Ulster. Bunch of gung ho squaddies, a law unto themselves. Something else that MI5 let run amok, let's not do it again.'

Inwardly Sir Basil was seething, but outwardly appeared calm, 'Major Lamont was one of our best assets, saved a lot of lives in the province and here on the mainland. You may have been a little young to remember that Rory.'

Campbell twiddled his cufflinks, a nervous habit he had when confronting authority.

Hashmi butted in, 'I believe that our man Jones needs to head this up. Henry Darcy can handover to him when he gets back from the Middle East. MI6 has the foreign connections and infrastructure to deal with this issue, yours is an internal service to the UK and has not.'

The seasoned DG of MI5 turned to look at the Foreign Secretary, 'I am sorry Tarique but I get my instructions from the Home Secretary and have done so as Director General of MI5 for fifteen years. Currently, that happens to be Edward Soames.' The hint at the temporary nature of politicians wasn't lost on anyone in the room. It was clear the Foreign Secretary was not used to being talked to in that way. He had failed in his rather obvious attempt to get agreement when the Home Secretary was indisposed, 'I will deal with Edward if you can't do this amicably Sir Basil. I am surprised by this continued rivalry you foster with MI6.'

'I can assure you sir, there is no rivalry fostered on my part. But I do realise after many, many years of being in this game that every project has its correct fit in the services we have in place to defend our country. I can also reassure you the *fit* of this particular one dovetails perfectly with MI5. I will ensure that Darcy continues to liaise with Rory's team so we have the best of all our resources.'

Hashmi shook his head, 'like I said Sir Basil, I will resolve this with Edward, as you have correctly outlined. You will get your instructions from him. I think that concludes our meeting.'

The men shook hands, albeit rather frostily, and took their leave.

*

Saeed Abdul Raheem had decided to use a car to travel from Port Sudan to Khartoum. It was much quicker to travel there by air than the rather poorly maintained eight hundred or more kilometers of road between the two cities, or by train which took even longer. He had taken the services of one of the hawkers that had offered "taxi service" in Port Sudan. The man was delighted to be offered five hundred US dollars plus fuel expenses to take Saeed to Khartoum in his beat up twenty year old Toyota. The purpose was two-fold, a flight, car hire or train ticket was documented and could be traced, by travelling in this way it broke up any trace that anyone could have on him. It also avoided video surveillance in airports and train stations that could be accessed by anyone hunting for him. The Palestinian was very aware of the technology that the West and in particular, the Americans and Israelis could use to track him. The sinking of the African Tide would have raised alarm bells and they would be on their trail somehow. It also allowed him some extended time to reflect on the plan before his meeting in Khartoum. It was an apt place for the Mubarizun to meet. It was where the Blue Nile met the mighty White Nile, the longest river in the world. It was where the great Muhammad Ahmad or "Mahdi" had defeated the Infidel General Gordon and had his head mounted on a pike which was paraded through the town.

Saeed had departed his dhow in Port Sudan. His men had sailed the vessel into the dhow harbour and discharged the cargo into another container mixed with wooden furniture for export, previously purchased by Makhlouf and one of his businesses.

They had simply left the dhow tied to the quayside with a local stevedore employed on board to look after it until they returned. They had no intention of returning. His men had flown back as seafarers going on leave to the West Bank where they came from, with the exception of Sia, his daughter and two of his men, who had flown to Rome.

He had considered taking the discharged dhow back out to sea and sinking it. But that would delay his men and possibly attract more attention in a busy shipping lane than simply abandoning it. He regretfully had to have Captain Al Shaffer and his crew executed, weighted with spare anchor chain and thrown overboard. It had not gone well, one man screaming had jumped over the side and had to be dispatched in the water by a burst from Miriam's AK47. They then had to recover him in the dark to weight his body, all the while the fuel was running down. They were almost running on air by the time they made port. Al Shaffer went to his death on his knees praying to God and pleading for his life and that of his crew. Saeed had assured him of his place in heaven and shot the dhow Captain in the back of his head with his Browning. Some of the salty blood stung his eyes and made him look as if he had shed tears of compassion for his business partner. He wiped his face with his head dress while his men wrapped chain around the body before throwing it overboard without ceremony.

Saeed had been driven through the night and was now two thirds of the way to Khartoum, they came upon the Nile to the west. The road roughly followed its east bank as he headed south-west to his destination. The river gave life, he had driven through desert and as he neared the Nile he could see the landscape turn greener where centuries of agricultural irrigation and natural flood had fertilised the area both sides of the river. Allah himself had given this artery of life to the population, a highway as well as bringer of sustenance. He could see boats going both ways as the sun rose over the horizon behind the car. It was a beautiful sight, he even commented on it to his driver. Towns now started to spring up as the population had grown, despite the problems that has plagued Sudan throughout its history. They stopped by a café near the river and ate some flatbread and rice mixed with goat meat. Saeed paid for the meal which they washed down with sweet chai tea. The driver took the opportunity to ask Saeed his business in Khartoum. The Palestinian politely declined to discuss anything alluding to some Sudanese oil deal he was working on with SUDAPEC, the state petroleum company based in Khartoum. He dropped into the roadside mosque near the cafe for his early morning Al Fajr prayer. He took pleasure in the interludes that he had in the much more serious and hectic business of winning a Holy War.

They continued on the road now, it became busier as the country woke up and started going about their business. As the sun rose higher and warmed the car, he regretted not getting a vehicle that was more modern. The air conditioning was non-existent despite the driver assuring him it worked perfectly when the left Port Sudan.

By the time he passed through the suburbs of Khartoum the sun was high in the sky and the car was stifling despite the breeze coming through the open windows. The driver seemed completely oblivious to the discomfort and drove along humming to himself through his brown discoloured teeth. They crossed the long truss bridge over the White Nile to Omdurman on the West Bank. Saeed directed the driver to its most opulent area. Hassan Makhlouf had a large walled villa with well-tended garden, swimming pool and a large majlis room which he used to hold his council on business as well as with Saeed and the Mubarizun. He had a sophisticated satellite communication system installed which he only ever used for legitimate business. Any Mubarizun meetings were conducted in person.

Makhlouf met Saeed at the door of the majlis building and after the customary Arabic greetings told him he could have sent his Mercedes to pick him up in Port Sudan. Saeed made a sarcastic remark about security being more important than luxury and went into the building to meet the others.

The Mubarizun Council consisted of seven men, five of whom were present at the meeting. It simply wasn't possible to get everyone there at the same time. Partly due to the difficulty in lining up schedules to avoid suspicion and partly for security reasons. If the secretive organisation was ever breached one drone strike could kill the whole council. Everything was done man to man on the council, there were rarely any couriers, often the weak point for jihadist leaders. Bin Laden and Al Baghdadi were two good examples, both compromised when communicating with couriers. The Mubarizun wanted as few points of communication as possible that could weaken the system. The seven men directed their own contacts and cells and cross communication was always between the council members themselves. There was no elected chairman or leader, no figure with his name brandished for the world to see. The Mubarizun dipped in and out of other terrorist organisations and used them when required to spread propaganda or carry out attacks as well as manipulated state security where it could. It had fewer than fifty jihadists who worked directly for the council members themselves. These men and women were highly trained, well paid and completely dedicated to the cause. They were also rarely used unless for major operations where the Mubarizun needed direct and exclusive control or when they could co-operate with banned organisations that were better known to security services.

The Mubarizun was a ghost organisation, the name has been heard of in the past by the agencies of the West but doubt existed whether it was even real. It hadn't conformed to the usual terrorist mode or doctrine used by ISIS, Al Qaeda or other jihadist organisations. It did not seek others out on social media or boast of its exploits. It had no "ego" so few, if any, believe that such a council existed. That was its strength for now.

Three other members of the council in addition to Saeed and Makhlouf were already there. Two were dressed in expensive suits, open necked shirts being the only concession to the hot weather. The third was dressed in Sudanese kandora and white cotton wrap around head. Dress that was common in the area. They spent a short while greeting each other before sitting down to Arabic coffee and dates. Makhlouf asked his servant to leave before closing the curtains and shutting the door to the majlis room so the meeting could begin.

*

KSA RoRo was a subsidiary of the national shipping company of Saudi Arabia. Its ships were painted in a dark green of the Saudi flag with a white superstructure and grey decks. While the Company had a vast array of vessels from tankers to livestock carriers, the roll on roll off ferry subsidiary operated a fleet of eighteen freight ferries on regular shuttles throughout the Arabian Gulf, Red Sea and Mediterranean. The Red Sea to Mediterranean route was a relatively new one for the Company and had been set up to break into the relatively lucrative market enjoyed by Italian RoRo vessels. The ships were configured to carry freight trailers and trucks on two internal decks and unitised container cargo on the external deck. It was on to one of these ships, the m.v. Shamal that the unaccompanied trailer unit was loaded by a tugmaster tractor unit. It was lashed to the deck securely and customs manifest checked which stated that it was the transported personal furniture and goods of an Italian oil executive re-patriating to Tuscany.

The ship sailed from Port Sudan, taking thirty six hours to reach the Port Suez anchorage where it waited for the assembly of a north bound convoy and its canal pilots to convene. It then sailed through the Suez Canal and Bitter Lakes, past the south bound convoy to Port Said where it exited the canal. It adjusted its helm north-west toward the Italian port of Brindisi. The Shamal reached its destination in less than three days from the canal despite some unseasonably inclement summer weather.

When the vessel's Captain requested a pilot and permission to enter Brindisi port's navigable waters, the Port Control Officer took his cellphone and texted the twin brothers who worked for one of De Bastiani's Capos, Stefano and Luigi. The text simply read "arrivato".

The two men who were "soldiers" in the Sacra Corona Unita were not identical twins though they looked similar, both dark haired men, who like their much older boss obviously worked out in the gym. But unlike him they were smaller, no taller than 1.7 metres, Luigi had tattoos adorning almost all of his body, Stefano less so. Stefano was identifiable by a badly misshapen nose and half of his left ear was missing above a sizeable scar on the side of his head and neck. He made no attempt to cover it by having cropped hair. Like many of the men on the ground in the organisation they were multi-functional. Both had heavy good vehicle licences. They were enforcers, using various weapons from coshes to fully automatic weapons. They were very comfortable using software on computers and cell phones while also being able to use remote devices to steal cars when required. They even had "company" credit cards to claim legitimate expenses for fuel or meals and hotels while travelling. The ability to drive almost any vehicle on the road was key. The Sacra Corona Unita used its own drivers for critical cargos of high value and smuggled in normal third party containers and semi-trailers for the smaller, lower value projects. With the advent of large narcotic shipments of enormous value or human trafficking where the trailer may need opened more frequently it was of paramount importance that the drivers knew what was in the back. There had been instances of tractor units breaking down or refrigerated units being plugged in by mistake, damaging a large narcotics shipment or freezing "illegals" to death.

Stefano would take the large Scania R Series tractor unit down to the port to await its discharge to the pickup area outside the vessel handling area. It had large twin bunks in the back for intercontinental travel so that two drivers could get their trailer delivered to its destination non-stop. Both men actually owned a legitimate haulage Company with ten tractor units and eighteen drivers. This was on paper. The money behind it came from their Captain who passed the majority of the profits up to De Bastiani. Stefano would follow in the unmarked Fiat Tipo station wagon owned by the firm, it would only be occupied by Stefano who would stay at arm's length from the clients' in the truck with Luigi. The plan was they would not know he was following the truck at a distance. Another car could be delivered halfway through the journey to Stefano in case his was spotted. Unlikely, as only Luigi could see in his mirrors and the car would be one or two kilometres behind the Scania and trailer.

The trailing car also allowed Luigi and his brother to take along a pair of the very latest Beretta PMX 9mm sub machine guns and spare ammunition. They were only 400mm long with a folded stock, weighed little more than three kilogrammes loaded and could operate fully or semi-automatic if required. The weapon had just been issued to the elite units within the Carabinieri, a few had found their way to the De Bastiani's men and were prized among the rank and file. Like any status symbol, it showed you were favoured amongst your peers in the unique and violent society of the Sacra Corona Unita. Both men also carried their Beretta APX handguns and were rarely without them. They were not going to take risks with this cargo, they had been summoned in person to see the Boss which rarely happened. They were told this had to go without a hitch and any problems immediately reported back to headquarters. They were told "not to fail", the brothers were under no illusion as to what this meant.

The information on the ship's arrival also worked its way up to Gianni De Bastiani. He was informed "arrivato" verbally by a young "runner" for the organisation who didn't even know what the word signified, while he was entering the doors to his gym in the basement of his office block. He nodded and walked past the boy at the reception. His mind went over the arrangement as he started his habitual workout by warming up on the step machine. He still hadn't heard from the Palestinian, the second twenty five per cent payment wasn't in his bank account and the two Pakistani British men had not shown face to pick up the cargo. De Bastiani had instructed his men to have a look in the back of the container before calling the two men to tell them that it was ready for shipment. The mafia boss had held back pushing for the payment because he wanted to examine the cargo first. He would do that in one of his warehouses before calling the Palestinian for the next payment. He didn't want his client knowing he's breached the cargo. His men were adept at unsealing container units so they could steal cargo and re-sealing them with a perfect copy of the official tag. This knowledge would allow him to make informed decisions on how to proceed. If no more cash were forthcoming he would simply keep the deposit and sell the cargo. Perhaps his client had no access to the further five million euros he was owed.

De Bastiani's men had been instructed accordingly, he was wary of which organisation he was dealing with but they had no fear of the two fools who had turned up to accompany the cargo. They would simply shoot them both and throw them into the sea to float around with all the illegals that had drowned out there while trying to cross from North Africa. He could claim that he had no knowledge of their whereabouts and if the Palestinian didn't pay he was legitimately expected to recover his losses. The Sacra Corona would keep the trailer for two weeks as a gesture of goodwill before that happened.

The big man could feel the sweat starting to break out from his body as he moved to the rowing machine, the next part of his workout. Gianni de Bastiani tried to push business from his mind now so that he could concentrate on his workout. One way or other he would make ten million more euros and would figure out how to invest it. As the flywheel wound up and started to whir on the rowing machine his mind drifted to how he could spend ten million euros. A much more pleasant occupation for the mind, he felt.

Chapter 29

Billy Franklin got home from his meeting on the USS John McCain, having flown directly from the ship to the US base in Qatar and boarded an unmarked jet used by his intelligence agency to Norfolk International Airport. He lived in Langley, Fairfax County, the home of the Central Intelligence Agency and was a native Virginian. His family could trace back its history in Virginia for two hundred years. Langley was named by Thomas Lee the Governor of Virginia in 1749 who, in turn, had named the land after his estate in Shropshire, England. Like Lee, Franklin could trace his English heritage almost to that time. He felt Virginia and the United States was part of his blood and its defence would be his life's work. He was a thin man of medium height and had a pock marked face from teenage acne which had aged over the following twenty years to give his complexion a rugged appearance. He had lost his hair early in adulthood and shaved the remaining strip on the back of his head regularly. One feature that stood out were striking light blue eyes, once seen, rarely forgotten, not a great attribute for a spy. He often wore tinted glasses with no prescription lenses or even coloured contact lenses should he desire to mask his appearance.

The spy had operated in the Middle East for most of his career. He had been involved as a junior operative in the first Iraq war, searching for the elusive weapons of mass destruction in the following invasion and had progressed to dealing with the evolution of Al Qaeda and ISIS. He had established many relationships around the Arabian Gulf and North Africa during the so called "Arab Spring". He had weathered the spring cleaning of the CIA after the twin towers attack because of his expertise. It had helped that Afghanistan wasn't in his portfolio of countries and he wasn't involved like the old guard with Bin Laden after the Russian invasion of the country.

Billy Franklin was happily married with two children at elementary school, his wife was used to his travelling and their relationship was one of running their lives according to his work schedule. His ambition was to be the head of his section and continue to specialise in the same region. Finding leads from other friendly agencies was much easier and less hazardous that building your own internally. The United States' position in the world and its ability to distribute huge amounts of aid was a comprehensive benefit to the CIA. Much of the information they had was offered my friendly countries, some trusted and others not. The other advantage they had was electronic information gathering and its interpretation. The National Security Agency had unrivalled amounts of funding to have world leading capability in monitoring worldwide traffic and chatter.

Franklin had been tasked to look into the sinking of the African Tide and also to evaluate what the British interest was in the affair. Sharing of information between the US and UK intelligence agencies had to be done via official channels so that control of information flow and its accuracy could be undertaken by both countries. Operational cells like Darcy's were not authorised to handover any information unless it came from the top. The United States had lost faith many years ago with the Kim Philby affair when he sold secrets to the Russians while being a senior operative for MI6. Reciprocally, UK intelligence services felt they had been undermined when Aldrich Ames, the CIA traitor had betrayed their top level KGB spy, Colonel Gordievsky. Despite the fact the CIA were never told of his identity, they had worked it out by spying on the British and failed to keep it secret on a need to know basis. More recently protocols had been put into place to share information, particularly after the twin towers atrocity and the growth of fundamentalist terrorism in the Middle East.
He had asked Darcy privately what was behind his questioning, the MI5 man had divulged little, saying it was part of a MI5 "internal security evaluation" which in reality had meant nothing to Franklin. He could ask officially for more information on the matter but needed a good reason to open up the channel of communication on the subject of the meeting. Ultimately if it was considered serious enough, it would have to go through the office of the US State Department and UK Home Office for clearance. Being a foreign CIA operative he had contacts within MI6 but little relationship with MI5 as he had never operated in the United Kingdom. He would talk to a couple of his old contacts in the Secret Intelligence Service. Perhaps a visit to Vauxhall Cross was worthwhile once he briefed his head of Middle East section on his visit to the USS John McCain.

Franklin would also get in touch with the NSA to intercept and monitor any communications traffic related to the sinking of the African Tide or other piracy in the region. They had already told him that satellite surveillance during the sinking was poor due to heavy cloud. Any drones despatched to the area were too late to pick up anything that the helicopter had not. They had actually picked up Kravits's rescue the next day when the cloud had cleared. The film had verified the Ukrainians story. There was a lot more satellite data to examine both before and after the suspected attack. He knew they should eventually find footage of the craft involved but there were so many ships and small boats in the region, it would take time to evaluate and the suspects would be long gone. He would get a summary on the African Tide sinking and what the NSA had thought had happened in a few days. They could combine this with the information that the CIA had from the USS John McCain. Meantime he could pursue getting more from the British.

Chapter 30

The train to Sofia had left Istanbul before nightfall. It had no first class but had bunks in compartments that folded down in three tiers. Normally the journey would take fourteen hours, but on the occasion of Khorasani's journey it had taken eighteen. There had been no buffet car on the train, only a supply of drinking water and some dates and nuts which could be purchased. By the time he had reached Sofia airport he was very hungry, tired and had got little sleep. The first priority on alighting the train was to get a good meal inside him for the rest of the journey. The long and winding trip to Zurich was necessary to cover his tracks. He had a number of passports while operating for VAJA and his intention was to use three different identities and modes of transport to make his journey difficult to trace. The more variety and modes of transport injected into in a journey meant that anyone attempting to follow it had more difficulty in tracking him. Khorasani had also purchased clothing in Istanbul more suited to a middle aged American tourist than someone from Iran. He wore cream chinos and Nike training shoes with a light blue polo shirt and a light brown/dark blue reversible blouson jacket. He carried two hats, a straw panama, and a dark baseball cap with no marks or logos clearly visible on it. He had only one suitcase and carried a camera bag over his shoulder, devoid of a camera, which he carried all his documents in.

His telephone had been switched off for the entire length of his journey to Sofia. He purchased a new SIM card in Sofia International airport. He then boarded a direct flight to Paris Beauvais Airport. It had been constructed for low cost European carriers and much less likely to be under observation by VAJA than Charles De Gaulle. At each stage of the journey he changed his chinos to a different colour, reversed his jacket and donned an alternate hat. He wore tinted glasses and was cultivating stubble into an eventual beard. Khorasani had even neglected to smoke when he thought there was a chance of being seen in video, few middle aged American tourists did so. He knew that most of Iran's enemies knew what he looked like. It was also possible they were on the lookout for him, particularly in light of Zarrins' telephone call while he was at the airport outside Tehran.

Khorasani could hardly believe he got out of Iran without being apprehended. As a senior and relatively trusted member of the little known VAJA within the Ministry of Intelligence he had a passport that allowed him to exit the country any time he wanted, unlike a normal Iranian citizen. He always maintained a visa for entry into nearby friendly countries such as Turkey and Syria and of course for the European Union. He thought that Ghaani or the head of VAJA would have immediately put an alert on his passport at all areas where he could exit Tehran. They had obviously been slow to react as he had been with the organisation for so long and been entrusted with a historical project.

Almost every official person he saw from the check in desk to the Turkish Airways lounge had concerned him. He had considered avoiding the lounge in case registration there raised an alarm bell but it kept him away from the cameras. The walk to board the aircraft seemed to take an age, while on board he was soaked in sweat once again. Even as he taxied he awaited the pilot's tannoy message saying they were going back to the stand. As the aircraft took off he felt a little more relieved. It took just under an hour, he estimated, to leave Iranian air space. It wasn't beyond them to launch an interceptor to make the aircraft return to Imam Khomeini airport. Khorasani watched the "flight path" screen on the back of the seat in front of him as the icon denoting the aircraft he was on moved millimetre by millimetre toward the Turkish border. He finally heaved a sigh of relief when it had. A few minutes later he felt almost elated and ordered a large two finger scotch whisky from the stewardess to celebrate his escape. He had a lot to do to avoid detection but the immediate threat was over.

His thoughts turned to Zarrin. What the hell was that all about? Had she been spying on him? Was she Mossad or CIA? It seemed to come out of the blue, he had not suspected a thing but it did throw another angle at the situation he was in. He was not only concerned about his own intelligence service being paranoid about him absconding. He also had the treacherous Palestinian Fakhoury who obviously had a very sophisticated network behind him and now his mistress! Khorasani had noticed a change in her, should have been more suspicious but had so much in his mind with the project. None of it mattered now, unless he could sell the information to a Western agency, in which case speed was of the essence before the information became old. He would also have to break cover to do so. It may be better to lie low.

As the veteran Iranian spy walked out of Beauvais airport in France and gratefully lit a cigarette which he shielded from the breeze with his panama hat, he looked for the car hire building for his final leg to Zurich. Having identified it he walked out on to the pavement thronging with holidaymakers who were getting out of buses and cars on their way to cheap holidays in the sun. He could easily have been a Costa del Sol retiree popping home to see his grandchildren or a tourist arriving on a low cost airline flight to experience the City of Light.

*

'Robert, how are you?'

'I am well, thank god'
'We know the client has gone on holiday now. We are endeavouring to find out where he has gone to so we can get in touch,' David led. 'We will need your contact to get in touch with him as its better for the business relationship we have.'

'He will not respond, his telephone is switched off.'

'Can you and the contact leave the country Robert?'

'I'm not sure, a visa will be required, it will take time.' Cohen wasn't sure if a visa could be granted for either of them and if it was, how long it would take to get them. In the past it had taken two weeks. He wasn't even sure of the rationale of them both going, it was difficult to discuss in detail on a satellite telephone in case it was being monitored. But the instruction from his handler was clear. 'I will try to get to where you require us to be.' He could encourage Zarrin to leave permanently for a better life, Cohen needed to return as he didn't want retribution to be taken against his family. The Mossad would also be keen on this. As a non-Jew with only distant relatives left alive it would not be such a problem for Zarrin. Cohen would hint to Zarrin that he too was absconding.

'OK, confirm in due course and we will rendezvous in Rome.' The previously agreed meeting point was Paris but the code word was "Rome" to throw any eavesdroppers off the trail.

Cohen hung up, he walked back to his car from the Lebanese restaurant he was in and drove back to his temporary office at his building site. He called Zarrin from his Iranian cellphone, 'Hello my love, how would you like a trip to Europe with me?'

There was silence on the line. Finally, Zarrin took it in, 'that sounds great, when do we go?'

'As soon as we can get visas, I will meet you at the cafe tomorrow and we can discuss?'

'Yes of course.'

Once again he hung the phone up, he remembered his training in Israel "keep it short and to the point". After discussing in the morning he would try and process as quickly as possible. His visa, as a businessman would be no problem, Zarrins' as a government employee would be more difficult. As they were unmarried in a strict Islamic country, their applications could not be linked, it may even be better to have different destinations.

"David" stood up from the desk in the soundproofed room in Tel Aviv, he had requested they leave without clearing it with his boss. He would have to clear it with the head of the Mossad, Director Yossi Avrahami. Meantime it did no harm to start the visa process for his team.

He lifted up the thick file on Khorasani. They knew his previous aliases, he had flown to Istanbul, a Mossad operative had tracked him shopping but had lost him in the famous Spice Bazaar. They were now trying to track his several names at the airport, main railway stations and bus depots. Not an easy task. They would find him, the question was when. His plan for Cohen and Rahmani was a flexible one. All he knew is they would be useful in finding Khorasani or luring him to a destination where his professionals could take over.

David was not his real name of course but for the purposes of the man he was handling it would suffice. Even his superiors in the Mossad who knew of the spies he was running had nicknamed him by that name. It would have been more secure to have multiple names but there was a danger of mixing the pseudonyms up when speaking to his operatives. The bond between handler and operator was critical, there had to be a trust between the two. He was the only support that Cohen could rely on. David had never met "the boy" as he called Cohen off line but he admired his courage. The boy was isolated in a country with a regime that would not hesitate to publically hang him in a square in the centre of Tehran and leave him there for the cameras to see. He had been in tight situations himself but never isolated in such a hostile country for such a very long time.

David felt that the boy should have been out of Iran a long time ago but neither Cohen or David's superior officers wanted it to happen. Until such time as the operative wanted out nothing would be done. He felt this was an ideal opportunity to meet the spy he had worked with for so many years. David was well past retirement age, he was getting frail, his injuries were a handicap now. The veteran spy wanted to spend more time with his family. He had gradually given up his operatives as projects had come to an end but couldn't leave the last of his men in situ and transfer to another handler. Not without having met Cohen. He would speak to the Director and ask if he could introduce another handler in person before finally retiring.

The old man was a legend in the Mossad. He was their greatest ever handler and polyglot, he could talk eight languages, most fluently. He could easily pass for a native speaker of English, Arabic or German as well as Hebrew. He had ran operatives in most European countries, the United States, Argentina, Brazil as well as many of the countries around the Arabian Gulf, Syria and of course Iran. He had experience of working double agents and handled spys of both sexes and of many cultural backgrounds. David had contacts in the majority of the large intelligence organisations around the world and commanded a great deal of respect from them.

He still had a boss though. He picked up his desk phone once again and pressed the button for his assistants' desk, 'get me Avrahami,' he said wearily.

Chapter 31

Luigi climbed up into the big unmarked Scania, he would drive and the clients' men could ride in the cab. The R series had a sizeable living quarters customised in the back with two bunks, a sink and a small cooker and microwave. He seriously hoped that the two men had washed since he met them last because they had smelled rather badly, he would insist that they travelled in a more hygenic condition. Luigi's command of English was not good but it was a lot better than Stefano's. He had taken the trouble to tape his Beretta holster under his driving seat with Gaffer tape for quick access and concealment while driving. It was empty for now but he'd get a handgun from his brother after leaving the port. He also kept a large shifting spanner with a rubber handle down the side of the drivers door, it would pass for part of a drivers toolkit but was an excellent cosh should he need it. Stefano would follow in the Fiat with the Beretta PMX's should he be required.

Luigi started the engine and drove the tractor unit through the morning traffic to the unaccompanied trailer holding area. There was a green, white and orange forty foot container with "Tuscan Traslochi" written on the side with a picture of the "Looney Tunes" cartoon roadrunner pulling the word banner along with great haste. Not the most discrete trailer but was very clear what it was intended for. He would have to get the truck painters in before they left.

Luigi presented his paperwork to the port checking supervisor who allowed him in the pick up the trailer. He hitched up the unit and connected his airlines, before setting off for the warehouse. He then called Stefano to ensure he was on his way to meet him.

Mumtaz and Abdul Ansari had spent two days relaxing in the Best Western Hotel in Brindisi. They had cleaned up, laundered their clothes and prepared their weapons for the trip north with the Italians. Mumtaz had explained to Abdul that there may be an altercation when picking up the cargo as he was unsure if Fakhoury had paid the agreed instalment. He also told him the Italians would not let them take the truck north unaccompanied. Both men donned their tracksuits and tucked their Tokarev handguns in the pockets of their jackets before setting off in a taxi for the warehouse with their rucksacks for the trip. As the taxi drew up to the security fence and through the gate they could see the large truck sitting inside the huge building. Both men walked cautiously through the massive warehouse doors. They could see no one around so Mumtaz Ansari tried the door to the Scania cab, it was locked.

'Hey, you try to steal my truck?' a voice exclaimed from an office door recessed in the side of the warehouse.

Both Ansari brothers turned from the drivers door on the side of the Scania to see a small but heavily built tattooed man strolling toward them from the side of the building. He was grinning but it was clear he was going to take control of the relationship. Mumtaz Ansari felt it was time for him to exert his authority, he had taken enough shit from these infidels, he would tell them how this was going to proceed. 'This is our cargo, we have paid for you to give us it - now give me the fucking keys.' He spoke with a thick Birmingham accent but slowly enough that Luigi understood what he meant. Ansari turned full on, legs apart to face Luigi, his brother did the same.

Luigi stopped five metres from the men, both hands hanging by his side. He could see the weight in both men's tracksuit pockets, they were clearly armed. He had his instructions from De Bastiani, don't let that truck go anywhere until they are paid and once paid you drive it out of Italy, 'the cargo, it don't go any place until I say,' his Italian accent made it sound almost conversational. Mumtaz Ansari lifted his hand toward his tracksuit jacket pocket. Suddenly and without a sound Stefano appeared from around the passenger side of the Scania and in a wide arc struck Mumtaz Ansari on the side of the head with an aluminium baseball bat. It made contact with a hollow thud. The elder Ansari's knees crumpled from under him and he fell completely unconscious to the warehouse floor. At the same moment Abdul put his hand in his pocket, Stefano swung a sawn off shotgun, which was held over his shoulder by a strap, around in front off him and jabbed it hard into the younger Ansari's right eye. Abdul Ansari's hand fell from his pocket. Luigi stepped forward and disarmed the young jihadist, patting him down for further weapons as well as his prone and unconscious brother.

'I think you have fucking killed him,' Luigi said to Stefano in Italian angrily, 'we weren't supposed to kill them.'

Stefano looked down at the prone figure, blood now seeping from his head, 'he's still alive, lets get them both in the office in case anyone comes in.' Abdul's eyes were wide with a combination of fear and rage, he was unaware of what the two Italian criminals were saying to each other. He eyed the now dented baseball bat with trepidation, his hands were shaking. The two Sacra Coruna men instructed Abdul to drag his brother into the warehouse workshop. They then handcuffed both men to a steel workshop bench and locked the door. They Italian brothers would have to tell their superiors what had happened. They had been told to assert their authority and lay down the law, both men hadn't allowed for two of the Ansari brothers being armed, they had no choice. Stefano and Luigi's instructions were to keep in touch with De Bastiani directly if a problem occurred. The brothers decided to toss a coin to see who would be the one to make the call. Stefano lost, justifiably Luigi thought.

First, Stefano would call Claudio Sarronni, their Capo. He would be furious but had to stand by his men or recommend their "removal" if the stakes were high enough in the Sacra Corona Unita. In this case they were not. When they phoned De Bastiani he was going to go crazy but at least their Capo would be listened to when the Boss contacted him for an explanation.

De Bastiani was just finishing his gym constitutional when Stefano called him. His leader actually took the news quite well in the circumstances Stefano thought. Apart from the expected "I told you not to fuck this up" and "I told you to keep that fucking monkey under control, not kill him" he was relatively calm. De Bastiani told him this would affect his Capo, Claudio's record and standing in the business and then calmed down a little. Stefano knew by this point continued protest on what little choice they had was futile, it was time to shut up. The Boss told him to get the organization's tame doctor to go to the warehouse to tend to the elder Ansari brother, feed them but keep them locked up until further notice.

De Bastiani reflected on the news as he showered himself. He wasn't concerned, in fact was rather pleased that the conflict had happened so early in the process. It would ensure he had the Palestinian's attention and showed him that he wasn't to be fucked around with. He would also have a free hand in getting his men to look in the back of that trailer. His cellphone started ringing where he'd left it on the bench in the gym changing room. That would be Claudio making his excuses on behalf of his men about the operation. He would call him back once out the shower and tell him to have the trailer searched.

Stefano was annoyed with his brother, Luigi had blamed him for getting in the shit with De Bastiani. Luigi wasn't upset with his twin because he hit the man too hard but because Stefano had rejected Luigi's plan of meeting the men off site to defuse any fight away from the wagon. They would have been more malleable if their cargo wasn't staring them in the face. It would not have been so easy to try to force the Italians' hand, he had said. Stefano felt he had resolved the situation by knocking the bastard's head with his bat, not to mention stopping them both from being shot. Now Stefano had taken the call from Claudio who had called him every bad word under the sun and told him to go and find out what was in the truck. That would mean moving all the cargo covering whatever contraband they had and it was a big trailer. Luigi had gone to get the doctor to tend to the now conscious Ansari as well as get them food and water.

Reluctantly Stefano decided to make a start. He left the office, sticking his Beretta handgun in his waistband and unlocked the workshop. Mumtaz Ansari was sitting up on the workbench, his back against the far wall. Abdul had a bucket of water and was wiping the matted blood from his brothers' face and neck with a paper towel. He had obviously applied a bandage to Mumtazs' head from the workshop first aid kit.

There was a lot of blood and the wounded man was looking very pale and listless. Stefano looked at Abdul, 'a doctor come to look at him, you don't try any stupid fighting with us, OK?'

Abdul stared back at his captive, 'OK, but he needs to come quick, my brother has lost too much blood.'

'He stupid man, you come here from England and fuck with Sacra Corona, you crazy, next time you maybe dead!' Stefano wagged his finger at Abdul Ansari, almost in amused admonishment, as he backed out of the room and secured the door. The younger Ansari faced the closed door with a look of sheer hatred.

Stefano called his brother and made sure the doctor was on his way before mounting a step ladder and carefully removing the seal from the Tuscan Traslochi container. He then undid the rear door lever and opened one side of the container up. It was loaded with furniture right up to the back door so he started up the Scania and reversed it onto an empty loading bay so he could have access at container level without using the ladder. Stefano then started to unceremoniously throw the furniture on to the empty loading bay ledge from the back of the trailer. After removing a considerable amount of furniture he found a narrow passage had been left on the right hand side of the container where he could crab sideways up to the front of the unit, taking a crowbar with him. He was sweating profusely now and stripped off his hoodie sweatshirt which he was wearing over the top of his t-shirt. Eventually he could see some boxes at the front of the container, some were cardboard marked with the name of the removal company and some were wooden, labelled "FOTMA". There was nothing obvious, he would have to start taking a random look. He looked in a couple of the removals boxes and found cutlery, some wine bottles and ornaments, all packed with bubble wrap and cardboard. There was nothing he could see that may contain a large amount of drugs. He then went back down the container and cut open a large sofa and mattress with the switchblade he carried, nothing. He then moved on to the FOTMA crates. There were six in total, two were longer and appeared to have a lot more volume than the others. He levered open the first one. It was full of bags of gold brown powder with no attempt at concealment within the box. He dug through the first few bags and picked one that was deeper inside, he pushed the blade of his knife into it and lifted it to his mouth. Stefano licked the switchblade, it was heroin, and there was a lot of it. Underneath the powder he could see a large round steel cylindrical beam connected to a box with electronic wires hanging out of it. It looked like the beam was connected to a large spherical gearbox or big end of a truck or tractor from what he could see. He replaced the packages which were packed around the machinery spares.

It seemed to confirm Stefano's feelings about this smuggling operation, these were not sophisticated people. There was no attempt to hide the contraband, should customs have done even a rudimentary search, they would have found the narcotics. He guessed that's why they needed to spend a lot of money with the Sacra Corona to get it to their destination. He wasn't sure how much but it must be a very large figure for the Boss to allow transit through his port and territory. It was unprecedented in his experience. He closed up the crate and the boxes he had been inspecting and left the container, shut the rear doors and re-installed the customs seal with the dexterity of years of practice. He would inform Claudio of what he had found, but first he would phone De Bastiani directly to inform him of what he had discovered. It would go some way to redeeming himself after the incident with Mumtaz Ansari. He took the Beretta from his waistband and placed it under the driver's seat in the Scania cab for his brother to use later on. There was another in the car.

Abdul Ansari had tried to keep his brother awake but he had fallen into a very deep slumber, his breathing was shallow and Abdul thought he was dying. He had tried banging on the steel workshop door to no avail. Finally he decided to give in to the will of God and sat back down, they will come when they are ready. He wrapped some more bandage tightly round Mumtazs' head hoping to finally stem any more bleeding.

Abdul had grown up with his brother in Aston, near Birmingham. Mumtaz was four years older than him. His parents were strict practicing Muslims, having come across from Peshawar when Abdul was only three years old. His brother had been his protector from the white English bullies on his street and at his school. He had helped both him and sometimes his parents with their English language and had taught Abdul to play cricket and football. When Mumtaz reached his mid-teens he had started to drink alcohol and hang around the park about a mile from his house. Around that time there was a prominent gang culture in the town and his brother had been swept up in it. He saw the trouble it had brought at home and Mumtaz was beaten on several occasions by his father. By the time his brother was eighteen he was on hard drugs, he smoked crack cocaine and had taken heroin. Eventually the tables had turned and it was Mumtazs' turn to beat his father which resulted in him being evicted from the family home. Abdul's father told him the West and its undercurrent of sin had influenced his brother and that Abdul must not take the same path. He had listened to his father.

When Mumtaz was living in a squat with a white girl and some other junkies, Abdul had taken him food and constantly talked to him about giving up his ways and finding God again. He had taken him to hospital when he'd overdosed and got him out of the local police station when he'd been caught stealing a car.

While in Strangeways prison for a housebreaking offence Mumtaz had met some jihadists on remand. Abdul had taken the train to Manchester every week to visit and noted the change in Mumtaz. He changed from a listless lazy youth who had met family advice and discipline with indifference to a zealot with fire in his eyes. Abdul was impressed by the doctrine he saw on the social media and by the rhetoric expounded by his brother. The population of the world would be one religion under one God, evil and its unbelievers or kaffirs would be eliminated and heaven would be everyone's destiny. Once his six month sentence was completed they both visited the local mosque in Aston together but the teaching there for them was too liberal. They had pilgrimaged to more radical mosques in Birmingham and London where the mullah's had fought the infidels in Afghanistan and in Iraq and had the scars to show for it.

It was at Finsbury mosque in London that they had met Cyrus Sia, he had told them his organisation was looking for some new recruits with no terrorist record for work abroad. He told them they would become jihadist household names like the men who had given their lives in vengeance against the "Great Satan" on September 2011.

Mumtaz, always overtly the leader of the two had immediately agreed to undertake anything that was required of them, he did not even consult Abdul about the decision. Abdul knew that Mumtaz was the impulsive one who stood out and always appeared to have Abdul two steps behind him as the lackey or underling there to do his bidding. Abdul knew that Mumtaz was weak in his mind and with his will, he could be fickle in his decisions and unsophisticated. Sia's approach could have been a sting operation for all they knew, such things had been undertaken in the US more than once. There was a word for his attitude in English, it was "boorish", he was rough, coarse, lacked intelligence. Abdul was not, he was a scholar in Islamic studies and had a first in Microelectronics from Birmingham University. He knew when they undertook this project he would have to step up at some time, that time was now. Even if Mumtaz could recover quickly from his injury he could no longer be the leader of the two. Abdul had told him not to confront these seasoned thugs on their turf, he obviously had learned little on the street and in prison. Despite what they had done to his brother and whatever the outcome of that awful blow to his head, Abdul vowed he would bide his time and retribution would come.

A sound at the door interrupted Abdul's train of thought. He could hear Luigi shouting at him to stand back from the door as a key rattled in the lock. He did as he was bid and the two Italian criminals walked in with an old man with a doctor's bag. Abdul stood to one side as the doctor knelt and examined his brother. Abdul explained Mumtazs' reactions to the blow but the doctor appeared to understand little English.

*

De Bastiani received Stefano's call with some satisfaction. At last he knew what these people were up to on his patch. He couldn't necessarily understand the economics behind it until he knew how much heroin was in the load but it didn't matter, this was a one off. If Fakhoury didn't turn up then the goods were his. He congratulated Stefano and told him he was glad he's appointed him to the job. Praise could work with his soldiers as well as threats. Next issue was to see if Mumtaz Ansari would survive and await Fakhoury's contact and cash transfer. As he stood up and contemplated going out to the warehouse to take a look for himself the Mafia boss's personal assistant walked through the door of his office. She excused the interruption, 'reception called up to say that two people, a man and a woman are here to see about your shipment from Sudan.'

'Put them through security and tell them to come up,' responded De Bastiani. He thought that he would get some news on the next move as he sat back down at his desk, perhaps it was Fakhoury. As he switched his computer monitor to the camera in his waiting room he saw that it was not.

Cyrus Sia and his daughter walked into the office, both greeted De Bastiani and were ushered to the meeting table and offered refreshments. The big Italian observed the two visitors as they sat down. The older man was of slim build and moved with an athletic assuredness, he had a sallow complexion and a receding hairline. He had a five o'clock dark shade to his jaw line despite it being early in the day. The other visitor was striking, though small she had a heart shaped face with beautiful fine features, olive skin tone and a slim shapely figure. Her auburn hair shone in the fluorescent light but the most striking feature she had were her eyes, they were such a shade of dark brown they were almost black. There was little to differentiate between the iris and pupil from a short distance. She carried herself with an upright and haughty composure, he couldn't help but stare at her for just a bit too long. She knew he was looking at her but met his attention with a well-practiced insouciance.

De Bastiani knew these two were a lot different, to what he felt, were an ignorant and impecunious pair that had already been presented as Fakhoury's representatives. His critical eye had noted they were both well dressed with expensive watches and her jewellery looked to be the very best quality, some of which he would have been happy to buy his wife. All of this came very quickly to the "Boss", it was how he survived.

Sia started the conversation in fluent English, 'firstly, Signore De Bastiani, I would like to thank you for seeing us without making an appointment, we like to keep digital communications to a minimum in our business. I am representing the organisation of Mr Omar Fakhoury. We are here to confirm our further twenty five per cent payment commitment is being processed as we speak and that we will also be escorting the shipment out of your area as agreed.'

De Bastiani smiled cordially and responded, 'welcome to Brindisi. I believe Mr Fakhoury told me you would be coming. I am glad you have confirmed the payment will be wired immediately.' He was indeed glad he was going to receive his money. His face suddenly became more serious, he continued, 'however we have had some unfortunate problems which I am sure you may have heard about. Firstly the second payment instalment is very late, it was supposed to have come in a week ago, prior to the shipment arriving in the port. Secondly, your men were very foolish, they tried to strong arm us and take the cargo without the stage payment being made and without our men being the primary escort. They were armed and we had to take steps to restrain one of them before my men were shot. This is not acceptable behaviour and cannot happen again or we will impound the shipment. My men have now been informed to react to such behaviour with lethal force.'

Sia's amiable expression as he responded did not alter though the woman's eyes glazed over with anger, 'the payment was simply an administrative oversight on the part of our bank. With regard to our men, we have had little contact with them. In fact nothing at all nothing over the past three days, perhaps you can help us there.'

'We have them under lock and key because of their behaviour. One has a head wound, he was lucky we didn't shoot him as the idiot was about to pull a gun on my men. They had to defend themselves. We have a doctor attending him now. I believe his name is Mumtaz, the other one, I forget his name, is unharmed.'

Sia glanced at his daughter and said, 'we need to see them and confirm we can move ahead with the cargo arrangements. We also need to inspect the container.'

'Well our arrangement has changed Mr Sia. You have delayed the payment by one week already. This is when you need your cargo moving, I am not confident you will pay us on departure at the Italian border. We will not move the trailer until full payment of the ten million euros is met. I made it very clear to Fakhoury that he needed to comply strictly with our requirements. Your organisation has failed on two counts, the escort you supplied and the money, we have lost confidence in our partnership. You will pay the remaining five million Euros now and you and your escort may accompany our men. You are very lucky I am not raising the price. Those two fools may accompany the cargo under our new arrangement, but unarmed. Those are my terms, take it or leave it.'

'Let me see my men and I will talk to Mr Fakhoury on the matter and respond directly.'

De Bastiani pressed the button on his phone to his personal assistant. 'Get me Claudio.'

Chapter 32

It had been more than three weeks since the sinking of the African Tide. Henry Darcy had summoned Finlay Lamont and Anna Siebert to a meeting in Millbank with the CIA agent they had met aboard the USS John McCain. Henry had cleared the communication through the official channels after the approach by the American. Both sides had given the meeting priority as they needed information from each other.

Billy Franklin needed the information that was obviously behind the MI5 and SIS investigation, he was further intrigued that his contacts in the SIS were reluctant to pass on too much and referred him to MI5. Apparently the instruction had come from the highest echelon of the UK government that Henry Darcy was the point of contact and any discussions had to be centred round him.

Henry, in turn, needed the wealth of information that could be extracted from US surveillance and interpreted by the NSA. The Americans were famously reluctant to give away the depth of their ability to track detailed movements across the globe. The ignorance of the degree of detail with which the United States' enemies could be monitored was part of the strengths of the NSA. It prevented sophisticated counter measures being undertaken by the foe in question. In particular Henry wanted to know what had happened to the dhow and its pirated booty after it had left the side of the African Tide. Otherwise the trail was lost.

The discussion was held in Henry's meeting office. The MI5 Officer outlined what they had been looking at, outlining in broad terms the killing of Dubois. He described the trail to drawings they had discovered in France, how it was linked to a drawing they found in Dubai and its link to the security services there. Henry knew that the "cousins" would have no hesitancy in taking the case over. It would be much quicker, the more detail that he provided to them early on. He left out much of the fine detail Franklin could follow up on without glossing over the main salient points. Franklin followed with some questions and timelines. Once he was satisfied, removed his laptop from his bag and asked if the room was "clean" from surveillance before connecting it to the large flat screen TV at the end of the conference table.

The first picture was an aerial shot of "hells' gates" or the area of sea between the end of the Arab peninsula in Yemen and Djibouti on the Horn of Africa, otherwise known in Arabic as Bab el Mandeb or "gate of tears". It was an area famously known over centuries as a hotbed of piracy, where any privateers could ambush a merchant vessel and disappear very quickly to nearby land on two different continents. More recently it was very well patrolled by naval vessels which had restricted most of these types of activities. It was also one of the most monitored parts of the world from the sky as well as a very busy sea lane for ships navigating the Suez Canal further north.

Billy Franklin pointed at the satellite picture. 'You will see here a satellite shot of Bab el Mandeb taken less than two days after the sinking of the African Tide, it shows shipping traffic in the straits. The NSA have taken it along with the information and footage they received from the USS John McCain. This is a picture they took of one nearby dhow it considered most suspicious from our last discussion.' Franklin flicked to the helicopter footage of a dhow with a large orange RIB on it, then back again to the overview of the straits, 'this is what we saw once we zeroed in.'

The picture moved from the large scale shot showing the shores of two continents to a direct overhead detailed view of a dhow without sails deployed and a canopy over the deck. The image of the RIB was even clearer than in the helicopter picture. It was obviously the same boat. Franklin flicked up a series of overview pictures and more detailed pictures of the dhow. 'We have tracked it here with other intermittent shots which showed it arrived at the loose cargo or dhow berth in Port Sudan. By this point we had launched drones to find out where it was. It remains in that dhow berth since it was tied up there. Our local operatives in Sudan tell us it hasn't moved, the crew appear to have abandoned it. One of our guys bribed the watchman who was on board and had a look around. He found blood on the starboard over-side bulwark and main deck and two AK47 rounds lodged between the deck planking and the base of the steering column.' Franklin flicked through some pictures the agent had taken on board the dhow.

He moved on, 'we have more pictures from the drone in the vicinity of the dhow. Here we see some shots of crates that appear to have been taken from the boat being loaded into a container.' The last pictures he flicked up on the screen were slightly obscured by haze from light cloud so were quite grainy. They clearly showed something being loaded into a container that appeared to be green and white from the angle the shot was taken from. The front of it was partially obscured and most of the shot was of the roof. No writing could be seen despite Franklin showing blown up pictures of the drone shots.

Henry stood up and tried to see more of the container by moving right up to the screen, 'I take it this is the best resolution you chaps could get of the container. If so did you manage to track it to anywhere?'

'We got it being lifted on to a trailer and moved to the ro-ro terminal the next day. Our guys on the ground got no more information on the trailer itself other than the night watchman saying the container had a bird painted on the side and some words in a foreign language. All we know is that subject to further surveillance of the ro-ro terminal it appears the trailer has gone. Our relationship with the Sudanese authorities is not the best as you know so everything has to be done clandestinely. We couldn't simply ask them for information on containers without going through extenuated and protracted procedures, for example. We have an office in Khartoum which has approached them but since the lifting of sanctions two years ago they have been less than helpful. We may or may not get something. The port authorities are corrupt and very suspicious of questions about their activities. We have, however, looked into which ro-ro container services could be used for the delivery of the cargo. We now know more about it since you briefed us. Direct ferry services are available to and from the following ports in the two days it took for the trailer to disappear. Jeddah, Aqaba, Brindisi and Sohar. It is not likely that they would take it to Port Sudan and then all the way back to where the crime was committed so we can discount Sohar in Oman. Aqaba could be a destination as it is in Jordan, right on the border with Israel. The African Tide was on its way to Bandar Abbas so very unlikely that the Iranians hijacked it before the container went to their own port. We believe the Iranians would be the only ones that would be behind sending it to Jeddah, any other organisations that may be anti-Saudi are small and fragmented or have bigger targets. Europe is a big target for jihadist terrorists so Brindisi is a very likely destination. As far as the people sitting round this tables' interests are concerned, we should be focusing on that destination.'

Henry sat down again, 'I agree, though we could inform the Israelis.' In exchange for information on the Fakhoury figure discussed with Colonel Sohail thought Henry, an ideal opportunity. 'If we can find out any more information from your chaps in Sudan, Billy that would be ideal. One question, is this ro-ro stuff transhipped, I mean could it go to one port and then be loaded to another destination?'

'Yes it could,' the American responded, 'and often does so we could lose it if we don't get more information on it. One more thing, there were other containers in the vicinity of the dhow that could have been loaded up with something but this one we have pictures of. We actually see the boxes being loaded with a forklift. More could have been loaded on another container that we didn't see in the cloud or in the dark.'

'I guess we can only follow the trail we can see,' said Finlay.

Henry stuck in one more point, 'our friends at Aldermaston have mentioned one thing to me. If there is a relatively unsophisticated nuclear device of any kind it will leave a radioactive residue behind all day long. Can your CIA guys in Khartoum get a Geiger counter or whatever it's called these days on that dhow?'

'Yes great idea Henry,' Billy Franklin said, and with a hint of irony, 'if we'd have known about this sooner it would have been done by now.'

The meeting was concluded with promises of further scheduled update calls in the near future so any developments, no matter how small, could be exchanged.

Once Franklin had left to catch a flight to Khartoum Henry summarised where they were and decide the next steps. Henry would call his contact in the Mossad and exchange information on the piracy of a threatening cargo which could be destined for Israel. He would also update his superiors and inform MI6 of developments. Anna would stay in London and run her AI software with new inputs to see if anything could be thrown up. This would help them with regards to the new destination of the possible device. Henry, while completely ignorant of anything involving a computer, suggested new inputs concerning Port Sudan and Brindisi should be plugged in somehow as it could bring up links. The other key inputs would be the information gleaned from Colonel al Qubaisi and Chief Officer Kravits.

Finally Henry turned to Finlay Lamont, 'now Finlay it is time to use your surveillance skills, you have been a little side-lined by our wicked ways in intelligence. There comes a point in any project such as this where we need men on the ground who can touch the flesh and smell the way ahead. I would suggest you get yourself over to Brindisi on a military flight and have a sniff around. You'll need to draw a weapon in case you come across anything. We are in a serious situation here, we can't announce this to the world as we have already been hauled over the coals about "weapons of mass destruction" in the past. There is no way we'll get permission to put out an "all-points bulletin" to Europe on the basis of the scant evidence we have at the moment. That will come, this could be chemical, a dirty bomb, conventional device or god forbid a full blown nuclear weapon. If we are wrong it will create mass panic. If we are right they could kill millions. The degree of our response will become a political decision as we get evidence. Meantime we need to do our job, if this thing is in Europe it could go off at any time from now.'

Finlay nodded, 'just get me the paperwork done Henry and I'll go back to the hotel and get my kit organised.'

*

'Does Henry know you're meeting me for dinner?' enquired Anna

'He's probably got the table bugged. You see that old dear over there scoffing oysters, that'll be one of his crew following us around Covent Garden.'

Finlay had time to kill while Henry was organising clearance on a NATO flight for Finlay to Italy and drawing any kit or ordnance that Finlay requested. He wasn't good at sitting around hotel rooms so once he'd gone for a run he telephoned Anna. He asked her if she'd like to join him in J Sheekeys fish restaurant in Covent Garden to "run through the next sequence of events". Anna had been hesitant, either concerned about getting too close to the old soldier or being concerned about her boss not approving of a personal liaison with his old compatriot Major Lamont.

'I take it that means no Finlay?'

'Are you worried he would disapprove?'

'No it's just that he'll think there is more to it if we don't tell him and he finds out.'

'I don't really give a shit what he thinks Anna, we're just having dinner and enjoying each other's company.'

Anna visibly relaxed, 'I'm sorry for being so stuffy, I'm not used to being asked for dinner.'

'No problem, that's what happens when you work for the intelligence services, you become part of the woodwork. It becomes engrained in your very soul. I remember when I worked with MI5 in Ireland, one guy told me that you never take anything at face value, always looking for the angle or the subterfuge even when it simply doesn't exist. Might even have been Monmouth himself that told me that. He'll never change. I don't think that Henry will ever retire, he'll die being a spook. Things are a bit more straight forward in soldiering.'

'Yet you seem to be coming back into it?' Anna enquired, one eyebrow raised.

'Yes, this is the last one Anna, a dead man fell in my lap, and I felt it was my duty. Henry didn't help, perhaps I should have told the police and kept out of it but they would have investigated me and it would have all dragged on. Then it would have come to the same conclusion. Phoning Henry was a lot quicker.'

'So full retirement is beckoning after this.' Anna pushed the point.

'Yes, straight after this is done, I'm going to see my son in Cyprus and go and see Elspeth, in San Francisco or possible Miami, she has an interview there I believe. She's a very bright girl, in a similar line of work to you. Perhaps you'll meet her one day.'

'I hope so, give me her perspective on her dad.'

'What about you Anna, what is your outlook in life?'

Anna smiled, pushing her brown hair back from her big green eyes and wrinkling her nose as if unsure how to answer, 'As far as work goes I'd like to push my AI programme to being more mainstream, both within MI5 and SIS. I think it's the future. I need to work with the digital security team to get it to become more accurate, get better results. It's all about mathematical algorithms which I am a specialist in. AI works like a brain, there are banks of "nodes" in series feeding into each other, many thousands, even millions. You have an input and the nodes weight each other as you "train" the system, at the end of it you have an output or a probability of something being identified. Like the nukeprof link to the African Tide sinking. That is the bit we need to be more accurate. It's like sorting the wheat from the chaff to get a result. We have had our budget more than quadrupled this year but we also have a lot of detractors. They would rather spend the money on agents on the ground, threats from home grown terrorism and so on.'

'Old farts like Henry,' Finlay laughed.

'Actually he has been very supportive of me. He saw the way ahead on AI years ago. In fact he was directly responsible for recruiting me from Cambridge when I finished my PhD.'

'I thought he thought Cambridge was a hotbed of communists.'

'He probably still does, it didn't seem to put him off as far as I was concerned though! If I can prove in more of our cases that this is a solid path to follow this will become mainstream. There are basically three things we are working on. Firstly access to inputs and data, all sorts of technical issues to overcome here and of course an ethical one. Secondly, how we write and develop the software to be more accurate and lastly we simply need a massive amount of computing power as the first two become larger and more powerful. Can't tell you much more than that I'm afraid.' Anna sat back, satisfied she had summarised her role in MI5 without giving away any privileged information.

'You have a lot riding on this,' Said Finlay

'It's all I have done in my working career for the last fifteen years, if we help resolve this, there will be no looking back, no recriminations from your so called "old farts".'

'And what about your personal life, you have brushed over that previously when we talked.'

'If there were ever a case of the pot calling the kettle black, this is it Major Lamont.'

Finlay smiled, they had talked a couple of times on the journey to the United Arab Emirates and he accepted he had been distant when the subject came to personal life. He as starting to really like this woman, her looks and mannerisms charmed him but there was more to her than that. Henry's "computer monkey" was highly intelligent, obviously at the frontier edge of artificial intelligence and how it could be used to defend the nation. She was understated, not at all conceited and hardworking. Miss Siebert sought to impress no one but her superiors and that was to promote her field. Finlay wanted to get to know the person now, not just the technologist and security operative. He decided to get straight to the point, 'never been close to marriage?'

She refrained from answering the question while the waiter took their order. The analyst waited until the waiter walked off with his notepad and leaned across the table so the other tables couldn't hear, 'I've had a couple of serious boyfriends, one that was in the service and one that was an economist with the World Health Organisation. The first didn't last too long on the grounds that I was hauled in by HR and told to desist. It wasn't going anywhere anyway, I was almost relieved. The other lasted two years. He went off to work in Abuja in Lagos followed by Nairobi. He seemed more distant each time he came home on leave. He knew I worked for MI5 but I find men don't like women keeping secrets – of any kind. He would question me on what I had been working on, I simply couldn't tell him. I'm only telling you because we're working together. It's like someone asking you what you did in the SRU around the world. You can't tell anyone.' She paused then said almost reluctantly, 'did you ever tell Ella what you did?'

Finlay pursed his lips before answering. This was like intelligence services trading information, she had opened up a little and the price was him reciprocating, 'I guess my job was a little different. I could tell her I was a soldier and approximately where I was working but I didn't ever discuss operational details. It wasn't just because it was classified but also, if I'm honest, because some of the unsavoury things we did. It is a dirty job sometimes, we have to clean up messes. I don't think Ella wanted to know about that. I was ever her caring husband and father of her two lovely children. I always had that part of it put to one side when I was home, to pick up soldiering again when back in active service. I suppose we had an unspoken deal, I would never tell of the nasty side of my job and she, in turn, could never ask about the clandestine activities I undertook. As far as everyone else was concerned I was in the first battalion Parachute Regiment supporting the SAS, no one was any the wiser. And that is about as much as I can say!' He smirked across the table. 'Henry would be having a fit if he knew we were discussing this in a restaurant.'

'We have not said much that isn't public knowledge.'

The conversation changed to growing up and friendships over the years as the starters and main courses were consumed alongside a good bottle of Chassagne Montrachet. They followed up with a couple of drinks in the bar after the second sitting theatre goers had cleared a space. Finlay walked Anna to the taxi rank and received a peck on the cheek and a brief embrace for his trouble. Neither wanted to push things too far too quickly.

As he walked back to his hotel taking in the night air Finlay was in a reflective mood, the overwhelming feeling of guilt was still there but had dissipated slightly. His mind then moved to the task in hand and his imminent departure for Brindisi.

The next morning He rose early with a slight hangover, went for a run around London embankment before the commuter crowds blocked the pavement and then ate breakfast. He then walked to Millbank and went into the weapons check facility in the basement with Henry.

He had checked out a fourth generation Glock 17 with four additional magazines and sixty rounds of ammunition. It was the standard sidearm of the British armed forces, light and easy to conceal. It used 9mm parabellum ammunition which was very easy to find the world over. Despite the popular rumour it was a plastic gun and undetectable by metal detectors it does contain metal parts and is indeed detectable. It was however, well proven and very robust. Every soldier would prefer a shoulder mounted weapon for accuracy but this wasn't practical for the type of work that Finlay would be carrying out. It would be up close and personal and needed stopping power and reliability. Finlay also drew thunder flashes and flares, compact pyrotechnics in case he needed to disorientate or show his location to the cavalry. He also drew a digitally coded telephone which would work on European networks. In addition he had requested dark Patagonia climbing clothing that would be warm, waterproof and comfortable, while he would also pass for a tourist. He already had his well-worn and trusted Scarpa walking boots, easy to wear casually in the street but would be comfortable and breathable in a hard "yomp" should it be required. He had to account for the weapon and every round used, the clothing was expensive but he was allowed to keep it, he only signed for receipt of it. In addition to that he drew dried rations and energy food. From habit his Bergen would be equipped like a combat operation, it could always be lightened by removing excess equipment. It was better than trying to find equipment in the middle of a fast moving operation.

Curiously he had also asked for an old overcoat, scuffed size nine brogue shoes, woolly hat and scarf with some old fashioned black rimmed glasses which had no prescription. The xquartermaster's section also supplied him with a light state of the art Canon digital camera and telephoto lens.

Henry also signed out the same model handgun along with a rucksack and clothing which he didn't already have in case he had to join Finlay in a hurry.

*

Mumtaz Ansari lay in a basement apartment on the Via Appia, the doctor had given him some blood and morphine to dull the pain in his head. The right side of his skull had swollen up like a football and the eye on that side was sealed shut. His head had been shaved where the blow had landed and he had received twelve stitches where the skin had split. He was on a drip to keep him hydrated and had moved frequently between being conscious and in a deep sleep. He hadn't uttered a word to anyone apart from his brother since Stefano had hit him with the baseball bat. The apartment was used as a safe house by the Sacra Corona Unita and the basement was a mini hospital used to treat any of the soldiers that had been injured in the service of the organisation. There was a limit to what the doctor could do and he wasn't capable of scanning the skull to see if the brain had swollen. Ansari's treatment had gone as far as it could without him attending a hospital.

Abdul Ansari had occupied a bed in the same room as his brother for two days, both men were confined to the room under armed guard, leaving only to visit the toilet. Abdul had pleaded that his brother go to hospital but neither the criminal organisation, nor his own, under the command of Sia wanted to attract the attention of the authorities at this stage in the operation. Sia had visited once and done little but offer words of encouragement to them both. Abdul asked to talk to Fakhoury but was denied by Sia on security grounds. Sia had reminded the brothers that this was a jihad operation against the infidel and they must act like soldiers, they were all expendable. Stefano and Luigi had stayed away to prevent further animosity occurring in the short term. Both Ansari brothers suspected the men were waiting for Mumtaz to die as he was a liability now.

De Bastiani visited with Cyrus Sia and returned to his office to discuss the operation subsequent to all of his terms being agreed with Cyrus Sia. Fakhoury had not been in touch but the funds had cleared the account as promised.

Both men sat across the meeting desk with no one else in the room, the Boss leaned across the table and squeezed Sia's arm. 'We are ready to move ahead now, Mister Sia,' he smiled as he spoke in English.

'Good, we need to be progressing the cargo through your territory and concluding our business after this unfortunate delay.' Sia had been utterly professional in his approach to the business in Brindisi. In truth he cared little for the Ansari brothers, they were a means to an end.

De Bastiani went on, 'we will wait three more days and move the cargo early on Sunday when the roads around here are very quiet and there are less police to interfere. We need to decide what to do with your men. I suggest that if the wounded one is still alive we put him in the truck, then when he clears Italy he is your problem. If he gets worse I think we finish him off.'

'I can't do that, his brother needs to be working with me, he will be needed in the future.'

'Well he's your problem, questions will be asked if the police stop the truck and see him with that injury. Better to leave him here,' retorted the underworld boss.

'His brother won't leave him with you, thinks you will kill him,' Sia surmised.

'Where is Fakhoury now?' De Bastiani changed the subject, he saw no point in denying the accusation. They would kill if him they had to.

'Busy elsewhere Mister De Bastiani. I am sure he will be in touch once we have completed our assignment.'

'It is disappointing he is not here during this critical phase of the operation…………but I am paid now so that is what counts.'

Both men agreed to meet again before the truck departed, Cyrus Sia stood and took his leave.

As Sia walked out of the office he nodded to three men who were waiting in the ante room outside, he wondered if they were De Bastiani's henchman for the escort of the cargo. They looked like tough characters, not at home amongst the mafia leader's expensive leather furniture and impression of legitimacy. As he nodded in acknowledgement he saw that the one with half his ear missing had a nasty rash or burn on his wrist and upper hand. When Sia exited the door to be escorted to the lift by the PA, he heard De Bastiani say loudly "avanti Claudio". One of the men stood and went in. His suspicions were correct. De Bastiani had already summoned him the last time he was leaving his office – sounds like he would head the operation. Perhaps the other man got the rash from the fight with Ansari.

*

Anne Siebert sat in her office, oblivious to the thunderstorm that was lashing the large drops of summer rain against her office window in Millbank. The computer room that she was in should not have had a window. It contained one of the world's most powerful single computer processors outside of the American NSA. The computer itself was in a pristine super-cooled environment remote from the office but the access to it was from her desktop. She knew that it should have been in an encased secure environment to minimise the risk of bugging and hacking, however human beings, she knew, were not computers. The human brain was still the most advanced intelligence system in the world. It needed natural light, a window and regular breaks to perform at its best. To successfully integrate with the massive processing power accessed on the screen and keyboard in front of her. She had stood ground during a heated debate on the subject with the IT security department and had won. Henry in particular had supported her, she suspected so he could hang out the window and smoke.

While she had been away a bank of over a million more nodes had been added to the already massive computing power. Mostly in parallel, making the processing power broader but also in series, making it more powerful and having a better and faster decision making ability. The machine still needed human inputs and ultimately guidance on the outputs before going further. The success in making the nuclear proliferation link was already a great step forward. Something they would be shouting from the rooftops once they had more proof – but they needed it to do more often and have a better success rate. Anna didn't want her software to be an *aid* to the process of deduction by human operatives, she wanted it to be the *guidance* with people merely having to confirm its deductions. That was the ultimate goal. She knew that this point in history was some time away but felt it was inevitable.

The sophistication behind her artificial intelligence system was not necessarily the size and power of the brain but how the software was written and how the machine was trained to think. Long and complicated algorithms taught the machine how to make decisions by weighting the nodes and influencing the outcome. Once it had been trained it would remember its successes, as fed back by the operators. Then it would expand physically by human masters adding more processing power and further developing the algorithms and software. Yet another iteration of power and software had been done by in house technicians during her visit to the Middle East and now she was ready to input more information. Once this information was added, the search words and data would trigger a search on the world wide web once again and not just with publicly available information. The system had the ability to hack into networks of both foreign and friendly security systems. Only the most secure firewalls could resist it, this tended to be financial and state security systems. Video surveillance networks in malls, railway stations and airports, for example, have little chance against the power of this artificial brain. It could do all of this with little or no threat to its own ability. It needed constant attention by operators however, and Anna had a shift of three people monitoring the machine twenty four hours a day when in operation.

She studied her notes and what she had learned from her recent meetings in the United Arab Emirates and in London. She used her own knowledge and experience to help the search. The first word she thought of was smuggling, she linked this to the African Tide sinking and the suspected proliferation issue. Next she entered the Chechyn link to the attack on Major Finlay Lamont. The details that they got from the Vasily Kravits interview were added. Two more keywords. She then entered the names of Mumtaz and Abdul Ansari, further searches were Islamic fundamentalism in the UK as well criminal network in Europe. Anna then entered the names of Omar Fakhoury and Hassan Makhlouf. Finally, she added the names of Yasser Arafat and Saeed Raheem. She scanned in any photographs she had of all the people in question.

Flicking through the last of her notes, she saw the information procured from Billy Franklin of the CIA. Port Sudan, Jeddah, Sohar, Bandar Abbas and Brindisi were all added. She also put something in about a green forty foot container with "a bird" on the side. She knew this was a long shot and you had to be careful about prioritising what goes in. Each word would have to link to the whole computer "briefing" and could add millions of further links for the processor to deduct. You could contaminate and dilute valuable links and outputs that the machine could make. Once all this was done and confirmed by the "brain" you then simply gave it time to think. It would throw summaries and suggestions at you and you had to respond knowledgeably. Often this would mean contacting field agents and asking them the questions. Many times these queries didn't make sense to the operatives and would lead to accusations of time wasting. Once again human relationships and interfacing were key to a successful outcome.

Anna had worked on some projects where the field agents simply did not want to spend time thinking about inputs for some type of new-fangled computer system. Anna had been met with hostility tinged with a degree of contempt on some projects. Various excuses had been thrown up by agents, more contact with head office could result in security breaches. The supercomputer had led them down the wrong path, simply wasted time, and on a couple of occasions the interface with the machine itself had allegedly led to the complete failure of the mission. Another concern, though valid, was the amount of people cleared for very privileged information. These were her "watch keepers" who operated the computer round the clock. She had fought the corner of the brain for several years, from when it was a simple data storage and access memory until now. It was currently at the cutting edge of its field in AI.

Henry had continued to be a champion for the machine he called "Skynet" after the malevolent AI supercomputer in "The Terminator" film. His idea of a joke though the thought of Henry even watching the film was the thing that most amused the people in the IT department of MI5. He had continued to be derogatory and pretended he did not understand one item of technical information he had discussed with anyone in the service. She had realised very soon after meeting the jaded old spy that his level of intellect was a match for her own. It was something he preferred to keep hidden, perhaps as a result of his trade.
Not only was the new project critical to the ongoing promotion of Skynet, it would be key to see how the information would interface with someone like Finlay Lamont. It was obvious the man was a trained and effective soldier with an enormous amount of practical experience. Finlay obviously commanded a lot of respect from Henry and his superiors to be entrusted almost single handily to

carry out surveillance in Brindisi. She wasn't sure how he would react and deal with the inputs from Skynet, if he cooperated fully and they were successful, no one could shut the machine down. Half of Anna felt that she wanted the nuclear threat to be real so they could prevail and prove her life's work. The other half felt a degree of guilt that the risk of it being real could kill millions of people.

She completed the data input, explained the story to the Skynet watch keepers and as with all binary processing systems, simply pressed a binary "enter".

*

Finlay had arrived at the large Italian NATO air force base, Aviano in north-eastern Italy. It was a ten hour drive down the coastal E55 highway but it was the only base he could be cleared in to with weapons. Going anywhere else would have caused longer delays and attracted too much attention. He felt that his visit may be a bit of a long shot but in the circumstances it was better than twiddling his thumbs in London or at home. The service had supplied him with an *unobtrusive* Fiat Panda as they had called it. Cheap and slow may have been better description in his view, he wouldn't be wanting to chase anyone at speed. At least it had four wheel drive in case he needed to go off road. He checked into a small *quaint* hotel near the port and immediately went out in the evening to have a look around and get his bearings. He was surprised how scenic the port area was, he'd expected something more industrial. It was a mixture of modern and old but there were very few high rise buildings, the new buildings were in keeping with the old streets and villas. It was a warm night but a gentle breeze blew across the Adriatic. He found a balcony on the first floor of an old bar from where he could look over the port area. He could see the passenger and freight ferry terminal less than five hundred metres away. A Grimaldi lines ro-ro was discharging trailers and accompanied traffic to a holding area near the link span ramp that was used to access the stern of the ship.

He ordered a beer and some food as he watched the operation, it was enclosed by a security fence and anything going in and out was checked at the kiosk by the gate. He noted that some articulated truck tractor units were coming in from the main road near the port and leaving with trailers that they had picked up. He couldn't see accompanied trailers leaving, it probably wasn't practical or economical for the tractor units to accompany the trailers on the ships even just across the Adriatic to Albania or Serbia. The drivers would have to be paid and to transit immigration successfully. Finlay imagined this would be even more inefficient with the long passage from Port Sudan. He would be looking for a trailer or container that had been picked up.

After finishing his meal he wandered across to the kiosk. The Grimaldi ship had discharged its cargo and the holding area had gone quiet. The checker in the kiosk was reading a book and looked up as he approached, his face betraying a look of annoyance at a passer by knocking on his window. He probably thought it was an inquisitive tourist. Finlay asked if he could recommend someone that could pick up his trailer that was coming from Port Sudan. The checkers' English was poor and after much arm waving and pointing he took a list and ran it through the photocopier. It was two pages long and in Italian but appeared to be a list of hauliers cleared to enter the port. Finlay didn't expect much but it was a start. He thanked the surly checker and went back to his hotel to get some rest.

The next morning, he checked his encrypted email system on his cell phone. He had sent a picture of the list of hauliers to Henry before going to bed the previous evening. A response had come back saying that Skynet had detected a link overnight on smuggling between the Middle East and North Africa region to the port of Brindisi as well as ports in Sicily and the west coast of Italy. The connection in south-east Italy was the Sacra Corona Unita. The email had given a list of mafiose members, starting from the top. It could provide more detail and bio's if required. It had also managed to identify one haulage company being linked to the criminal organisation that was on the checkers' security list submitted by Major Lamont. It was called Toro in Carica or "Charging Bull", it had a mixture of owned tractor units, black with a gold rampaging bull on the sides and back, or unmarked rental units. Interpol had identified it as being one hundred per cent owned by a subsidiary of the Sacra Corona Unitas' boss's holding company. The email contained possible links to the other ports mentioned by Franklin but they were much further down the list of possibilities. Franklin's CIA had also obtained a sketch of the bird allegedly on the side of the container from the Port Sudan watchman. Unfortunately he spoke no English and wrote only in Arabic so the text on the side was lost for good.

Finlay now had something to work on. He asked for further information on the locations of Sacra Corona Unita facilities and for a Geiger counter to be sent to him. A "particle detector" as he phrased it in the communication. Preferably a small one if there were such a thing. He could start work on his own, he had De Bastiani's name and the parent company he owned known simply as Toro. His subsidiaries all contained the bull name notation, if it wasn't prefaced by "charging" it was "sitting" or "sleeping" and so on. The logos depicted the action of the same bull graphic and relevant name. Apart from various news stories surrounding De Bastiani's previous court appearances, there was a website containing his legitimate businesses around the south-eastern region of Italy, most prominently in Taranto and Brindisi. He found the locations of the head office in Brindisi and the haulage business in the industrial estate in the suburbs of the city. The head office was less than three kilometres away. He donned his Patagonia shorts, walking shoes and a white T-shirt with "Italia" on the front. He also wore a dark baseball cap and what appeared to be clear prescription glasses. He took his emptied Bergen and put his jacket, camera, laptop and his Glock in it. The Sykes Fairbairn went in a side pocket of the Bergen, the handle accessible through the slightly unzipped side pocket. For all the world he looked like a middle aged tourist, possibly looking for his long lost ancestors. He carried a genuine British passport with the name David D'Angelo in it. On inspection it would make an Anglo-Italian connection.

He walked inland from his hotel and the port until he got to the six story building with a large neon bull lit on the top floor. The entrance was across the road from a sizeable café with a balcony, tables and umbrellas on the outside. Very useful, this was easy surveillance. He sat down at a table nearer the back of the balcony so he wasn't easily seen from the Toro building and took out his laptop.

Several other customers also had laptops out as he waited, a combination of tourists and businessmen. The pictures of the Sacra Corona capos and soldiers hadn't come through from Millbank yet. He went on to the café Wi-Fi and found a couple of pictures of De Bastiani leaving court three years ago in an online newspaper. He copied them for future reference, memorised his features and took them off his laptop screen.

Now came the boring part, reconnaissance on your own contained an element of luck, it was not possible to undertake it constantly, you simply had to maximise your chances. He had no idea whether his man was even in town. He knew the office would open at nine o'clock as per the website, chances are the boss of such an organisation would go in to work in the morning and possible leave at lunch time. He sat down opposite the office at eight a.m. before the first of the office workers would arrive. He hadn't that long to wait before people in the vicinity would start to notice how long he'd been there. His camera would be too obtrusive if he stood up to take pictures of the front door. He had a high resolution camera in his cell phone, he could easily take pictures with that without attracting attention and blow them up later.

Finlay was in luck, several cars dropped people off at the front door of the building, most he assumed were office workers. He had only been there about half an hour when a large black Mercedes S Class with dark tinted windows pulled up and a large well-built man got out in an expensive dark suit carrying a gym bag. He handed the bag to the doorman and glanced back at the car. He'd forgotten his sunglasses. He turned and walked back to the car and opened the back door, leaning in to get them. For the few seconds he turned, Finlay took a burst of shots from the cell phone camera, while pretending to speak to an image on the phone. He kept an eye on the door and sent the pictures to Anna and Henry.

Finlay spent the next two hours taking camera shots in a similar fashion, mostly of men entering and leaving the business. Several looked like tough men, almost caricatures from a mafia movie. Around lunch time he decided to go and take a look at the two truck yard locations on the outskirts of town. He used the café Wi-Fi to transmit all the pictures he took and walked back to the hotel to pick up his car.

He drove for some fifteen minutes through heavy and somewhat unpredictable Italian traffic. The first location was simply another office. The area in front of it was deserted, the access was via a normal swing door on to the pavement, there were no cars parked apart from around the back of the building. Any surveillance would raise suspicion. He got out the car which he parked further down the street and walked up and down past the office entrance, he couldn't do anything here. Finlay drove to the yard which was only about one kilometre away, and like the office he had just been to, had the charging bull logo on the front gate and office window. This was different, it was a very large yard with several trucks and trailers in the parking area. It had a small despatch area and café for the drivers which was opposite a massive warehouse which you could store cargo or load trailers undercover. The whole yard was enclosed by a high security barbed wire fence. There were video cameras at every corner. Finlay suspected these were to detect any police activity as anyone foolish enough to break in and steal from the mafia would not last very long.

The front of the yard entrance was opposite wasteland next to a damp and undrained marshland. A stream meandered behind a hillock full of long grass about three hundred metres away. This was more like the surveillance he knew as a young man in Ireland. Finlay drove the Panda to a rough track that passed behind the hillock over a dilapidated old wooden bridge. He parked the car behind some gorse bushes and climbed to the top of the hillock, the last few yards on his hands and knees. He parted the long grass and placed the camera and telephoto lens angled directly at the front gate. He would have to move between there and the door of the warehouse and drivers cabin. This would be worthy of some help if he could get prove a link to the container from Sudan or persons identified by their intelligence contacts.

Over the next few hours he observed and photographed several wagons and drivers going back and forth. Some drivers who had finished shifts were picked up and the front gate by cars or they entered their own in the car park. Finlay pretty much got it all, though he couldn't directly identify them from where he sat. He knew the extremely high resolution camera and powerful zoom lens would allow facial recognition as briefed by Anna. He would simply take as many pictures as he could and send them back overnight to Millbank, hopefully they could get a lead.

The flies and mosquitos had started to gather around the old soldier lying in the grass. He had no camouflage and certainly hadn't come equipped with mosquito nets or repellent as he would have done in his SRU days. He thought this would be suburban reconnaissance. More fool he, Finlay reflected as he slapped the back of his neck and covered himself with the jacket from his Bergen.

*

Anna rubbed her eyes in the dark office in London's Millbank. She hadn't had much sleep. After speaking to Henry she had managed to get a camp bed put in a nearby empty store room and catnapped when her watch keepers were working Skynet. Once, a number of years ago she was allowed to visit the NSA and see the resources they had to hand. It was exceptional. It simply dwarfed what the UK intelligence services had. She would put a month's wages on the fact that her equivalent at the FBI or NSA wouldn't be sleeping on a camp bed at night.

She had changed into a fleece and pair of track bottoms and now moved through to the cupboard bed for a couple of hours rest after going through the data that Finlay had sent through to her from Brindisi. It was then handed over to her team to process in the AI system. She found herself wondering about what Finlay was doing and if he was safe. She would like to talk to him on the phone but needed an operational excuse. It wasn't just Skynet that was causing her to lose sleep, she was being distracted by the beginning of some kind of relationship. Anna wasn't sure how it could progress, if it could be allowed to develop. There could be no risk to her life's work, no failure due to a relationship with a man who may not be there a year down the road. No one had noticed apart from Henry who had said nothing. He was an old school spy, she half suspected that Major Lamont's surveillance trip to Italy had killed two birds with one stone. Henry had got him out of the way.

She forced herself to move her thoughts to her work. Finlay had sent through a lot of pictures. They had identified Gianni De Bastiani very quickly indeed along with several of his henchman, almost all of whom had been in police custody at one time or other. There were five or six individuals who had gone into the building with these men that they could not identify. That could be a key as they ran it through the massive processor in the MI5 headquarters.

Anna dozed for a couple of hours but couldn't fall asleep. She hear the footsteps move toward the cupboard before the light tap on the open door. It was Jake, one of her watch keepers. The caricature of a computer geek, short, fat, acne despite being in his late twenties and wore a brown and yellow tank top jumper. 'I think we may have a link boss,' he said with a smirk on his face.

Anna sat up quickly despite her weariness, 'OK I'll take a look.'

Jake explained as they walked toward his station actually inside the large secure space where Skynet was, 'the machine did a search on Kravits' information, searched the Port of Singapore Authority or PSA surveillance database. Got in real easy. Picked up video surveillance of the immigration office where any passengers or crew go through to board these big container ships. We put a range date that we knew the African Tide was in. It's picked up three men and a woman broadly fitting the description given by Kravits. Particularly interesting as not a lot of women go through this surveillance system, only ship's crew and dockyard workers.' He was sitting at his station now pointing at the screen and going through the footage slides, one by one. 'This tallies with information given to us by Singapore Intelligence, these two in particular, the older man on the left is Cyrus Sia and this is supposed to be his wife Miriam. Kravits didn't think it was but those were the names on their passports. They appear genuine. They are on the passenger list of the African Tide.'

'Get me Kravits on the phone, I don't care how we do it. I'll call Henry,' said Anna. This was the breakthrough they needed - please, please let Kravits verify this, she thought.

Henry lived in one of the new apartment blocks in Ilford at the end of the soon to be constructed Crossrail project. He had purchased it with a view to paying suburb prices much lower than central London but yet would have quick access into the Millbank office. A more central location was too expensive on a MI5 salary. The continual delay of Crossrail meant he had to take a slow surface train into the office and the service could be patchy.

His scrambled cell phone rang loudly in the main bedroom. Henry rolled over, almost automatically, still semi-conscious, and answered it, 'Henry.'

'Hi its Anna, we have a visual image of the suspects on the ship.'

'Does it match with anything Major Lamont has sent?'

'We're running them now,' Anna responded.

Henry could hear the excitement in her voice, that didn't happen often. He sat up, placing his feet on the floor. 'I'm on my way.'

That bloody train again if there was one.

Chapter 33

Around the same time as Finlay had called a halt to his mosquito infested surveillance, an old man wearing casual clothing sat in a hotel lobby of the Claridge close to the Champs Elysees. He looked very old, in his eighties perhaps, pale but with large liver spots on his arms and hands having spent many years under the heat of the desert sun. He had no hair and wore silver legged rimless glasses over his long nose. The eyes behind the lenses were a pale grey, still as bright as they were when he was a teenager. He had clearly been a tall man, although the weight of his years had weighed on his back causing a slight stoop exacerbated by a limp when he walked from damage to his leg. When he had asked the receptionist for a quiet table to await his meeting attendees he had talked with a whisper. His voice rasped as if he had a chest problem or perhaps some infection or damage to his voice box.

David had arrived, as was his custom, half an hour early for the meeting. He knew that others generally would arrive on time or perhaps ten minutes early. Years of espionage had taught him to arrive promptly, even for a friendly get together involving your own. It would allow you to scout the area for exits and see if anyone was observing the area already. He would often get up and walk out with fifteen minutes to go to see if he would be followed before returning on time. It was always best to be unpredictable, particularly if you had no backup. He also knew that "Bob the Builder" and his girl had no idea what he looked like for their first meeting so he could watch their body language before making his presence known. He had purposely picked a lobby which was small and quiet, where it would be difficult to put them under surveillance without being noticed.

He had just ordered a coffee when they came in ten minutes early. Moshe looked like a builder, stalky with big hands and a square jaw, close cropped hair but an intelligent face with a ready smile. Zarrin looked the opposite, she was undoubtedly beautiful. Tall and elegant with striking green eyes set in an olive complexion but she looked sullen and scared. Normally he would just have met his operative, the less people that saw him the better but this operation was critical and David was to retire soon. There was little risk of him ever being involved in any espionage after this project was completed.

As agreed previously with his operative David lifted a pipe to his lips and took a lighter out of his pocket, he attempted to light the tobacco but was unsuccessful. Moshe saw him and walked across, 'Father you're not allowed to smoke in here.'

'OK I'll wait until I get outside.' They had confirmation.

David stood and embraced Moshe, patting him on the back as he did so. He also embraced and kissed a reluctant Zarrin before sitting back down and ordering them all a refreshment. It was obvious the girl was out of her depth and was only there because of her feelings for Moshe Cohen.

The old Mossad agent turned to Zarrin first, 'have you managed to get a hold of Khorasani yet?'

Zarrin shook her head, 'no he didn't answer his phone since we spoke in Iran, now its unobtainable.'

'He probably doesn't want to be tracked by your security services. He will have got himself a telephone though, under one of his other identities, of which he has several.' David kept addressing Zarrin, 'Do you know if he has strong links here or even another relationship?'

'I believe most of his money is in Switzerland, over the years he was always talking to Geneva or Zurich. I also saw he had access cards to Swiss banks. I remember UBS was one of them. I don't know much else,' Zarrin recollected.

'He'll go where the money is, Khorasani will be reluctant to communicate by telephone or internet and the banks won't allow any access without telephone verification. As far as we know he has no other phone. To transfer cash or get access to it he will have to attend in person. My guess is he will be in Zurich. Our people have details of his banks and finances, all are in Switzerland, between three banks, UBS, Credit Suisse and Zurich Cantonal Bank. We know which branches he uses. I have men on their way there now. This is a big operation for us, I have called in a lot of favours so both of you need to help me.'

Zarrin continued to look undecided, her sullenness was morphing into being uncooperative. David, glanced at Moshe, 'how much have you told her?'

'I have told Zarrin of the threat that faces the world if Khorasani isn't found and the information he possesses isn't extracted from him.'

'The threat that faces Israel you mean,' this was directed from Zarrin to Moshe.
David interrupted, 'my dear it does of course threaten Israel and that is why we are here, but it also threatens the Western world in entirety. Despite their differences with us over the years, we need them. If it were revealed we knew something but did nothing and a calamity overcame the West they would never forgive us. It is also an opportunity to apply ever more pressure to the Iranian regime and I know you want that to change.'

'You have both made me a traitor, I will have to look over my shoulder for the rest of my life.'

Moshe smiled at Zarrin and put his hand on her arm, 'you were looking over your shoulder anyway. I have my family to think of, I have to go back.'

David raised his hands, palms toward them as if they should stop and take stock, 'listen, at the moment they know nothing of your involvement, that is how we intend it to stay. We find Khorasani, then we resolve what is going on and apply pressure to Iran, that is your best chance of complete freedom. It is entirely possible we succeed.'

Zarrin shrugged, 'OK what do we do next?'

David looked at Zarrin once again, 'there are two ways to do this. One is we simply conduct surveillance at the banks, when he turns up we render him. Always a risky business, it can go wrong. Second option is for you to make contact and persuade him to come over to us, tell him we can protect him and so on.'

Zarrin laughed sarcastically, 'there is more risk for me in the second option!'

'Not if it's in a public place, watched by my men. He doesn't know Moshe, he can also be in the background, you will be safe.'

'And how am I supposed to contact him?' She responded.

'Simply leave a message for him at each of his banks saying to call your number due to a family emergency. Tell him you are in Switzerland.'

'And if he ignores it?'

'He won't, but if he does then it's back to option one.'

The emerald green eyes glanced at Moshe, held his gaze for a while, then she slowly, and reluctantly, nodded her head.

Chapter 34

Finlay had slept well after finishing his previous nights' surveillance and gone for a one hour run around the port when he rose in the early morning. He had checked his email before he left and there had been no missives from Henry or follow up from Anna. As he ran he planned the morning's activities. He would try the café across from the office again for a couple of hours. It would be the last time as he would attract attention with continual visits, any further surveillance would have to be more covert. He would then return to his spot on the hillock next to the truck depot. He had little choice until he got more from London.

On returning from the run, he checked again, there was a very big file which he downloaded from Henry. It was a file that had been forwarded from Anna to Henry who had added his instructions on the matter. The Skynet system had found a match between a man named Cyrus Sia and someone who had exited the main office building yesterday morning. Sia had been with a man called Luigi Gianetti and another called Claudio Sarronni, the latter was a Capo in the Sacra Corona Unita organisation. The key though was Sia, he had been matched as being on the African Tide with his daughter Miriam so finally they had that key link. It had been verified by Kravits. Finlay's heart skipped a beat when it finally sunk in, this evidence was hard to refute unless you didn't believe Anna's box of tricks actually worked. There were a series of photographs of Sia from Singapore and both Gianetti brothers from Taranto court and police archives. They had also supplied pictures of Miriam, Sia and the two henchmen passing through security on the way to African Tide. As yet the names of the other two men had not been supplied due to a glitch in the PSA's database in Singapore.

The rest of Henry's email outlined what the next steps were. Henry and Anna would join him in Brindisi after Henry had elicited more help from MI5. Anna would provide local guidance to the watchkeepers on Skynet. Henry V would co-ordinate his intelligence organisation's process with any support he needed from MI6 or anyone else. Finlay's priority was to find and track Cyrus Sia and his daughter. The Gianetti's were secondary. The ultimate goal of course was to find the trailer and its contents.

Finlay decided not to change his plans for the day but instead of general surveillance he would try and find Sia. He remembered the three men that he had photographed, and had been matched, vaguely from the many others. They had left De Bastiani's head office the preceding morning around eleven a.m. The old soldier responded to Henry's email with a simple acknowledgement. He showered, packed his usual items into his kitbag and headed down to the café for his breakfast. As he strolled down the street to his car he could feel the excitement of the chase starting to get to him along with a slight pang of guilt. He hadn't thought of Ella since he'd arrived in Brindisi.

While the surveillance position was not far away Finlay wanted the rental car to hand in case he had to follow his subject. He drove down to the café and parked the car as close as he could to it. The café itself was very busy. He couldn't find a table in the relative coolness of the morning when the patio was in the shade so had to sit inside at a table near the window. He had a poor view of the front of De Bastiani's office but it would have to suffice. Finlay had an old trick which he had used in the SRU - smoking. He carried a pack of cigarettes in his bag, when he wanted to take a look around a public area he would use it as an excuse to go outside and smoke. It was a familiar site in Europe where smoking was banned inside buildings and never attracted attention. After having his breakfast he sat on a wall near the café and smoked a cigarette, very slowly. It gave him an unobstructed view of the buildings entrance across the road. As he was about to light a second a car pulled up and two men exited the building. This surprised him as they must have been there very early, before he had commenced his surveillance. One was clearly Sia, the other was probably Luigi Gianetti. He would have to check that later. Finlay raised his cell phone and pretended he was talking to someone on the screen and took a photograph. He couldn't identify the driver as the light was reflecting off the windscreen. It was a red Fiat Tipo. As the two men talked to the driver through the side window,

Finlay started to stroll the two hundred metres to his car parked around the side of the café. A quick glance back saw both men getting in the Tipo. He sprinted to his car as he disappeared from view, hastily started the Fiat Panda and manoeuvred it round toward the front of the café. As he turned on to the street he saw the Tipo turn a corner toward the road which led away from the port toward the industrial area in Brindisi. They were probably going to the truck yard and warehouse. He made sure that his car hung back while keeping the red Tipo in sight best he could.

The centre of town gave way to the suburbs and Finlay was starting to think that the three men were going to somewhere other than the industrial area as he was not familiar with the route. Then suddenly, he turned a corner behind the car and he could see the back of the mound he had been using for surveillance. They had simply used a quicker route that had not been picked up by his map on the phone he was using. He tracked the car round to the front of the waste ground and saw the red estate car turn into the compound he had been watching. Finlay drove his car past the yard and round to the back of the surveillance mound. He parked the Panda in a small copse of trees in the shade and took his rucksack and equipment back up to the mound, training his camera on the gates once again, while covered in his jacket. This would go some way to warding off mosquitos again and the heat of the sun which occasionally poked through the light cloud cover.

*

Mumtaz Ansari was conscious now, though the swelling on his head and face looked even worse. Abdul had taken some solace from this and held out more hope for his elder brother's survival. The Italian called Luigi and Cyrus Sia had come through the night and helped the doctor and Abdul get Mumtaz into an estate car with one rear seat folded down, where he lay covered in a dust sheet. The doctor had sat on the other back seat. Abdul and Luigi had got in the front and driven back to the yard where the truck was in the warehouse.

Abdul had watched the buildings of the Via Appia give way to the suburbs and industrial area while he contemplated the situation he was in. He knew these men regarded him and Mumtaz as being disposable. Sia would kill them as quickly as the Italian criminals if it was easier for the mission. They had no way of defending themselves. Perhaps the only way of saving his brother was to escape and take him to hospital. He would look for a moment to do this.

While removing Mumtaz from the car inside the warehouse he had woken and started to murmur something and raised his arms in the air, he was asking for his mother. Abdul thought this might be the end for him. They had sat him down in the office and given him some water, while they propped him up. Mumtaz had calmed down when he opened his good eye and seen Abdul. His senses appeared to be coming back to him, he gulped the water greedily and asked for more. Abdul had not spoken to his brother for some time. Had moved away to more general conversation after the doctor had confirmed Mumtaz knew his name, location and which month he was in. When he appeared comfortable they moved Mumtaz into the bed in the back of the Scania truck cab. It was more spacious than Abdul had imagined. It had a large bunk bed, a cooker, sink, a cupboard for utensils and even a bench seat where two could sit. It looked custom made for long journeys.
His brother lay on the bottom bunk and the doctor secured a hydration drip to the side of the bed and into Mumtazs' arm. He left some medication with Abdul and instructed him in broken English as to how it should be applied. A combination of powerful pain killers, anti-inflammatory drugs and antibiotics for the large laceration on his scalp. The doctor told Abdul he must ensure his brother should drink plenty of water and try and eat something before he dispensed the drugs. It was obvious that the Italians had agreed that Mumtaz could travel with them. Abdul had requested the doctor travel with them also. Sia had told younger brother that was not possible.

As the doctor had left the warehouse, Sia's daughter had arrived in another car. Her dark striking eyes took in the situation, the face betrayed no emotion. She did not even acknowledge Abdul's presence on the bench seat as she went in the back of the Scania cab to look at Mumtaz. She simply regarded them both as if they were an annoying inconvenience.

Luigi climbed into the driver's seat, 'we are leaving in ten minutes, make sure you have all your things,' he said to both Abdul and Miriam.
Sia climbed in the passenger side, 'Abdul you and your brother stay in the back, Miriam will ride in the passenger seat and Luigi will drive. He will also do all the talking should you stop and speak to anyone. Before you cross the border you need to go in the container, it will take one day to get there. Is this clear to all of you?'

'I need my weapon and our luggage,' responded Abdul.

Sia looked across at him as he turned in the passenger seat. 'I have agreed you will get you're weapons back when the Italians leave after the border. They don't want a repeat of what happened with your brother, that is fair. Miriam and I are armed. The luggage is in the office. I will be following in a red Fiat Tipo.'

As Abdul walked around the back of the articulated rig to fetch his belongings he could sense the strong smell of paint, he looked up and the container was now all dull dark green. No logos were on it, the "roadrunner" logo had been completely painted over while he was in the tenement building in downtown Via Appia. He took his own luggage and made himself comfortable on the back of the truck. His brother was sleeping again, this time it was a deep slumber after eating a small amount of food. Miriam climbed in after throwing a large holdall in the back and covering the rear cabin by drawing the curtain. He then heard the growl of the big twelve cylinder diesel starting and the semi-automatic gears being engaged. The large truck then edged its way on to the yard apron and toward the gate. Abdul looked down at the holdall that Miriam had thrown in the back. He would give it some time and try to see what was inside, he could see an angular shape poking the holdall material near the zip. It might be an assault rifle, he doubted if she just carried a handgun.

Chapter 35

Henry Darcy had been summoned to a crunch meeting at Whitehall. He had been told by his boss Sir Basil to attend as a matter of urgency and to bring his "AI computer wizard woman" with him. Sir Basil Cudlip rarely remembered anyone's name below his direct reporting line or indeed their titles. His sharp mind, however always recalled where they fitted in his sizeable organisation, and he referred to them thus.

It wasn't Henry's first meeting in the wood panelled rooms. He'd been doing this too long to be nervous about it but he had done his homework and gone over the whole scenario with Anna and her team of watchkeepers. His one Achilles heel was he had not heard from Finlay for twenty four hours when things were getting interesting in Brindisi. His strengths were he had the Americans working with him and Anna had come up trumps with Skynet. He felt it would be even more difficult for MI6 nukeprof section to take over. Sir Basil had been excellent and was very much on board. The one concern he had was that the two government secretaries who wielded all the power in the negotiation had come to an agreement to appoint the responsibility to MI6. Henry, like most spies had an inbuilt distrust and dislike of politicians, verging on revulsion. They were there in a short term post trying to make a name for themselves and their appointment with destiny. They would trade their souls for advancement. Behind the scenes deals were often brokered for political gain. Soames and Hashmi were no different from their many predecessors, Henry felt. He had said so to Sir Basil who had chuckled knowingly on the telephone call.

Anna sat at the large old fashioned mahogany table. Anna fidgeted and looked nervous. Henry smoked by an open window though it was strictly banned in Whitehall. He threw the cigarette out the window and waved his arms around when he heard footsteps in the corridor outside. The door opened and it was clear everyone was being ushered in at the same time. Henry immediately became suspicious that there had been a pre-meeting to decide his fate. Perhaps he was getting paranoid.

Sir Basil came in first, his booming voice thanking them for attending at short notice as if they hadn't even spoken at length before the meeting. He made a point of positioning himself at the table between Henry and Anna. Tarique Hashmi then entered the room with Rory Campbell and Charlie Jones, coming in behind Sir Basil in his demob suit they almost look like three small uniformed elves dressed in the best cut of expensive suits Henry had ever seen. He made a mental note to relay his humour to Sir Basil later.

While they were making their introductions to Anna, Edward Soames walked in, he was probably the oldest man in the room. A veteran conservative politician who had been involved in politics from his days as a senior minister with the Thatcher government. He didn't even bother introducing himself and sat at the top of the table away from everyone. Before anyone could speak he addressed them all, almost as if they were his subordinates. 'Good morning everyone, sorry I couldn't attend the last meeting but Tarique decided to call it while I was indisposed up north.' His unfashionable cut and clipped upper class accent was a source of pride to him while middle class politicians in parliament tried to give the impression of coming from impoverished backgrounds. He went on, his hands sweeping over his shaved head as if laying back the long lost hair, 'I have talked to both parties and see no reason to move the responsibility for this operation to MI6, unless a more compelling case can be made now.' He glanced at Hashmi and Campbell positioned across the table from Sir Basil, Henry and Anna.

Tarique Hashmi's face filled with blood, he was not used to being spoken down to, 'I have already made the case clearly to Sir Basil as has Rory who clearly feels this should be headed up by his Nuclear Proliferation section. I believe there have been developments where the perpetrators have landed in Italy. The details of this have yet to be passed on to the section head in MI6 which is frankly unacceptable.'

Soames looked over at Henry to prompt a response. Henry cleared his throat, 'this is a fast moving investigation, that information is barely twenty four hours old. I was about to brief Charlie before I was summoned to this meeting. I…'

Hashmi butted in, 'he should always be your first point of contact, if we have confirmation this is real we need live updates. Sir Basil, your team is not conducting itself professionally.' Hashmi looked at Soames, 'if we don't have a resolution to this I will go to the Prime Minister.'

Soames calmly stared back at Hashmi, he raised a hand to prevent an angry retort from Sir Basil, 'Tarique, the PM is fully aware of what is going on, I don't think it's wise to show discord between our two departments.'

'Well we settle this now or I will call him this afternoon.'

'OK a compromise, how about we you put someone from SIS into the team,' responded Soames.

Hashmi looked at Campbell, the MI6 Director General nodded, 'I would put Charlie himself in. He goes along and rides shotgun with Henry and reports back to me in real time.'

Henry was on the verge of raising an objection but catching Sir Basil's eye decided against it. The veteran spy didn't want to be carrying a deadwood analyst with no field experience. He was already training up Anna, one more reporting outside of his organisation was nothing but a hindrance and an added security risk. He did feel that SIS were relinquishing their claim on leading the investigation, however, at least for now. He gave an almost imperceptible nod to Sir Basil.

'OK agreed,' the DG of MI5 leaned back assuming that was the end of it.

'One more thing,' continued Hashmi, 'any information from your new AI box of tricks is relayed to Charlie at the same time as Henry.'

Henry was completely against this, he had hoped the relatively brief negotiation and acceptance of the Foreign Secretary's demands would suffice but now he was trapped. He couldn't deny that information to Jones if he was on the team. He could brief Anna, however to feed him the information first though, it was manageable.

Again Henry gave a brief nod of acknowledgement to Sir Basil who picked up the confirmation, 'yes that's acceptable to us,' he said while raising his eyebrows to Soames.

The Home Secretary nodded then stood up to indicate the meeting was over, 'fine let's bloody well get on with it then.' Without so much as a departing gesture the ageing politician opened the door and wandered off down the corridor leaving the rest to make their farewells.

Charlie Jones stayed behind with Henry and Anna after the more senior figures had left. Anna de-briefed the MI6 operative on what had been identified by Skynet and left the rest of the overall briefing to Henry. He touched on the way ahead and told Jones to make himself ready for immediate travel. He told him very little, omitting as much as he could about his conversations with Billy Franklin and Major Lamont. If Jones was to accompany them he could find that out for himself.

Anna and Henry took their leave and headed back to Millbank, as the car made its way through the busy lunchtime traffic in London, Henry had something nagging at his mind. Hashmi and Campbell had given in all too quickly on the change of leadership issue. There could only be three reasons for this. Firstly, they thought that the operation would not be a success and MI6 could claim they had tried their best but MI5 had cold shouldered them. Secondly, they knew something that would come to fruition soon and it would inevitably fall to them to resolve leaving MI5 with egg on its face. Lastly, they were up to something internally that could circumvent the home intelligence service while they kept an eye on what they were doing. There was something that was gnawing at his gut about the meeting that just wouldn't go away.

Anna snapped him out of his reverie, 'what are we going to do now boss?'

'Pack our bags and get a flight to Italy after I get a hold of Finlay, he's gone very quiet. You speak to your Skynet team and put someone in charge while you're away. That individual talks to you only and you talk to me first. Once we are fully organised we'll tell golden boy Jones and he can run around trying to catch up. The more he has to logistically arse around the less time he has to poke his snotty fucking nose in our business.'

Anna nodded. She was nervous, these were the most exciting days of her career, a lot was riding on it. While she felt the stress it created she also felt elated though wasn't sure why.

*

Finlay had taken several pictures in the heat of the afternoon. Mostly of trucks leaving the compound of *Toro in Carica* trucking company. They all had the charging bull logo on them and were of similar design, articulated tractor units towing trailers of various lengths and colours. He couldn't see many distinguishing features on them as he was too far away. No doubt Anna could get them blown up and examined. Unfortunately he was not in a position to get number plates without being seen quite easily. The entrance was at an oblique angle to the mound. When the wagons turned toward the exit, which must leave to a motorway, they were obscured by trees at the front of another business.

He was getting adept at transferring the pictures to his laptop and transmitting to Millbank very quickly while keeping an eye along the telephoto lens for more picture opportunities. He was also ready to move quickly should the red Fiat Tipo appear. For all he knew they may be halfway to the Italian border in a truck by now and the car may not exit for days. Once again he had to hedge his bets. He had come down off the mound and strolled past the yard to see if he could pick anything up that was out of the ordinary. He saw the Tipo parked outside of the warehouse through the slots in the fence but the large buildings' massive sliding door was closed. A trailer could have exited and left without him being aware it had come from inside. There were another dozen or so unaccompanied containers in the yard but none that fitted the vague description from Port Sudan. If he had a Geiger counter he could have broken into the yard and seen if any trailer could be detected. He would take another tour around in the car.

As he walked down the back of the mound to avoid being seen and to put his kit in the car, Finlay saw through the wooden copse that a red car was leaving. It had to be the Tipo. He sprinted to the Panda, tossed his Bergen in the back and threw the car around the rough road until he got on to the tarmac road in front of the warehouse. He had raised a lot of dust but that couldn't be helped. He had to get a line of sight on that car so he could see what route it would take. He cursed the fact that Henry wasn't there with his box of tricks to track the car with electronic surveillance. Finlay used the gears to best effect in the underpowered Panda to get past the yard entrance and in the direction of his prey. At the last moment before he thought he would have to take a guess at the junction he saw the Fiat turn in the opposite direction from Brindisi. They were heading for the highway E55 which snaked up the back of the boot shape which was Italy to Bari and beyond.

Finlay dragged his Bergen over into the passenger seat while still trying to use the gears to catch the Tipo, his hand felt past his Glock, camera and laptop and found the satphone. He pulled it out in a tangle of charger cables, eventually freed it and pressed the speed dial for Henry. His old friend answered almost immediately. Finlay didn't wait for any pleasantries, 'Henry, I'm on the trail of a red Fiat Tipo heading north from Brindisi. I think in contains Sia and Stefano from the Sacra Corona, I need backup urgently.'

'OK got it, I've been delayed with political bullshit at this end, I'll get there as soon as I can. I have got the gear you requested. I can be at Aviano in three or four hours as flight is already standing by, I'll update you then, things are moving fast now. Turn your satellite tracking on the satphone, we can pick you up on it when we land. Millbank will keep an eye on it meantime.

'I'm heading in that direction now but who knows, get here as quick as you can and make sure you're tooled up. And get a fucking car with some poke in it!' Finlay hung up, he needed to think.

The Tipo was now on the highway about one kilometre ahead as he pulled off the ramp on to the main road, he put the car into its highest gear, not wanting to get too close. There were a couple of cars between the red Fiat and the Panda. Finlay could be leaving the terrorist weapon in Brindisi or he could be following the terrorists to rendezvous with it. If Sia was in the car he was on the right track. He had to take a chance and get eyes on it close up. The Panda hung back for another ten minutes until he saw an off ramp sign indicating a town a few kilometres ahead. Once again he went
up through the Panda's gears to close on the car he was pursuing. After a couple of minutes he was slowly approaching the Tipo, another car pulled out in front of him to overtake. He kept a reasonable distance behind and as the Panda moved past behind the other car he could clearly see Sia in the passenger seat of the Tipo and another driving. The same man he had seen drive into the yard – bingo! The other man appeared to be Stefano, Luigi's brother whom he recognised from the pictures he'd been sent. He would pull off at the next exit and get back on the highway behind them. As Finlay accelerated to get well beyond his target he saw a green articulated unit in the distance, who knows perhaps they were driving behind as a security tail, they were moving at approximately the same speed as the truck, well below the car speed limit. Maybe he'd hit the jackpot.

The Panda pulled off the exit ramp and negotiated a roundabout slowly to allow the Tipo to get past it on the main highway, then it edged back on to the E55. The red Tipo was out of sight. Once again Finlay hurriedly accelerated the little car, the engine was screaming in protest as it reached its limit with each gear change. After five minutes the Tipo edged into view around the sweeping bend in the road. There was no sign of any trucks from where he was around one kilometre behind Cyrus Sia and the Stefano. Once the car was sighted by Finlay he relaxed more into his seat, feeling his heart rate go down, he had time to gather his thoughts now. The old soldier positioned his Glock, knife and phone for easy access underneath the

Bergen and settled back for what he assumed was going to be a long drive.

Chapter 36

Saeed Abdul Raheem sat on the balcony of the little chalet high in the Alps above Chamonix and enjoyed the sweet tea he had made himself along with a breakfast of eggs and beef sausages with houmous and Arabic bread. He had come to this part of the world before as Omar Fakhoury to rest and plan his next move in the game of violent chess against the West and the "Great Satan" in particular. The Mubarizun had met here on a few separate occasions. He loved the crisp clean air and the view unobstructed by atmospheric pollution and sand as it was so often in the Middle East where he operated. It reminded him of the Mount Lebanon range in some ways, though it was cooler and more mountainous. He had even seen some Cedar trees in the valley further down, obviously they had not been native to France or the alpine mountains but the smell brought back memories. He owned a mountain hut near Mount Lebanon itself, nestling in the very trees that were on the flag of Lebanon. He loved their smell. The Mubarizun committee had met there over a decade ago, free from surveillance and interference. This would not be the case now, there were too many spies trying to make a fast buck in Lebanon, allied to technological advances such as advanced drone technology. Their lives could be wiped out and their cause eliminated in a single second from above.

Here in France the selfish enemy would never dare to launch such a strike on its own soil. It would have to come up the valley in vehicles or via a noisy helicopter giving some warning. He had two of his men positioned in a village at the bottom of the valley road that led to his rented chalet. They posed as mountain bikers enjoying the summer in the Alps. It gave them excuses to keep watch on the road from above on the longer summer days. His means of escape would be through the mountains in the area to Switzerland. He had devised a route many years ago before the first Mubarizun meeting so could always return to the area when he could.

Saeed sat on in a recess under the eaves overlooking the drive to his chalet which was filled by a large Carthago Chic luxury motorhome. He had acquired it from money wired to him by Hassan Makhlouf three months before and had kept it at his long term let. He had chosen it because it had a payload of over a tonne in weight, slept four people comfortably if it needed to but was small enough to drive in the streets of a town or city. He had made some changes to the vehicle, the axle at the back had been replaced with a double wheel axle to take more load and the engine uprated from the one hundred and eighty horsepower diesel to a two hundred and eighty horse power, ten cylinder truck engine. A new heavier duty close ratio gearbox and larger calliper disk brakes had been added. The whole project had all been done legitimately through a German dealer who specialised in designing motorhomes for long term use for remote and mountainous areas. The "garage" floor under the double bunk had been strengthened accordingly allowing almost three tonnes to be placed above the axles. The bunks, toilet and cooking arrangements were standard. He had personally converted the cupboards to have false backings to store weapons in them behind the clothing and food stores. The windows were heavily tinted and he had ensured that he had the requisite driving licence to drive the vehicle. Saeed could have easily bought a much more heavy duty motorhome, the type of vehicle that was based on a truck chassis, but as always his planning had been meticulous. The means of delivery of his device needed to be unobtrusive. The coach builder in Germany has asked if he could put the logo of his reputable business on the sides and front of the vehicle which, along with the vehicle certificate, would enhance its value. Saeed had declined. He wanted it to look like the stock model externally. This was his means of weapon delivery to its target. The beauty of such a vehicle is you can put it in any caravan park for any length of time you wish and live in it ensuring security from prying eyes. He didn't want motorhome "anoraks" asking him questions about the conversion and wanting to look around. A truck, trailer or car was less flexible and questions would be asked if left to for too long. You also had to live remote to where the weapon was stored. With his relatively compact motorhome all these problems were resolved.

Saeed finished his breakfast, he would take a shower and drive the Carthago down to the nearest fuel station to fill it up in preparation for the rendezvous. He also needed a bit more practice in driving the vehicle on the mountain roads.

Chapter 37

The big Scania rig had just passed Pesaro, they had been on the road for over seven hours. Mumtaz had slept soundly, even Abdul had slept well for a couple of hours on the top bunk. He could see the top of Luigi's head over the partition curtain from the top bunk. He couldn't see Miriam as she was smaller but had heard her ask a couple of brief questions about the route to Luigi. The cab was very well insulated and quiet with an efficient suspension which had encouraged the brothers to sleep, there was little else to do in the back of the tractor unit. Abdul had jumped down from the bunk a couple of times to check on his brother. The second time he sat for a while on the bench seat and when he heard no movement from Miriam he softly unzipped her holdall. He immediately uncovered a CZ scorpion sub machine gun, a very light and compact weapon he knew made mostly from polymer. He could also see a thirty round magazine inserted in it and a spare lying along its length. His only problem was he had never fired one. He couldn't see a bolt to pull back, perhaps it was on the other side. He could see that the safety was on. He had hoped it was an AK47, something he had trained on in Pakistan, simple. He couldn't risk using it if she had a sidearm on her and Luigi was undoubtedly also armed. Abdul couldn't save his brother so quickly by overpowering them both. Sia and that animal Stefano were also following and Abdul wasn't sure how to drive the truck. His brother was supposed to take over the wagon after crossing the border, he had a Heavy Goods Vehicle licence, but was in no fit state to do so. Perhaps they thought Abdul could drive or had made other arrangements. The truck had stopped at a roadside rest facility once for ten minutes to use the toilet and get a coffee but that was all. There had been no sign of the red Fiat, he hadn't asked why.

Abdul got down from the top bunk once again and drew the curtain back on Miriam's side, 'are we going to stop for the night or are we driving all the way to the border? I need to take my brother to the toilet and change his dressings.'

Luigi looked over the cab as he was driving but Miriam spoke, 'we'll be stopping once we get past San Marino, there is a truck stop just before Imola, we can eat their and use the facilities. That's when we start to cut across from east to west. We sleep in the truck though, no hotels.' She kept her eyes on the road, not glancing at Abdul once.

'Is Mr Sia and the other Italian still following us?'

Miriam didn't answer, Luigi looked over, 'yes of course but they don't make contact with us, in case we have a tail. That's what they are there for. The same will happen next stop.'

Two kilometres behind the Scania R, the drivers had changed. Sia had struck up a conversation with Stefano about the process of following the truck and keeping their distance. They could have put a tracker on the unit but the possibility of security forces picking up the signal was prohibitive. It had to be done the old fashioned way of speeding up occasionally to actually see the wagon then dropping back. Sia asked how Stefano had got the sizeable red rash on his right hand and wrist, he could see it clearly on his arm while Stefano drove. The Italian had responded saying it was an allergy of some kind to something he had eaten. Sia note it was getting worse, it occurred to him that he may have got a dose of radiation from the weapon if he had been snooping. He would mention it to Saeed when they met, perhaps he needed to be eliminated along with the other one, though he doubted if the man would know what he was looking at. It was his leader's decision. He also noted that the man had a Beretta down the side of his door in a plastic bag, he had made no attempt to cover it up and had taken it round to the passenger side when they had swapped driving duties. Sia knew he carried a sizeable overnight bag which could also contain weapons.

Another two or three kilometres behind the Tipo, Finlay yawned as he shook his head and concentrated on the road ahead. The red Fiat had stopped at a large truck stop in the car section well away from where all the wagons were parked. They had simply waited for a while and pulled away after Sia had got out to get coffee and some food. They had not gone to fuel the car. Finlay figured his Panda with a small engine should have a better fuel consumption but it was starting to run low now. The last thing he wanted was for them to leave when he was in the middle of re-fuelling. He hoped that he could fill the car in tandem at a sizeable station unnoticed by the two men he was tracking.

Henry had called Finlay when he arrived at Aviano. Of course neither were sure of the destination of the red Fiat but Henry said he would head south-west toward Bologna. That way he could turn for the east coast if their prey had gone that way or for the west coast if that were their preferred route. Henry had splashed out and hired or borrowed a BMW 550. A large and powerful car with four wheel drive capable of keeping up with any car on the road while remaining relatively unobtrusive. They agreed that they would use both cars to track the two men. They would have much more flexibility. One could go ahead and look to see if there were a trailer or truck unit ahead while the other car remain tailing the Tipo. Fuelling or stopping for any reason would not be a problem as it could be alternated. Finlay could hear Anna shouting hello in the background, hardly the behaviour of a spook. Henry didn't sound approving at all and talked over her background greeting. Finlay smiled.

Henry had updated him briefly on the latest state of affairs over the phone but was unwilling to go into too much detail. The British government and secret services had started to wake up to the threat, they understood that they were on to something serious. Before briefing other European entities they wanted confirmation of "dirty bomb" or some live threat pertaining to a nuclear device. Confirmation with a particle detector would suffice. As yet they had heard nothing from Billy Franklin who was attempting to get a Geiger counter on the dhow in Port Sudan. Rumours of serious threats were given monthly in the west. The British government was already aware of the false rumours of "weapons of mass destruction" in Iraq and the part it played in public confidence when it was proven they never existed. Inevitably there would be leaks from any foreign agencies they informed. Finlay knew that the CIA and MI5 were leaky enough without involving the rest of Europe.

Henry had also managed to lose Charlie Jones before he had even got the chance to get on board. He was supposed to join them in the next forty eight hours once he's got himself a flight into Italy or wherever their destination was to be. Henry was to keep SIS updated as promised. As the sun commenced its decline into the western horizon, Finlay sipped the last of his service station coffee, now lukewarm, and cracked open a window to let in some fresh air to keep him alert. It had already been a long day and he strongly suspected an even longer night forthcoming. At least his fuel problem would relieve the monotony, whatever the outcome.

Chapter 38

Zurich had been inhabited by humans for thousands of years. Its position at the north end of Lake Zurich was a naturally good point to inhabit. The river Limmat flowed north from the lake's shores and provided access to a valley that led down and away from the Alps to France and Germany. The Romans had used it for a taxation pointy for goods trafficked on the river into Germany. After the fall of the Roman Empire German tribes settled on the Swiss plateau and the German language was used predominantly in the city from then until now. As the largest city in Switzerland it had benefitted a great deal from the success of Swiss banks, known famously for their discreteness when dealing with clients. Despite modern regulation and many scandals that aura persisted and investment continued.

Ebrahim Khorasani, now dressed in a suit like any Swiss banker, walked through the narrow ancient streets of the city with an umbrella keeping the summer rain from getting him wet. He had booked into a cheap hotel by Zurich's standards and decided to clear his head and enjoy a couple of cigarettes before going to Paradeplatz to visit the first of his banks. He loved Switzerland. He had little reason to come here through his work unless he was following a target or meeting an informer. He often used these reasons as an excuse to check on his accounts and invest money. He also used it as an unofficial holiday, away from the goldfish bowl that could be Tehran. Khorasani had stayed in a backstreet hotel called simply "The Persian". His instinct was to use another hotel as the link to Iran could cause him to bump into someone he didn't want to meet but he had decided to stay there one more time before he made his new life elsewhere. Swiss immigration laws were too prohibitive. He would struggle to get nationality or residency here, he would have to live elsewhere.

Paradeplatz, was a square with several banks on it crisscrossed by tramlines. It was one of the most expensive areas of real estate in the world. He walked carefully over the pedestrian crossing and up and into the grand building that housed Credit Suisse, one of the country's largest banks. He asked to see the Manager that looked after his accounts and was shown to the waiting room. While he sat sipping a coffee the Managers' secretary came in and gave him a message. It was from Zarrin telling him she was in Zurich and wanted to meet him urgently. She had left a telephone number. He read it again. He felt as he had in Imam Khomeini airport and on the Turkish Airlines flight, trapped! Khorasani could feel himself starting to sweat despite the coolness of the bank waiting room and his damp socks from walking in the pouring rain. What in God's name was going on? How could this inexperienced dizzy girl know where he was? She was being ran by a puppet master. But who? Not VAJA or the Revolutionary Guard, he would never have got out of Iran. It must be foreign intelligence.

The turmoil of his thoughts was interrupted by his account manager. He sat through the meeting and did his best to discuss how to move some of his money out of the account, failing that he wanted easier access to moving large amounts quickly. He couldn't absorb what was being discussed. The man had to repeat himself several times. He even asked Khorasani if he was OK. The Iranian made his excuses about feeling ill and asked if he could meet with him to go over the options at a later date. Khorasani hurriedly stood up, refused the offer of using the washrooms, and walked hurriedly out of the bank into the pouring rain. The deluge was getting worse, almost echoing his predicament.

Chapter 39

Finally, just after Imola the red Fiat Tipo had pulled off to a large motorway rest stop which catered for all types of vehicles. It had two low cost hotels which had obviously benefitted over the years due to their proximity to the famous Formulae One racetrack. Finlay cautiously followed the car in to one of the hotel car parks. He watched the men exit the vehicle and go into the hotel. The old soldier then drove his Fiat Panda to the fuel station, filling it up with petrol, before returning to in the hotel car park. He took the opportunity to grab some food in the service station as he didn't know what would come next. He hoped they were staying in the hotel. Finlay parked the Panda in the furthest corner of the car park where he could still see Stefano's car near the reception area. He called Henry and settled back to await his arrival.

Unknown to Finlay, the large Scania and its load were less than a kilometre away in secure parking for trucks behind a fenced area surrounded by trees. The area was accessed via a security gate and covered by surveillance cameras. The primary reason for this was to dissuade both theft from trucks and to prevent illegal immigrants from accessing the trailers overnight whilst the drivers slept.

Luigi and Miriam were resting in the bunks while Abdul took his brother to the washing facilities. He had given his brother a double dose of pain killers so he could walk to the shower area. Abdul took Mumtaz into the cubicle and stripped off after removing his brothers' clothes. He put the changing room bench in the shower and let Mumtaz sit on it while he washed him and changed his dressings. He then saw to himself. As he dried himself with a towel, he addressed his brother in Urdu, 'I need to get you out of here Mumtaz, you are in danger of dying of that head wound.'

'I am still in pain but we must go on Abdul. We cannot fail. Allah has given us this task.'

'We can fight another day, Mumtaz, we are being used as tools by Fakhoury and Sia, they care nothing for us.'

'Do you think we joined the Jihad so people would care for us, my brother?'

'No but I do not intend that you and I sacrifice our lives fighting the Italian mafia, that would be pointless. I can get a weapon and kill both the Italian and that cold hearted bitch. We can be gone from here tonight and get you to a hospital.'

'And then where would we be. Failures. We have an opportunity to strike against the unbelievers, against the crusaders who have killed our people for a thousand years. Then we can truly bring Islam to Europe after we have turned its people to ashes.' Mumtazs' words were slow and deliberate due to the grogginess from the head wound damage but it was obvious he was thinking clearly.

'I think they may even try and kill you once we are in a more secluded place as you are a hindrance.'

'Then they will also have to kill you Abdul and they won't because they need you. That is why we are both alive. I have been thinking this through while lying in that truck.'

'You know more about this mission than you are telling me. We were to plant this bomb and set a timer, anyone can do that. Why not Cyrus Sia or Miriam or any other men that Fakhoury or Makhlouf have?'

Mumtaz looked up at his brother from his bench seat, his eyes moist, 'because there is no timer Abdul, just a switch I have to close.' Abdul Ansari suddenly understood and sat on the bench on his towel next to his brother, still naked. 'You have agreed to be a suicide bomber.' He started straight ahead at the wall. 'Why could you not tell me of this?'

'You would never have agreed to join me.'

'And where does this leave me?' said Abdul. His momentary realisation that he was going to lose his brother anyway gave way to anger.

'Your job is to be with me in my final hours and then to leave me to do my job. To tell the world of the great jihadi I am and follow in my footsteps. You told me you'd be willing to give your life to the will of Allah. Are you scared now it is coming to fruition?'

'I am not scared. I am also not an idiot who is kept in the dark by his own brother.'

'You are not in the dark, you know everything now. Keep close to me in the next few days, I am feeling better, I have a destiny, please don't ruin it by doing something stupid. I have an emergency number I can call Fakhoury on. I will ask him to give instructions to get our weapons back.'

Abdul did not respond but simply glared at his brother as he got up from the bench in the small cubicle and dressed himself. As they left the large toilet facility, they saw Luigi sitting on the bench by the door, next to the cashier's entrance. He obviously didn't trust the brothers' intentions and had followed them from the Scania. He was stripped off with a towel round his heavily tattooed torso. Mumtaz greeted him and told the Italian he was feeling much better. Luigi went to use the shower as the two brothers made their way to the truck. Miriam watched them from the rolled down passenger window as they headed back to the vehicle.

As the sun set there was no sign of either Sia or Stefano. Finlay had dosed a little but he still managed to keep an eye on the car. The car park was lit so he could see anyone coming out of reception. He had eaten all his fast food without enjoying it and gone to use the toilet in the hotel on one occasion. Just as he got out the Panda to stretch his legs a BMW circled round the car park and pulled in next to his space. It was Henry and Anna.

Finlay jumped quickly in the back of car and Henry drove the BMW to the rest stop car park away from the hotel to prevent both vehicles being seen together from the hotel. They greeted each other warmly, both Finlay and Anna were almost awkward when they said hello. Henry went on to brief Finlay in more depth on events. They needed confirmation on the Geiger that Henry had brought with him to mobilise help from European agencies. They needed to get a tracker on the red Fiat and of course positive identification on the truck was the absolute priority. Harry had a tracking device monitor glued to the BMW's dashboard. All agreed that Anna would keep watch on the red Fiat for any movement, Henry would get a chip on the car and Finlay would do his best to try and identify the trailer. While Finlay was gone Henry and Anna would occupy the Panda for their tasks.

Mumtaz sat on the passenger seat of the truck while Luigi slept in the top bunk. Miriam had gone to use the wash facilities. Abdul had also tried to sleep in the bottom bunk but had got up and sat in the driver's seat, he would keep watch with Mumtaz until Miriam returned. The elder Ansari brother made a telephone sign with his thumb and little finger and gently opened the door of the Scania. He lowered himself down clumsily but quietly on to the ground and closed the door, leaving it off the latch for re-entry.

Abdul sat in the dark watching his brother shuffle round behind some trailers in front of them and fumble around for the phone in his pocket. He obviously couldn't see very well and moved from the trailer into a spotlight arc in the truck park to dial the number he was looking at on a piece of paper. Fakhoury forbade them all to commit numbers to the telephone memory.

Ann had felt her heartbeat rise when she was told that she would be responsible for tracking the movements of the occupants of the Fiat. She now kept watch as Henry walked toward the target car to place the magnetic tracking device. She watched as he approached the car. As he did so a car pulled into the hotel car park and started to drop off some occupants and their luggage. Henry changed direction and walked into reception. The car moved off and the driver found an empty space and returned to join his passengers in the rest stop hotel. Henry re-emerged walking slowly, looking around as he did so. With the aplomb of a veteran spy he dropped his telephone at the back wheel of the Fiat Tipo and bent down to pick it up. While he did so he fitted the magnetic tracker under the wheel arch and walked back to the rest stop car park to test he had a signal in the BMW. Ten minutes letter he texted an "OK" to Anna and Finlay.

Finlay had left the BMW after donning his dark climbing gear he had taken from the Panda, tucking his Glock into the jacket pocket and attaching the knife to his belt. The Geiger was a bulkier item which he slung over his shoulder. He climbed the embankment that separated the truck park from the hotel and rest stop and lowered himself down on his belly. He crawled around the perimeter fence to find a way in. They had chosen a good place to stop if the articulated truck was in here. It was completely fenced off, had a number of security cameras and a guard on the gate. One other guard was patrolling the parking area which was huge. There must have been one hundred wagons parked here of various shapes and sizes. It would be hard to find his target in the dark if it were there, most of the vehicles were obscured by others or by the shower, cafe and toilet facilities in the centre of the area. He would of course be looking for the bull logo but he knew it could be in an unmarked truck, he had seen several leave the *Toro in Carica* yard in Brindisi. He would have to systematically work his way around from the spot that he managed to get in and also avoid the cameras monitored from the check-in point.

The grass on the embankment was damp, he crawled along the fence for around ten minutes and found a section where it was not firmly connected to the ground. It looked as if it may have been used as a shortcut to the more comprehensive facilities in the rest stop, or by illegals trying to get in the trucks. He lifted the fence easily and crawled under, pulling the particle detector behind him. It was an area without any cameras. He crawled under a trailer and switched on the Geiger counter, turning the volume as low as it could go. It started to click softly as it picked up natural background radiation, the analogue dial was still well within the green zone. Finlay started to work his way around the trailers from where he had entered. He occasionally stopped in a shadow of a truck to swing the counter 360 degrees to see if there was a stronger signal in any particular direction.

Abdul yawned in the cab as he continued to watch his brother. Mumtaz had obviously managed to dial the emergency number to Fakhoury into the phone and had moved between two trailers to have the conversation. He had come out again and was pressing the buttons, he assumed redial, on the phone, must have problems getting a signal. As he looked around he caught movement over to the right in among some trailers. He saw a shape in the distance pointing a device at the trailers, it was moving toward his brother. It may be immigration looking for illegals, he'd better warn Mumtaz to get back in the cab to prevent complications. Abdul looked around for something to use in case it got rough, there was a large shifting spanner in the cab door, he picked it up. Almost as an afterthought Abdul felt under the seat, his fingers felt around the shape of a handgun. He pulled it and it made a tearing sound as the tape pulled away from the floor surface. He stopped and listened, there was no sound from Luigi behind him in the bunk. Abdul replaced the spanner, tucked the Beretta his waist band, dropped down from the Scania and walked toward where his brother was making the call. Finlay cautiously went from trailer to trailer, then swung the counter in an arc once again, he could hear the particle detector pick up on his right hand side. He pointed it back in the area he had heard the increase in clicking. The meter started to climb into the amber zone occasionally edging into red and setting of the warning light in one particular direction. As he edged underneath the cover of a trailer he could hear someone talking in English on a telephone. He muted the Geiger counter and slowly and softly walked toward the person making the call and listened.

'……. I have suffered a painful head wound Mr Omar and neither the Italians nor your people will give us our weapons. How can we be jihadis with no guns?' There was silence as he listened to the response.

'Yes, but we will be at the border tomorrow, we need the freedom to operate and take on the project, you must trust us we are dedicated people……….' He was obviously being interrupted on the call.

Finlay decided to wait to hear the outcome of the call and hopefully follow the individual to his target. The sixth sense he possessed just returned to Finlay as he ducked to go under the trailer but a bit too late, a blow intended for his head glanced off his shoulder. He swivelled round and saw a slim shape lurch to his right as the force of the glancing blow carried its momentum further than the assailant intended. He had felt a metal shape hit him, smelled gun oil and knew instinctively it was a firearm. Using his left heel of his hand he drove it upward and under his attackers' jaw, Finlay felt a vertebrae crack and the man's head snap back. At the same time the man had grasped Finlay's hood firmly and thrown his weight at the crouching soldier, knocking them both under the trailer. The seasoned paratrooper managed to roll out from under the weight of the man, jumped on him and delivered a short but very hard punch to his face. He felt the hold on his jacket ease off and the body go limp.

Finlay let go of Abdul and stood up, he couldn't see the gun in his attacker's hand. He looked around for it and the heard someone's feet move.

'Put your fucking hands above your head where I can see them or I'll blow your head off!'

Finlay did as he was told, it struck him that the statement was a Hollywood cliché, but effective nonetheless. He turned as he did so and saw a dark skinned dishevelled man with a large bandage wrapped around his head. It was the same voice that he had heard on the phone. The man was unsteady on his feet and pointing a distinctive Beretta semi-automatic pistol less than one metre from his head. Finlay didn't know that it was the same one that Abdul had dropped. He had to assume both men were armed.

'Step back and away from him.' As Mumtaz spoke he put his cell phone torch on with his free hand to light up Finlay's face. Finlay peered in the glare of the torch. He could no longer see the man but he had the phone torch positioned behind the Beretta he had in his other hand. It was a Beretta M9, an excellent weapon used by the US military. Finlay had used one on the firing range many times. It had a safety on the automatic slide that could be used by left or right handed people. He looked and saw the white notch was uncovered by the switch, not the red. The weapon's safety catch was on. Finlay jumped forward with his right foot to get within reach of the weapon. His left arm swept upward hitting Mumtazs' forearm pushing it and his body away from him to the right. In the same movement the old soldier's right arm pulled the Sykes Fairbairn from its sheath and stabbed the jihadist under the rib cage. The knife was buried to its full extent then twisted on removal to cause maximum bleeding. As Mumtaz, already weak from his head injury, went limp, Finlay pulled his second assailant's body in front of him and in one deft movement cut the man's throat. He stepped away from Mumtaz as he dropped and looked around for the Beretta as he took the Glock from his pocket. He surveyed the scene, it had only taken a few seconds. The first man had gone, he must have crawled under the trailer. Finlay looked around the yard for a couple of minutes there was no sign of the first man. He saw the security car driving around the perimeter from the main gate and decided to abort the rest of his mission. He took a picture of the dead man's face with his phone and searched him for belongings such as a wallet or identification. He had none. Finlay pushed Mumtaz under the fifth wheel of the truck they had fought near. The soldier cleaned his knife on the dead man's tracksuit, picked up the Beretta, switched off the Geiger counter and made his way back to the fence.

*

Henry had made himself busy while sitting in the BMW. Anna had joined him for a short while and brought him some coffee from the Costa in the rest stop. The tracking device gave them a little more freedom to operate as they could see if the red Fiat moved from the confines of the BMW. After she had left to go back to the Panda he had called Billy Franklin. There was still no news from his agents in Port Sudan on particle detection of the dhow, Billy felt sure it would follow in the next forty eight hours. While he had been on the call a text had come through from "NH". Nadav Harel, the Director of Shin Bet, the Israeli equivalent of MI5, the home security service. Henry liked the fact that he could deal with the top men in Israel, they were very much hands on compared to other Western security services. He had got the introduction through, Yossi Avrahami, the head of Mossad whom he knew from his MI6 days in the Middle East. He hadn't met Harel but had relayed his request for information on Fakhoury after briefing Avrahami on the dhow and the cargo's unknown destination from Port Sudan. He gave the information freely and requested detail on the pictures of Fakhoury. Whether he was the same man that had stood with Yasser Arafat on the old picture he had from Major al Qubaisi in Abu Dhabi. The man called Saeed Rahim.

He returned the call immediately.

'Mr Darcy, I assume,' said the voice with a clear American accent on the other side of the telephone.'

'I appreciate the promptness of your call, Director Harel.'

'Please call me Nadav, Mr Darcy. To get straight to the point, this is the same man. We have been tracking him any time he gets near Israel or the West Bank. What do you need to know?'

'Really some background on him and his organisation.'

'Well he is a very careful and clever man, I'd prefer not to discuss this by telephone but I know speed is of the essence. His organisation is called the Mubarizun, you may know this. It consists of less than a dozen members with access to large amounts of capital. They fund, rather than carry out terrorist activities themselves and they are always looking for the big one. They want another nine eleven. They feel that this woke up Arabian Islamic consciousness and another attempt would set the ball rolling on all-out war with the West. If you remember, Al Qaeda was also so secretive in the early nineties before they managed to commit some major attacks. The more they claimed credit the closer they came to being penetrated. These people will only claim credit for one major attack it seems. We have struggled to find out the identity of the others in the Mubarizun, they are very secretive, with almost little or no connections outside of the organisation. We believe they may have access to information inside the security services including yours and the CIA. Hell, we wouldn't rule out a mole within Mossad or Shin Bet. This is also something new.'

'Is Raheem and his group capable of such an operation as I outlined to Yossi?'
'Yes they are. It is rare for Raheem to become closely involved. If he is then it is the big one they have sought. If there is a dirty bomb or

such device that may be why he has raised himself from his lair. The last we knew of his whereabouts was that he was in the Yemen, around Hudaydah or Sanaa. He disappeared two or three months ago. We lost track of him, he probably did leave by boat as air and land travel would be very hazardous. He may have crossed the border on foot into Oman, but boat most likely.'

'Do you have more footage of him or a recording of his voice?' asked Henry.

'We have more pictures, some very clear, with and without beard, but no voice. He has never spoken in public to our knowledge and we have never traced a call,' responded Harel.

'I may be able to help you with the voice. He was tracked and filmed in Dubai.'

'We would certainly appreciate that data Mr Darcy, as you know we don't talk too much to the rest of the Middle East which is a pity. I would also be grateful if we are kept updated. We are tracking someone who may have been involved in the African Tide cargo. We will of course reciprocate. Have you tracked the cargo from Sudan?'

Henry didn't want to give away too much, 'yes we have…. we are pretty sure it's Southern Europe. We'll keep you updated.'

'Thank you. We're keeping an eye on our borders anyway. As always. Pleasure to make your acquaintance Mr Darcy. I hope we can meet some time, perhaps have a beer together in Jerusalem.'

'Likewise. And the beer sounds like a good idea Nadav. Please call me Henry. Goodnight.'

Henry reflected on the information. It was all adding up to a big one. He just needed that meter reading. No one could criticise them if it were a positive one and he could up the stakes and support.
Meantime he needed to try and get that car to lead them to the truck. He hoped it wasn't a decoy and the truck was either still in Brindisi

or about to make Rome radioactive for the next thousand years. Perhaps the seat of Christianity was their target. They didn't have a huge beef with the Italians though. They did with the French and the British. Paris would be easier than trying to cross the channel. It kind of depended on whether they thought the security services in Europe were on to them. They may set the bloody thing off in a layby if they thought their number was up, another good reason to watch rather than blow their cover too early. He'd see what Fin had discovered in the truck park.

His phone rang again. It was Anna.

*

Abdul lay in the bunk of the Scania as the truck pulled out of the Imola rest stop in the early hours of the morning. He had some paper towels he had found next to the sink held to his nose. It was swelling up. His back was in agony, the blow to his jaw must have done something to the top of his spine. He had taken a couple of Mumtazs' painkillers. He had staggered back to the truck and met Miriam climbing out of the cab coming to look for him. She had obviously come back from the showers and found he had gone. Abdul explained what had happened. She cursed him and woke Luigi, telling him in no uncertain terms to move the truck back on the highway before someone raised the alarm. Abdul had been bundled in the back and told to clean himself up. He had objected and wanted to get his brother's body. Miriam had stuck her Scorpion in his face and clicked the safety to "off". The younger Ansari had backed down, he knew his brother was dead, he had been dispatched like a sacrificial goat. By the time he had backed off Miriam into the back of the Scania living quarters Luigi had the rig in on the way to the security gate. They were behind another vehicle that was leaving. The traffic coming in and out was continuous so their particular vehicle would not necessarily be seen as complicit to anything that had gone on in the yard if they left immediately. As he drove out Miriam could see the security vehicle heading toward the gate from inside the compound, probably to check the cameras.

'Where is my fucking gun?' Abdul could hear Luigi shouting, furious that the Beretta had been removed when he felt under the seat after he left the on ramp on to the main highway.

'I took it to find Mumtaz, I dropped it when I was attacked.'

'You are fucking amateur, boy,' shouted Luigi in broken English. 'Lose my fucking gun, I break your nose too.'

Miriam swept the curtain back and came in and sat beside Abdul. She appeared more conciliatory now, probably so she could find out what happened. He explained what had occurred when he went to find his brother.

'You should have waited for me,' she said, shaking her head.

'If we had our weapons this would not have occurred, we are not familiar with Beretta, never trained on it. If we had the Tokarev's this would not have happened. We trained with them and the AK. This man would have been dead.'

'Yet he beat you and killed your brother, with only had a knife. This man is a professional. His job is to kill quietly. We are being followed by the best. At least we know now. He must have been looking for the truck and its cargo. I will call my father.'

*

Before Henry could even talk into his cell phone Anna said, 'they are on the move Henry. I am watching them get into their car. In a hurry.'

'Shit, our man is still in the truck park, you call him wait for him there, then follow me. I'll wait for them to leave and track them in my car.'

'Henry….' He had already hung up. Anna had used his name, she cursed herself. Henry had told her not to do that more than once. As she picked up her phone she heard someone pull the passenger side door handle of the Panda which she had locked from inside. It was Finlay.

He threw his equipment in the back, 'let's get out of here.'

'Yes it appears that the red Fiat and its occupants are on the move. So is Henry. How did you know?'

'I didn't, I had to deal with a couple of Tangoes who jumped me in the truck park. One got away, must have raised the alarm.'

'Oh my god, are you OK?'

'Yes fine, I reckon that truck is there though. Blew our cover, not good, they know we're on to them now. Was listening to one on a call and the other bastard sneaked up on me. I should have seen him.'

Anna could tell he was furious with himself, she would have simply been relieved. 'What happened to the one that didn't get away?' she was beginning to realise the implications of what he had just said.

'He's dead,' said Finlay, 'he had a handgun, it's in the back. I wasn't in the position to take him in unfortunately. The one I killed had an English accent. The other one didn't talk. I have a picture of the dead one.'

While they were talking Anna had started the car and manoeuvred on to the north bound highway. Her hands were shaking a little as she changed gear but she was determined not to let Finlay see her shock at what had transpired so quickly. 'Can you send the picture to the watchkeepers on Skynet via your Satphone, the number is on my phone in the glove compartment.'

The old paratroop Major looked across at her and smiled. She really was keeping it together. 'Yes of course, quick thinking.'

He doubted if his old compatriot would be keeping it together quite so well once he'd told him what had happened. He stowed his kit where it couldn't be seen and removed the rounds from the Beretta before making the call.

*

'Fuck, fuck, fuck!' exclaimed Henry Darcy at the very top of his voice on the hands free in the BMW, 'this is not good Major, not good at all! They may set that thing off at any time now and we'll be to blame.'

'What's done is done Henry, it wasn't intentional I can assure you. I doubt if the weapon is in a state of readiness if it's in the back of a trailer.'

Henry took some deep breaths, there was a pregnant silence on the phone.

'Hello, hello…,' came from Finlay.

'Just get the car up behind me will you, I'll have to consider our next move. We can only tail them for now.'

'Henry, it was definitely the men we are after. I overheard a conversation where one was complaining that his comrades had taken the weapons from him. He also had a swollen face and a fucking great bandage round his head. He didn't know how to operate the weapon, was not familiar with it. I don't think we're dealing with the masterminds here. There also appears to be disagreement in the ranks.'

Henry rang off. He needed to think. The fact that the tail car took off as soon as Finlay had his altercation proved that it was linked to a team of men most probably in an articulated unit in the truck park. That showed they were on the right path and this was not a decoy. They had to keep that tail without being spotted. They two men in the Tipo would be on high alert now, so they had to keep out of visual range. Thank god he had that tracking device on. They could well be looking for it though. He would have to get a visual if they stopped. There was an alarm if someone pulled or moved the magnetic device from its position. He didn't want it attached to another innocent vehicle and head off on a wild goose chase. He kept the track on the Satnav about two kilometres ahead. The target was moving at one hundred kilometres per hour, the truck speed limit. Finlay had told him that is what it had done since Brindisi. He kept one eye on the tracking device location as he drove north-west on the E45 toward Milan. He could see the Panda in the mirror two cars behind.

The phone rang again, it was Finlay. 'Head office has come back, the dead guy needed a bit of work because of the state of his face. It was the elder Ansari brother which matches up with the fact that he had a Birmingham accent. I suspect the other guy was the young one, difficult to tell in the dark, he didn't speak.'

'Ok, well let's try and find out somehow if the truck is ahead of us. We must not get blown again. Would you know the wagon if you saw it?'

'It may or may not have a charging bull on it, I didn't see it. They won't have seen your BMW, my Panda may have been clocked. It's probably worth changing cars and letting me take a look once it gets light, won't see much in the dark. It'll most likely be well in front of the red Fiat.'

Chapter 40

Saeed had spent the day down in the valley. The sun had been shining as he changed down through the gears on the way down through the switch backs. He drove the Carthago Chic carefully. Halfway down from the escarpment where his chalet was to the village two mountain bikers cycled down a rough track on to a viewpoint. They had stood and watched the motorhome zig zag down the mountain, greeted Saeed warmly and with deference. He offered them some food and water before resuming his journey. They were good men, Yemenis, used to the mountains, small, slim and very fit. They could live on nothing. They two warriors had served him for ten years and their loyalty and courage were not in question.

He had filled the motorhome up in the village, with the sharp peak of the mighty Aguille Du Grepon high in the distance on the clear day. Saeed then parked the motorhome in the village square and went into a nearby café and had lunch on the balcony. He enjoyed the peace and tranquillity of the day, it was like he didn't have a care in the world. He had sat and gathered his thoughts. He would rendezvous tomorrow or the following day with his men and transfer the device to the motorhome, then he was in the final leg of his mission. It would be less than a week before it came to fruition, had taken years of organisation and hundreds of millions of dollars.

The Palestinian had got into the habit of silently reciting his prayers five times a day at the requisite time without doing it openly. He had placed his sunglasses over his eyes and prayed at the designated hour for Dhuhr before he ate. To a bystander he was simply staring straight ahead, as
always he wished not to attract attention. He had closed his eyes and prayed for the success of his war against the infidel. To free his lands. To kill and wreak as much havoc as he could with his device. He wished with all his heart for the complete destruction of the west and the ascent of strict Sharia law over all peoples of the world. He also prayed that his team could keep it together after his call with Ansari, he's been cut off after issuing his instructions and hadn't

heard from them, best to keep calls to a minimum. Now he could eat, it took less than one minute.

After a long and relaxing lunch Saeed had walked around the village before driving the Carthago back up the mountain pass to the chalet. Before his evening meal he had read the Koran and taken exercise on the paths that made their way up to the Mont Blanc massif. He knew the mountain air would make him sleep well. After the final Isha prayer of the day he went to bed, going over the plan once more in his mind. He would call Cyrus Sia in the morning.
Saeed had barely dosed off in his bed when his telephone wrung out with a loud shrill, it was Sia calling him, something was wrong.

Chapter 41

Charlie Jones was seething. He had not heard a word from so called "Henry V" or from anyone else on the MI5 team. He'd eventually got a hold of Jake Slater who was in charge of the Artificial Intelligence program being developed in MI5 and he was tight lipped saying "nothing had been authorised to be released". That smacked of evolution of the situation but Jake being told to not tell MI6 until Henry gave the go ahead. He had been summoned by Rory Campbell after the meeting at Whitehall and asked what the latest was. When Charlie said he had no update he'd been told that he needed to update the SIS DG every day. Two days had gone past with nothing despite several calls, he was supposed to be on site with Henry Darcy by now. The final straw came when he was summoned by both the DG and Tarique Hashmi, once again to Whitehall, and given a roasting by both. The final comment by Hashmi was "get fucking moving on this or we'll find someone else to do it and he'll be the next head of section". He had never heard Hashmi swear before. It seemed to Jones that his whole career had just come crashing down around his ears - or was about to.

He had walked back slowly from the meeting along the banks of the Thames. The summer weather had encouraged all the local young ladies to wear scant summer dresses as well as some tourists clad in next to nothing. Normally Charlie had admiring eye for such beauty but not today. He very much regarded himself as a ladies man, and was always at the forefront of flirting at the office. He walked, head down, buried in his thoughts, trying to find a way to get back on this case. His only option was to keep trying Henry. Slater refused to give out Anna or Finlay's number, he didn't expect anything from the latter anyway. He'd seen the hard bitten ex soldier's mentality in Lamont. Seen it before in other military people. It didn't really exist with Campbell who'd been ex-navy. He was too ambitious and had developed the diplomacy at a young age. Lamont was different. He was an ex Major that was nearly sixty, an operational man that was embittered and over the hill. That combined with him being a bloody stubborn Scot had caused Jones to write him off for any kind of discussion. Anna would not react to any flirting or olive branches from him he knew. That threw him in the hands of another embittered old git, Henry. He had no choice. He took his telephone out of his jacket pocket to try again.

Jones stopped at the crossing near Vauxhall Bridge, as he looked up at the signal a siren close by made him jump. A police car followed by an unmarked Jaguar XJ with flashing blue lights behind the engine grill pulled into the middle of the crossing in front. The front passenger window rolled down and a plain clothes policeman showed his identification and beckoned him at the same time, 'Mr Jones jump in the back please.'

Jones bent down and looked through the passenger side window. Tarique Hashmi was in the back. The Foreign Secretary was already talking as he got in the back. 'I wanted to catch you in person before my next meeting Charlie.'

'Oh I see, how did you know I was here?'

'I didn't. I was on my way to wait for you at VC and spotted you at the crossroads.'

Jones noted that Hashmi's tone was friendlier than it was almost an hour ago. 'How can I help you Foreign Secretary?'

'Look I was a bit hard on you in there but there is a lot riding on this. I'm not convinced the DG is really grasping how much, but he has a lot on his plate. I really need you to get across there and feedback information, don't hesitate to give it directly to me. I will clear it with your DG, don't worry.'

'Sir that is very irregular, I can't miss out the DG….'

'I'm not asking you to miss him out just tell me immediately what is happening, give us both the same update. Look, I don't trust Sir Basil or Soames, they are glory hunters. The most important thing is we nip a major terrorist act in the bud. It is clearly in our remit in a foreign country despite what those people say.'

'I wholeheartedly agree sir, but I simply cannot get a hold of anyone who will tell me the latest.'

'How can I help? You want me to talk to Soames.'

Charlie saw his opportunity, 'yes sir that would be excellent, I feel they are blocking us, if you can lean on them to keep to their word that would be ideal. I have my gear packed and am ready to fly within a couple of hours, all I need to know is there whereabouts.'

While they were talking Hashmi had gone into his briefcase and removed a small cell phone and charger which he handed to Jones. 'Here take this, my number is programmed into it. If you need any help, anything whatsoever, call me. Also give me a verbal report on it every day. Couple of minutes is fine….and listen - I do apologise for my outburst earlier. You are a good intelligence agent. If you get this right it could be DG one day. Rory won't be there forever you know.'

'Thank you, Mr Foreign Secretary. Grateful if you could let me know once you've had a word with the Home Secretary, then I will know to try Darcy again.'

The car had driven to and waited outside the MI6 building as they were talking. Henry said his farewells to Hashmi and strolled up to security. He felt considerably better now, it was very unconventional but hell, he was an analyst not a field agent. Perhaps these types of things happened all the time at the sharp end.

Chapter 42

The Mont Blanc tunnel is almost twelve kilometres long. At its lowest point it is two thousand eight hundred and forty metres below the peak of the Aguille du Midi, making it one of the deepest tunnels in the world. The idea to build a tunnel to circumvent high mountain climbs between Italy and France dated as far back as the nineteenth century when the development of the railway first lent itself to the idea. The idea didn't attract much attention until 1908 when the first design was put forward to both governments. The advent of two of the world's greatest wars and a collapse in economies in between put paid to any building programme until 1959. It was finally opened in 1965 by both Presidents' of Italy and France. It links Courmayeur in Italy with Chamonix in France and transports as much as one third of Italy's freight to Northern Europe.

It was this tunnel that the massive truck with *Toro in Carica* emblazoned on it headed toward. It had taken over seven hundred tonnes of TNT to build the tunnel. The explosive device that had been sold to the Iranians by the North Koreans, that had now found its way into the back of the "Charging Bull", was the equivalent of twenty five thousand tonnes of TNT. This was larger than the "Fat Boy" bomb dropped by the Americans on Nagasaki. If it exploded in the tunnel it was capable of collapsing the whole mountain, causing catastrophic landslides around the area and extensive loss of life.

Finlay had swapped cars with Henry, Anna had joined him in the BMW. Once the sun had risen above the rear of the car as they headed north-west toward the tunnel they accelerated past the red Fiat to see if they could identify a truck. As Anna kept an eye on the tracking device they saw themselves pull up to five kilometres ahead of the Tipo. They passed and photographed five trucks from a distance. Anna sent each picture to Jake in the Millbank office to see if Skynet could make a link on the number plate or container. Finlay pulled up to ten kilometres ahead. There was no tractor unit with a bull on it. Either their targets were using another vehicle or they had pulled much further ahead. Eventually Henry called them back as they had given him regular updates. He then instructed them to pull off the road out of sight until the Tipo had passed them and rejoin behind. He knew the range of the tracking device was limitless but needed two cars within chase range should they turn off and abandon the vehicle for any reason.

While driving the Panda Henry had received a call from Sir Basil Cudlip. It was very brief, telling him to let Charlie Jones in on the act immediately as things were heating up in Whitehall. He knew that he had several missed calls from the MI6 operative so finally decided to return the last one. The rather frosty discussion resulted in Jones rushing to board a flight to Geneva. He would try to rendezvous with them in the Chamonix area at the end of the tunnel assuming that's where their destination lay. Henry was irritated by the outcome, not least as he was attempting to multitask between smoking, steering, changing gear and the telephone. This resulted in most of the driving seat and his clothing being covered in cigarette ash and the view out the windscreen being considerably restricted. His eyes nipped and he felt very tired. He couldn't see an end in sight if they couldn't get a positive reading on that bloody counter and call in the cavalry. Then it hit him - the Beretta Finlay had got from Ansari! It was possible that its reading could be considerably higher if it had been near the device. He looked in the back, feeling around in the foot well behind him for the counter, cursing as he dropped his cigarette on his lap between his legs, before retrieving it again. Shit, it was in the back and Fin had the firearm in his Bergen. He grabbed the phone again.

Abdul sat in the passenger seat of the Scania while Luigi drove. Miriam was sleeping in the back. The initial adrenaline rush of leaving the truck stop in a hurry and the death of his brother had worn off and he felt very tired. All three of them were running on empty. No one could drive the truck now apart from Luigi. He had been speaking to his brother in the trail vehicle in Italian. Sia had talked to Miriam, it appeared he had received instruction from Omar Fakhoury and they would meet him soon.

Abdul's rage had turned from the Italians who had injured his brother to the infidel scum who had murdered Mumtaz like a sacrificial animal. He would fulfil his brothers' dream of striking them in the centre of their lair. He would do what was required of him by Sia or Fakhoury. He ran when his brother was being killed when he should have saved him. He had never been in that situation. It had terrified him. He knew by the way Miriam and Luigi had looked at him occasionally that they

regarded him with contempt. Abdul had returned to the Scania with a burst nose and a sore neck, hardly the wounds of an accomplished jihadist. He felt disgraced and ashamed but that is what would drive him on. His name would be celebrated across the world by aspiring soldiers who would join the holy war. Like the men who had taken the American planes to the Twin Towers and the Pentagon. Abdul Ansari would not fail again.

Once again he thought of his brother. His eyes had filled with warm salty tears, he wiped them with his fists as if rubbing away the tiredness so the Italian driver wouldn't see.

*

'Give me that fucking Beretta.'

Both cars had come to a screeching halt in the layby of the E25 near Courmayeur, Henry had sprinted from the Panda, grabbed the Beretta which was in a plastic bag and thrown it in the passenger seat of the Panda. He jumped in the drivers' seat and switched on the Geiger counter. It immediately jumped into the amber setting, way above atmospheric background radiation.

Henry grabbed his phone and informed Sir Basil Cudlip after despatching the BMW to continue surveillance of the Tipo. It was a borderline reading but the only excuse he needed to mobilise some help. The Director General supported his reasoning and told him he would request assistance including more manpower and surveillance for the team.

The old spy had put his neck in the noose. If this went the wrong way he would probably be out the service or forced into early retirement. He wasn't concerned, knowing he was right. This was the most serious live threat to Western Europe since the Second World War.

*

Trucks including articulated units travelled in five vehicle convoys once they reached Aosta on the Italian side of the tunnel. Cars and smaller vehicles were stopped to allow these convoys through. This system was put in place after the infamous fire of 1999 when thirty nine people died. Around forty kilometres from the tunnel on the Italian side trucks and trailers were checked by thermographic gateways for "hot spots" that could exist in faulty machinery or loads and may cause combustion. The vehicles also had to get a pass before they could proceed to the tunnel. Categories of dangerous goods were not permitted and the Italian traffic police conducted random checks. It was the one weak point in the Mubarizun plan to ship their cargo north to France but considered an acceptable one. It was also the single place where a particle detector could have been used to check every single truck without raising suspicion had there been a political will to do so.

Henry had pleaded with Sir Basil Cudlip by this point to tell the French and Italian authorities to search the trucks and to involve their respective secret services. Sir Basil had agreed and gone through the correct chain of command which was Edward Soames. The decision here, however, lay with the Foreign Secretary Tarique Hashmi. He had been the main block over passing the information on to the French and Italians. He wanted his man on the ground to gauge feedback. Finally he had given permission due to unrelenting pressure from Soames who had eventually called the Prime Minister.

The *Toro in Carica* unit exited the thermographic gateway successfully. Miriam Sia sat in the back of the cab, two men in the truck would attract the least attention. The original plan of the Ansari brothers going in the trailer was now redundant. Luigi then drove the wagon to a check point which was occupied by security guards doing the checking and supported by police. Luigi produced the papers and wandered round the truck with the inspectors. He was asked to open the trailer. Luigi did so. The inspector took a photograph of the furniture and signalled to the driver to close the doors and move on to join the next five vehicle convoy. It was around that time that the Commissario Capo of the Autostrade police got a call in his office in Courmayeur telling him that the government had requested urgent checks on trucks going into the tunnel. More men and equipment were being mobilised. He was also told to look for a tractor unit with *Toro in Carica* emblazoned in it with a charging bull emblem. He passed the information on down the chain of command.

Luigi turned up the air conditioning as his vehicle sat on the busy truck convoy holding area near the tunnel. The sun was shining through the large windows increasing the temperature in the cab - or that is what he was telling himself. All the occupants of the Scania were tired and looking forward to getting through the tunnel to the rendezvous point. Miriam, as cool and deadpan as ever, was fast asleep in the lower bunk.

A traffic policeman looked up at Luigi in the cab and asked for his papers. The mafia man greeted the policeman warmly from the rolled down window and handed over his tunnel pass and manifest. The policeman briefly checked the documents and waved Luigi on. At around the time the *Toro in Carica* reached the tunnel entrance, third place in a convoy of five, the heavy goods vehicle checkpoint forty kilometres behind them got the call to check for it.

The big rig kept its distance from the wagon in front and commenced its limited speed journey through the tunnel with the convoy vehicle leading. Luigi and Abdul were completely silent, almost mesmerised by the fluorescent lines and reflectors in the tunnel road popping up from underneath the trailer in front. As they neared the exit Abdul could almost see the Italian visibly calming down, he even offered him a piece of chewing gum which Abdul declined. He knew why

Luigi was relaxing, it was almost time for him to hand the vehicle over having fulfilled his duty to his mafia boss. The pressure for him was easing off. For Abdul it was only going to increase, alone, without the help of his elder sibling. He guessed that the police would have found his body by now and would be trying to identify him. That would take time as he had no means of identification on his body. Then they would be looking for Abdul Ansari.

By the time the *Toro in Carica* left the convoy at the French end of the tunnel the Autostrade Police at the Italian end were checking for the truck entering the tunnel and opening up every vehicle at the convoy holding park. They were also attempting to source particle detectors which they were told would be needed for detecting "contraband cargo".

Meantime Anna's team were beavering away in London, feeding more information into their AI system as the information was being fed to them. Just as the Autostrade Police were starting to search trucks, Skynet had accessed the video surveillance system at the thermal gateway on the Italian side and found a picture of a charging bull on a Scania truck. The net was starting to close in.

Chapter 43

Ebrahim Khorasani left the Persian Hotel in a hurry. He had made no attempt to phone the number that Zarrin had left in the note. He half expected her to be waiting in reception for him or even his room. The room had been tidied by housekeeping but nothing seemed out of place. His papers and clothing appeared not to have been interfered with. The VAJA veteran knew that credit card activity could easily be traced so he paid the bill in Swiss francs, apologised for cutting his booking short and left the hotel with his trolley bag and camera case. The rain had continued and there were no taxis outside reception when he asked the doorman to get him one. Impatiently he raised his umbrella and walked down the narrow one way street toward the main street where the taxi rank lay or he could jump on a tram. He wanted to put space between himself and the hotel. He would jump on and off different forms of transport and lose any tail he may have. One side of the street had parked cars on it and a pavement, it narrowed to a corner where there was no room for a pavement or parked cars. As Khorasani stepped on to the road a large dark Mercedes Sprinter van pulled up beside him and the sliding door flew open. Khorasani dropped his bag and ran back on to the pavement which started again as the narrow street widened. Two figures stood in front of him between the building and more parked vehicles. He turned, two further men were out of the sliding door. He turned again and ran at the men in front of him. He felt a sharp blow to the side of his head and his legs were kicked from under him. His head hit the pavement as he fell and he could feel his consciousness slip from him momentarily. Khorasani was lifted easily and thrown in the back of the van on a seat behind the driver. A man sat either side of him and a hood was placed over his head from behind. A large plastic cable tie secured his neck to the headrest and others went round his wrists and ankles. He could hear the van driver change through the gears as it navigated the narrow streets. No one had spoken a word in the few seconds it had taken to get him in the van or as it had started its trip to its destination.

Ebrahim Khorasan's worst fears had become reality.

Eventually he tried talking in English, 'Who are you?' There was fear in his voice.

A gravelly voice came from the third row of seats in Farsi, as if he had laryngitis or some problem with his voice box or lungs. 'Who do you think it is Ebrahim?'

For a moment his heart sunk even lower, 'I have no idea?' In English.

The raspy voice responded in English this time. 'Well if I was part of your security apparatus that would be you're worst case scenario. But you know that don't you?'

'I have no idea what you are talking about.'

'Don't be a fool Ebrahim. We know you inside out, better than you do. You are a senior VAJA operative, have been aligned with your old friend General Soleimani for decades. That is before the Americans got him in Iraq. He was an arrogant man, thought he was untouchable. You have sowed violence and hate in the Middle East for more years than even I can care to remember. You have killed westerners, your own people, it must amount to tens of thousands indirectly. But you were in the middle of a big operation when Soleimani was assassinated. Perhaps that's why the Americans took the gloves off with Soleimani? Who knows. We know you were out in the market for a nuclear weapon, had been for years. Please don't sit there and go into the good old "deny everything" spy mode. Tell us what we need to know, why did you leave Iran and hide, what have you done that has upset your leaders?'

'You have the wrong man, I have no idea what this is about.'

'Listen to me Ebrahim. You can help us. To us you are worth a lot, we can de-brief you for days, get the information we need and then we will let you go. No need for recriminations as you will be hunted for the rest of your life. We are fine with that. Do you know what your choice is?'

The VAJA spy shook his head despite the cable tie restraint.

'The choice is we get what we want from you by force which will not be pleasant and then simply give you back to your bosses. Repatriate you through Hezbollah in Lebanon. That's what decent people we are. We are humane. Unlike you and your compatriots Ebrahim, we're not gangsters and crooks. We'll send you home, you can re-kindle your acquaintance there with your bosses. Hezbollah can tell them where they got you from.'

The Iranian's English wasn't good enough to understand all of it but he got the basics of what the man meant. The answer was starting to dawn inside Ebrahim Khorasani's head. This was Mossad. Only they could have the contacts and confidence to hand him over in Lebanon. The man's accent was Israeli Hebrew, he spoke from the back of his throat like and Arab. The Israeli knew he would be handing Khorasani a death sentence if he was given to Hezbollah and the Revolutionary Guard. He was stuck between a rock and a hard place as the Americans would say.

The Iranian's head was spinning. Better to keep quiet, the more they talked the more he could learn. When they were at the point of hurting him he could make the decision as to whether he should talk or not. Meantime he would deny everything.

The rasping voice spoke once again, 'you remember Youssef Al Noury, Ebrahim, used to be one of your suppliers of transport to Hezbollah in Lebanon?'

The VAJA man didn't utter a word, the hood didn't move in acknowledgement, though he had some room within the cable tie.

His inquisitor went on, 'he was one of ours, a Christian who hated you people. He was fitting tracking devices to the cars for us and making you a rich man with kickbacks as I recall. We killed a minimum of thirty senior Hezbollah when we tracked those cars to a house in the Lebanese mountains. And that was just one strike. You remember what you did to him when you found a tracking device in a car?'

Still no response.

'That was in 2006. He was my friend, my operative. One of the best I had in five decades. You crucified him Ebrahim. You ordered it to cover your crimes and set an example.'

Ebrahim Khorasani's heart sank, he knew precisely what the man was talking about. He also suspected he knew who this man who sat in the third row of seats was. He was in the hands of his worst nightmare. The Mossad spy handler David, Khorasani had been trying to kill him for twenty years.

Chapter 44

By the time Henry, still driving and cursing the Panda, reached the end of the tunnel he could vaguely see the big BMW in the distance. He couldn't see the Tipo. It eventually turned left into Chamonix and they parked in a small hotel just off the main street. Sia and Stefano exited, took their luggage from the boot and went into the hotel. Henry and Anna, who had not been seen at any point while tracking the two men checked into the hotel as man and wife. Finlay kept an eye on the outside of the hotel in case the men left without the car.

Anna and Henry had taken the tracking device and laptops into the hotel with them and started to go through the information just in from Skynet. Henry then left Anna and took over from Finlay in the Panda, the latter then went to conduct a reconnaissance of all the truck stops in the area with the BMW. By this time Henry had received a call from the DGSI who had two men on their way to assist. They had already mobilised the local Gendarmerie to look for the *Toro in Carica*. More men and resources were on their way from Lyon to assist in the search. This was followed by a call from Charlie Jones who had just arrived in Geneva and was on his way. Henry reinforced to everyone he was liaising with that he didn't want them near the hotel. He would meet them in Chamonix out of sight. Any searching of vehicles was to be done as routine load checks on truck units. The red Tipo was to be strictly left alone. He felt that this was still his best chance to find the truck.

The old spy dozed with one eye open in the Panda until the early evening when his old comrade in arms returned in the BMW. They both jumped in the larger more comfortable vehicle.

'Anything?' enquired Finlay.

'No movement, the DGSI want to stick sound monitoring and cameras into the room. I told them to fuck off but we're on their territory, it's going to be a battle. We must not alert these people it's our only sure chance of getting to the device. If we grab them now it'll take days to get the information out of them. The trailer is around here somewhere. Its bloody huge surely we can find it.'

'Not if it gets disconnected from the tractor unit.'

'They're now stopping every articulated unit on the two roads out of Chamonix under the guise of conducting load tests and tyre checks. A DGSI guy in police uniform is checking the trailers with a particle detector.'

'We can't stay here forever Henry, in any recce we need a cut off period. We could be staring at our navels while the mission is being accomplished elsewhere.'

Henry V nodded, 'I agree let's give it twenty four hours then we pull these guys in. We'll need an armed response unit as backup.' He made sure he met the SRU Majors' eyes, 'Finlay, we need them alive, especially Sia. If not we have a big fucking problem.'

'Then we need to split them up, getting one alive is hard, two impossible, if they want to fight.'

'They'll fight, believe me. I'll see if the DGSI guys can use a Tazer.'

Finlay shook his head, 'count me out if you're dicking about with a Tazer. Round in the back of the knee when he's not looking – it's an old Irish trick. That will take anyone down, drop like a sack of potatoes. We can't be shouting "armed police" and all that shite. My view - shoot the other arsehole in the head, not sure how much he knows.'

It was Henry's turn to shake his head. 'No. Both alive. I don't care how you do it.'

'Well you'd better not involve the police with all their response procedures or they'll both end up dead, perhaps take a couple of coppers with them to. It's your call Monsieur Darcy.'

'We have to split them up.'

*

There was no movement in the Aiguille Verte Hotel until later the next day. Charlie Jones who'd arrived late the previous evening was on watch from a room which overlooked the target car. His counterpart in MI5 had told him to get some sleep and he could take a shift the next day. He had relieved Major Lamont at lunch time and sat on the room balcony above the red Tipo. The DGSI had attended with plain clothes police and told the proprietor to lock all the fire escapes so the only means of access or egress to the hotel was via the reception and front door. The French secret service was determined to take over the operation. Henry let his seniors take care of the politics. So far they had been nothing but helpful.

Jones had received a gruff and uninformative handover from the old paratroop officer which basically amounted to "nothing's happened son, don't fuck it up". They had decided to call time on the surveillance and bring the two men in for questioning at five p.m. At three-thirty Cyrus Sia and Stefano left the building with their luggage and walked toward the car. Charlie Jones jumped out of his seat and ran to the room door opposite his in the second floor corridor and thumped on the door.

As the red Fiat pulled out of the car park and turned right through Chamonix toward Argentiere and the mountains, Henry and Finlay jumped in the BMW followed by Anna and Jones. About two kilometres from the ski village of Argentiere the Tipo turned right and drove up to an isolated chalet on route to the Argentiere glacier below the Aiguille du Chardonnet mountain. They were high in the Alps now where the air had started to become rarefied. Henry's team parked their cars further down the track under a massive buttress which overlooked the narrow road. Finlay and Charlie took their equipment, weapons and rucksacks and cautiously made their way up the narrow road while Henry and Anna would call for backup and await its arrival. Finlay found a hiking track that made its way up around the back of the chalet. The area was rocky and interspersed with areas of grass and scree. The chalet was situated in an area cut out from the side of the mountain and commanded a good view south of the access road along its last two kilometres. The track cut along the mountainside and then went west up a series of narrow steep switchbacks before carving a path east again above the chalet. They could observe the building from there and block off any escape.

The traverse to that point should take them less than an hour Finlay thought. He had set a quick pace carrying his Bergen and had purposefully left his warm clothing in the rucksack despite the cold mountain air. Charlie Jones hadn't followed suit. He was cold when he got out the car and had donned his mountain clothing. He spent a lot of time in the gym and thought he could keep up with the old dinosaur ahead of him. Charlie was wrong, he was falling behind the old soldier's "yomp" and if he stopped to take off his clothing he would fall further behind. He satisfied himself by unzipping his jacket fully and removing his woolly hat. Finlay, pulling clear ahead was muttering about having to work with an amateur. He would have preferred not to work with an operative he didn't know, who quite possible had no military training. He'd spend more time looking after this mug than himself. He stopped and waited. The MI6 man caught up breathing laboriously in the thin air.

"Take your jacket off and strip down to your shirt." said Finlay

Charlie nodded and did as he was told. He bent down to stuff his fleece and jacket in his backpack.

"Where's your firearm?" enquired the soldier.

"In my rucksack."

"Well it's no fucking good there is it?"

The spy pulled a Glock out of the bottom of the rucksack sheepishly snagging it on the webbing.

"Is it loaded and do you have an extra clip?"

"Yes."

"Do you know how to use it?"

"Yes." Charlie wasn't asked to elaborate, if he had he would have had to tell Finlay it was the only weapon he'd ever fired and even then only about a hundred 9 mm rounds on the range. Though he felt he'd done quite well at 25 metre range, even managed to get one round on the bulls' eye.

Henry knew from the way he handled the weapon, like he was scared of it, that Charlie Jones wasn't proficient with it at all.

'Look son I'll tell you this once. You haven't shot anybody therefore you'll hesitate and get you or me killed. These men are killers, this Sia guy has been responsible for killing a whole ship's crew and god knows what else. Once you've killed you won't hesitate, you need to overcome that reluctance right now. Do you understand?'

Charlie Jones nodded.

'Let's keep it simple when I shoot, you shoot too. You don't point that thing at me…. ever. If there are two men, I'll take Sia, you take the Italian. You know the difference, you've seen pictures?'

'Yes.'

'We're supposed to take them alive, that is going to be bloody difficult now.'

Finlay turned and commenced his walk at the same rapid pace, 'and keep that fucking Glock where you can grab it quick.'

He didn't want to treat this guy like an idiot. He knew as an ex paratroop major he had to, the boy needed to be on his toes to stay alive.

Further down the valley Henry had told the DGSI to search up at any altitude that a large truck could get to, beyond that there was little point. An armed response unit known as the GIGN, an elite unit of the Gendarmerie was on its way from Paris by helicopter to the helicopter landing pad in Argentiere.

He spent the remainder of the time going through any further information that could be plugged into Skynet with Anna.

Finlay and Charlie reached the end of the escarpment above the chalet and found a flat spot behind a rock jutting over the pathway that curved behind them and then on toward the glacier. Finlay had no idea where the path led to and conveyed this information to Henry to try and get a map of some kind. They wrapped up in warm clothing, ate some food and took turns to keep watch on the target building.

At around nine pm, as the sun was setting, they saw some movement down in the chalet. Both men had exited wearing mountain gear and had rucksacks. Finlay could see through binoculars what looked like a Czech Scorpion sub machine gun hanging from Sia's shoulder. His mafia companion had a Beretta PMX with the stock extended. He took a photograph and sent it to Henry via his satellite phone, to show him the challenge he faced more than anything else. The two men appeared to be having a heated argument. Stefano was gesticulating toward the mountain path as if he were reluctant to start the long journey. His whole posture was of a person that was stooped over and unwell. Sia finally shrugged, turned on his heel and commenced climbing the rocky path as the sun cast long shadows over the mountain landscape. Stefano followed reluctantly at a slower pace.

Finlay turned to his companion, 'if Sia gets up here without the Italian we let him go past and I'll take down Stefano. There is something wrong with him, he is weak. Then we isolate and track Sia. He may come back for his friend if he doesn't catch up, then we can take him too. If not we'll track him.'

'How are we going to keep Stefano quiet?' responded Charlie, already whispering despite the two targets being half an hour away.

'We probably can't, we'll have to hurt him, tie and gag him and move on. Once we've done that I'll let Henry know. The priority is Cyrus Sia. I'm guessing this guy Stefano doesn't want to be here, he isn't a fanatic, simply wants to avoid the police and get back to Brindisi. He'd probably have preferred to head back down the road and drive back through the Mont Blanc tunnel. Sia's probably told him the cops are on his tail and this route is the way out.'

Both men made sure that they and their belongings were hidden from the path. They moved any small loose rocks that they may kick in the failing light, checked their weapons and waited to hear the sound of footsteps. Charlie would keep an eye down on the path to see how far the targets were apart and signal to Finlay further up the slope when they walked past him concealed behind a large boulder.

Soon Finlay heard the sound of footsteps on the loose rock that constituted the path that led its way to their hiding place. He could only hear one set. Charlie had signalled a distance of three hundred metres. The crunching got louder, Finlay lay pressed under the overhang of a large boulder his Glock in his right hand. And his knife by his side. He saw the boots, the top of which was wrapped in a waterproof gaiter, move past him and turn up steps cut roughly in the rock. In a few metres the man would turn on another switchback up the mountain toward the glacier plateau above. He could see the figure move away from him and the condensed breath being emitted from his heavy breathing in the poor light of the dusk. After the sound of reverberating footsteps dissipated there was brief silence. He signalled to Charlie to come up and join him behind the boulder. As he did so he could hear the faint sound of more footsteps coming up the path but as yet couldn't see Stefano from his concealed position. Where the hell was Charlie? He looked around, the MI6 man had taken too long to retrieve his binoculars and rucksack. He was looking around for something, then bent down to pick it up. His Glock. Charlie Jones slowly and carefully made his way up the scree slope to Finlay's concealed position. Finlay signalled with his arm furiously to get a move on before he was seen. There was a gap in the cover of large boulders up to the position the old soldier was in. Finlay could do nothing else without giving away his position. Charlie saw him and picked up his pace. Finlay lay on a large flat area which was the mountain bedrock, the bottom of which was wet with the mountain dew that had formed as the sun dropped. Charlie Jones reached this area moving quickly. Stefano's crunching steps moved closer. Finlay slowly rolled out from the boulder overhang, raised himself to his knees, Glock in right hand. He left held the old commando dagger. As he got to his feet, he turned one last time to see Charlie. The young MI6 spy slipped on the wet rock, his feet went out from under him on the angled rock and he landed flat on his face. The weight of his rucksack compounded the slip. As he did so, the Glock spun from his hand and clattered on the rock before he managed to grab it. The crunching footsteps stopped. Silence, no one moved. Finlay heard the click of a safety catch but still couldn't see his target from his angle to the path between the boulders. Charlie could see Stefano's shape on his right against the light coloured mountainside in the evening dim. He saw the Italian raise his weapon but wasn't sure if he had been spotted. Then Charlie Jones felt a hard thump in his side, heard the rat-a-tat of machine gun fire and briefly saw flames barely supressed coming from the Beretta as he fell. Nine millimetre rounds pinged off the bedrock as Charlie slumped on to the rock.

Stefano was firing down on Charlie Jones to the right of the large boulder that Finlay was behind, he stepped quickly to the left lifting the Glock 17 as if it were an extension of his anatomy. Finlay dropped the knife. His hands closed around the grip, right three fingers round the handle, left supporting the right, both thumbs down the left of the weapon, clear of the recoil slide. The safety was double trigger, slight squeeze pulling the safety mechanism off, the remainder of the pull firing the round. Major Lamont registered none of it. On the range he could get the first round within three centimetres over twenty five metres and the second within five. In half a second. Double tap. So could many others. The difference was he could also do it in combat while moving. He needed a headshot in case the target was wearing a ballistic vest. The first round hit Stefano in the right cheek as he was still looking down toward Charlie. The second went right in through the side of his head. Either would have killed him immediately. The volleys of shots could still be heard echoing around the mountainside. The Italian flew back, head slammed the ground, feet in the air, before they also clattered down on the path.

Finlay moved quickly while listening for the returning footsteps of Cyrus Sia. He checked Stefano was dead and ran down to Charlie. The lad was barely breathing, he had the pale pallor of a dying man in Finlay's briefly lit torch. He took his satphone, pressed the SOS and laid it down beside the MI6 man. Henry would pick that up straight away. There was no time for first aid, he could be dispatched while attending to his compatriot or Sia would escape into the mountains with his critical information. Neither choice was worth the outside chance of saving Charlie Jones' life in the circumstances.

Finlay went back to Stefano and checked his weapon after holstering his own Glock. The Beretta sub-machine gun had a spare clip which he could see was full through the plastic material. He replaced the partially spent clip and quickly examined the weapon. It was still sticky with the wax used to store new weapons so would be reliable. The old soldier knew he'd be outgunned again unless he used it. Slinging it over his shoulder, he retrieved his knife and rucksack and headed cautiously up the path. He knew that Cyrus Sia was much more likely to run than come back and help someone who was essentially a non-believer and a criminal, a means to an end. He had to take that gamble and increase his pace.

*

Less than half an hour after Henry saw the Helicopter fly overhead to Argentiere, a dozen tough looking and very well armed Gendarmes appeared out the back of two police mini vans where the Panda was parked. Henry briefed the DGSI officer in charge informing him there had been shots fired and effectively that stealth was no longer required. Half the men headed up the chalet road on foot, the other half returned to the police helicopter to lend support to the men on the ground. Henry and Anna followed the Gendarme team up the mountain. Henry had received the SOS and given his telephone to the French DGSI agent so he could tell his men the location. He hoped his men were OK but he knew at least one if not both were injured.

By the time the ground team reached the chalet the Gendarmerie Eurocopter had arrived overhead shining its spotlight on the building, there was a flat space for it to touch down and disgorge the full complement of GIGN armed response gendarmes before providing cover again. In less than ten minutes windows had been broken, loud "flashbangs" had been thrown in and the building was cleared. The French appeared to care little for any booby trap devices. Six armed response men then climbed into the helicopter again and it took off, its spotlight following the path which ascended toward the glacier from round the back of the chalet. Once again Henry and Anna followed the remaining six officers who went up on foot. As they left Henry could see more police driving up the road to the chalet below since it had been cleared.

The helicopter now hovered above a boulder strewn area above. Henry heard chatter on the French VHF radio, a person could be seen lying on the ground with a telephone and a pistol lying near him. Henry saw the look of utter despair in Anna's face when he told her and put a reassuring arm round her briefly as they strode up the path. When they reached the area the massive spotlight shone down on the body, the down draft blowing long hair over his forehead. It wasn't Major Lamont. It was Charlie Jones and he looked dead. Further up the mountain they could see another shape lying on the path. As Henry walked toward the corpse he could see two almost innocuous entry wounds in his head and face but there was no mistaking the distorted and scarred ear. It was Stefano.

'Charlie's dead', he heard Anna say behind him, her voice shaking. Henry guessed she'd never seen a dead person before. He barely heard her soft voice in the thump from the helicopter engines above.

Henry, down on one knee, looked up at the slight woman, her hair completely covering her face from the helicopter wash, 'So is Stefano, looks as if your man nailed him perfectly.'

'I heard a Gendarme saying the area is clear, the helicopter can't land, its going ahead to light the path.'

'Well it looks as if Major Finlay is on the hunt for Sia, he managed to split them up after all. Not quite what I intended my dear Anna.'

The veteran spy turned his attention to Stefano, he searched his belongings and shone a torch on his head and body. The mafia man did not look well. He had a rash on his neck that was red and livid. One hand had a bandage on it, the dressing was weeping through on the back of his hand. Henry rolled the sleeve up and his arm was in a similar condition. Henry took a Geiger counter from his pack and switched it on. It immediately jumped into the lower end of the red zone. Stefano was radioactive. He informed the nearest gendarme and turned his attention to Charlie Jones further down the hill.

He took two telephones from Charlie's body, primarily so the French wouldn't get their hands on them. One was the state issue secure phone for secret service work, the other a pay as you go mobile phone. It only had one number on it. Henry dialled it. The voice answered, 'Hello Charlie, what's the latest?'

It was the unmistakeable voice of the British Foreign Secretary on a pay as you go unsecure telephone. Henry pressed the end call button without speaking and stared thoughtfully at the handset.

*

Finlay Lamont's walk changed from a cautious gait aimed at minimising any noise to a yomp. He then heard a helicopter much further down the mountain, saw the spotlight from the aircraft and changed to a jog. Sia would not be hanging around now. The path started to climb almost vertically up a cliff face, ice and snow patches were getting more pronounced as he climbed. He was now using his hands to assist clambering on the steeper rocks made slippy with snow melt from the glacier which he was now climbing parallel to. He could see its wide white girth snaking up the mountain to his right as he climbed in the moonlight. The clear sky offered no insulation and it was becoming bitterly cold. The wind started to pick up. Eventually he reached what appeared to be an extensive plateau. He could see a mountain hut, a square shape silhouetted against the skyline in the dark. He approached it slowing down once again to a cautious walk. Normally these huts would be left open for climbers to shelter in. He circled the hut, Beretta PMX raised to his shoulder, nothing. One way in and one way out. He kicked the door open, threw a stun grenade in and stood back as it detonated with a sharp crack. He ran in, the torch now taped to his weapon showed him an empty space with some rough wooden furniture. Nothing.

Finlay moved on up the hill following the path, he could have walked past his target hiding anywhere, he would leave that to the French gendarmes further down the mountain. Cyrus Sia was heading for Italy or Switzerland, moving to a different jurisdiction always helps in a situation such as he was in. As he moved the paratroop Major could hear the helicopters' noise recede, they were either refuelling or replacing the helicopter and taking their time about coming up the mountain. There was no way to communicate with them as his satellite telephone was by Charlie Jones' body and his cell phone had no reception.

As time moved on he moved across the plateau and started climbing the mountain again. The path appeared to be moving up toward a col between two peaks. It had become pretty difficult, was no longer a walk but a serious vertical climb. The early morning summer sun was about to rise, the path was going directly east. It would soon rise in the direction Finlay was climbing. They must be getting near Switzerland now where the French had no jurisdiction. Suddenly in the distance behind him he heard the thwack of helicopter blades. He couldn't see below him as he had climbed over a cliff edge in the rise to the col but he assumed the French had found the hut and were searching for a place to land in the flat plateau. The climbing was becoming very difficult now. Finlay had to sling the Beretta behind his back, he'd be an easy target if caught climbing up the cliff face or from behind if Sia had hidden along a ledge somewhere. As the sun rose slightly above the horizon scuff marks on the soil, rocks and snow were now visible, the target had come this way very recently.

The SRU man doubted that Sia could stretch the distance from his too far, though he had the advantage of not having to be cautious about an ambush. Not many people in the world could out climb the accomplished mountaineer. He knew he was catching him. He was now starting to climb in ice without the required crampons and ice axe, it was getting to the point of being impossible. Finlay stopped and listened. He could hear breathing above him. Then a thump and what appeared to be a curse in a foreign language. He glanced round the side of some snow on the ledge he was on. Sia was there. The Iranian was trying to negotiate a narrow icy ledge to bypass a rock overhang above and had slipped and fallen on the ice. As Finlay glanced round, he reached behind him for the Beretta. Just at that point Sia saw him and like lightning grabbed the Scorpion beside him and let off a burst of fire. Finlay was too slow in diving back into the snow and felt a thump on his left shoulder, throwing him on to his back. He grabbed his Beretta and returned a burst of fire, aiming between his own feet so Sia would keep his head down. Sia stood and raised his Scorpion to his shoulder and simply walked toward where Finlay was lying firing short bursts at his target. The soldier had fallen into deep snow on the ledge and most of the rounds had deflected on this missing him. One hit his sub-machine gun strap. Finlay simply sat up and one handed fired half his clip at the advancing jihadist. He saw Sia thrown back off his feet as if hit by a heavy weight. He'd got him, hopefully alive.

Finlay Lamont struggled to his feet, starting to feel the pain in his shoulder, couldn't raise his left arm. One handed he pointed the sub-machine gun at the Iranian. Sia's Scorpion lay a metre from his outstretched right hand, he started to move toward it, Finlay leapt forward and stamped his right foot hard on his hand and brought the other boot to stamp down on his face. Three hard stamps on Sia's head made the jihadist fall back unconscious. The Major threw the Scorpion over his back after removing a flare and plastic cable ties from his Bergen. The flare was fired in the direction from whence he came. He strapped Sia's hands and feet together, searched him and identified a wound to his ribs and stomach. With a first aid kit from his rucksack he did what he could to staunch the flow of blood. The stomach looked like and entry wound and ribs just looked grazed and possibly broken. Sia was then held by the collar and unceremoniously dragged down the cliff face one section at a time so that Finlay could get breath in the thin air. The whole operation was slow with one hand but he had to get him to a flat area where the helicopter could lift the terrorist to receive quick medical attention.

The squad of Gendarmes walked rapidly on the path above the mountain hut. They had checked it and moved on quickly. Henry V was following them up the hill. Anna remained at the hut to check in with Millbank. As the plateau started to climb toward a cliff face they saw a green flare fired into the sky just ahead of them. Green for go. Looks Henry's old compatriot had killed or captured the Tango. Henry smiled with some relief but also felt trepidation on the fate of his target, there was a strong chance Sia was dead and they were back to square one. A mountain police rescue helicopter was followed by the Gendarmerie Eurocopter. He saw the rescue machine disappear over the rise in the col and heard it hovering for at least fifteen minutes. It reappeared with a stretcher slung below its squat body, slowly flew over to the mountain hut and lowered the stretcher to the waiting police below. The chatter confirmed that it was the target in the stretcher and the British operative was still up the mountain and descending injured. Henry headed back to the mountain hut leaving the team of Gendarmes to move up the mountain to find Finlay.

*

Further down the valley helicopter surveillance had found a disused mountain road just outside of Chamonix. It had been used to access an old crystal mine and they could see new deep tyre marks in the previously undisturbed grass that had grown over the path. They sent a patrol in a four wheel drive to take a look. Just inside the large mine entrance they found *Toro in Carica*. The large articulated unit had been driven into the mine cave cab first as there obviously had been no room to turn on the narrow road. The back doors lay open and many items of furniture lay strewn about the mine entrance. Several crates with Chinese writing on them had been smashed open. They were the first thing the two policemen saw when they cautiously entered, weapons drawn. They immediately informed the helicopter above that they needed backup.

While they were waiting their inquisitiveness overcame their fear and they slowly made their way along the mine on either side of the trailer. They could see nothing in front of the cab but confirmed with the helicopter that the truck had the bull logo on it. They policeman on the left carefully opened the drivers' side door. He smeared his hand with what appeared to be congealed blood from the door seal, looked up and saw a heavily tattooed man slumped across the steering wheel. The man had a massive exit wound from a bullet on the left side of his head.

They then confirmed the cave was clear and searched the cab of the Scania tractor unit. They found very little apart from two 9 mm shell casings and some old bandages, a drip and medication.

*

Cyrus Sia awoke when a bucket of frozen snow was placed upside down on his head, then removed. His head was throbbing, vision blurred. He felt bonds securing his hands and feet, he was lying on a raised surface, perhaps a table. A pale middle aged man with yellowing teeth and a receding hairline stared down at him, 'hello Mister Sia, we meet at last.'

He could smell smoke, yes the man was smoking. His vision cleared a little, as he lowered his eyes he could see his own nose swollen, it felt broken. Sia looked to the right and saw the window of the mountain hut. He had entered previously and thought of resting for a while but there had been no time. Turning to the left he saw the man that had been pursuing him. He nodded his acknowledgement and respect, half smiled through cracked and swollen lips.

Yellow teeth went on. 'We need you to tell us where the device from your truck is Mr Sia.' The Iranian ignored the man, stared straight up at the rotting wooden eves that held up the hut's roof. 'I don't need to tell you that we are not here to abide by any human rights bullshit when your regard for life itself does not exist. We don't have much time. Where is the bomb going and when is it going to be detonated?'

Sia didn't moved, just chuckled through his swollen lips. The man went on. 'OK Mister Sia, may I call you Cyrus? I am going to inject you with a lovely concoction called SP117, invented by our Russian friends, you can take it orally or we can inject it. Suggest in the interests of time we do the latter. I'm not an expert in injecting people, in fact this is a first, so I suggest you don't struggle.'

'I'll do it.' Sia looked over to the man standing against the wall who had spoken, he stepped forward. 'I've had to use needles on people before. I won't mange to use my left arm to hold him anyway.' He gestured to his arm in a sling.

Sia wriggled as hard as he could. His hands had been secured to cable ties, in turn roped under the table tightly so he had little room to manoeuvre. His ankles were strapped together and also tied down. As his assailant held the needle up he arched his back and tried to turn sideways. Yellow teeth jumped up on the table and sat on his chest. Then, a woman appeared from nowhere and pinned his left arm flat to the table. He was weak and his struggles were feeble. Sia felt the nip of the needle as it entered his arm opposite his elbow and a slight pressure. The Iranian gave up and lay back trying to get his breath and slow his pulse down to prevent the drug from getting round his system too quickly.

If you'd have asked Cyrus Sia how long his ordeal in the mountain hut had lasted he couldn't tell you if it was a few hours or a week. All he knew is that he had awoken in a French hospital bed in Paris that specialised in securing violent mental patients. He was restrained in a large adjustable hospital bed with two gendarmes guarding the door to what was effectively a cell. He had been operated on and his wounds had been dressed. Though he was heavily sedated he could recall conversations with his captives in the mountain hut. His difficulty was separating the reality of possible discussions from his dreams. He can remember laughing and telling yellow teeth that his capital city was finished, that Britain was done. A country that had supressed his people for centuries and placed despot dictators in charge of his people was about to meet its end. But he could also remember having a distinct floating feeling while talking and then he was sipping a hot sweet tea. All of it was blurred, the past and the present mixed in a confusing jumble.

Chapter 45

Edward Soames sat in his cabinet office meeting room with Sir Basil Cudlip and his field team who had just returned from France. Sir Basil looked worried, Henry Darcy impatient, the girl was tapping away on a laptop and the tired Lamont was nonchalantly resting his sling encompassed left arm on the shiny mahogany meeting table. The Home Secretary peered at Sir Basil over the top of his old repaired reading glasses, 'So please tell?'

Sir Basil looked at Henry, 'Go on Henry, may as well come from the horse's mouth.'

'Sir, we have tracked down two of the terrorists and found the vehicle responsible for hauling the nuclear cargo as far as Chamonix in France. Despite extensive searches over that last forty eight hours we haven't found the remaining occupants of the truck, we believe it has been transferred to another vehicle. Of the two terrorists we caught up with one is dead. We believe he is linked to the Sacra Coruna Unita mafia in Brindisi where the cargo arrived. The other is a Sunni Iranian linked to a new terrorist organisation we have identified, the Mubarizun. We questioned him at length. He told us three things. Firstly that the weapon has a huge potential destruction, he didn't confirm that it was a nuclear device but we believe it is. Secondly the target is London, we don't know where. We believe he probably doesn't know. Thirdly we have a leak at the highest level in our intelligence services, he knew almost everything we have done to track him. My tardiness in keeping people informed probably prevented his escape.'

Soames turned his head toward Sir Basil, 'how do we know this terrorist is telling the truth?'

'We don't,' Sir Basil replied. 'Not for sure but the chemical we administered…'

'I don't want to know,' interrupted the Home Secretary.

Henry responded, 'let's just say the interrogation process we used has a strong tendency to produce reality, gives the recipient an urge to divulge a conspiracy to his friends in the room after some time. Even if it's not true it's likely that any target in the UK will be London. We have to start somewhere. The French are dealing with their own country and now only a matter of time now before this gets out into the public domain.'

'We really think this is an actual explosive device? Not just a dirty bomb that will spread radioactivity?' Soames eyebrows were raised in doubt.

Henry carried on, 'Sir we have detected high levels of radioactivity in the truck and on a sidearm. The Americans have confirmed now that the dhow is extremely radioactive and it appears the terrorist killed near Chamonix was in an advanced stage of radiation poisoning. Indications are from the advice that we received from Aldermaston are that this is a crude but effective plutonium bomb.'

Soames, for so many years, a calm veteran politician used to attending disasters and putting other's lives on the line went white as a sheet, paler than Sir Basil had ever seen him in the harsh fluorescent light of Whitehall. He rubbed his hands over his face lifting his glasses of with his fingers as they slid up his wrinkled visage until they fell on the table, one leg askew. 'We need to shut access to this city down, now.' He stood and picked up the telephone. 'Get me the Prime Minister, tell him its code red … and I want the head of the Met in my office … yes now … like fucking five minutes ago.'

Chapter 46

Finlay and Anna walked back to Millbank to see what Skynet could have picked up on any surveillance combined with new information inputs. Henry stayed at Whitehall to brief the Prime Minister and his cabinet in the Cabinet Office Briefing Rooms, often referred to by the media as COBRA.

Finlay took the opportunity to go through several messages on his personal smartphone. He had a number of texts from Eli and two missed calls. He also had a message from Bruce in Cyprus. Eli was at the airport on her way for an interview with a tech company in Miami. He took the opportunity to tell her he was working ay Whitehall with an AI expert he could introduce her to in the future and to say he would call back shortly. Bruce was talking about coming over to see him after chatting with Eli when she visited him. Finlay said he would go to Cyprus and that he was busy, and it was best not to come across to London until his project was finished.

He sat for a moment of contemplation as he looked out into the grey and wet London weather. People were running in the street below to avoid the rain, some with umbrellas were walking to their destination occasionally bumping into those walking in the opposite direction. Employees on their way to work were stoical and looking grim, some tourists laughed at the weather and simply got wet, a large group of Chinese had plastic bags from their packed lunches over their heads. All went about their everyday lives without the knowledge of a massive threat that lurked in a vehicle

on its way to the City. They could all be snuffed out in an instant. The summer rain turned into a squall as wind blew up the Thames from the east. The street seemed to almost magically empty as the large drops of rain filled the streets and gutters started to flow taking some of the street litter with the deluge of rainwater. Curiously the sight seemed to aid the self-evaluation of the remainder of his life, there was a beauty to it worth living for. His relationship with Anna was hardly a romance yet, but something worth pursuing. He made a vow. Finlay would start living his life again once this was all over.

He would visit his children regularly and ask them to visit him in the mountains of Scotland. He would and ask Anna to visit to show her the rugged granite peaks and the wild desolation of the Grampians. Assuming the bomb wouldn't go off under their arses.

Chapter 47

Saeed Abdul Raheem sat outside the Carthago Chic motorhome in the Lee Valley Caravan Park in Essex. It was nearly time to fulfil their mission. The beauty of the device they were assembling in the back of the converted motorhome was that you didn't need to accurately deliver it. Central London was less than ten miles from where he had berthed the vehicle. All he had to do was successfully put the parts together and trigger the device, that was devastation enough. They would get as close as possible to their target and if stopped by the enemy would simply press the button. That electrical charge detonated the spherically shaped conventional explosive, causing an implosion compressing the plutonium which caused the nuclear reaction. It would of course be better to be as accurate as possible. To deliver such a weapon into the heart of the city would be historical, even the twin towers legend would be in his shadow. He would have delivered it like the Mubarizun of old, not hide in cave in Afghanistan whilst others gave their lives.

The one setback that they had was that Dubois was dead. He was supposed to assemble the bomb in Europe at his chalet but had disappeared. Miriam was Saeed's secret weapon. She had been an understudy of the clandestine nuclear programme and had impressed the predominantly Shia dominated scientific wing of the Revolutionary Guard from a young age. Despite their concerns about her loyalties they had taken her from the university in Tehran and let her study and work under one of the leading Iranian nuclear physicists. He had long since been assassinated by the Mossad as had many of his colleagues over the years, both abroad and in the heart of Iran itself. They were desperate for the knowledge and Miriam had risen up the ranks very quickly indeed. They had failed to recognise the beginnings of her hatred for the regime that had persecuted her people. Her father or other members of immediate family had no historical record of activities undertaken against the state. Cyrus Sia had been careful but had been acting against the regime almost all his life, encouraging his daughter to penetrate the regime was one of his clandestine activities. Miriam's main knowledge was on the electronic and conventional explosive side of the weapon, she wasn't an atomic scientist as such. The timing and rapid detonation of the sphere to allow immediate compression of the fissile material was key. Abdul was also an electronics engineer and had been coached in the wiring system in Dubai by Dubois prior to his disappearance, though was informed it was on a timer. Saeed had learned through his intelligence network that the two Ansari brother had been careless and some diagrams had been left in the apartment in Deira. This discovery had been passed on to the UK intelligence services. No matter, the boy would soon make amends.

While Saeed sat at his camping table outside the motorhome Miriam and Abdul were wiring the bomb up for detonation. The two Yemenis were able mechanics and had bolted the whole contraption together. They had done the heavy lifting in the cave prior to placing the machine in the garage space of the Carthago after removing from the trailer of the truck. The girl had insisted on dispatching the Italian criminal. Miriam and Abdul were now in the back finishing off the wiring and checking the circuits with a meter before connecting up the large battery that would send the current through the detonation switch to the explosive. The Palestinian moved his folding chair, further under the canopy as the rain became heavier. It reminded him of the rain that fell in Dubai when he had met with Makhlouf. It seemed like a generation ago, not just a few weeks. He decided he may allow himself to break his vows of daily abstinence and have a cigarette. He had bought some on the P&O ferry when they crossed the English Channel.

*

London had never been subjected to such a mobilisation since 1940 when the Blitz had commenced. All police, army and intelligence services had leave cancelled, every able body was recalled. Aldermaston was manned up and kept on standby. A red warning was put out to the public that a terrorist threat was imminent somewhere in the UK. All major cities were now on alert. The public was asked to be vigilant, in particular of suspicious activity of large load bearing vehicles such as trucks or buses in the centre of large cities. Such terrorist warnings were rarely so specific. The public became alert. More so than during any previous warnings. The call centres became red hot with activity, the security services had to answer and monitor any serious possibilities that came from the public over the telephone. Trucks and buses were stopped and searched. One individual ran from an articulated unit in the port of Liverpool when caught by the side of the road opening the container on his trailer. He was shot dead when turning a street corner but the wires hanging from his jacket belonged to the earphones of his telephone. His truck was full of Iranian immigrants. Another woman was tasered when her van failed to stop for a roadblock in south London. After ramming a police car she also tried to escape. The van contained a mixture of class A drugs. People reported everything from the "militant looking white van man" to truck drivers who had flashed their lights at them on the motorway.

All of this did much to assist Saeed's route down the A104 toward the City. He had heard on the radio that central London had essentially been cordoned off to anything other than light vehicles, London Transport buses and taxis. There were very few heavy goods vehicles on the road. He would get as close as he could to his target. The Houses of Parliament. The heart of colonialist evil in the West. The Yemenis had gone to hire a van and create a diversion elsewhere with a wooden crate with some wires hanging out of it constructed from the remains of the FOTMA tractor parts containers. That left him with Miriam and Abdul. Miriam and he would leave the vehicle an hour before detonation and take a taxi out of town and make their escape, hopefully eventually to the mountains of the Yemen. Abdul would avenge his brother and all of his people and set the fire that would cleanse the world. They could not be stopped now, they were close enough.

*

Finlay's reverie was interrupted by a squeal from Anna, both her and Henry walked into the meeting room occupied by Finlay. 'Finlay, we've picked up a video surveillance facial recognition from Skynet. Saeed Raheem and Miriam Sia were spotted in a caravan park in North London. The AI has tracked them down to a road entering London five minutes ago. They are in a large motorhome, not an HGV, we have the registration. We're about to send the location out to our armed response teams.'

Finlay looked up at both of them. 'Tell them to stand off the motorhome. Let it make slow progress through the traffic. We must not do anything to cause them to detonate. Makes no difference now where they set it off. It's going to kill a lot of people anyway if it goes off now. Give them some hope of reaching their target. Slow the traffic, don't stop it. Henry, get me there now!' The old Major knew that you need to set the ambush on your terms, not scare the enemy away or let him fight on his terms. Finlay removed his sling and swallowed some more painkillers.

Within five minutes two unmarked KTM light trials motorbikes arrived and Finlay and Henry became the pillion passengers. The motorcyclists were plain clothes anti-terrorist SAS men. The soldiers were armed with H&K MP5 submachine guns secreted in their satchels strapped over their backs. Both were seasoned off-road bikers, the pavements and narrow streets of London was now their obstacle course. They took no prisoners with pedestrians and fellow security service personnel to get to their destination.
They pulled off a side street on the Kingsway and crossed the street to Lincoln's Inn Fields. A large fifty two seat bus with tinted windows was sitting next to a hotel as if it had just discharged its load of tourists. Finlay dismounted and thanked the biker.

'What's your name son?'

'It's Eddie. Major.' Finlay had no idea how this lad knew his title. 'The command centre is on that big white bus.'

Finlay gestured to Henry and they boarded the bus with their two escorts. On climbing the front steps past a driver wearing a white shirt and a tie. He walked into an area covered with computers, a couple of TV screens, telephones and a large table with a map of London on it. The rear of the bus had tables and chairs which were occupied by a dozen SAS men mostly dressed in black fatigues, heavily armed and ready for combat. A team of four wore casual clothes and carried cycle courier bags. A Captain wearing the famous beige beret was the only soldier in more formal uniform. He ignored Henry and walked straight to Finlay shaking his hand, 'Captain Farnham, Major Lamont delighted to meet you.'

Henry butted in before Finlay could respond, 'My name is Henry Darcy Captain, Military Intelligence, I am heading up this operation, Major Lamont has been tracking these individuals from day one. You must do as directed by him. Time is off the essence so I suggest you brief us on what you know.'

'Certainly Mister Darcy. We believe the target vehicle is approaching the junction here.' The Captain pointed to the map on the table. We had planned to take it on the Kingsway by approaching from these two side streets and attacking the vehicle from both the front and behind, standard vehicle boarding tactics. We have three SAS squads of four men, the lads in civvies approach the vehicle from the front as if they are crossing the road, the other eight will hide behind parked vehicles. Unless you have a different idea, we plan to execute shortly.' The Captain looked at Finlay.

The SRU Major responded, 'we can't do that Captain. For your information this is a massive suicide bomb. While difficult to attain we must take these guys out, kill them immediately before they get a chance to press a button. We need to do this without detonating the device. The traffic is being directed down the Kingsway, let's get this bus on the road on the left and park it. We go from the bus. They must suspect nothing. I will explain. I also need your biker lad Eddie so make sure he doesn't bugger off. We will need something with more punch than an MP5. We need a larger round that will kill these fuckers through the windows.'

The Captain summoned a sergeant from the back of the bus. He held a G3 H&K assault rifle which used a larger 7.62mm round. 'We have four of these Major, biggest calibre we have on this bus.'

'It'll have to do, son, get all four up the front and lined up to fire through the windows. It needs to be a quick kill, no fucking about or we're all dead.'

*

Saeed turned the motorhome through the junction on High Holborn passing the Rosewood Hotel on his left and then left on to the Kingsway road. The street was busy, mostly with London Transport buses and taxis making their way to the bridges over the Thames. He kept to the right. Out of the bus lanes. Miriam was at the back of the vehicle looking out of the small window at the traffic behind and Abdul Ansari was sitting on top of the device. The mattresses had been pulled off the access to the garage below and used as another means of protection along the side of the left of the vehicle nearest the pavement. There was a two-step detonation process to make sure the device did not explode prematurely. Firstly, there was a small circuit breaker that would supply the power from a battery on the floor of the garage compartment. Secondly a simply toggle switch that would close the circuit to detonate the conventional explosive. This would implode the nuclear material and cause the chain reaction that would destroy a significant part of Britain's capital city.

As he approached the London School of Economics on the left hand side he saw a large white bus with dark tinted windows parked on the left next to the entrance, he assumed it was dropping or picking up students. They could be near Parliament Square within thirty minutes. A line of traffic ahead of him was waiting for the lights to change to green at a junction. The Carthago motorhome edged past the bus, he could see a motorbike moving between the lines of traffic behind him.
Saeed reached forward for a drink from the bottle of water in a cup holder on the dashboard. As he reached out he felt a thump on his left shoulder which knocked him bodily across the vehicle against the passenger door. He then registered a cacophony of noise, the window next to the drivers' side of the motorhome had shattered, glass lacerated his face, blood ran into his mouth as he lay slumped against the door. His old Browning was in a space in the dashboard but he didn't have time to attempt to get it. His hands fumbled for the door handle as a massively loud explosion blew in his eardrums and the motorhome filled with smoke. He heard screams. From behind him.

*

Finlay rode pillion on the KTM, Eddie's MP5 in his good hand across his chest. Ahead he could see the motorhome pull alongside the bus slowly. It struck him momentarily that this assault was being executed on the basis of visual verification from a computer. While Anna and her team had been through the data and verified its authenticity, no one had done an "eyeball" verification. It was too late now. He saw a team of four men move out from the pavement side behind the special force's bus as the Carthago inched passed. Some pedestrians started to run when they saw the armed soldiers dressed in black fatigues and masks. It was a matter of seconds before the alarm was raised inside the motorhome.

Suddenly the side windows of the white bus exploded like a broadside from a battleship of old. Four men with the high calibre weapons had opened fire from inside. The four man teams then went at the front driver's position and in the back window. They couldn't go round the other side or they would be hit by friendly fire. Someone had already thrown the flash bangs in to disorientate the enemy. Unfortunately they had also thrown smoke bombs, this was standard procedure to protect the assailants but not the right thing to do when trying to kill a suicide bomber. As the KTM pulled up behind Finlay jumped off, crouched down and started to make his way on all fours to avoid any fire through the side of the vehicle. Pain shot through his shoulder. The smoke was now filling the street around the motorhome as passengers in the other vehicles started to exit their cars and run. Less than ten seconds had passed since the men had started firing. Finlay made his way up to the drivers position between the two vehicles, sporadic fire was still going into the motorhome above his head. He screamed to cease fire to the men above him as he pulled open the drivers' door on the left hand drive vehicle. The seat was flecked with blood but empty. As he jumped in the motorhome, crouching behind the driver's seat aiming his MP5 into the rear, two SAS troops in gas masks entered the right hand side full length access door. The first man swept his sub machine gun to the left and fired two three round bursts into something he saw in the smoke. Finlay, his eyes now streaming from the smoke canister saw a figure lying behind the driver's seat, he fired a burst into the figure. The two SAS men shouted to the men attempting to board the vehicle from the rear, to hold back. Then more rounds were fired before a few seconds of complete silence. The lead SAS man further back, now almost hidden by thick white smoke from Finlay, lifted his mask from his face briefly and shouted, 'Clear!'

Finlay could hardly see now, he exited the motorhome and walked round to the pavement side of the large white security bus, sat down and waited for his eyes to clear. Captain Farnham tapped him on the shoulder with a bottle of water, 'Rinse your eyes Major and we'll take a look at the target vehicle. The bomb disposal boys are a couple of minutes away. The Met are urgently clearing the area.'

*

Henry was walking to the front of the bus, now almost empty of men to speak to Finlay before taking a look at the target vehicle. As he descended the steps his cell phone rang, the ringtone was an emergency siren, almost lost in the surrounding siren noise on the Kingsway. He looked at the phone to make sure, "NH" was flashing, 'Good afternoon, Mr Harel.'

'Henry, I have some urgent news. Please listen carefully. We have captured and interrogated a VAJA operative. He has revealed something we believe to be true. There are two devices, not one, I repeat two devices.'

Henry felt a lump in his throat, he looked at Finlay as he spoke. 'Do we know where the second device is Mr Harel?'

'We believe it was shipped from Port Sudan also, but as yet we have no idea where. We have been in touch with Mr Franklin, they have assured us from surveillance footage they have reviewed that the dhow only went there. Two devices were taken from the African Tide as there were two in the container. They have been spreading their bets Henry – like the twin towers. I will let you know if we find out more. We are convinced the operative knows little more of the destination. Perhaps if you find the terrorists in the UK you will find out more.'

Henry looked at the motorhome, 'we have just intercepted them Mr Harel, situation is live, we will let you know how it unfolds. I will update you later.'

'Appreciated Henry. Good luck.'

Henry was now sure the Israelis had killed Dubois, they would not confirm it of course - they never did. They knew a hell of a lot more than they were revealing. He looked back at where Finlay was seated, the old soldier had gone.

*

Finlay had heard most of Henry's side of the conversation, at the point Henry mention "second device", he had jumped to his feet, checked the safety on his MP5 and gone around to the main door of the motorhome. The smoke had cleared. The SAS Captain followed him in. Miriam lay behind the driver's seat. Most of her head was missing down to her bottom jaw. All he could see was her lower set of teeth and some brain tissue. There was surprisingly little blood around her head. The 7.62mm rounds had done their gory job at point blank range. Abdul Ansari, by contrast looked relatively untouched, the smaller rounds from the team's sub machine guns had hit his body several times but his head and face seemed relatively unscathed. He lay across the top of the device, the soldiers were attempting to look underneath him to see if he lay on any kind of switch. The Captain instructed his men to leave him where he was until the bomb squad could take a look. There was no sign of Saeed Raheem. He must have escaped when the smoke bombs were at their thickest. He felt like admonishing the Captain for allowing his men to throw smoke canisters but they had achieved their objective in spite of this. He knew mistakes were always made in the heat of combat.
Finlay saw some spots of blood trailing across the wide road to the other side of the street, he followed the trail. It gradually disappeared as he turned on to a side street near a television and audio shop with TV's playing live television. The staff were cautiously peeking over the television at the events further up the street. A news flash on a large plasma TV caught his eye, he switched his gaze from the street

ahead to the picture on the screen. He could see a picture of a huge cloud of black smoke above a city obviously taken from someone's phone camera. The news strapline running along the bottom of the screen read "Breaking News - Massive Explosion in Miami – more to follow". He sensed someone near him, it was Henry. 'There were two bombs Finlay, I sincerely hope that wasn't the other one.' Finlay barely heard him, both men stood with their mouths open staring in the shop window as the sound of sirens in London grew even louder.

Printed in Great Britain
by Amazon